WOMEN IN GERMAN YEARBOOK

13

EDITORIAL BOARD

Leslie A. Adelson, Cornell University, 1992–2000
Angelika Bammer, Emory University, 1992–2000
Barbara Becker-Cantarino, Ohio State University, 1992–2000
Jeannine Blackwell, University of Kentucky, 1992–97
Gisela Brinker-Gabler, State University of New York, Binghamton, 1992–97
Helen L. Cafferty, Bowdoin College, 1992–97
Jeanette Clausen, Indiana University–Purdue University Fort Wayne, 1995–2000
Susan L. Cocalis, University of Massachusetts, Amherst, 1992–97
Gisela Ecker, Universität-Gesamthochschule-Paderborn, 1992–97
Ruth-Ellen B. Joeres, University of Minnesota, Minneapolis, 1992–97
Anna K. Kuhn, University of California, Davis, 1992–97
Sara Lennox, University of Massachusetts, Amherst, 1992–2000
Ricarda Schmidt, University of Manchester, England, 1992–2000
Inge Stephan, Humboldt-Universität zu Berlin, 1995–2000
Arlene Teraoka, University of Minnesota, Minneapolis, 1995–2000
Susanne Zantop, Dartmouth College, 1995–2000

PAST EDITORS

Marianne Burkhard, 1984–88
Edith Waldstein, 1984–87
Jeanette Clausen, 1987–94
Helen Cafferty, 1988–90

WOMEN IN

Feminist Studies in German Literature & Culture

GERMAN

Edited by Sara Friedrichsmeyer & Patricia Herminghouse

YEARBOOK

13

University of Nebraska Press, Lincoln and London

© 1997 by the University of
Nebraska Press. All rights
reserved. Manufactured in
the United States of America.
Published by arrangement
with the Coalition of
Women in German.
♾ The paper in this book
meets the minimum require-
ments of American National
Standard for Information
Sciences – Permanence of
Paper for Printed Library
Materials, ANSI Z39.48-1984.
ISBN 0-8032-4784-2 (cloth)
ISBN 0-8032-9803-X (paper)
ISSN 1058-7446

Birgit Dahlke's essay and the interview with Elke Erb that follows it have been extracted from her recently published book, *Papierboot: Autorinnen aus der DDR—inoffiziell publiziert*, Würzburg: Königshausen & Neumann, 1997, and are published in translation here with permission of the press.

CONTENTS

Acknowledgments vii
Preface ix

Herta Müller 1
The Red Flower and the Rod

Libuše Moníková 7
Some Theses Regarding Women's Writing

Karin A. Wurst 11
Elise Bürger (1769–1833) and the Gothic Imagination

Daniel Purdy 29
Sophie Mereau's Authorial Masquerades and the Subversion of Romantic *Poesie*

Lynne Tatlock 49
Recollections of a Small-Town Girl: Regional Identity, Nation, and the Flux of History in Luise Mühlbach's *Erinnerungen aus der Jugend* (1870)

Barbara Hyams 67
The Whip and the Lamp: Leopold von Sacher-Masoch, the Woman Question, and the Jewish Question

Katharina Gerstenberger 81
Her (Per)version: *The Confessions of Wanda von Sacher-Masoch*

David A. Brenner 101
Neglected "Women's" Texts and Contexts: Vicki Baum's Jewish Ghetto Stories

Birgit Dahlke 123
Avant-gardist, Mediator, and...Mentor? Elke Erb

Elke Erb 133
Not "Man or Woman," But Rather "What Kind of Power Structure Is This?": Elke Erb in Conversation with Birgit Dahlke

Beth Linklater 151
Erotic Provocations: Gabriele Stötzer-Kachold's Reclaiming of the Female Body?

Jutta Ittner 171
Jigsaw Puzzles: Female Perception and Self in Brigitte Kronauer's
"A Day That Didn't End Hopelessly after All"

Annette Meusinger 189
The Wired Mouth: On the Positionality of Perception in Anne Duden's
Opening of the Mouth and *Das Judasschaf*

Monika Shafi 205
"Between Worlds": Reading Jeannette Lander's *Jahrhundert der Herren*
as a Postcolonial Novel

Heike Henderson 225
Re-Thinking and Re-Writing *Heimat*: Turkish Women Writers in Germany

About the Authors 245
About the Translators 249
Notice to Contributors 251
Contents of Previous Volumes 253

ACKNOWLEDGMENTS

In addition to members of the Editorial Board, the following individuals reviewed manuscripts received during the preparation of volume 13.

We gratefully acknowledge their assistance.

Beth Bjorklund, University of Virginia
Ute Brandes, Amherst College
Barton Byg, University of Massachusetts, Amherst
Albrecht Classen, University of Arizona
Ruth Dawson, University of Hawaii, Honolulu
Friederike Eigler, Georgetown University
Elke Frederiksen, University of Maryland, College Park
Margy Gerber, Bowling Green State University
Katharina Gerstenberger, University of Cincinnati
Sabine Gölz, University of Iowa
Kay Goodman, Brown University
Marjanne Goozé, University of Georgia
Alyth Grant, University of Otago, New Zealand
Sabine Gross, University of Wisconsin, Madison
Susan Gustafson, University of Rochester
Brigid Haines, University College of Swansea, Wales
Gail Hart, University of California, Irvine
Barbara Hyams, Brandeis University
Joey Horsley, University of Massachusetts, Boston
Nancy Kaiser, University of Wisconsin, Madison
Lynda King, Oregon State University
Erika Kluesener, Clarion University
Susanne Kord, Georgetown University
Elizabeth Mittman, Michigan State University
Leslie Morris, Bard College
Brent Peterson, Ripon College
Cora Lee Nollendorfs, University of Wisconsin, Madison
Karen Remmler, Mount Holyoke College
Christiane Zehl Romero, Tufts University
Lisa Roetzel, Eastman School of Music, University of Rochester
Ferrel Rose, Grinnell College
Brigitte Rossbacher, Washington University, St. Louis
Monika Shafi, University of Delaware
Katrin Sieg, Indiana University

Gabriele Strauch, University of Maryland, College Park
Katie Trumpener, University of Chicago
Jacqueline Vansant, University of Michigan–Dearborn
Margaret Ward, Wellesley College
Linda Worley, University of Kentucky

Special thanks to Victoria Hoelzer-Maddox for manuscript preparation.

PREFACE

In last year's preface to Volume 12, we commented on the important work that members of Women in German have undertaken in questioning and expanding traditional notions of German literature and culture, a development that has also become evident in contributions to the *Yearbook*. It can, in fact, be traced through the history of our publication, beginning with Volume 1 (1985).

This tradition is readily apparent in the present volume, which opens by maintaining another tradition as well: contributions solicited from the special invited guests at WIG's annual conference, which in 1996 was focused around the theme of gender and German identity. Herta Müller, in a previously unpublished autobiographical essay, recalls her brief experience as a preschool teacher in Romania under Ceauşescu. Accustomed to corporal punishment and indoctrinated to respond only in terms of official expectations and slogans, the five-year-olds of whom she writes had already forfeited the capacity to respond to nature and to use language authentically—capacities that for Müller the writer are essential human qualities. Our other guest, Libuše Moníková, who was introduced to readers of *Yearbook 12*, insists on the importance of evaluating women's writing *as writing* and not as therapy for experiences of victimization. In asserting that "misery is not a criterion of truth, pity not a basis for judging quality," Moníková seems to be expressing her hope that her texts—and potentially others that are now included in our expanded understanding of German literature—earn their place in the new canon on their intrinsic merits and not on the basis of some sort of "sympathy bonus."

Literature around 1800 is the focus of the first two of the following articles: Karin Wurst probes Elise Bürger's Gothic imagination and the freedom it offered for an unconventional vision of reality beyond the narrowness of the domestic sphere and its value system. Using Bürger's narrative "Dirza," Wurst demonstrates the emancipatory potential of a genre that allows its author to explore "phenomena and potentialities of experience that...would be too troubling or menacing to contemplate" under the conventions of realist writing. Daniel Purdy then takes up the case of Sophie Mereau. Her translations of the writings of Ninon de Lenclos, he suggests, served a strategic function in her own feminist agenda of asserting a tradition of female authorship in European literary history and positioning her political critique of Romantic and Classical denigrations of the feminine. Mereau, he argues, does not merely transfer Lenclos's words into German, but herself masquerades as Lenclos, rewriting the older woman's text as an intervention in the gendered ontology of her own times.

Focusing on a prolific nineteenth-century writer who was the object of much more attention in her own time than in ours, Lynne Tatlock sets out to examine Luise Mühlbach's 1870 memoirs of her nineteenth-century childhood in Mecklenburg and demonstrates how that author's representation of the past served as a defense against a disturbing present. In this provocative reading, Mühlbach's nostalgic depiction of provincial Mecklenburg emerges as the attempt to imagine a feminized and domesticated nation as an alternative to the power politics of a Prussianized nation of blood and iron.

Another cluster of articles provides new insights into fin-de-siècle culture: Barbara Hyams suggests that Leopold von Sacher-Masoch's career as editor of the journal *Auf der Höhe* casts new light on his attitudes towards Jews and women. Although Sacher-Masoch is remembered today primarily as the author of a work that provided a model for what Krafft-Ebing described as a pathological condition, Hyams indicates that for his journal Sacher-Masoch selected texts that represented a multicultural and cosmopolitan Hapsburg empire. Katharina Gerstenberger then turns to the confessions of Wanda von Sacher-Masoch, whose autobiographic text is revealed as a subversive countertext to her ex-husband's infamous "Venus in Furs." In the years of their marriage, she had even adopted the name of the protagonist of that work, Wanda von Dunajew, as a pen name, but in the confessions, Gerstenberger argues, she writes herself free of the authority of the master text and asserts female subject positions that provoked the wrath of her critics. David Brenner then examines two relatively unknown "ghetto novellas" published by popular author Vicki Baum in the first Jewish magazine, *Ost und West*, as documentation of Baum's ambivalent attitude towards her own Jewish heritage. Brenner deftly situates these texts in the tension between the magazine's—and Baum's—project of establishing cultural respectability for Eastern European Jews in Imperial Germany and the concurrent phenomenon of Jewish self-hatred generally associated with Baum's contemporary, Otto Weininger, whose *Sex and Character* had been published just a few years earlier.

East German women poets of two generations, Elke Erb and Gabriele Stötzer-Kachold, are the focus of the following three contributions. Birgit Dahlke's examination of Elke Erb's texts claims a place for the writer as a mediator between different generations and literatures. Both here and in the interview with Erb that follows, Dahlke seeks to explain why Erb, like so many GDR women writers, resists identification as a feminist. Against a background of GDR notions of sexual taboos, Beth Linklater discusses Gabriele Stötzer-Kachold's use of a provocative sexual vocabulary, particularly her references to female genitalia. This vocabulary, according to Linklater, was intended to challenge and provoke readers to a new understanding of the female body.

Subsequent articles explore the works of other contemporary writers: Jutta Ittner offers an analysis of Brigitte Kronauer's "A Day That Didn't End Hopelessly after All" as an odyssey of female maturation. Comparing Kronauer's story to a jigsaw puzzle that offers readers fragments of an ambiguous reality in language that is precise and clear, Ittner argues that the reader who accepts the challenge posed by the countless details, distracting detours, and intricate reflections of this text will ultimately arrive at a higher plane of perception. Annette Meusinger enters the ongoing discussion of racist elements in feminist aesthetics by considering two novels by Anne Duden. She argues that the novels, both of which present their female protagonists as victims, reproduce essentialist notions of woman and the female body. Monika Shafi's examination of Jeannette Lander's recent novel *Jahrhundert der Herren* (Century of the Masters) in the contexts of postcolonial and travel literature traces the conflicts confronted by a young German woman who settles in Sri Lanka. Although able to critique the (neo)colonial master's discourse, the protagonist comes to realize that she herself is deeply implicated in it and must continue "playing the role of the independent, entrepreneurial Westerner, [although] she has lost faith in linear progress and the future-oriented pace of the European self." Arrested in a permanently liminal state, she slowly recognizes the impossibility of attaining a state of authentic intercultural hybridity.

A final contribution to the on-going project of expanding our definition of German literature is offered with Heike Henderson's examination of challenges to traditional notions of family and homeland in German texts by four Turkish women: Aysel Özakin, Alev Tekinay, Saliha Scheinhardt, and Zehra Çirak. As Henderson asserts, their texts provide us with concepts of *Heimat* that reject geographical definitions and instead allow for cultural differences.

From the many submissions received, the articles in this volume have been chosen to reflect the quality as well as the genres, periods, and critical approaches that characterize feminist studies in our field. For the editors, this selection process has been a source of deep satisfaction, as we recognize the many important ways in which these articles complement one another in addressing current scholarly concerns and raising new questions for further examination.

Although the final word has not been spoken on the *Yearbook*'s all-English policy, we offer once again a volume completely accessible to English-language readers. For their generous efforts in this endeavor we thank our translators. Our readers will be aware that the publication of an all-English volume coincides with another development: the continuing internationalization of Women in German and the *WIG Yearbook*. This trend is evident not only among our contributors and their range of topics, but also among those on whom we rely: members of the Editorial Board and the truly international roster of readers whose thoughtful advice benefits authors and editors in equal measure. We also gratefully acknowledge once again the alert and reliable professionalism of Victoria Hoelzer-Maddox, who formatted the volume, and the indispensable local base of support provided by our own institutions, the University of Cincinnati and the University of Rochester.

Sara Friedrichsmeyer
Patricia Herminghouse
July 1997

The Red Flower and the Rod

Herta Müller

Rumanian-born Herta Müller was one of the two invited guest speakers at the 1996 Women in German annual conference in St. Augustine, Florida. She has been awarded a number of prestigious prizes for her writing, including the "aspekte" Literaturpreis in 1984, the Förderpreis des Bremer Literaturpreises in 1985, the Marie Luise Fleisser Prize and the Ricarda Huch Prize in 1989, and the Kleist Prize in 1994. At the editors' request, she contributed this previously unpublished autobiographical essay, titled "Die rote Blume und der Stock" in German, to the Yearbook. The translator of this story, Sieglinde Lug, has recently completed the translation of a collection of Müller's stories, *Niederungen*. The translation is forthcoming with the University of Nebraska Press. A bibliography of the author's book-length works is appended to this essay.

The meetings in which people spent a great portion of their time during the dictatorship gave the clearest picture of the manner of speaking in Romania when it was under constant surveillance. Probably not just during this dictatorship. Anything halfway authentic, any personal touch, any individual finger twitch was purged from the speakers. I watched and listened to interchangeable figures who had retreated from their individuality into the smooth mechanics of a political position in order to conform to a career pattern.

In Romania, the whole ideology of the regime was connected to the cult of personality around Ceaușescu. The village priest used the same method to drive the fear of God into me when I was a child that the functionaries used to spread their socialist religion. Whatever you do, God sees you; he is infinite and everywhere. The portrait of the Dictator placed in many thousands of locations throughout the country was reinforced by his omnipresent voice. His speeches were broadcast on radio and TV for hours, so that every day his voice would hover in the air as a control. This voice was as familiar to everyone in the country as the rustling of wind or the falling of rain. His manner of speech and the gestures accompanying it were as well known as the lock of hair on the Dictator's forehead, his eyes, his nose, and his mouth. And his rehashing of the same prefabricated phrases was as familiar as the sounds of everyday utensils. The repetition of the prefabricated phrases did not quite guarantee the appreciation of the speeches any more. Therefore, at public appearances the functionaries also tried very hard to imitate Ceaușescu's gestures. The highest speaker in the regime had finished fourth grade and had problems not only with complex content but even with the simplest grammar. In addition he had a speech impediment. With changing vowels and a quick sequence of consonants his tongue would get stuck and he would mumble. He tried to distract his audience from noticing it by barking out chopped-up syllables and by constantly waving his hands. So the imitation of his manner of speech resulted in an especially striking, tragicomic distortion of the Romanian language.

I used to say in those days that the youngest functionaries in the country were the oldest. That's because they managed the imitation of the Dictator effortlessly, as it seemed, and more perfectly than the older ones. Of course, they had more need of it, since their careers had just begun. But after I took care of preschool children I was forced to come to the conclusion that the young functionaries were not just imitating. That's who they were; they didn't have any different gestures of their own.

For two weeks I was a preschool teacher and noticed that even with five-year-olds the imitation of Ceaușescu was unmistakable. The children were obsessed with party poems and patriotic songs and the national anthem. I came to that preschool after a long period of unemployment because factories and some schools were laying off people. None of them wanted me any more because of "individualism, nonconformity in the collective, and lack of socialist awareness." The school year had long since started and I was supposed to substitute for a preschool teacher who had gotten jaundice and was not expected to recover very soon. When I accepted the position, I thought it couldn't be as bad as in the schools. At least there had to be a little childhood left in this state; there couldn't be the steady empty destruction through ideology with such young children, there would still be building blocks, dolls, and dances. In addition, I didn't have any money; instead I had debts and loan installments to be paid every month. I knew that in my situation you shouldn't slip into the dependency of becoming a renter. Because any landlord would have thrown me out on the street at the first threat from the secret police. I had to lean on my mother, an LPG farmer (LPG = *landwirtschaftliche Produktionsgenossenschaft,* a producers' cooperative in socialist countries), who had to work very hard to keep my head above water.

On my first day of work, the preschool principal took me to my group. When we entered the classroom, she said almost cryptically: "The anthem." Automatically the children formed a half circle, pressed their hands straight to their thighs, stretched their necks, and raised their eyes. Children had jumped up from their little tables, but it was soldiers who were standing in a half circle singing. What they were doing was closer to screaming and barking than singing. The main thing seemed to be how loud it was and how they held their bodies. The anthem was very long, since it had gained some more stanzas in recent years. I think at the time it had reached a length of seven stanzas. Because of my prolonged unemployment, I wasn't up to date; I didn't know the text of the new stanzas. After the last stanza the half circle dissolved, and after standing at attention the children reverted to boisterous, squealing unruliness. The principal took a rod from the shelf: "You can't do without it," she said. Then she whispered in my ear and called four of the children. Look at them, she said, and then she sent the four back to their seats. Then she explained to me their parents' and grandparents' positions. One boy was even the party secretary's grandchild, you had to be especially careful with him, she said. He wouldn't tolerate any back talk, and you had to stand up for him against the others, whatever he might do. Then she left me with the group. On the shelf there were about ten rods, twigs as thick as pencils and as long as rulers. Three of them were broken.

Outside that day it was snowing big irregular flakes that were the first to stay on the ground that year. I asked the group which winter song they wanted to sing. Winter song? They didn't know any. Then I asked them about a summer song. They shook their heads. Then I asked about a spring or fall song. Finally one boy suggested a song about picking flowers. They sang about grass and fields. So there was a summer song after all, I thought, even though they were not familiar with those classifications. But soon, it was the same old thing. After the first summer stanza, the second stanza turned to the cult of personality. The most beautiful red flower was presented to the beloved leader. In the third stanza the leader was happy and smiled, because for every child in the country he was the best.

The children's minds didn't seem to form an image of the details of the first stanza, the fields, the grass, and the picking of the flowers. Starting with the first word, their singing sounded feverish, the children seemed driven. The closer they got in the text to presenting the flower and to the smile of the leader, the louder and faster and more like barking their song became. This song, which allowed one stanza for the summer, did not allow for any real comprehension of the landscape that gave rise to it. But, likewise, it didn't allow for any comprehension of gift-giving. Even though Ceauşescu often held children in his arms, they were quarantined for days beforehand to rule out the danger of any contagion. Singing this song called for a mental void. Everything that happened at the preschool was governed by this mental void.

I remembered a few winter songs from my own childhood. The simplest was: "Snowflakes, white capes" ("Schneeflöckchen, Weißröckchen"). I sang, explained the words, and encouraged them to watch how the snow was falling out of the sky over the city. Their little faces didn't communicate anything. The kind of marveling that shelters even as it frightens, and the kind of listening and watching that's condensed in poetic images and provides emotional support even if it makes you sentimental—this was all kept from them on purpose. The beauty of falling snow, which has been contemplated by human beings from time immemorial, was simply irrelevant. Even in this realm, the country had pulled out of the history of emotions. Verbal images like "white capes" or "you live in the clouds" were prevented from settling in the children's minds. In addition, this snow song was too quiet for those already corrupted children. Their emotions weren't touched until they could stand at attention and bark. They were not allowed to conceive of themselves as individuals or to confront the details and things around them from that perspective, as is necessary for socialization into a civil society. This suppression of anything personal made it impossible for each individual later to cope with life in any way. And that's exactly what the state wanted: weakness was supposed to begin where your skin was thinnest. The flight from weakness that was offered by the regime meant accommodation to the force of power, self-abnegation, and subservience as a chance of furthering yourself. A sensorium capable of reviving itself, of coping without this flight, was not supposed to develop.

This first day at the preschool I asked the children to put on their coats, hats, and shoes so that we could go out into the yard, into the snow. The principal heard noise in the cloakroom. She tore open the door of her office. I explained that we had learned a snow song and so I wondered why we should stay inside the building while I told the children about falling flakes. In half an hour we would be back inside. "What could you be thinking," she screamed, "that song is not in the curriculum." We had to return to the classroom. Games, a break, a snack, then the song again.

First thing the next morning I asked if anybody had watched the flakes "that live in the clouds." Here I was the one who was the child, I had done so. To muster courage for the day on my way to work, I had even sung the song in my head, without a sound. Ill at ease, I asked if they remembered the song from yesterday. Then a boy said: "Comrade, first we must sing the anthem." I asked: "Do you want to or do you have to?" The children shouted all together: "Yes, we want to." I gave in and let the children sing the anthem. And like the day before, they quickly formed a half circle, pressed their hands to their thighs, stretched their necks, raised their eyes, and sang and sang. Until I said: "Fine, now let's try to sing the snow song." Then a girl said: "Comrade, we have to finish the anthem." It would have been no use to ask again about the wanting, I just said: "O.K., then finish it." They sang the remaining stanzas. The half circle dissolved. Everybody except for one boy sat down at the little tables again. The boy came towards me, looked me in the eyes, and asked: "Comrade, why didn't you sing with us? Our other comrade always sang with us." I smiled and said: "If I sing along, then I can't hear if you sing right or wrong." I was lucky, my little guard wasn't prepared for my answer. Neither was I. He ran back to his little table. He wasn't one of the four higher beings in the group. For the moment I was proud of my lie. But the circumstances of how I had to and how I came to tell this lie deprived me of my peace of mind for the rest of the day.

Every morning my aversion to going to the preschool increased. The children's eyes, constantly watching, paralyzed me. I could understand that it was impossible to expect a conscious decision for a snow song instead of the party songs from five-year-olds. But it was conceivable that unconsciously and instinctively, without complicity, they might have liked the snow song better than the barking and standing at attention of their songs. Objectively, it was forbidden to offer anything personal to the youngest, the three-year-olds, but subjectively it would still have been possible with them. With the five-year-olds it was impossible even subjectively, it was too late. Every day I understood that more and more unequivocally. The abuse of the human spirit had been internalized, it had created an addiction for continuation. The destruction was complete with the five-year-olds.

That was half of the facts. The other half was the rod. Except for the higher beings whose backgrounds I had been introduced to for their special protection, all the children automatically ducked no matter how or when I approached them. I didn't have the rod in my hand, but they were so used to beatings that their scared faces stole a glance at me, begging: "Don't hit me, please don't hit me." And those who were not in reach shouted: "Now you'll get it, now you'll get it."

I didn't ever use the rod. The result: Whether asking, explaining, or shouting, I was never able to get their attention for even five minutes. It was too late for that too. The normal spoken word, whatever its pitch, was not a means of communication. Only the rod corresponded to the trance of endless empty phrases.

Those children tried to force me to satisfy their need for beatings. They felt let down, they were suspended in hysterical emptiness because they didn't get their beatings. For them, crying under the rod was the only way to feel human. It raised them out of the collective.

Passing half-open doors of other classrooms, I heard the rods beating and thrashing and the children crying. In the eyes of the principal and colleagues who did the beating, and possibly even more so in the eyes of the children who wanted to cry, I was incompetent, and for the same reason: in one case I was not willing, in the other I was not able to use the rod.

But I was increasingly unable to cope with myself. Not able to become like the others and not able to remain who I was—this conflict could not be resolved. I gave notice after two weeks.

The spoken word arising intuitively in our heads, allowing seemingly natural relationships, is not innate. It can be learned or prevented. During the dictatorship, education prevented it in the children. And in the adults who still had some memories of it left, it was wiped out.

Translated by Sieglinde Lug

Selected Bibliography of Books by Herta Müller

Niederungen. Bucharest: Kriterion Verlag, 1982; Berlin: Rotbuch, 1984 (rowohlt paperback, 1988).
Druckender Tango. Bucharest: Kriterion Verlag, 1984 (rowohlt paperback, 1996).
Der Mensch ist ein großer Fasan auf der Welt. Berlin: Rotbuch, 1986 (rowohlt paperback, 1989).
Barfüßiger Februar. Berlin: Rotbuch, 1987.
Reisende auf einem Bein. Berlin: Rotbuch, 1989 (rowohlt paperback, 1995).
Der Teufel sitzt im Spiegel: Wie Wahrnehmung sich selber erfindet. Berlin: Rotbuch, 1991.
Der Fuchs war damals schon der Jäger. Reinbek: Rowohlt, 1992.
Eine warme Kartoffel ist ein warmes Bett. [Essays]. Hamburg: Europäischer Verlagsanstalt, 1992.
Der Wächter nimmt seinen Kamm: Vom Weggehen und Ausscheren. Reinbek: Rowohlt, 1993.
Herztier. Reinbek: Rowohlt: 1994.
Hunger und Seide: Essays. Reinbek: Rowohlt, 1995.
In der Falle. [Bonner Poetik Vorlesungen] Göttingen: Wallstein, 1996.

In English translation:

The Passport (*Der Mensch ist ein großer Fasan auf der Welt*). Trans. Martin Chalmers. London: Serpent's Tail, 1989.
The Land of Green Plums (*Herztier*). Trans. Michael Hofmann. New York: Metropolitan Books, 1996.

Some Theses Regarding Women's Writing

Libuše Moníková

Born in Czechoslovakia, Libuše Moníková was one of two invited guest speakers at the 1996 Women in German annual conference in St. Augustine, Florida. Her works have been recognized with numerous prizes, including the Alfred Döblin Prize in 1987, the Franz Kafka Prize in 1989, the Adalbert von Chamisso Prize in 1991, and the Berliner Literaturpreis and the Johannes Bobrowski Medal in 1992. This essay was previously published in *Die Zeit*. A bibliography of the author's book-length works is appended to this essay.

What has changed since the emergence of "women's writing" in the seventies?

A lot, I hope. Women no longer have to reveal and validate their body for literature, or to thematize the social and physical injuries that have been done to it. The first phase of women's writing was marked by these experiences; the impulse to communicate and to write usually started with them. For the taboo zone of one's own sexuality there was no language; for its literary treatment, no traditional form.

The first attempts to touch our own bodies led to naming, to comparisons and images that were no less uncertain and awkward, but that were recognized by an entire generation as "authentic" in their emphasis.

The "pumpkin-breasts and -bellies" (*Kürbisbrüste und -bäuche*) phase, this aggressive declaration of physicality, ought to have given way in the meantime to the recognition that women also have a head. Sensations and sensitivities are no longer primarily dealt with (I hope) on the level of physical suffering and insult, but instead reflected on and dealt with intellectually.

Some things I am able to understand through my own writing: For my first book *Eine Schädigung* (Injury, 1981), I garnered approval from the women's movement primarily because the protagonist—a young woman who is raped by a police officer and then kills him in the heat of the moment—was above all a victim with whom most readers (women as well as men) could feel solidarity and with whom many could also identify. They could get emotionally involved, because this role was familiar to them.

The second book, *Pavane für eine verstorbene Infantin* (Pavane for a Dead Princess, 1983) bewildered my original supporters and scared off many of them. This time the woman was an intellectual who does not put up with the everyday, unreasonable expectations of her environment, who also thoroughly and rationally analyzes them and finally "strikes back" in her own way. (She sits, although "healthy," in a wheelchair, blows off literature seminars and instead writes a continuation to the story of the Barnabas family in Kafka's *Castle* in which she searches for a social solution for them.) This book was formally more advanced and more complicated than the first. New readers appeared, among them supporters who paid more attention to the construction of the text, but on the whole, the "comfortable pit of our misfortune," where it is so easy to complain, was missing—an intellectual woman was not a welcome theme in 1983.

Since then I have also been writing about men. As a rule they turn out more convincing and realistic than my female figures, who are usually too dominant and therefore appear less credible. My feelings for them betray wishful thinking. It is an authorial weakness.

I place demands on myself and my fellow writers: in this day and age I not only want women to see (and represent) themselves more clearly and convincingly as intellectuals rather than as weak, manipulated victims, but above all to fulfill expectations of form when doing so. A private history does not interest me if it is not of high literary quality. Then the woman represented can even be weak. The main thing is that the writing is strong.

What I still miss for the most part is literature by women that is funny, humorous, biting, satirical. Self-pity has diminished, but self-irony is still rare.

Women lack a certain ease and, furthermore, tenacity and economy of effort when dealing with larger thematic areas and quantities of material: beyond the horizon of the personal.

More humor.

More subversiveness in material and form. Why not write about men, make them the object of our literary desire? They used us for their creative fantasies for thousands of years (and those were not the worst ones).

More desire to experiment, incursive forms: cabaret, carnivalia—masks, "red noses"— *femmes fatales* as comrades, and comrades as intellectuals. I am not satisfied when women work off their feelings through writing (experiences from my seminars); that is self-therapy at best, but as a rule it is mush: diarists write diaries, rarely literature.

Self-criticism, based on a sound ability to make comparisons. Men might serve as a basis for comparison and competition—they have been developing the form for a longer time; art has its own rules and is dependent neither on ideologies nor bellies.

More professionalism. The constant complaints about women's "double role" have no place in art. It always comes down to "exceptions" when one deals with "women's literature," "minority literature": Women just write, and that's all there is to it.

I claim for women, for their writing as a social practice, full earnestness and full commitment; I do not want to have to take children into consideration, not in my own writing and not when judging others' texts. I can respect in addition that a woman is working under the more difficult conditions that a family means for her. This is not my primary interest, however. When judging art there are no extenuating circumstances.

We are not victims, and if we do not make progress, it is because of us, and because we are not able to get past the persistent stereotypes that we find confirmed in history and in our own childhood. I do not want any pity for women, especially self-pity.

There once was a woman, mother of several children, who died from hunger and mental fatigue at the age of forty-two. First, however, through her prose she advanced Czech as a literary language. Božena Němcová. Such achievements are unique. Still, I would have preferred if she had suffered less and written a few more books.

Misery is not a criterion for truth, pity not a basis for judging quality. Women who write must free themselves from misery, from their own, and also from the misery of an amateurish form; only then can they contribute with their work to reducing misery in the real world as well.

We ought to discuss the conditions of our literary production, as well as its weaknesses, without looking for excuses.

Translated by Lynn E. Ries

Selected Bibliography of Books by Libuše Moníková

Eine Schädigung. Berlin: Rotbuch, 1981 (dtv paperback, 1990).
Pavane für eine verstorbene Infantin. Berlin: Rotbuch, 1983 (dtv paperback, 1988).
Die Fassade: M.N.O.P.Q. München: Hanser, 1987 (dtv paperback, 1990).
Schloss, Aleph und Wunschtorte: Essays. München: Hanser, 1990.
Unter Menschenfressern: Dramatisches Menü in vier Gängen. Frankfurt a.M.: Verlage der Autoren, 1990.
Treibeis. München: Hanser, 1992 (dtv paperback, 1997).
Prager Fenster: Essays. München: Hanser, 1994.
Verklärte Nacht. München: Hanser, 1996.

In English translation:
The Façade. Trans. John E. Woods. New York: Knopf, 1991.

Elise Bürger (1769–1833) and the Gothic Imagination

Karin A. Wurst

By challenging the limits of the natural, predictable, and reasonable, the Gothic offered a certain amount of freedom from the referentiality of realist texts, creating an unconventional vision of reality through conventional narrative. This article explores the productive tensions between Gothic elements and realist narrative forms, which were predominantly influenced by developmental novels in the sentimental, moralistic, and didactic traditions. Bürger's use of the Gothic not only allowed for the creation of unconventional female protagonists; it reacted against the obsessive focus on the domestic sphere and its value system and expressed formal displeasure with the increasing staleness of the possibilities of realistic writing conventions at the end of the century. (KAW)

At the end of the eighteenth century, the Gothic became popular and fashionable in several national literatures. While many examples from English literature have become canonical (e.g., Horace Walpole, *The Castle of Otranto,* 1764; Anne Radcliffe, *The Mysteries of Udolpho,* 1794; Mary Shelley, *Frankenstein,* 1818) and have consequently attracted serious scholarly attention, in German literary historiography most examples have been relegated to the realm of "trivial literature" and are virtually unknown today.[1] The Gothic movement in literature displays a widespread interest in archaeology, antiques, and ruins, particularly those of the Middle Ages:[2] fortresses, ruins, cloisters and monasteries full of secret chambers, locked rooms or towers, and dungeons. Plot structures such as incest and violent struggle along with preferred icons (skulls, daggers, moving curtains, and flickering lights) constitute other hallmarks of the genre. Having gleaned its inspiration from medieval Romantic literature, the Gothic revival can be read as a reaction against earlier eighteenth-century order and formality and the tempered, balanced, and tamed emotions of *Empfindsamkeit* ("sensibility").[3] The Gothic fostered a new attitude toward nature and sentiment; "wildness and boldness came into vogue" (Bayer-Berenbaum 19–20).

The Gothic expresses dissatisfaction with the possibilities of conventional literary realism. In this article, realism is not used in the sense of *Realismus*, which in German literary historiography is traditionally associated with the later nineteenth century, but rather to denote those literary forms at the end of the eighteenth century that favor the non-symbolic, the empirical, and the probable. If the Enlightenment novel initially consisted of an analogy between symbolic and realistic systems of signification, by the end of the century the novel had split into two main strands. On the one hand, we find the *Bildungsroman* ("developmental novel") in its classicist or romantic formations, which strives for a union of anthropological and physical realities and is characterized by the correspondences between philosophy and aesthetics. Most of the novels produced around the turn of the century, however, fall into a different category, for which we lack an adequate terminology and classification. These novels and prose narratives were labeled "dilettantish" by Goethe and Schiller in their study on dilettantism (1799), dismissed as philistine by the romantics, and categorized as "trivial literature" by literary critics.[4] By borrowing the more value-neutral convention from English literary criticism to label these prose texts "realistic," I not only wish to avoid the designations *Trivialliteratur* ("trivial literature"), *Massenliteratur* ("literature for the masses"), or *Unterhaltungsliteratur* ("entertainment literature")—I also want to stress the common denominator: their realistic system of signification. These texts are non-autonomous and communicatively oriented around practical matters of everyday life, serving as an experimental arena for social practices and behaviors and allowing for identification.

By challenging the limits of the natural, predictable, and reasonable, the Gothic offers a certain amount of freedom from the referentiality of realistic texts (Backscheider 156), creating an unconventional vision of reality through conventional narrative. As we shall see, it challenges traditional assumptions about the relationship of self to Other, about good and evil, masculine and feminine, and cause and effect (Day 4).[5] Backscheider characterizes the Gothic hero—who is usually male—as "pushing the absolute limits of what the audience imagines to be possible in nature. He is subject to cataclysmic passions, has committed or is contemplating unspeakable crimes that reek of ancient, sacred taboos, and is engaged in a magnificent struggle with himself" (163).

The writer and actor Elise Bürger (1769–1833) used Gothic touches in several genres: in her chivalric play (*Ritterschauspiel*) *Adelheit, Gräfinn [sic] von Teck* (1799), in her autobiographical sketch "Begegnung im Walde" (Meeting in the Forest, 1826), and, above all, in her prose text "Dirza" (1799). Yet her works do not entirely fit the fixed cultural pattern or conventionalized parameters of the Gothic genre. Bürger does not fully engage the Gothic sense of power reeling out of control or unleashing the horrors of passion and madness; rather she uses the Gothic to experiment with the unfamiliar, the unforeseeable, the essentially ominous nature of humanity. These Gothic elements problematize familiar limits and show their eventual collapse in her narrative "Dirza."

This article explores the productive tensions between Gothic elements and contemporary realist narrative forms, which were predominantly influenced by developmental novels in the sentimental, moralistic, and didactic traditions. My focus is on discursive events, on texts and writing practices, and not on the biography of the author.[6] However, since this article also introduces an obscure text, a brief methodological consideration might be in order. It is not my intent simply to deconstruct the traditional "male-centered" canon by constructing an alternative or parallel canon of women's literature because that would obscure the complex dependencies and hierarchies of literary production. Instead, my project reflects the tensions between the various discourses constituting the position of women's texts at this particular point in (literary) history. Beyond the focus on intertextual relationships, this article will remind us of the marginalized, precarious position of women writers in the literary marketplace, their socialization and education, and how these factors influenced their writing practices (cf. Wurst, *Frauen* 14–26).

By representing what is not supposed to exist, the Gothic can provoke interesting questions regarding the construction of the gendered self as a response to the conventional concepts of identity and family that dominated late eighteenth- and early nineteenth-century middle-class life. It has been argued that most women's prose writing around 1800 did not directly challenge these patriarchal values (Runge 195; Brandes 50)[7] but instead employed various strategies of more or less subtle subversion (Gallas and Heuser 7; Zantop; Kontje 236).[8] Bürger's experimentation with the Gothic imagination ultimately functions as a strategy of subversion. All her texts that display Gothic elements focus on a non-traditional female protagonist. Or more precisely, it seems that Bürger employed these elements to provide a wider range of action for her female protagonists than was possible in the domestic realm of the realistic novel in the sentimental or moralistic tradition or in bourgeois drama.

In the chivalric play *Adelheit, Gräfinn von Teck,* the unconventional heroine Countess Adelheit has been forced into a loveless marriage. While this prehistory is the stuff of bourgeois tragedies, the plot—shifting the focus—shows her as a widow taking her fate into her own hands. When threatened by a suitor who hopes to gain access to her land and fortress, she defends her right to self-determination and property.

On the stage, the Gothic elements create an opportunity for special effects. Bürger, who was financially dependent on the success of her works, used them to provide the audience with a specular/spectacular event. As an experienced actor, she knew what audiences wanted and as a dramatist she responded to their tastes. The genre of the chivalric play, which has certain features in common with the Gothic, allowed her to depart from the dominant convention of bourgeois drama (Wurst, "Negotiations"). In addition, in the Gothic setting—the fortress with its secret passageways, haunted towers, locked doors and dungeons, the wilderness of the forest—the female protagonist can strive for self-determination. Here she can dress as a knight and take up arms in defense of her son and her property. An apparition, which we have come to associate with the Gothic tradition, not only externalizes her parapsychological premonition of impending danger in an eye-catching manner,[9] but also sets the plot in motion after an impasse.

In Bürger's autobiographical fiction "Begegnung im Walde," the narrator, an actress—the persona that Bürger creates for herself—travels independently to visit friends whom she had met professionally, constructing a life away from home and family. The narrator finds herself leaving her coach and walking on Bohemian soil. Immediately the history of the soil, the violent battles of Bohemia's history, reveals itself to her imagination.[10] Seeing the heroes come to life again in each tree, she feels connected to this past through the soil. This peculiar occurrence sets the mood for an unusual encounter with a stranger, who evokes fear and curiosity in the narrator. He turns out to be a count and playfully takes her hostage for a strange mission of mercy: he wants to take her home as a "remedy" for his ailing father. Depressed and brooding for years, his father miraculously comes alive for a brief period of time when he gazes into the clear eyes of beautiful women, especially those who speak French to him. His family is thus always on the lookout for such eyes. The narrator's eyes indeed do have the power to improve his outlook for a short while. We are told that excessive passion for a French dancer who betrayed him incited this bizarre deportment.

In this text the Gothic touches are least pronounced. Where they are utilized, they add touches of the extraordinary and the unique to an otherwise ordinary event in the narrator's life story. In a non-logical, non-rational fashion, the Gothic mood weaves past and present together without having to rely on causal relationships. The uniqueness of the events provides a sense of adventure to conventional structures of autobiographical writing. Elise Bürger saw her works as distinctive versions of "autobiographical" writing because, she claims, all of them sprang from a true or actual emotional experience of sorrow or joy in her heart and are based on actually lived experiences (*Lilien-Blätter und Zypressenzweige* v).[11]

Despite this almost stereotypical defensive strategy,[12] the author goes on to present her contemporaries with the "images" of her inner life (*Lilien-Blätter* [vi]), obviously considering them to be worth sharing in a poetic autobiography (*poetischer Lebenslauf*) (*Gedichte* ixx [sic] [xix]).

This is not "women's autobiography" in the conventional sense, which would most likely focus on the chronology of her life, emphasizing childhood, courtship, marriage, motherhood, etc. (Meise; Goodman; Niggl). Instead it is a chronologically arranged collection of poetry and prose. The "life-story" emerges in the web of poetic texts, autobiographical fictions, and—in the case of *Gedichte*—a few footnotes commenting on and providing background for the poetic texts. In a sense, the fictional constructs of her life-experiences take the place of the historical account of her life.

The Gothic elements are part of this experimentation with an alternate form of autobiographical writing. These forms of poetic autobiography or "autobiography in fiction" foreground the textuality, the constructedness of (auto)biographical writing, thus participating to a certain degree in a metafictional discourse. As Patricia Waugh reminds us, metafictional writing is "fictional writing which self-consciously and systematically draws attention to its status as an artifact in order to pose questions about the relationship between fiction and reality" (2).

The Gothic non-realistic elements draw attention to themselves, provoking questions regarding their status within a genre labeled autobiographical. As has been noted elsewhere, eighteenth-century women did not write poetological treatises (Heuser). Their thoughts on aesthetics, on the role and function of literature, and on the relationship between text and reader are frequently contained in prefaces, less frequently in letters. Bürger's text raises questions about how a woman's autobiography could be written that does not follow the traditional structuring pattern of women's lives. While men's autobiographies derive their significance from the integration of public and private self, of individual subject and collective history, women's texts in the eighteenth century more often than not lacked this dimension of integration. Without a tradition, women's autobiographical writing that opts to go beyond the realm of the family struggles to find a voice and a form.[13] The somewhat artificial and arbitrary utilization of Gothic elements in this example of Bürger's autobiographical writing has to be read as experimentation with narrative patterns or plots that allow for the emergence of extrafamilial aspects of women's lives, such as friendship, artistic and creative pursuits, professional experiences, and a sense of adventure.

In *Adelheit, Gräfinn von Teck* and in "Begegnung im Walde," the Gothic elements are more external than in the narrative "Dirza," where they are most pronounced. Not surprisingly, "Dirza" is also the text with the most unconventional female protagonist. From the beginning, the narrator sets up an ambivalent image of Dirza, labeling her a woman who is not without charm (*nicht reizlos*) despite being reckless (*unbesonnen* 1). Since the character Dirza deviates from the moral and ethical positions traditional heroines occupy, the text challenges reader expectations that are alluded to by the narrator.

The text also contests other reader expectations. The narrator, for example, sets out to draft a picture (*Gemähld̃e*) of her life, which suggests that the author does not promise a developmental plot or tale but rather a (visual) depiction or sketch. Deemphasizing development, the text thus seems to elude the by now popularized enlightenment challenge to individuals to take responsibility for their own development and to transform themselves from a state of immaturity to one of complete individuation. Central to the formation of the self is the integration of experiences to achieve an ever-increasing level of self-awareness, i.e., of development or, ideally, of "Bildung."[14] According to the narratological address to the reader that frames the fictional text, this "picture" delineates the outer and inner content of the protagonist's life (1); however, the latter is for the most part missing. The description of the protagonist's inner life is severely curtailed, creating a distance between reader and protagonist that precludes identification, which, of course, would hardly be appropriate considering the unconventionality of the (anti-)heroine.

The narrator does not speculate about the motivation and reasons for the protagonist's actions beyond repeatedly referring to her desire for adventure. Providing little insight into the protagonist's inner values, the narrative prevents a definitive moral evaluation of its central character, ending with the vague and ambivalent address to the reader: "What a shame that this plant had to grow in such poor soil" (1, 35). Withholding any explanation of Dirza's unconventional behavior raises the possibility that Dirza is guided solely by her nature and that this nature is essentially selfish. The text foregrounds a heroine who is driven only by self-interest, by her hunger for adventure, power, fame, and fortune. What distinguishes this character from traditional anti-heroines is that she is not fashioned as a negative foil to an actual or implied virtuous main character.[15] The Gothic elements are used to attribute an element of evil to this experimental character. The narrator's formulations suggest that she intends this character to be both fascinating and evil. Furthermore, she avoids explanations for the heroine's behavior and ultimately avoids value judgments. By suggesting that she is unique and not representative, the writer is able to distance herself from her character. In this way the Gothic allows the author to imagine an unconventional heroine and thus to subvert the contemporary value system governing the role of women.

The orphaned Dirza was placed in a convent where she is unhappy and bored. Worldly literature, Voltaire, Rousseau, poetry, and the latest novels provide the only pleasurable diversions. Her uncle, a prior at a nearby monastery, is equally bored and discontented with his celibate life and thus joins her in these unspiritual reading sessions. Soon the young girl and her middle-aged uncle create their own romance. The setting of a dreary convent, monastery, or cloister, where innocents are held against their will or where horrid crimes are committed, is part of the Gothic imagination. What makes these places so attractive as a setting for crimes is the traditional distance between the sacred and sacrilege. In a place dedicated to celibacy, carnal (incestuous) relations are the ultimate sin. In the Gothic utilization of the setting, good and evil—while seemingly worlds apart—are shown to be uncomfortably close together. Incest and sacrilege push the limits of reader expectations as the text collapses familiar limits of behavior. Desire and self-interest are interpreted as the great equalizers between the sexes. This is not a story of seduction, or besieged womanhood, not even of the older man seducing the younger woman. Instead both are equally discontent with their lives and motivated by self-interest to seek the pleasures of the flesh.

When their relationship becomes known, they escape with money stolen from the coffers of the cloister. Enroute to Italy the uncle—in a case of mistaken identity—is murdered. Dirza leaves for Florence, gives herself a new name, and rewrites her history as she schemes to find her way into the best society. Despite her pregnancy, she participates in as many festivities as possible and seduces a Marquis with her beauty. In stark contrast to the contemporary cult of motherhood, Dirza's pregnancy is downplayed and ignored; the birth is described solely as a life-threatening illness. There is no mention of maternal feelings; and as her newborn son displays the perfect tonsure, Dirza's plans fall apart.[16] Frightened by this mark, she is pressured into telling the truth and is consequently dismissed from polite society.

She flees with her son to Switzerland where she immediately tries to attract a rich count. Fashioning herself as a sentimental heroine, she displays herself for him with "Abelard and Heloise" in her hand. He is not easily seduced but his friend Vaubreuil is. She continues her flirtatious relationship with Vaubreuil in order to be close to the count, who eventually asks her for information about her past in order to clear the way for a marriage. Again she rewrites her personal history; but as she sees herself close to her goal of marriage with the rich count, she has second thoughts—her attraction to Vaubreuil interferes. Before she can make a decision, it is made for her, as the count witnesses a secret meeting between Dirza and Vaubreuil and banishes them both from his sight. After their expulsion they marry and live in Geneva.

After several years, the supernatural stigma of the tonsure changes Dirza's fate again. The Marquis from Florence has a chance encounter with her son, Antoine, and reveals her past to Vaubreuil, who leaves her. Blaming her misfortune on her son, she gives him away and leaves for Frankfurt, initially to look for Vaubreuil. However, the hustle and bustle soon capture her attention and her desire for fame and fortune reawakens.

When she meets a prince who has the reputation of being a womanizer, she agrees to serve as his daughter's governess. For six years she leads a quiet life—summarized in half a sentence—then becomes the prince's mistress. Finally she has all the luxury and power she always craved. During a trip to the spas in Italy, Dirza, who has passed herself off as the prince's wife, is arrested for bigamy and sorcery (*teuflische Künste* 29). Vaubreuil and the Marquis force her to choose between entering a convent or living quietly in the country—Dirza chooses the latter.

Around her fortieth birthday, her son reappears and—despite the fact that she had given him away—lovingly invites her to live with him and his wife in Geneva. Dirza accepts and, again, the next few years are glossed over as uneventful. But during the French Revolution, Dirza's desire for fame and title leads her to become politically active. Her endeavor costs her son his family as he and Dirza have to flee to France, where she starts a politically risky journal. This time her activity costs her son's life, while she is able to escape the executioner. Again, neither Dirza nor the narrator offer any explanation. The contemporary audience raised on sentimental and moralistic novels would have expected a description of the motivation for this callous behavior.

The latest event plunges the protagonist into deep financial crisis; she is forced to become a beggar. But just as the reader might expect traditional poetic justice punishing Dirza for her lifestyle, the plot twists and turns again, and Dirza finds a lottery ticket worth 60,000 Dutch Gilders. This avoidance of the topos of "just rewards" destabilizes narrative conventions and reader expectations by withholding moral evaluation. Furthermore, this *deus ex machina* solution departs from a (moral) cause and effect structure. It offers freedom from the need for careful motivation required by realistic writing conventions. Coincidence as a poetic device suspends causality and creates an opportunity to rethink not only traditional causal relationships, but also concepts such as justice, reward, and punishment.

With her new-found wealth, Dirza retreats to a remote estate where she is shown to disregard conventional, gender-specific behavior. She despises children, who are not allowed on her property, and she treats her servants harshly. As a monstrous "non-woman," she is stripped of all feminine virtues such as the capability for nurturing and relating to the needs of others. She is mean-spirited, combative, tight-fisted, and prone to speak ill of others (34). A recluse, she dresses only in plain peasant clothes, disregarding cultural differentiations marked by clothing (for example the distinctions between Sunday and workday clothing), and selecting garb beneath her economic means. Other behavior such as drinking only beer and eating peasant food also indicates that she does not live according to the standard that she could afford and that decorum requires. Her female body is shown to take on grotesque qualities.

Furthermore, this conduct suggests a certain witch-like quality. Eventually, she gives her estate away and takes the rest of her money to live with Gypsies in the Bohemian forests. The Gypsies are said to admire her because of the money she gives them.

The narrator combines the Gothic with ethnic stereotyping to denote the sinister quality of the main character. The Gypsies are declared the lowest form of human companionship that Dirza could possibly select. They are referred to as the scum of the earth or the abject (Kristeva) of humankind ("der Auswurf der Menschheit" 35). By drawing on this ethnic prejudice, Bürger, without going into much detail, is able to conjure up an image of civilization's Other. The Gypsies represent chaos, wilderness, lack of ethics and morality, as well as lack of cleanliness—in short, lack of culture. They are made to represent all that needs to be suppressed or rejected in order to achieve cultural order as a basis for and part of subject formation. The fact that Dirza embraces this Other instead of expelling it is both a confirmation and an interpretation of her behavior throughout her life. Disorderliness, chaos, all that precedes culture—the Semiotic in Kristeva's terminology—is part of her character in which chaotic wishes and desires are not abjected but retained.

Processes of abjection underlie, for example, the establishment of the incest taboo, as incest would threaten to dissolve social and ethical laws (i.e., culture). In "Dirza," the transgression of the cultural (symbolic) laws prohibiting incest sets a whole host of events in motion, destabilizing cultural laws: "This thoughtless moment created a series of mishaps for Dirza" (4). Determined by her selfish pursuit of pleasure and power, she does not fully participate in this process of abjection, i.e., she does not completely subject herself to the laws of culture and subject formation.

Since the protagonist is not primarily focused on the family,[17] the author needs to experiment with a value system appropriate for her character's circumstances. This requires a different setting than that of the middle-class household. Compared to conventional realistic domestic fiction, the female protagonist embraces a wider range of possibilities and positions, challenging the distribution of conventional gendered virtues and vices. When compared to characters from the dominant narrative genre, the realistic novel, Dirza, more than Bürger's other women characters, would have to be categorized as a negative character who does not embody the dominant value system. Realistic novels, however, hardly concentrate on a sole negative character. Instead, negative characters are usually foils for the protagonist, thus embodying the struggle of opposing value systems; this is not the case in "Dirza." Instead, her non-traditional characterization and lack of appropriate feminine behavior is underscored by the Gothic sense of evil—the allegations of sorcery and the witch-like qualities she takes on in her old age. At the same time, this atmosphere of evil produced by the Gothic elements precludes a moral evaluation.

If her negative character is not conceptualized as a warning to women, as a story of how not to live their lives, then this form of characterization ultimately also calls for modification of the narrative convention; in short, it requires a different genre. The realistic novel, especially in the sentimental or moralistic vein, the forté of women's creativity (Schindel),[18] more often than not confined its virtuous female characters to a narrow range of action. Lacking genuine possibilities for action, their potential for agency is limited. Kate Ferguson Ellis detects a similar problematic deemphasis of female agency in the English sentimental novel, where a woman was confined to passivity, where she was unable to "determine her own actions, or even influence in any active way what other people think about her" (30). Reading the sentimental novel as a "vehicle for protesting 'the wrongs of woman,'" she surmises that it "owes much of its popularity with woman readers to this fact." She also notes the lack of opportunity for decisive action associated with this genre: "But its heroine cannot even imagine, much less act upon, liberatory alternatives" (30). Ellis thus considers the feminine sphere at the center of sentimental plots as a "power vacuum" (219).

All of Bürger's texts ventured to depart from this power vacuum created by the realistic domestic novel. Experimentation with Gothic themes, icons, and structures is only one of her strategies of resistance. One could speculate that, in general, interest in the Gothic was a reaction against the obsessive focus on the domestic sphere and its value system. The Gothic seemed to emerge in the heyday of the domestic sentimental novel. For the English context, Ellis notes: "The initial popularity of the Gothic novel at the end of the eighteenth century thus comes at a point in the history of the novel at which the sphere of virtuous action has narrowed to a very thin line" (30), a phenomenon that can be detected in German literature during the same time period as well.

In order to foreground the uniqueness of her female protagonist and to call into question the convention of positioning woman exclusively in the domestic sphere, Bürger experiments with certain elements from the Gothic tradition without fully engaging the cataclysmic demise, the obsessive neuroses, the violent madness that we have come to associate with the genre. However, the sense of the unfamiliar, the erratic, "the essentially threatening nature of the world," and especially the disintegration of accepted boundaries (Backscheider 157) that underlies the Gothic experience also underlies Bürger's narrative "Dirza." For example, the text challenges the limits of the "natural," foreseeable, and rational. Seemingly natural gender boundaries are transgressed. The attributes traditionally associated with femininity—passivity, modesty, an ability for empathy and nurturing, and the acceptance of the domestic sphere as the primary range of social action—cannot be found in Dirza. Her feminine appearance does not "speak the truth"; it does not reveal her true character, which lacks "feminine" qualities.[19] Most shocking—and yet possibly intriguing—to a contemporary audience must have been her disregard for the sanctity of marriage, her contempt for familial relations (the incestuous relationship with her uncle and the abandonment of her son), but also her egoistic hunger for adventure, fame, and fortune.

Dirza's life in the domestic sphere is purposefully excluded with summary remarks. Instead, as we have seen, the narrative emphasis is on a broad sweeping plot spanning a lifetime in a few pages, accentuating the many unique moments and events. In short, only those events that propel the plot forward are foregrounded. This emphasis on action, typical of the Gothic tradition, results in frenzied motion from one detail to another, and has been likened to the structure of the Gothic cathedral with its frenetic movement in ornamentation and the larger sweeping, rising movements of construction (Bayer-Berenbaum 55). Dirza's decisions propelling the plot forward are not conceptualized as stages in her development leading to greater awareness and to integrated experiences. The character does not learn from the events in her life. Instead, similar decisions are made repeatedly—and apparently at random—producing an incessant repetition of seemingly interchangeable decisions. Bayer-Berenbaum submits that these repetitious patterns evoke a sense of infinity: "In Gothic art...a ceaseless pounding of identical strokes suggests the infinite persistence of a particular form" (67); she goes on to argue that "[b]eyond the suggestion of infinity, repetition functions as an organizing principle in Gothic art that replaces symmetry" (70). In Bürger's text, this Gothic repetition of a particular form is indicative of a refusal to show the protagonist as undergoing a learning experience or a development. This lack of development distinguishes Bürger's narrative form from the developmental novel. When compared to these realist modes of writing, Bürger's plot seems repetitive and the characters psychologically underdeveloped. The reader is whisked through a web of recurring obstacles that seem to resist a teleological structure and the rules of credibility. In "Dirza" it would be difficult to locate a conventional climax toward which the action builds or from which it declines; the plot lacks all symmetry. A swift protracted chain of events replaces development.

The integration of Gothic elements into Bürger's narrative problematizes not only the developmental narrative form but also its underlying idea of a self striving for individuation and autonomy. Furthermore, the Gothic elements tend to dislodge causal relationships and remove the insistence on a developmental narrative with its belief in the protagonist's growth and maturation. Lacking the element of development, Bürger's narrative is a significant departure from realistic writing conventions, especially the sentimental, moral, didactic, or developmental novels so dominant in her time.

The traces of the Gothic imagination provide a safely distanced means of making sense of phenomena and potentialities of experience that under normal (i.e., realist) writing conventions would be too troubling or menacing to contemplate. They allow the writer to create an experimental, atypical character without giving moral explanations.

In "Dirza," Bürger's use of the Gothic as a method of inscribing meaning, of accounting for disturbing phenomena and dealing with uncertainty, is linked to her formal displeasure with the increasing staleness of the possibilities of the realist writing conventions at the end of the century. The Gothic imagination provides her with a certain amount of independence from the referential context of these forms of realist writing, resulting in an attempt to produce an unconventional vision of reality through conventional narrative.

Notes

[1] In the German cultural context, texts belonging to *Schauerromantik* have been discussed for the most part in the context of research on *Trivialliteratur*: Appell; Greiner; Schulte-Sasse; Christa Bürger; Christa Bürger et al.; Plaul; Nusser. The discussion thus focuses on issues of canon formation and its exclusionary strategies, on the binary oppositions between "high" and "low" literature, or between "art" and "entertainment." In the context of eighteenth-century literature and culture, the complex relationship between women's texts and *Trivialliteratur* and the issue of exclusion of women's literature from the canon has haunted most feminist scholarship of the last twenty years. Yet an analysis of this relationship and its consequences for feminist methodology remains to be written; this is certainly not the place for it. The issue has been discussed in the following general studies: Gnüg and Möhrmann; Becker-Cantarino; Weigel; Brinker-Gabler; and in studies with a specific focus on the eighteenth century in Germany: von Hoff; Wurst (*Frauen*; "Negotiations"); Kord (*Blick*); Cocalis; Meise; Gallas and Heuser; Goodman and Waldstein. The positions have recently been summarized by Lange and Kord, who also address the perennial question of the aesthetic value of women's literature at the end of the eighteenth century (Lange 18; Kord, *Anonymität* 173).

[2] The relationship between *Schauerromantik* ("shudder romanticism"), which is similar to the genre of the Gothic in English literature, and *Romantik* would warrant further exploration which goes, however, beyond the interest and scope of this paper. The discussion of this genre in the secondary literature is limited by the fact that *Schauerromantik* is associated with trivial writing traditions.

[3] Jäger's study on *Empfindsamkeit* still offers the most comprehensive discussion of the concept and period. See also Wegmann (especially 100–02).

[4] With respect to a specific group of women's novels, Christa Bürger has referred to these products as belonging to a "middle ground" between autonomous texts and trivial literature (*Leben* 27, 31). However, I do not consider her definition representative for novels written around the turn of the century. Therefore, the analytical category of "mittlere Sphäre" is of limited value.

[5] Day has a longer list, which in its entirety does not apply to Bürger's texts.

[6] On a very general level, this study is informed by Sigrid Weigel's *Die Stimme der Medusa,* where she calls for the historical description of women's literature in the context of other (literary) discursive practice (9).

[7] Brandes attests to the predominantly affirmative character of women's writing because their contributions had to meet contemporary expectations in order to be commercially successful. There are of course a few exceptions, especially among the women of the Romantic circles, for example Bettina von Arnim and Sophie Mereau.

[8] See also the standard works on women's novels in the eighteenth century: Touaillon; Beaujean; Meise; Schieth; Christa Bürger (*Leben*); Lange.

[9] In addition this creates a pleasurable spectacle on stage, increasing the entertainment value of the play.

[10] In Bürger's texts, Bohemia comes to represent an exotic place at the border of civilization, associated not only with adventure but with danger and a lack of civilization and culture.

[11] Of course, this emphasis on the "naturalness" of the creative process "straight from the heart" is a common form of preventive self-containment used by many women writers of the time. It suggests that the author is well aware of her position within the cultural hierarchy. In an earlier collection of poetry her perceived need for gender-specific "modesty" was even more pronounced: "Keines dieser Gedichte habe ich machen *wollen*; Wehmuth oder Scherz, Gefühl oder Laune, haben sie gezeugt, und es ist ihnen daher auch nie erlaubt, Ansprüche, welche gelehrten Männern misfallen müsten, zu machen; zwar sind unter den gütigen Unterzeichnern sehr gelehrte Männer, aber diese kennen mich und wissen, wie weit ich entfent bin, mich über die Gränzen [sic] des beschränkten weiblichen Wissens hinüber wagen zu wollen. Gefühl, Fantasie und Sprache sind mir geworden, und mehr als diese drei hervorbringen, will ich nicht aufstellen, und wie viel mehr wird noch erfordert, um klassisch werden zu können" (*Gedichte* xviii).

[12] How much of it is tongue-in-cheek, we can only guess; comments by contemporaries portray Bürger as strong-willed and demanding; Friedrich Schiller, for example, commented to Goethe that her demands made her quite intolerable (*ganz unausstehlich*).

[13] See also Elisa von der Recke's autobiographical writings. Von der Recke also departs from structuring her autobiographical life as solely based on the conventional stages of womanhood in the private sphere (youth, courtship, marriage, motherhood, old age). Especially in the second volume, she not only

attempts to integrate her public and private self by focusing on her public tasks but she also analyzes and comments on her life story. Both narrative strategies strive to give meaning to that part of her life that exceeds that of the context of family. For an analysis see Goodman, Meise ("Autobiography"), and Wurst ("Recke").

[14] The question, of course, is whether the demand for a process of individuation, often associated with Kant's summary of Enlightenment thought in his essay *An Answer to the Question: "What is Enlightenment?,"* has any relevance for women, who were clearly not included among Kant's independent beings in civil affairs. This issue concerns not only the creation of an integrated (female) subject in novels, in developmental novels in particular, but also in autobiographical writing. The developmental novel *par excellence,* the *Bildungsroman*, achieves the highest prestige within the hierarchy of the genre.

[15] Although Dirza is technically a member of the impoverished nobility, this class status is downplayed. Delineated as a representative of neither the aristocracy nor of the middle class, this indeterminacy adds to the ambivalence of this character.

[16] It has been noted elsewhere that the trauma of giving birth, the experience of pregnancy, women's physicality and sexuality, as well as the trope of giving birth to monsters, are frequent themes in women's Gothic writing. See also Fleenor, especially the essays in part IV, "Maternity—The Body as Literary Metaphor" (227-79).

[17] Whenever the character is linked to a traditional family situation, the narrative summarily dismisses these years as uneventful.

[18] For a description of the strategies Schindel utilizes to contain women's writing, see Wurst (*Frauen* 49-52). He considers women especially suited for romances in the domestic genre because of their more refined moral sensibilities and sense of social decorum (xvii-xx): "Ehre den Frauen, die durch ihre Schriften wirklich das Gefühl für das Schöne und Gute ansprechen, unterhalten, und besonders für ihre Mitschwestern lehrreich sind: sie mögen fortfahren zu erfreuen und zu nützen" (xxvii). His description is important because he is the foremost biographer of women's literature at the beginning of the nineteenth century and offers as close to a contemporary systematic account as we can get given the material available.

[19] This statement refers only to her youth; in her old age, her "non-feminine" appearance mirrors that of her actions. The character drops her feminine mask.

Works Cited

Appell, J.W. *Die Ritter-, Räuber- und Schauerromantik: Zur Geschichte der deutschen Unterhaltungsliteratur.* Leipzig: Wilhelm Engelmann, 1859.

Backscheider, Paula R. *Spectacular Politics: Theatrical Power and Mass Culture in Early Modern England.* Baltimore: Johns Hopkins UP, 1993.

Bayer-Berenbaum, Linda. *The Gothic Imagination: Expansion in Gothic Literature and Art.* London: Associated UP, 1982.

Beaujean, Marion. *Der Trivialroman in der zweiten Hälfte des 18. Jahrhunderts: Die Ursprünge des modernen Unterhaltungsromans.* 2nd ed. Bonn: Bouvier, 1969.

Becker-Cantarino, Barbara. *Der lange Weg zur Mündigkeit: Frau und Literatur 1500–1800.* 1987. München: dtv, 1989.

Brandes, Helga. "Der Frauenroman und die literarisch-publizistische Öffentlichkeit im 18. Jahrhundert." *Untersuchungen zum Roman von Frauen um 1800.* 41–51.

Brinker-Gabler, Gisela, ed. *Deutsche Literatur von Frauen vom Mittelalter bis zur Gegenwart.* 2 Vols. München: Beck, 1988.

Bürger, Christa. *Leben Schreiben.* Stuttgart: Metzler, 1990.

———. *Der Ursprung der bürgerlichen Institution Kunst im höfischen Weimar: Literatursoziologische Untersuchungen zum klassischen Goethe.* Frankfurt a.M: Suhrkamp, 1977.

Bürger, Christa et al., eds. *Zur Dichotomisierung von hoher und niederer Literatur.* Frankfurt a.M.: Suhrkamp, 1982.

Bürger, Elise. *Adelheit, Gräfinn von Teck.* 1799. Jena: Voigtsche Buchhandlung, 1812.

———. "Begegnung im Walde." *Lilien-Blätter und Zypressenzweige.* 111–30.

———. "Dirza." *Irrgänge des weiblichen Herzens.* Hamburg: Buchhandlung der neuen Verlagsgesellschaft, 1799.

———. *Gedichte: Als erster Band ihrer Gedichte, Reise-Blätter, Kunst- und Lebens-Ansichten.* Hamburg: Conrad Müller, 1812.

———. *Lilien-Blätter und Zypressenzweige von Theodora* (Elise Bürger, geb. Hahn). Frankfurt a.M.: Heller & Rohm, 1826.

Cocalis, Susan. Introduction. *Thalia's Daughter's: German Women Dramatists from the Eighteenth Century to the Present.* Ed. Susan Cocalis and Ferrel Rose. Tübingen: Francke, 1996.

Day, William Patrick. *In the Circles of Fear and Desire: A Study of Gothic Fantasy.* Chicago: U of Chicago P, 1985.

Ellis, Kate Ferguson. *The Contested Castle: Gothic Novels and the Subversion of Domestic Ideology.* Urbana: U of Illinois P, 1989.

Fleenor, Juliann E., ed. *The Female Gothic.* Montreal: Eden, 1983.

Gallas, Helga, and Magdalene Heuser. Introduction. *Untersuchungen zum Roman von Frauen um 1800.* 1–9.

Gnüg, Hiltrud, und Renate Möhrmann, eds. *Frauen Literatur Geschichte: Schreibende Frauen vom Mittelalter bis zur Gegenwart.* Stuttgart: Metzler, 1985.

Goethe, Johann Wolfgang, and Friedrich Schiller. "Über den Dilettantismus." *Gedenkausgabe der Werke, Briefe und Gespräche: Schriften zur Literatur.* Zurich: Artemis, 1950. 729–54.

Goodman, Katherine. *Dis/Closures: Women's Autobiography in Germany between 1790 and 1914.* New York: Lang, 1986.

Goodman, Katherine, and Edith Waldstein. *In the Shadow of Olympus: German Women Writers around 1800.* Albany: State U of New York P, 1992.

Greiner, Martin. *Die Entstehung der modernen Unterhaltungsliteratur: Studien zum Trivialroman des 18. Jahrhunderts.* Reinbek: Rowohlt, 1964.

Heuser, Magdalene. "'Ich wollte dieß und das von meinem Buche sagen, und gerieth in ein Vernünfteln': Poetologische Reflexionen in den Romanvorreden." *Untersuchungen zum Roman von Frauen um 1800.* 52–65.

Hoff, Dagmar von. *Dramen des Weiblichen: Deutsche Dramatikerinnen um 1800.* Opladen: Westdeutscher Verlag, 1989.

Jäger, Georg. *Empfindsamkeit und Roman: Wortgeschichte, Theorie und Kritik im 18. und frühen 19. Jahrhundert.* Stuttgart: Kohlhammer, 1969.

Kontje, Todd. "Socialization and Alienation in the Female *Bildungsroman*." *Impure Reason: Dialectic of Enlightenment in Germany.* Ed. W. Daniel Wilson and Robert Holub. Detroit: Wayne State UP, 1993. 221–41.

Kord, Susanne. *Ein Blick hinter die Kulissen: Deutschsprachige Dramatikerinnen im 18. und 19. Jahrhundert.* Stuttgart: Metzler, 1992.

———. *Sich einen Namen machen: Anonymität und weibliche Autorschaft 1700–1900.* Stuttgart: Metzler, 1996.

Kristeva, Julia. *The Powers of Horror: An Essay on Abjection.* New York: Columbia UP, 1982.

Lange, Sigrid. *Spiegelgeschichten: Geschlechter und Poetiken in der Frauenliteratur um 1800.* Frankfurt a.M.: Helmer, 1995.

Meise, Helga. "'I owed my diary the truth of my views': Femininity and Autobiography after 1784." *Impure Reason: Dialectic of Enlightenment in Germany.* Ed. W. Daniel Wilson and Robert Holub. Detroit: Wayne State UP, 1993. 203–20.

———. *Die Unschuld und die Schrift: Deutsche Frauenromane im 18. Jahrhundert.* 1983. Frankfurt a.M.: Helmer, 1992.

Niggl, Günter. *Die Geschichte der deutschen Autobiographie im 18. Jahrhundert: Theoretische Grundlegung und literarische Entfaltung.* Stuttgart: Metzler, 1977.

Nusser, Peter. *Trivialliteratur.* Stuttgart: Metzler, 1991.

Plaul, Hainer. *Illustrierte Geschichte der Trivialliteratur.* Hildesheim: Olms, 1983.

Recke, Elisa von der. *Elisa von der Recke.* Ed. Paul Rachel. Vol. 1 and 2. Leipzig: Dieterich, 1900–1902.

Runge, Anita. "Nachwort." *Caroline Auguste Fischer: Der Günstling*. Hildesheim: Olms, 1988.

Schieth, Lydia. *Die Entwicklung des deutschen Frauenromans im ausgehenden 18. Jahrhundert: Ein Beitrag zur Gattungsgeschichte*. Frankfurt a.M.: Lang, 1987.

Schiller, Friedrich. "Brief an Goethe." 5 May 1802. *Nationalausgabe*. Vol. 31. Ed. Stefan Ormanns. Weimar: Böhlaus Nachfolger, 1985.

Schindel, Karl Wilhelm Otto von. *Die deutschen Schriftstellerinnen des neunzehnten Jahrhunderts*. 1823-25. Hildesheim: Olms, 1978.

Schulte-Sasse, Jochen. *Die Kritik an der Trivialliteratur seit der Aufklärung: Studien zur Geschichte des Kitschbegriffs*. München: Fink, 1971.

Touaillon, Christine. *Der deutsche Frauenroman des 18. Jahrhunderts*. Wien: Braumüller, 1919.

Untersuchungen zum Roman von Frauen um 1800. Ed. Helga Gallas and Magdalene Heuser. Tübingen: Niemeyer, 1990.

Waugh, Patricia. *Metafiction: The Theory and Practice of Self-Conscious Fiction*. London: Methuen, 1984.

Weigel, Sigrid. *Die Stimme der Medusa: Schreibweisen in der Gegenwartsliteratur von Frauen*. Dülmen: tende, 1987.

Wegmann, Nikolaus. *Diskurse der Empfindsamkeit: Zur Geschichte eines Gefühls in der Literatur des 18. Jahrhunderts*. Stuttgart: Metzler, 1988.

Wurst, Karin A. "'Begreifst Du aber / wie viel andächtig schwärmen leichter, als / Gut handeln ist?' Elisabeth (Elisa) Charlotte Konstantia von der Recke (1754-1833)." *Lessing Yearbook* 25. Ed. Richard Schade. Detroit: Wayne State UP, 1993. 97-116.

_____. *Frauen und Drama im achtzehnten Jahrhundert*. Köln: Böhlau, 1991.

_____. "Negotiations of Containment: The 'Trivial' Tradition and Elise Bürger's 'Adelheit, Gräfinn von Teck' (1799)." *Thalia's Daughters: German Women Dramatists From the Eighteenth Century to the Present*. Ed. Susan Cocalis and Ferrel Rose. Tübingen: Francke, 1996. 35-51.

Zantop, Susanne. "'Aus der Not eine Tugend...': Tugendgebot und Öffentlichkeit bei Friederike Helene Unger." *Untersuchungen zum Roman von Frauen um 1800*. 132-47.

Sophie Mereau's Authorial Masquerades and the Subversion of Romantic *Poesie*

Daniel Purdy

Hermeneutic understanding purports to penetrate a spiritual depth imbedded within texts. Historically when a subject's engagement with a text has not attained hermeneutic insight that encounter has been characterized as a mere performance, an unsuccessful attempt to empathize with a content or character not wholly one's own. In the following paper, I wish to investigate how masquerade disrupts an aesthetics that predicates meaning on its own ability to invoke a reality behind the surface of representation. The early fiction and late translations of Sophie Mereau demonstrate that literary masquerade served as a strategy for women writers to counter the gendered ontology implicit in early Romantic aesthetics. (DP)

At the end of the eighteenth century, translations were integral to the formation of a national literary tradition in Germany. Virtually all canonical male writers—Lessing, Schiller, Tieck, Hölderlin, Goethe, Friedrich and August Schlegel—practiced the art. These efforts did more than introduce foreign works to German readers, they also placed German writers in a comparative European context. By transforming *The Iliad* or *The Decameron* into German, these eighteenth-century translations suggested that domestically produced literary works could be integrated into a broad European culture. Translations naturalized foreign works, thereby eliminating the requirement that a cosmopolitan reader be proficient in many languages. Far from encouraging parochialism, the eighteenth-century flood of translations allowed middle-class readers to perceive their own literary culture in relationship to the movements and achievements of other literatures. For the German writer, translations suggested an implicit continuity between their own creations and foreign traditions. Thus, translations of Cervantes became more important for understanding Tieck's fantastic tales and dramas, just as the first German edition of Homer was able to make Goethe's *Die Leiden des jungen Werthers* (*The Sorrows of Young Werther*) more accessible to sentimental readers.

Sophie Mereau, like the male authors around her, employed translations as a strategic adjunct to her own writing. She translated seventeenth-century French women authors to provide an historical precedent and cosmopolitan context within which her own feminist writing could be understood. Her rendering of Ninon de Lenclos's letters into German, as well as her translation of Madame de Lafayette's *La Princesse de Clèves* (*Die Prinzessin von Cleves*) sought to place literature by German women within the broader European context of female authorship. Like German male authors who used translations to position their own works in relation to what were increasingly understood as national traditions of literature, Mereau sought to reinforce her own, what we might today call feminist, agenda by introducing foreign women authors to the German reading public. After discussing the manner in which Mereau posits a continuity of female authorship within European literary history, I will consider how her translations also provide a political critique of Romantic and Classical figurations of the feminine.

Mereau's literary allegiances lay somewhere between the Sentimentalism of Sophie von la Roche and the Romantic epistles of Bettina von Arnim, Rahel Varnhagen, and Caroline Schlegel (Fetting 74).[1] A popular salon figure who had divorced her first husband in 1801, Mereau drew the intense affections of Friedrich Schlegel and then Clemens Brentano, whom she married in 1803. During her entire literary career, Mereau was very active as a translator. She introduced Italian, French, and Spanish texts to German readers. She died during childbirth in 1806, a tragically ironic fate, given her lifelong effort to escape the constraints of bourgeois domesticity.[2]

Her interest in Ninon de Lenclos was not based on biographical similarities. The differences in their environments were too great for Mereau to draw a direct correspondence between their lives. Lenclos's personal philosophy, more than her biographical partners, attracted Mereau. Lenclos was the only daughter of a noble family thrown into relative poverty by the exile of her father Henri de L'Enclos because of a politically sensitive love affair. Ninon de Lenclos's mother was an extremely pious Catholic who struggled with her husband over the education of their daughter. In general, one can say that her father had the strongest influence on her. Lenclos's own sexual emancipation was based upon her insistence that she be allowed the same privileges as the men of her class. The center of a prominent Parisian salon during the reign of Louis XIV, Lenclos felt no compunction to hide her changing desires from her lovers, freely exchanging a new amour for an old one. More than a defense of free love, Lenclos's position asserted a female emancipation from social restriction (Hammerstein 59): "I see that the emptiest and most hollow expectations are set before us; and that men reserve the right to strive for the highest and most dignified goals, so that from this moment on I declare myself a man" (Mereau, *Kalathiskos* 60). For her entire adult life, well into her eighties, Lenclos practiced an open female libertinage that disregarded aristocratic concerns for preserving clear family lineage and alliances through marriage. Twice she gave birth to a son, each of whom was raised by the father. In the first instance the two claimants were forced to settle the question of fatherhood through a duel. The second son was taken by the father under the condition that Lenclos never reveal her relationship to the boy. We shall see that Lenclos's casual, aristocratic disdain for motherhood made her writing a particularly potent counter to the bourgeois model of the nuclear family and its accompanying celebration of the "natural" mother.

The impact of Mereau's translation of Lenclos is felt on three decisively different registers. In terms of literary history, it helped constitute a tradition of female authorship. By its very existence, the translation posits an historical continuity between German women around 1800 and seventeenth-century French female authors. In addition, by reflecting on the nature of writing, the text presents a critique of the Romantic and Classical denigration of women's writing as dilettantish and lacking in depth. Through her translation of what she claims to be Lenclos's theory of "feminine writing style," Mereau provides an ideological framework within which women authors can situate their own artistic projects.

Finally, through its own masterly manipulation of often contradictory nuances, Mereau's translation and criticism of the correspondence provide a prime example of precisely that mode of writing Lenclos purportedly describes. By synthesizing divergent and often antagonistic philosophical categories into a coherent epistolary form, Mereau's translation subtly integrates Lenclos's courtly arguments into the aesthetic debates of the Romantic period. The act of translation placed an old text within a new context, thereby creating two distinct temporal effects. On the one hand, Lenclos's views provided a sharp contrast to the figuration of women common to Germany in 1800. In that sense, her letters appeared within that discursive field as a potentially disruptive alternative to the prevailing representation of femininity. On the other hand, Lenclos's letters were already a hundred years old when Mereau translated them into German, and, accordingly, they represented a position that, within the progressive narrative of conventional political history, would have been termed "pre-revolutionary" or "outdated." As a defender of French absolutism, Lenclos was obviously unmodern, and yet her insistence on gender equality was more progressive than the politics most nineteenth-century German women dared to articulate. Mereau's translations integrate and subordinate divergent categories, such as French versus German, aristocratic versus bourgeois, and progressive versus reactionary, within a single continuous tradition of female authorship. As Uta Treder suggests, the "untimeliness" of Mereau's translation suggests a higher code of feminine existence, one removed from the ideologies of any particular era (183).

In 1805, Mereau's translation of Lenclos began to appear at varying intervals in the first issues of the Weimar *Journal für deutsche Frauen*. This project had, however, already been announced in a stunningly provocative biographical essay on Ninon de Lenclos published in the 1801–02 almanac *Kalathiskos,* in which Mereau argued that Lenclos's writings ought to be interpreted as an example of how women could live out their assertion of sexual equality. She clearly hoped that they would serve both as an interpretation and a redeployment of Lenclos's philosophy against the gendered metaphysics of nature that had come to dominate Romantic discussions around Weimar.[3] In her biographical essay, Mereau argued that Lenclos's claim to equality must be interpreted through her actions and not according to universal claims about femininity. Lenclos's letters were, for Mereau, an ethical model; their translation introduced a radical new mode of identity into the German context, while simultaneously legitimating the position of women such as herself. Mereau deploys Lenclos in much the same way that a fictional character serves the interests of a story. Lenclos functions as an independent voice that reinforces Mereau's own position. In a sense, Mereau masquerades as Lenclos when she translates her work, and in so doing she rewrites Lenclos's actual text. The empathetic engagement between translator and original is invoked to justify Mereau's appropriation of Lenclos's identity as an author. Mereau does not merely transfer Lenclos's words into German, she writes a new text, one that at key moments does not correspond to anything in the original. The boundary in Mereau's writing between literary translation and creation is often indistinct. The author Mereau speaks through Lenclos as much as through any figure in her novels. This orchestration of fiction and translation through the artistic "vision" of a single author was a prominent component of Romantic aesthetics. Mereau's inventive translations of Lenclos anticipate Bettina von Arnim's later epistolary reevaluations of her friendships with Karoline von Günderode and Goethe. Despite this legacy, Mereau's invention of different voices has been treated as a false masquerade, one which deserved to be stripped away in order to reveal the actual woman behind the literary representation. I wish to make a case against such "unmaskings" by arguing that they violently disrupt the play of ambiguities inherent in textual personas. By claiming to expose a depth behind a representation, the critic forecloses the possibility of multiple meanings, while reducing the text to a single usually highly ideological interpretation.

Already in her first, anonymously published novel *Das Blüthenalter der Empfindung* (The Blossoming of Sensibility), the question of how an author deploys alien voices led critics to insist that Mereau ought to write only in her own "real" voice as a woman. Utopian in its conception, *Das Blüthenalter* depicts two sentimental lovers who struggle to escape a patriarchal legal order that denies women their natural rights. Frustrated at every turn, the lovers Nanette and Albert escape Europe for the New World. The novel ends with the idealistic hope that in America women can become equal partners with men.

While modern scholars now place *Das Blüthenalter* and Mereau's subsequent writing in a fairly well-established canon of female authors, that sense of historical lineage was far from evident in the eighteenth century. As Sigrid Weigel notes: "The content and narrative mode of women's writing cannot be called original expressions of female experience *tout court*. Rather they are attempts to find some leeway within male culture and steps towards liberation from it. The beginnings of the female literary tradition are primarily inauthentic (*uneigentlich*) self-expressions of women, expressions of the second, not the first sex, and so are not genuinely autonomous expressions" ("Focus" 64).[4] Weigel goes on to cite Mereau's narrative voice in *Das Blüthenalter* as an illustration of how female authors cautiously disguised themselves in order to participate in literary culture. *Das Blüthenalter* has an ambiguous first-person narrator who is identified as male, yet whose characteristics remain strangely undefined throughout the novel. For Weigel this half-formed male voice functions as a mask for the feminist voice of the author, and, in her recent study of Mereau, Katharina von Hammerstein directly reiterates Weigel's position (257). This insistence that the vaguely masculine narrator of *Das Blüthenalter* is nothing more than a mask forced upon a woman writing in a masculine literary society presents all too stark an opposition between feminine subjectivity and the inherently fictional quality of literary characters. In her intense concentration upon authentic feminine subjecthood, Weigel sweeps past the question of how writing in general, both in literature and non-fiction, constructs "figures" that refract and distort the identity of their authors. Even when Mereau writes about female figures in her novels and her historical essays, she posits them as possible configurations of female identity rather than as mimetic representations of her own true self. Furthermore, in Mereau's "feminist" prose the contingency of her characters' relation to real historical conditions is used to doubly and deliberately mark as ideal inventions these literary figures who in their irreality cast a critical gaze upon existing historical conditions. Her fictional characters are often deliberately implausible representations of their own era.

In *Das Blüthenalter* the hyperbolic sentimentalism of the narrator underlines the emancipatory "falseness" of the text's representation. Contemporary readers, such as Friedrich Schlegel, an intimate friend and critic of Mereau, commented on the "feminine" tone of the male narrator. Writing to his brother August, Friedrich Schlegel starts to summarize the novel but ends up commenting on Mereau's "failure" to write in a masculine voice: "The novel opened with the depiction of a young person, in whom all manner of emotions swam together with purple intensity. It sat all alone in the grass. I use the word 'it' because I believed that the narrator was really a girl, although it was supposed to be a boy" (278). For Schlegel, the ambiguity and ultimate transparency of the narrator's gender indicates that Mereau was incapable of writing as a man. He recommends that she confine herself to female representations, suggesting that they would flow more "naturally" from her pen. Schlegel's conception of a successful female artist is one who intuitively and almost unavoidably portrays her own sex. He concludes his remarks on Mereau by comparing her to the painter Angelika Kaufmann: "If she could really depict properly, then she would do it like Angelika Kaufmann, for whom breasts and hips just flow from her fingertips" (279). Weigel and Schlegel clearly have different sympathies for female authors, yet their mutual insistence that women write foremost as women is predicated upon a shared assumption that an essential or authentic feminine identity cannot or should not be disguised in fiction. Weigel prefers Mereau to write about female figures because the progressive emancipation of women would seem to require it. Schlegel maintains that Mereau cannot write about anything but feminity because her natural condition as female precludes it. With regard to *Das Blüthenalter* both critics write from ideological positions that rule out the possibility that an ambiguously gendered fictional character might have an emancipatory quality.

The narrator's discourse certainly allows the reader to suspect that his feminist convictions are not really his own, i.e., that of a man. For Schlegel, this meant that Mereau was not a convincing writer; for Weigel, it meant that Mereau was trapped in an inauthentic masquerade. I would argue, however, that by allowing the male narrator to be taken for a female, *Das Blüthenalter* foregrounds the performative quality of gender in the text. By allowing a purportedly male character to be identified as female, the novel draws attention to the manner in which discourse, as opposed to the natural body, determines our assumptions about gender. The reader's doubt as to the narrator's true gender leads to the conclusion that a woman has inserted herself into a masculine literary convention of the desiring narrator. Instead of concluding that the novel was written by a woman, the suspicious reader might decide that the narrative voice belongs to a woman. The implications of this maneuver are manifold. By seeming to tip the mask of the male narrator, the novel suggests that he might indeed be a woman masquerading as man, opening up the further possibility that the novel could be read as a coded tale of a "passionate female friendship." While provocative, such a reading would again look past the inherently ambiguous status of the narrator's voice. By keeping our attention on the implausibly emancipated male speaker of *Das*

Bluthenalter, the novel depicts a literary character who fails to seem "real," i.e., truly masculine, because he expresses his desires in a passive manner (Schlegel's complaint) and because he makes overt statements against patriarchal marriage and inheritance laws that strip women of their property and personal freedom. The "falseness" of the narrator's character is directly tied to the idealized thoughts he utters. The irreal, or unconventional, quality of Mereau's narrator derives from the utopian impossibility that a male lover in the eighteenth century would have expressed the political views that Albert is made to speak in *Das Blüthenalter.* What Weigel and Schlegel describe as a mask for authentic female subjectivity is in fact a radical reconfiguration of gender norms, one so extreme that to readers with fixed gender ideologies it could only seem "fake." Following the same line of analysis, Treder concludes: "The feminine-androgynous narration, which draws masculine and feminine perspectives into itself, highlights the unjust and outdated condition of women more clearly than any other eighteenth-century women's novel (175).

A similar correlation between social critique and visibly false representation appears in Mereau's translations of Lenclos's correspondence with her paramour, the Marquis de Villanceau. Only in this case, the question of a character's irreal speech does not involve a debate over the implausibility of a fictional representation; rather it comes in the form of a scholarly debate over the historical accuracy of Mereau's translation. In her introduction to Lenclos's letters, Mereau acknowledges that some were more likely to have been written in the spirit of Lenclos than actually to have been composed by the historical person herself. Noting the editorial debates surrounding previous French editions of Lenclos's correspondence, Mereau suggests that she herself might have supplemented Lenclos's work in her own capacity as collector and translator: "There are those who doubt the authenticity of these letters: such concerns are irrelevant to the female reader of these fragments, for they are such that they could have been written by that inspired woman" ("Briefe" 142). Her point is that veracity matters less than the transmission of a philosophical ideal expressed in the original, a statement not far removed from the theory of translation posited by Mereau's contemporary, Novalis: "Translations depict the pure, perfected character of an artwork. They do not give us the actual artwork, but rather an ideal version" (quoted in Benjamin 65). Much like Mereau, Novalis relates literary criticism, artistic creation, and translation as interchangeable and mutually interdependent.

In her biography of Sophie Mereau, Dagmar von Gersdorff has already suggested a similarity between Mereau's translations and Novalis's equation of translation with artistic creation. Von Gersdorff begins her chapter on translation by citing Novalis's famous letter to Friedrich

Schlegel: "Translating is as good as composing [*dichten*], as creating one's own works, indeed it is more difficult and rarer" (Hardenberg 237). As uplifting as his pronouncement may seem to those who toil in two languages, Novalis's claim that all art involves translation did little to affirm the literary activity of eighteenth-century women. Like Schlegel's reading of Mereau's novel, Novalis's conception of the literary enterprise was grounded in a sharply divided gender ontology. In his *Discourse Networks* (*Aufschreibesysteme*), Friedrich Kittler provides a theoretical context within which to interpret Novalis's assertion, "In the end all poetry is translation" (Hardenberg 237). What seems like a vindication to those who have historically been accorded a secondary place within literary culture is in fact a proposition about the relationship of poetry to a metaphysical point of origin that lies beyond language. According to Novalis, the task of the poet is to translate this mythic realm into the medium of intelligible discourse. All value and beauty ascribed to literature exists, he claims, only in its ability to transform the hidden depths of nature into a rational system of signs. The translation work of *Poesie* really amounts to a movement from speechlessness into language. Translations from one language to another, from English to German for example, are evaluated on the basis of how successfully they transmit the mythic truth of a literary work across different languages. The interaction of these two types of translation—from speechlessness into language and then from one language into another—is arranged hierarchically, so that interlanguage translations are adjudicated by a standard that applies to all works of art, namely, how well do they translate the beauty and truth of transcendent reality into language. An interlanguage translation is thus evaluated on the basis of its representation of a higher truth already embodied in the original work of art.

Because all poetic works have the potential to portray the eternal, it is conceivable under Novalis's scheme that the translation of a given work from one language to another could produce a manifestation of the transcendent that outdoes the original work of art. Novalis asserted quite directly that it was possible for a translation to enhance the beauty and truth claims of an artwork. Thus he praised August Wilhelm Schlegel's rendering of Shakespeare into German as poetically superior to the original English version (Hardenberg 237). Novalis's claim may sound outrageous to native speakers of English, yet one should be careful not to interpret it as an assertion about the superiority of German as a langauge or Schlegel as a poet. Rather, Novalis's cosmopolitan notion of reading, criticism, and literary production presumes that the truth manifested in particular works of art exists beyond the mediation of any one language. Successful translation between languages simply reconfigures the mythic relations represented within the text. The value of an artwork lies not in its own language, but rather in its references to the inarticulate realm of myth. Translation requires both the preservation of the original work and its reformulation into a new language, a process that evolves with the historical reception of the artwork. For this rather difficult maneuver to work at any given moment in time, the translator must become one with the original text. According to Novalis, the translator must grasp the coherence of the original as a whole, rather than as a succession of linguistic statements. Andreas Huyssen's description of this process reveals the erotic potential within hermeneutical understanding. The translator reads the original text in order to meld with it. From this union arises an intuition of the unspoken relations that inform the artwork's linguistic form. "An 'unfaithful' [*verändernde*] translation is possible only when the author and the translator flow together into each other and are thereby transformed [*sich einander anverwandeln*]. Needless to say, this union occurs on the level of the 'Idea' of the whole, and not on the level of the various translated manifestations of the original" (131).

Kittler touches on the homoerotic desire implicit within this Romantic model of translation and reading between male authors; however, he argues that the discursive networks of the *Goethezeit* operated according to an oedipal model of male desire for the mother. The position of mythic wholeness that lies beyond literary production was, according to Kittler, represented within the discourse by three synonymous terms—Nature, Love, Woman. The poet's task was to translate these originary points of transcendent knowledge into the channels of language.

Within this metaphysical framework of poetic production, the figure of woman stands at the outermost poles, either as the maternal source of natural transcendence and love or as the erotically receptive reader of male authors. According to Kittler,

> Woman, insofar as she persists as One, remains at the originary ground of all discourse production and is thus excluded from the channels of distribution as these are administered by bureaucrats or authors. She remains this unapproachable ground in order to confine women, in their existence as plurality, to a domesticated reading, which, as reverence for divine texts, is indeed religion. In this respect the division of the sexes in the discourse network of 1800 was quite simple. Because the Mother produced authors as the unifying principle of poetic works, women had no access to any such unity. They remained a manifold grouped around the authorial lodestar (125).

What distinguishes Mereau's hermeneutic model of identification through translation is the conscious absence of a transcendent maternal figure. Rather than celebrating the inexpressible, Mereau's and Lenclos's texts suggest a wholly different model of poetic signification, one in which female silence is a function of male blindness to the social forces which shape speech and a gender-specific clumsiness in reading the gestural language of the body. Within this second poetic order the inarticulate symbol is redefined as a sign that simply has not been properly understood. In the place of the "powerful thoughts," "evocative images," and "fantasy" that are said to typify masculine literary discourse, Lenclos's (and Mereau's) discourse posits the existence of "a thousand tiny nuances...that elude your eyes" ("Briefe" 142). Inarticulate and undecipherable signs are not, accordingly, clues to a transcendent Romantic sphere wherein Nature, Love, and the Maternal exist as an harmonious unity; rather they are the effects of a feminine masquerade. Behind the half-understood signs of literary discourse lie concrete social relations that produce inarticulate speech, namely women's inequality and dependence. The reader's identification with a text involves, according to Lenclos and Mereau, a recognition of the political interests that underlie any discourse.

Mereau's translations follow Novalis's concept of translation to the extent that they claim to embody the "feminist" spirit of Lenclos, even if certain passages are themselves Mereau's inventions. However, the content of her translation work consciously puts forth a paradigm for a female literary discourse that is inherently oppositional to what it represents as a dominant male culture. As I wish now to argue in the remainder of this essay, one of the most important features of the alternative female mode of writing represented in and by Lenclos's writing is its distinct rearticulation of maternal identity as a privileged and articulate subject position.

Mereau's interest in defining women's writing is apparent from the very start of the translation project. She begins the series with a letter entitled "Feminine Epistolary Style." In all likelihood the letter is Mereau's invention, for it does not appear in any other collection of Lenclos's correspondences. This manifesto-like letter certainly begins as if it were plucked from a stream of letters; however, the reader soon becomes aware that buried within the seventeenth-century literary terminology lies an unambiguous critique of Romantic gender ideology: "I have already asserted that we women write better letters than you men. Today I want to explain why" ("Briefe" 142). While this claim for a female writing style would certainly have found a sympathetic response within the corresponding circles of Weimar Romanticism, the rationale the letter provides in support of its thesis makes no reference to an essential maternalism; indeed its discussion of femininity makes little recourse to nature. Instead the letter defines feminine style as an effect of women's dependence upon their husbands. Mereau's fictional Lenclos argues that women train themselves to examine more carefully the nuances of statements and to guard assiduously the visible manifestations of their passions: "Read the letters of a woman passionately in love—they are not as fiery, not as enthusiastic as those of her lover, and yet you can recognize her love all the more clearly" ("Briefe" 143). Mereau's inventive translation argues for a feminine style in the language of a seventeenth-century moral philosophy that praises the mastery of what are called *Affekten* or passions.[5] Seventeenth-century courtiers were practiced in the art of physiognomic readings of the body, the examination of surface appearances on the body as signs of internal passions. As a practical form of social knowledge, physiognomy was an ancient art first described by Aristotle. It assumed the existence of both a conscious and an unconscious correlation between bodily appearance (facial features, gestures, speech intonations, dress, overall deportment) and the mind. The opening letter links the bodily control of these affects and the ability to interpret them with a specific feminine skill in reading and writing. Both physiognomic interpretative skills and the ability to mask one's own passions were, according to the author, more refined in women because of their dependent social position:

> It is easy to understand, my dear Marquis—*our* entire happiness or misery is decided through friendship and love; through them *our* life gains its highest meaning, which is why we think more about relationships, and learn to evaluate them better than you. We grasp their qualities with all their subtle turns far better and can depict them much more accurately—add to that (just between the two of us!) the need to hide our feelings, indeed even to deny them.... Surely this must have multiple influences on our style ("Briefe" 143).

Whereas the letter's gendering of epistolary style would in a seventeenth-century context be understood as an opposition between physiognomy and rhetoric, this division would have had little immediate relevance for German readers of the early nineteenth century. Rhetoric was by then a disreputable form of knowledge, described by Schiller as an unreliable ornamental feature more likely to distort an argument than to give it persuasive appeal (Schiller 657; Wellbery and Bender 5–22). The situation with physiognomy was more complex.[6] The popular resurgence of interest in the art of reading facial features inspired by the writings of the Swiss clergyman Johann Kaspar Lavater had ebbed by the turn of the century, yet the terms this science employed would have been familiar to all those participating in fashionable society. Readers might still recognize the contest between physiognomy and rhetoric in Lenclos's text, but the debate would have seemed outdated in the discursive fields of 1800.

However, a second gendered distinction presents itself through Mereau's translation. The terms are again organized through sexual difference, although instead of a courtly game of seduction and alliance formation, the opposition operates in a field centered upon the nuclear family and its ideological justifications for a sexual division of social labor. Physiognomy and rhetoric would have been translated into a struggle between a political claim for personal rights and a Romantic metaphysics of art. The shifting horizon of expectations between the seventeenth and early nineteenth century would have meant that terms such as "fantasy" and "evocative images" would have had totally different connotations. In Mereau's translation, the barbs Lenclos aims at masculine rhetorical flourishes are redirected at Romantic celebrations of imaginary transcendence:

> And so our letter-writing style acquires that alluring variety, that soft gradual transition that your style lacks. You are more brilliant with powerful thoughts, richer in evocative images than we are; however, your fantasy ultimately harms you. Your intensity tears you along from one thought to the next. We instead hold onto a single one in order to represent its dignity and clarity in a single word. Your heat fails, our leisurely approach finds the fitting phrase. You lose yourself in high-toned phrases; we find the meaning with one little word. In the end we have been painters, while you have been mere orators ("Briefe" 144).

This passage begins with several clear references to Romantic aesthetic terminology. In the last phrase, wherein male writers are described as orators, Mereau allows herself a nuanced play on connotations. The unflattering parallel between fantasy and rhetoric strikes directly at Romantic pretensions to depth. Mereau equates the transcendent signified alluded to by *Poesie* with Romanticism's antithesis, the rhetorically maneuverable signifier. In place of the flattened Romantic claims to poetic depth, Mereau introduces a critique that describes literary discourse as an effect produced by the relative sexual differences in social power.

The differences in style spelled out in what purports to be a letter by Ninon de Lenclos closely match Mereau's assessment of her own correspondence with Clemens Brentano. As Herta Schwarz notes, Brentano's letters seemed as if they were "written in a hallucinatory rush...mystical, elevated yet not inspired, spiritual but not spirited" (34). Mereau, in contrast, preferred a more restrained style. She wrote, "A letter is for me like a novel—and I would rather say too little than too much" (quoted in Schwarz 34). The publication of Lenclos's correspondence provided Mereau with an opportunity to consider how these two styles reflected the socially conditioned genders of the correspondents. By writing her own experience into the translations of Lenclos, Mereau posited an identity between women across time, predicated upon the continual recurrence of gender discrepancies.

Mereau augments her theoretical elaboration of a female, non-Romantic mode of writing by retelling the story of Lenclos's second son. The centrality of this dramatic incident both in Lenclos's life and in her role as a model for German women writers is made clear by the fact that Mereau repeats it twice, once in her biographical essay on Lenclos and then again in her translation of Lenclos's letters. The incident amounts to a reversal of the incestuous fantasy that pervades male Romantic aesthetics. Instead of figuring poetic transcendence as a son's imaginary reunion with the maternal, Mereau depicts radical sexual emancipation in terms of a mother's imaginary liaison with an amorous son. The failure of this encounter is treated as a stage in Lenclos's *Bildung*. The tragic death of the son is recuperated within the biographical trajectory of Mereau's essay on Lenclos. Like Wilhelm Meister's relation to Mignon, the tragic affair between Lenclos and her son is portrayed as just one (admittedly very important) moment in the overall formation of Lenclos's character. This two-step process—the representation of fantasy and its ultimate renunciation—distinguishes Mereau's text from Romanticism, while allowing her to claim Goethe's narrative of *Bildung* for women.

The simple story runs as follows: Ninon de Lenclos gave birth to a son who was taken and raised by the father. As a precondition to this arrangement, the father insisted that Lenclos never reveal her true relationship to the boy, who was educated in Parisian society and known as Chevalier de Villiers. Given the elite circles within which all three persons moved, it was inevitable that Lenclos, whose salon drew many ambitious young aristocrats, would often find the young Villiers among her own company. She avowed her own special interest in his fortune, and he sensed that she paid him special attentions. Mereau described their salon relationship in the terminology of a Romantic encounter, suggesting veiled desires. "She always granted him favors in preference to the others. She enjoyed seeing him stay a little longer than the others, and her eyes bespoke a tenderness that the young man could not explain to himself" (*Kalathiskos* 106). Dramatic irony transforms the text's promise of transcendence into a fateful threat. Mereau's description suggests the passionate intensity of early Romantic literature. Unlike Romantic tales of incestuous liaisons, such as Tieck's "Der blonde Eckbert," in Mereau's account the reader acknowledges from the very start the moral law that requires the veiling, if not repression, of desire. Awkward, shy glances are not merely indications of attraction. Having already learned of the young man's origins, the reader shares with Lenclos an ironic understanding of the romantic situation. The reader recognizes the young man's desire because Mereau has spelled out the situation. Lenclos is described in the text as also recognizing the amorous intentions implied by the young man's gestures because she is, as the letter on feminine style asserts, an expert in the interpretation of "body language": "Ninon was disturbed in her innermost self, for she was all too familiar with this language, which was daily becoming more explicit. Against this inclination, she raised every weapon available to severity, including detachment" (*Kalathiskos* 107). The reader's critical distance comes through an appreciation of the unconscious dynamic of this oedipal play. For if the young man misreads the intentions of Lenclos's affection, the reader is also aware that he is not misreading them entirely.

Mereau's biographical narrative produces a tragic irony very much at odds with the self-referential irony employed in the Romantic stories of male authors. The "Romantic irony" of stories such as Ludwig Tieck's "Liebeszauber" and E.T.A. Hoffmann's "Der Sandmann" involves a dim recognition by the male protagonist that his position as lover or artist has been compromised by larger, unseen forces that condition and determine his own identity. Recounted from the male protagonist's perspective or focalization, these Romantic narratives are plotted so that the larger framework is revealed to the reader and the protagonist at the same moment, thereby producing a devastating psychic blow to the literary character and an intense aesthetic experience of identification and alienation for the reader. The machinations of fate performed before the audience in classical tragedy are experienced by the Romantic reader as a vague and uncanny intuition.[7] The irony is not experienced in reading the text so much as it is acknowledged by the narrative's conclusion as a structural principle in the story's unfolding (Fuchs 94). By suspending the reader's knowledge of the story until the final moment of revelation, Romantic irony sustains the reader's identification with the protagonist's misperception.[8] Mereau's biography of Lenclos consciously avoids the Romantic affirmation of misplaced desire and the intensity that such misperception produces. The reader of Mereau's text is informed from the very beginning of the Chevalier de Villiers's relation to Lenclos. The dramatic irony is not confined to the reader, rather it is shared by Lenclos herself. Prohibited by the father from speaking against desire by announcing her true identity, Lenclos is placed in the position of a reader. She recognizes the signs of desire but is unable to prevent their production or redirect their intended meaning. The reader's alignment with Lenclos is predicated upon a shared knowledge of the boy's identity and a prescribed passivity in the face of his growing desire. This mandatory inactivity increases the sense of sublime horror, just as it allows both the reader and Lenclos to contemplate the possibility of an incestuous liaison.[9] The father's prohibition against revealing the incestuous character of the Chevalier's affections enables them to develop up to the point of sexual gratification. Indeed, Lenclos's efforts to distract the boy only heighten and extend the experience of desire, both within the text and for the reader. Mereau's retelling of Lenclos's relation to her son indulges in the fantasy of an incestuous sexual liaison from the position of the mother, who recognizes the illicit character of her affair, but is forced to allow its development. Far from oppressing the mother, the imposed passivity allows her an imaginary pleasure, which, in the name of the oedipal father, she is able to renounce at the last moment.

Desire and dramatic irony work together to split the maternal subject.[10] Lenclos orders the Chevalier to leave her, to cease his affections. She points out that she is sixty-five years old and warns him that his affections seem ridiculous—"Get a hold of yourself, Chevalier, and learn how ridiculous your feelings and expectations are" (*Kalathiskos* 108)—all to no avail. The sense of fate is only heightened by an appreciation of the oedipal dynamic at play. The son's interpretation of his mother's gestures is incorrect as far as Lenclos's intentions are concerned, but presumably accurate on the level of unconscious desire. That Lenclos's protests fail proves all the more, within the code of courtly love, that her son's passion deserves gratification. Her veiled diversions serve as quite effective enticements. Nevertheless, the young man cannot grasp the nuances of his mother's gestures. Believing all too strongly in a promised gratification, he does not consider the social relations that condition Lenclos's speech, thereby giving added weight to the literal meaning of her words. Focused only on what lies beyond the veil that covers Lenclos's body, he does not perceive that the repression of desire has its own justifications.

The culminating moment of sexual fulfillment is coupled with the final triumph of the prohibition against incest. Mereau brings the story up to the last possible moment. After repeated efforts have failed to dissuade the young man, Lenclos apprises the father of the situation and requests that she be freed from her vow of silence. He agrees quickly, whereupon she sends for the young Chevalier, who, of course, believes that Lenclos has ended her opposition to his advances and that she will finally agree to consummate an affair: "The young man flew to her; he dreamed only of reconciliation, love, joy. What care he took in his appearances! What soothing images he carried in his breast!" (*Kalathiskos* 111). Their encounter is tumultuous. The narration alludes to Lenclos's desire for her son as well as her horror of the incest taboo: "Ninon, stormed by terrifying, contradictory feelings, sank into his arms. There exists, she said, in a suffering voice, a fate, which despite all human cleverness, proceeds on its unaltering path" (*Kalathiskos* 111). Lenclos finally reveals the Chevalier's parentage. She explains that his father kept his origin secret because he knew that the young man's reputation would have suffered from having a disreputable mother: "To preserve your self-confidence, so that your safe passage through the world would in no way be disturbed, you were never supposed to know" (*Kalathiskos* 112). The coincidence of his libidinal desire with the sudden revelation of his maternal origin is explained as a manifestation of the father's pervasive presence. The shock to the young man's identity comes not only with the realization that his two most powerful desires contradict each other, but he also learns that his father is responsible for both their constitution and their opposition. The father educated the boy in the absence of his mother, sent him to Paris to experience the world, and then stripped him of his love object at the moment of his imagined happiness. Faced with the realization that his entire identity has been both constructed and stymied by the father's authority, the Chevalier is stunned into silence. "Pale, quivering, soulless, the son's lips barely uttered the word 'mother.' His heart remained moved by it. Passsion and horror filled it—heat and cold had completely consumed him" (*Kalathiskos* 113). The Chevalier tears himself away, runs into a nearby garden, and falls on his sword.

Mereau's account emphasizes how devastating the boy's suicide was for Lenclos, while the Chevalier's subject position receives scant attention. The point of the incident is not to depict the collapse of the young man's aspiration, but to demonstrate Lenclos's development as an individual. True to the Goethean tradition of *Bildung*, the suicide marks a crossroad in the refinement of Lenclos's *Lebensphilosophie*, without, however, approaching the devastation of high tragedy. Lenclos's identity had never been constituted through any particular ideology of motherhood, aristocratic or otherwise. For her to despair in the face of her son's death would have implied the repudiation of her life-long sexual emancipation. In continuing the biographical narrative, Mereau assumes the long-term trajectory of a *Bildungsroman*. She describes the affair as a decisive, though not final, moment in Lenclos's ongoing personal development:[11]

> For a long time she let herself be overcome with the strongest bitterness, and only slowly did some consolation return to her. From then on it was her sole aspiration to experience her joys again and after she had known everything that life's intoxication and fire offers, she strove for nothing more than peace and ease (*Kalathiskos* 114–15).

Mereau's biographical account of Lenclos's liaison with her son reiterates the distinctions between masculine and feminine styles, while acknowledging the inability of either to control fully the interpretation of representation. Mereau's portrayal of Lenclos seeks to claim an ethical superiority for the female position in its ability at least to acknowledge the operation of unconscious motivations. However, Lenclos's corrections of the "misunderstandings" produced by her communications with the Chevalier suggest a different, non-ethical interest at play, namely the elaboration of an unsanctioned sexual fantasy. Mereau recuperates the privileged position she ascribes to Lenclos's feminine style through a temporalized understanding of the female subject, thereby transforming tragedy into formative personal experience.

Two conclusions can be drawn from the manner in which Mereau frames maternal relations within Lenclos's biography. On the level of intentional differences in style, Mereau represents the maternal position within the incestuous circle of Romantic *Poesie* by providing a perceptive critique of the social conditions that determine speech. This argument is spelled out in Mereau's translation of Lenclos's letter on style. However, when Mereau follows up on her claim to use Lenclos as a model for action, the neat critique of discourse is supplanted by the more radical, maternal appropriation of incestuous *Poesie* in the formation of female subjectivity. In this version, the feminine subject incorporates parenting into a larger aesthetic whole. The child, in this case a Romantic young man, functions as a transitory commitment in the development of an autonomous subject. The relation between mother and child is further aestheticized by the mother's sublime fantasy of incest. Mereau's representation of Lenclos's liaison positions the mother as the detached observer before whom the fearful and fascinating drama unfolds. Her dramatic irony is derived from her superior knowledge; it enables her simultaneously to protest and enjoy the prospect of incest. Unlike the male protagonists of many Romantic stories, Lenclos's self-understanding, her investment in the symbolic order—the transcendence Novalis sought—remains intact.

Notes

I am very grateful for the encouragement and commentary of Katharina Gerstenberger and Bettina Brandt. Unless otherwise indicated, translations from the German are my own.

[1] Christa Bürger develops this biographical fact into an argument about the status of Mereau's literary production within the developing notion of artistic autonomy ("Sphäre" 366–86); Bürger's thesis that women writers failed to produce artworks that respected the theoretical terms of Classical aesthetic theory as developed by Schiller and Goethe has the unfortunate effect of replicating their characterization of women writers as dilettantes.

[2] Gersdorff's biography is noteworthy only because it covers a wide range of Mereau's writing. A shorter treatment is provided by Riley.

[3] When Riley describes the essay as "feminist in a limited sense" she does so on the basis of a narrow definition of feminism, and not because Mereau's essay fails to provide a radical critique of gender roles. "Mereau is not really concerned with the emancipation of women, although she does represent this position. Her primary interest is in the liberation of both sexes from the coercion of socially determined roles" (79).

[4] The English translation of Weigel's article omits any direct interpretation of Mereau's writing, as well as that of virtually every other German woman mentioned in the original German essay. To understand Weigel's complete argument see "Der schielende Blick."

[5] For a discussion of the broad seventeenth-century understanding of "physiognomy" as including permanent bodily characteristics, expressive, and *Affekten,* see Campe (292–304).

[6] The eighteenth-century enthusiasm for physiognomy deserves a more detiled discussion than can be provided here. See Grey and Shortland.

[7] One of the frame characters in Hoffman's *Die Serapionsbrüder* defines the uncanny explicitly in terms of an unrecognized fate, "...the uncanny, i.e., the actions of an invisible entity upon our external sense, would certainly drive me insane. It is a feeling of utter and complete helplessness that crushes the spirit entirely" (327).

[8] Comic irony in Romantic texts does not strive to produce the uncanny as an experience while reading. Instead it draws attention, in the middle of the narrative, to the larger framework that surrounds the work of art. See Walter Bausch's discussion of *Parekbase* (110 ff.).

[9] Incest can be added to the list of "sublime" experiences indulged in by the passive observer. "This position of 'powerless witness' is also a crucial component of the experience of the Sublime: this experience takes place when we find ourselves in the face of some horrifying event whose comprehension exceeds our capacity of representation; it is so overwhelming that we can do nothing but stare at it in horror; yet at the same time this event poses no immediate threat to our physical well-being, so that we can maintain the safe distance of an observer.... And the lesson of psychoanalysis is that one has to add to torture and murder as the sources of possible experience of the Sublime *intense (sexual) enjoyment*" (Žižek 74–75).

[10] "Why, then, is the observer passive and impotent? Because his desire is split, divided between fascination with enjoyment and repulsion at it" (Žižek 75).

[11] Martin Swales notes the ironic tone of *Wilhelm Meister,* which asks for the readers' assent to the protagonist's human capacity for "error" (60).

Works Cited

Bausch, Walter. *Theorien des epischen Erzählens in der deutschen Frühromantik.* Bonn: Bouvier, 1964.

Benjamin, Walter. *Der Begriff der Kunstkritik in der deutschen Romantik.* Frankfurt a.M.: Suhrkamp, 1973.

Bürger, Christa. "'Die mittlere Sphäre.' Sophie Mereau—Schriftstellerin im klassischen Weimar." *Deutsche Literatur von Frauen.* Vol. 1. Ed. Gisela Brinker-Gabler. München: Beck, 1988. 368–88.

Campe, Rüdiger. *Affekt und Ausdruck: Zur Umwandlung der literarischen Rede im 17. und 18. Jahrhundert.* Tübingen: Niemeyer, 1990.

Fetting, Frederike. *"Ich fand in mir eine Welt": Eine sozial- und literaturgeschichtliche Untersuchung zur deutschen Romanschriftstellerin um 1800. Charlotte von Kalb, Caroline von Wolzogen, Sophie Mereau-Brentano, Johanna Schopenhauer.* München: Fink, 1992.

Fuchs, Peter. *Moderne Kommunikation: Zur Theorie des operativen Displacements.* Frankfurt a.M.: Suhrkamp, 1993.

Gersdorff, Dagmar von. *Dich zu lieben kann ich nicht verlernen: Das Leben der Sophie Brentano-Mereau.* Frankfurt a.M.: Insel, 1984.

Grey, Richard. "Sign and *Sein*: The *Physiognomikstreit* and the Dispute over the Semiotic Constitution of Bourgeois Individuality." *Deutsche Vierteljahrsschrift für Literaturwissenschaft und Geistesgeschichte* (1992): 301–32.

Hammerstein, Katharina von. *Sophie Mereau-Brentano: Freiheit—Liebe— Weiblichkeit: Trikolore sozialer und individueller Selbstbestimmung um 1800.* Heidelberg: Winter, 1994.

Hardenberg, Friedrich von. *Schriften.* Vol. 4. Ed. Paul Kluckhohn and Richard Samuel. Stuttgart: Kohlhammer, 1975.

Hoffmann, E.T.A. *Die Serapionsbrüder.* München: Winkler, 1979.

Huyssen, Andreas. *Die Frühromantische Konzeption von Übersetzung und Aneignung.* Züricher Beiträge zur deutschen Literatur- und Geistesgeschichte 33. Zürich: Atlantis, 1969.

Kittler, Friedrich. *Discourse Networks: 1800/1900.* Trans. Michael Metteer, with Chris Cullens. Stanford: Stanford UP, 1990.

Mereau, Sophie. "Die Briefe der Ninon de Lenclos." *Journal für deutsche Frauen, von deutschen Frauen geschrieben.* Ed. Christoph Martin Wieland, Friedrich Schiller, et al. 1.1 (1805): 142–46.

———. "Ninon de Lenclos." *Kalathiskos.* 1801–02. Heidelberg: Lambert Schneider, 1968.

Riley, Helene Kastinger. *Die weibliche Muse: Sechs Essays über künstlicherisch schaffende Frauen der Goethezeit.* Columbia, SC: Camden, 1986.

Schlegel, Friedrich. *Friedrich Schlegels Briefe an seinen Bruder August Wilhelm.* Ed. Oskar Walzel. Berlin: Speyer und Peters, 1890.

Schiller, Friedrich. "Über die notwendigen Grenzen beim Gebrauch schöner Formen." *Werke.* Vol. 2. Ed. Paul Stapf. Berlin: Deutsche Buch-Gemeinschaft, 1958. 656–77.

Schwarz, Herta. "Poesie und Poesiekritik im Briefwechsel zwischen Clemens Brentano und Sophie Mereau." *Die Frau im Dialog: Studien zu Theorie und Geschichte des Briefes.* Ed. Anita Runge and Lieselotte Steinbrügge. Stuttgart: Metzler, 1991.

Shortland, Michael. "The Power of a Thousand Eyes: Johann Caspar Lavater's Science of Physiognomical Perception." *Criticism* 28 (1986): 379–08.

Swales, Martin. *The German Bildungsroman from Wieland to Hesse.* Princeton: Princeton UP, 1978.

Treder, Uta, "Sophie Mereau: Montage und Demontage einer Liebe." *Untersuchungen zum Roman von Frauen um 1800*. Ed. Helga Gallas and Magdalene Heuser. Tübingen: Niemeyer, 1990. 172–83.

Weigel, Sigrid. "Double Focus: On the History of Women's Writing." *Feminist Aesthetics*. Ed. Gisela Ecker. Boston: Beacon, 1985. 59–80.

———. "Der schielende Blick: Thesen zur Geschichte weiblicher Schreibpraxis." *Die verborgene Frau*. Berlin: Argument, 1983. 83–137.

Wellbery, David, and John Bender. *The Ends of Rhetoric: History, Theory, Practice*. Stanford: Stanford UP, 1990.

Žižek, Slavoj. *The Metastases of Enjoyment*. London: Verso, 1994.

Recollections of a Small-Town Girl: Regional Identity, Nation, and the Flux of History in Luise Mühlbach's *Erinnerungen aus der Jugend* (1870)

Lynne Tatlock

Luise Mühlbach's recollections of her Mecklenburg childhood demonstrate the productive capacity of remembering, or rather, how representation of the past can serve as a defense against the present. In reinventing the province as the reserve of the eccentric and originary, as the place where desire is expansively expressed, Mühlbach posits an alternative to the power politics of imperialist Prussia, that is, a feminized and domesticated nation more inviting to women readers and to a public in other German-speaking principalities (including Austria) who lacked Prussian sympathies. In the end quirky Mecklenburg represents not the particular, but the universal, and thus stands not on the periphery, but at the center of an imagined German nation. (LT)

"*But your majesty knows well that we cannot with impunity rob a people of their inalienable and noblest rights—of their nationality —give them arbitrary frontiers, and transform them into new states. [The Fatherland is born along with the person and] nationality is a sentiment inherent in the human heart...*" (Queen Luise to Napoleon in Tilsit).

"*Possibly others may be more readily consoled for such losses,*" said the king: "*those who are only anxious for the possession of states, and who do not know what it is to part with hereditary provinces in which the most precious reminiscences of our youth have their root, and which we can no more forget than our cradle.*"
"*Cradle!*" exclaimed Napoleon, laughing scornfully. "*When the child has become a man, he has no time to think of his cradle.*"
"*Yes he has,*" said the king, with an angry expression. "*We cannot repudiate our childhood, and a man who has a heart must remember the associations of his youth*" (Friedrich Wilhelm III to Napoleon in Tilsit).[1]

As her daughter told it, young Clara Müller (1814–1873), later known to her readership as Luise Mühlbach, was only too eager to quit Neubrandenburg, population 6,300, where she had been born and raised, a town too small to contain her lively spirit (Ebersberger ix). Indeed, as soon as she respectably could, she left behind the brick Gothic walls of the Mecklenburg hamlet, became Clara Mundt when she married the notorious Young German Theodor Mundt, wrote nearly a hundred short stories and novels as Luise Mühlbach, and lived most of her adult life in Berlin.[2] Neubrandenburg hardly merited a backward glance. Yet in January of 1870 at age fifty-six, shortly before the outbreak of the Franco-Prussian War and the founding of the German Reich, Mühlbach began publishing in the liberal Austrian newspaper *Neue Freie Presse* a series of recollections in which she reconstructed not her adult life at the center of the empire that would soon be, but her childhood at its margins.

That memory always constitutes an approximate and subjective reconstruction, not an exact reproduction, of historical fact is now widely understood. Yet while Mühlbach herself defends the novelist's privilege to subject historical fact to authorial intention ("Jugend" 21–22), she displays rather less self-consciousness where her reminiscences are concerned. Indeed, even as she asserts in her *Erinnerungen* that the Mecklenburg of her childhood is irrevocably separated from the present by enormous political changes, she also suggests that this Mecklenburg nevertheless remains always available to the present in the form of personal memories that are recoverable at will. Her text leaves no doubt about her view of the quality of these recollections; they are genuine, pristine, monumental, even sacrosanct: "We, the children of modern times, should all at least embrace one religion, should bow down before it in pious reverence: the religion of memories." Mühlbach's "religion of memories" reveres the lived past as the individual's salvation in the present: "For this [religion of memories] is the shield and refuge (*Hort*) of our life and it accompanies us in the present and regulates and orders our existence" ("Jugend" 1). Our recollections of that past, she insists, will protect us in the present; the act of remembering will make transparent the principles that have shaped us and will preserve us from error. While in 1870 Mühlbach may consider her assumptions about the accessibility of the lived past unassailable, in the late twentieth century they invite skepticism: her narrative cannot recuperate a regional childhood "as it really was"; rather, it can only reinvent it.

The character of such reinvention raises for the present-day critic the question of the significance of the recovered primal and peculiar land of Mühlbach's childhood for the present of its invocation, for, as Andreas Huyssen asserts in *Twilight Memories,* "[t]he temporal status of any act of memory is always the present" (3). In his interrogation of time and memory, Huyssen deftly debunks the notion of an authentically remembered past and articulates the need for examining the modes of recalling and representing the past. He maintains that

> [a]ll representation—whether in language, narrative, image, or recorded sound—is based on memory. *Re*-presentation always comes after, even though some media will try to provide us with the delusion of pure presence. But rather than leading us to some authentic origin or giving us verifiable access to the real, memory, even and especially in its belatedness, is itself based on representation. The past is not simply there in memory, but it must be articulated to become memory. The fissure that opens up between experiencing an event and remembering it in representation is unavoidable. Rather than lamenting or ignoring it, this split should be understood as a powerful stimulant for cultural and artistic creativity (2–3).

This last point in particular relates to the present investigation, for even the unremarkable business of recording a few childhood memories can become the occasion for inventing nation. How, then, was the sunny past connected to the iron and blood of the moment of writing? How did Mühlbach reincorporate her regional childhood into her national(istic) adulthood? What emerged when she began to remember home?

As we shall see, Mühlbach's present prompted not an escape into the past, but rather a reinvention and reintegration of it; indeed, Prussia's and greater Germany's changing fortunes gave this popular and prolific author both practical and personal reasons for re-collecting her regional past. By 1870 she had become aware of the difficulties of the writer who wrote for a German nation but lived in a time of power politics. While a Bismarck might claim that "there was nothing special about territorial and national identities, or about the 'swindle of nationalities'" (James 66), the historical novelist sensed that when she spoke of nationality she was traversing a thorny landscape.

* * *

Before examining the *Erinnerungen* themselves, let us first consider the exigencies of the moment in which Mühlbach wrote them, for these precipitated the series of reminiscences and determined their mode of publication. In particular, Mühlbach's situation as widow; breadwinner for two daughters, a mother-in-law, and two sisters-in-law; and writer of historical novels in the decade in which Prussia consolidated its power with a series of wars merits consideration. As William McClain and Lieselotte Kurth-Voigt have noted in the introduction to their edition of Mühlbach's letters to her publisher, Hermann Costenoble, and as quickly becomes clear upon reading the letters themselves, Mühlbach, given her financial obligations and her liberal spending habits, needed money—constantly. To secure herself financially she relied on her own astonishing productivity and on a sturdy, indeed expanding, market for her historical novels. But she could not always count on the market in times of power politics. Indeed, as her letters, especially those written in the years 1866–1871, make clear, the politics of the German-speaking territories tangibly affected not only the sales of her historical novels but also her honoraria.

From the mid-1860s on through the Austro-Prussian War, Mühlbach worked steadily on a tetralogy that she eventually titled *Deutschland in Sturm und Drang*. She had invested a great deal in this work, both literary ambition and hope of present and future earnings. In her letters to Costenoble, she despaired of her ability to do the material justice, frequently reiterated her hope that she would produce a work of lasting importance, and worried that the tetralogy would not sell well when it finally appeared.[3] This last worry in particular deserves our attention for it points to a peculiar difficulty faced by those who would represent German history to an as yet non-existent and still-to-be-created unified and homogeneous German reading public. Much like the historical novelist Willibald Alexis, who had insisted that when he wrote the history of the Mark Brandenburg he wrote German history, Mühlbach had presented *Prussian* history as *German* history.[4] Moreover, her novels had frequently featured Prussia as the genius of the German nation and hence the legitimate engine for the unification of all Germans. In the mid-1860s, however, even as she put the finishing touches on the tetralogy, she began to display a heightened awareness of the political sentiments of those other German lands that did not necessarily identify their interests with those of Prussia. In January of 1866 she explicitly expressed her wish to write a German book, not a Prussian one: "I don't want to write a Prussian book, but rather a *German* one, and I'm afraid that if Friedrich Wilhelm III is in the title, then the South Germans won't be particularly interested in the book. We've got to make the title more general..." (McClain and Kurth-Voigt 1025).[5] While this statement can of course be understood principally as a reiteration of the position that *Prussian* history is *German* history, it also exhibits Mühlbach's awareness that her Prussian sympathies did not necessarily mesh well with her desire to write for all Germans.

Two months later, in April of 1866, she continued to worry about the title and this time made more explicit that her concerns related specifically to Prussia's foreign policy:

> And then I listened to the course of the era, and I find that a powerful change has taken place in people's feelings. Thanks to our miserable politics Prussia has become less and less popular in the rest of Germany, and if I now write a work called *Friedrich Wilhelm III and His Times* then that would mean writing a work for North Germany and thus losing all appeal for South Germany. For me: unpopularity; for you: poor

sales. So I presented my wish to change the title and to give it a more general character... (McClain and Kurth-Voigt 1030).

In the end Mühlbach felt compelled to add an introduction to part one (*Der alte Fritz und seine Zeit*), explaining anew her literary mission. In this introduction, written in September of 1866, two months after Prussia's defeat of Austria in the battle of Königgrätz, she pointedly characterized the history she was writing as for the German people; her goal was "to give an agreeable and popular form to our national history, which may attract the attention and affections of our people, which may open their understandings to the tendencies of political movements, and connect the facts of history with the events of actual life" ("The Historical Romance" 2). Although Mühlbach might have objected to charges of fictionality, she clearly aimed with her historical writing, as Brent O. Peterson has maintained, to provide "a disparate and isolated reading public with a fictionalized common past" (209) and, we might add, herself with as broad a reading public as possible.

Power politics and particularly war not only affected the reading preferences of the public, but also impeded this writer's career in additional tangible respects. Indeed, even as Mühlbach repeatedly insisted that right was on the side of the Prussians (see, e.g., McClain and Kurth-Voigt 1196), she also saw herself as a victim of the Prussian wars. In 1866, shortly before the outbreak of the Austro-Prussian war, for example, her publisher intimated that he would have to alter an existing contract "in the case of a war" (McClain and Kurth-Voigt 1040): "It would be nice and convenient," she fumed in her reply of 1 May 1866, "if in adverse times one could suspend the obligations one has incurred and I would, for example, love to do that with my rent" (1040).[6] A month and a half later when war had come, she wrote, "I've suffered a lot mentally and lost a lot—materially" (1043) and told of the financial losses she had sustained as a result of the unstable wartime economy.[7] In July of 1866 her publisher's suggestion that, in view of her frequent invitations to contribute to various newspapers, she could supplement her income by writing more frequently for periodicals provoked an indignant response: "The periodicals that did [invite me to write for them] are in Austria and in Würtemberg, and you understand that I can't work for them right now and can't offer them anything" (McClain and Kurth-Voigt 1050). The demise of the possibility of a "Großdeutschland" had for the moment at least considerably reduced Mühlbach's audience. Four years later, in August of 1870, she lamented in a similar vein:

> So now we're in the middle of a war again and all the misery and worry is back again! Certainly we're sure of victory and rejoice in it, certainly we hope that the war won't last long. But with all its exaltation the present still has its heavy burdens and miseries and has us by the throat.

> Unfortunately I belong to the group [of writers who are not journalists living from the politics of the day], and thus for me a difficult time of troubles is approaching once again! All those people who need to be paid want to be paid immediately... (McClain and Kurth-Voigt 1195).

While she did not make her living from contemporary politics per se, politics nevertheless affected her earnings. After having cited the impossibility of writing for Austrian journals in 1866, during the ensuing years she in fact rebuilt her bridges to the Austrian liberal bourgeois press. By 1870 her novel *Kaiserburg und Engelsburg* was scheduled for serial publication in the Viennese *Tages-Presse* and, most importantly for our purposes, in January 1870 her *Erinnerungen* began appearing bimonthly in the Viennese *Neue Freie Presse*. In September, two months after the French declaration of war on 19 July 1870, she reported that the *Tages-Presse* had postponed the publication of her novel on account of the war and that she herself preferred that it be postponed still longer; she did not wish her name to be associated with the virulently anti-Prussian sentiments of the paper.[8] The *Neue Freie Presse* was similarly unsympathetic to Prussia and thus the self-styled Prussian patriot felt compelled to take drastic measures: "For this reason I have suspended my *Erinnerungen aus meinem Leben*...for the moment despite repeated urgent pleading for their continuation, for these recollections are very much enjoyed (*goutiert*) in Austria" (McClain and Kurth-Voigt 1208). And although Mühlbach was still contemplating "four nice little volumes" when she interrupted their publication in the Austrian newspaper, the reminiscences were never completed and earned her not a penny more.

* * *

What is the nature of the recollections the Austrians allegedly so enjoyed? A woman's memories of a regional childhood were of course unlikely to offend the political sensibilities of an Austrian reading public or, for that matter, of the broader German public that Mühlbach hoped to reach. Indeed, these reminiscences present a sunny and humorous, harmless and easily digestible alternative to the tense politics of the historical moment of their publication. If, however, we simply dismiss them as trivial and escapist, we misapprehend their productive quality, that is, we fail to see that through them Mühlbach constructs an alternative community and that this alternative community also supports a national project of sorts.

In *On Longing* Susan Stewart has compared the remembrance of childhood to a view through a tunnel: "We imagine childhood as if it were at the other end of a tunnel—distanced, diminutive, and clearly framed" (44). Mühlbach's *Erinnerungen aus der Jugend* present no exception to Stewart's characterization, but in Mühlbach's narrative the framing is accomplished not only by time but by the geographically particular. In her recollections Mühlbach conjures up the sunken landscape of Mecklenburg, "a distant, long since sunken land, separated by centuries from us, a land that is separated from today by unbridgeable abysses" (60). The Mecklenburg of her memories initially seems cordoned off not only from the present and from the adult she has become, but also from greater Germany—in the case of Mecklenburg, specifically from Prussia—not to mention the rest of Europe. Mühlbach's forgotten land separated from the present by unbridgeable abysses has the character of a walled city isolated from the rest of the world by a hopelessly wide moat; indeed, it seems an exaggerated image of her hometown Neubrandenburg with its nearly intact medieval wall. Be that as it may, Mühlbach seizes on a proportionately even more impressive metaphor to bring home her point about the isolation of Mecklenburg: the Great Wall of China.

This outsized metaphor exhibits a certain ambiguity. While in 1870 Germans could read in any lexicon that the Wall had been constructed to keep out barbarian invaders (see, e.g., "Chinesische Mauer" 1865), it had taken on other meanings over the course of the century as the German view of China had become increasingly negative: a petrified culture, a culture without history (Fang; Schuster). The Great Wall was thus understood not as protecting civilization against barbarians but as isolating a backward nation from the modern world, that is, Europe. None other than Karl Marx, for example, "had the Wall stand for the whole stagnant (as he thought) Chinese social and economic system" (Waldron 212).

When Mühlbach initially imagines Mecklenburg behind a Great Wall, she does indeed write from the superior vantage point of the woman of letters in the present, a vantage point that is not without a certain ironic distance—she, for example, is only too willing gently to poke fun at the foibles of the province (see, e.g., "Jugend" 90). The reader may therefore expect the story of her childhood to be chiefly one of breaking through the Wall to the modern world. In fact she does write of her longing for the world outside. "For me the Chinese Wall hadn't fallen yet, and I sat behind it and listened to every strain, every sound from the alien world that back then I did not yet know and for which I longed so unspeakably" (42). And while at one point she declares that she forgives Mecklenburg its annoying propensity to cling to feudalism (24), she otherwise makes clear, particularly in her description of her relations with her fellow Mecklenburger Ida von Hahn-Hahn, that her political sympathies lie with the liberal program, not with the politics of backward Mecklenburg-Strelitz.

Nevertheless, her perspective on her Great Wall shifts. In the end this wall does not so much imprison as protect and preserve. Even as she insists on the radical isolation of Mecklenburg, she also notes an extraordinary vitality and originality behind this Chinese Wall: "...a vigorous [*frisch*] and original [*ursprünglich*] life with its own special properties [*eigentümlich*] grew and throve behind this wall" (51). In the following passage in which she returns to the wall, we can observe her critical perspective softening mid-sentence: "as if surrounded by a Chinese wall that separated it from the entire rest of the world. No highways, no industry, no export of its products, a medieval existence, safely enclosed [*eingefriedigt*] in the family, in daily exchange and the day-to-day business of earning a living" (60). What is more, when there are fissures in this Chinese Wall, they inevitably provide the occasion for contagion or social disruption (31, 66), not for increased freedom and progress. In the case of somnambulism, the modish and dangerous disease of upper-class women, "the modern disease" (72), for example, the radical isolation of Mecklenburg makes it possible to identify the first sufferer of the disease as well as its original carrier, a tutor, a newcomer to the Grand Duchy (68). But even as she constructs a Mecklenburg that is all but hermetically sealed off from the rest of the world, her narrative, so to speak, turns the inside out; it makes her reading public privy to the secrets and quaint ways of a place that once would have been inaccessible to them. In short her text constructs an imaginary barrier of enormous proportion only magically to destroy it in the process of narration.

I noted that Mühlbach's Great Wall constituted a disproportionately large fortification against the outside. Her tendency to magnify this barrier becomes clearer still when we observe that she tends, on the other hand, to minify an already diminutive Mecklenburg-Strelitz, the smallest of the Grand Duchies to join the North German Confederation in 1866. The text repeatedly refers to Mecklenburg-Strelitz as "my little fatherland" ("Jugend" 24, 25). Even the frequent use of the adjective "dear" (*lieb*) reduces the Grand Duchy to the tiny, familiar, and intimate. And if Mühlbach's hometown, Neubrandenburg, seemed a small, closed society, how much more so neighboring Penzlin, population 2,000, the locale of parts of four of the twelve installments of the recollections. Here the inhabitants are so intimate with one another that when Mühlbach's uncle organizes a theater production, the audience, with considerable hilarity, recognizes the costume of one of the players as the uncle's cast-off dressing gown (95).

Those familiar with nineteenth-century tales of petite personages—Daumerling, Daumesdick, Tom Thumb, Thumbelina—will quickly note that the text figures the tininess of the North German province in two tales of thumbs. In the first, the Devil, hoping to tempt Christ, holds up his thumb so that it casts a shadow over Penzlin; otherwise, so the humorous anecdote has it, Jesus would have immediately rejected a world "in which there was such a boring and godforsaken spot" ("Jugend" 124). The second story concerns one of the several eccentrics in Mühlbach's own family. It is a tale of cannibalism, comically tragic for the perpetrator, who cannot overcome his guilt over having eaten the thumb of a corpse during the campaign against Napoleon—"He never managed to digest the thumb he'd eaten" (53).

In Mecklenburg even the revolution of 1848, which Mühlbach elsewhere in the text characterizes as an avalanche (168), is markedly diminished. The Mecklenburgers storm the Grand Duke's palace demanding that he send away Countess Rossi, a.k.a. Henriette Sonntag, and that they be granted the right to catch crayfish wherever they please (13-14). The tendency to minify, manifest even in the digestible bites (newspaper installments, vignettes, anecdotes) in which Mühlbach presents her reminiscences to the public, produces a remote corner of a greater Germany as thoroughly palatable. But the tiny Mecklenburg of Mühlbach's recollection is more than merely palatable; it engages the reader in a particular way.

Here Stewart's characterization of the miniature, commonly featured in memories of childhood, is helpful. Stewart suggests that it creates in the viewer a sense of transcendence; the miniature "presents the desiring subject with an illusion of mastery, of time into space and heterogeneity into order." Furthermore, she observes, "[f]rom the privatized and domesticated world of the miniature, from its petite sincerity, arises an 'authentic' subject whose transcendence over personal property substitutes for a strongly chronological, and thus radically piecemeal, experience of temporality in everyday life" (172). The production of just such an "authentic" subject is crucial to Mühlbach's project, for, as we shall see, Mecklenburg occupies an unexpected place on the imaginary national map.

If Mühlbach thinks of memories in general as a *Hort,* a refuge, her tiny Mecklenburg takes on the aspect of an enchanted toy box or of a *Guckkasten* (nineteenth-century peep-show) where one can catch a glimpse of the archaic and originary—"that otherwise no longer happened anywhere else on earth" ("Jugend" 96), "vigorous and original life with its own special properties" (51). These *Erinnerungen* specialize in the resurrection of eccentrics—*Originale*—who, as she notes, "are becoming extinct throughout the world, the way pugs are becoming extinct" (51).[9] The primary meaning of the German word for eccentric, *Original,* deserves remark, for this very originality occupies a central position in Mühlbach's presentation of Mecklenburg, indeed in her presentation of her own family and also of herself. In Mühlbach's rendition, the province appears to foster just such originality, despite a certain social rigidity which, to give her credit, the author does not fail to note ("Jugend" 35).

A reinvented Clara Müller of course occupies the center of Luise Mühlbach's narrative of childhood and clearly she, too, is original. While some present-day readers may find tedious the accounts of events in which the cheeky and precocious child inevitably occupies the center of attention, precisely the enormous latitude, the room for play and exploration that this child experiences, her ability to move freely from one social sphere to another, from the Grand Duke of Mecklenburg-Strelitz himself to the master weaver in Penzlin, lend the memories and hence the Mecklenburg of this text a particular charm. Renate Möhrmann, the first contemporary scholar to devote attention to Mühlbach, quite rightly notes the immense personal freedom that Mühlbach, along with her siblings, "the darlings of the whole town" ("Jugend" 23), appears to have enjoyed (Möhrmann 61). I am, however, more hesitant than Möhrmann to assume that these recollections constitute a true picture of Mühlbach's past. As indicated at the outset of this paper, Mühlbach's own biography—her initiating contact by letter with Theodor Mundt, the then prominent and politically suspect Young German author whose works had been banned in 1835; her eagerness to leave Mecklenburg; her living of her adult life in the Prussian capital—suggests otherwise, i.e., that she chafed at the surveillance and monotony characteristic of small-town life.[10] Nevertheless, the child of Mühlbach's recollection sings "in a resounding voice" on various occasions and is never told to hush, routinely leaves her grandmother's house in Penzlin by jumping out the window, and has the capacity to enter any space she desires including the sickroom, the weaver's cottage, and the home of the mysterious and highly suspect Frau von Kinsky. Indeed, this child functions as the genius of the narrative, traversing the fictional landscape of Mecklenburg at will; it is she who divines the secrets of local personalities—particularly of the women—, the secrets that her adult counterpart reveals to what she hopes will be an eager reading public.

* * *

McClain and Kurth-Voigt have remarked on Mühlbach's tendency in her historical novels to feature the influence of important women (931). But Mühlbach not only revives historical women but also weaves minor plots of romance into the central narrative of historical events and thus introduces many more women into her historical narratives than are ordinarily found in history books. While Mühlbach's letters to her publisher nowhere indicate that she aims to appeal principally or even specifically to a female audience, an American biographical note from the *New York Herald* of 1 May 1873 nevertheless effuses:

> Where is the boudoir in that land of philosophy and music where some tender-hearted woman has not shed tears over the loves of Frederick and Joseph? Where is the young school girl who has not dreamed of some hero with "flaming eyes" and all that perfection of manly beauty with which every lover is endowed by Luise Mühlbach? Besides, there are thousands of persons in Germany who would never have looked at an

historical work had they not first been interested in the glowing romances of Louise Mühlbach ("Our Correspondents" 3).

This comment makes an important point about the inclusion of romance and its wide appeal, especially to women. With this inclusion Mühlbach made political history palatable to a broader audience—but not merely political history, national history. Indeed, another Luise from Mecklenburg, Queen Luise (1776–1810), daughter of the Duke of Mecklenburg-Strelitz and mother of the man who in 1870 would soon be Emperor of Germany, had often figured in Mühlbach's historical fiction, most prominently in *Napoleon and the Queen of Prussia* (*Königin Luise und Napoleon,* 1858–59), the work quoted above in the epigraph. The potential of this perennially popular and saintly daughter of Mecklenburg and mother of Prussia for putting an appealingly feminine and familiar face on a nation built of blood and iron cannot be missed; a feminized and domesticated nation was eminently more inviting to women readers and to a public in other German-speaking principalities (including Austria) who recoiled at Prussian coercion.[11] Such an attempt at universal appeal (inclusive of women) also characterizes Mühlbach's memoirs, alerting us to the sense in which Mühlbach constructs a German nation therein.

While narration of childhood, of family life, of the province, does perhaps lend itself more to the inclusion of women than does the narration of political history, the preponderance of installments in the *Erinnerungen* that focus on women's stories is nevertheless striking. These anecdotes, including those in which Mühlbach herself is the central character, pertain to any number of female personages, including Princess Luise of Mecklenburg-Strelitz; Ida von Hahn-Hahn; an aristocratic somnambulist; Henriette Sonntag; Frau von Kinsky; Trine Schalubben, a woman who fought in the Wars of Liberation; Mühlbach's nursemaid; her mother, aunts, and grandmother. Mühlbach's vignettes by no means present a uniform picture of a harmonious and happy life within the security of the province; quite the contrary. Most of these women suffer from thwarted desire of some kind. Taken as a whole, however, the women's stories effectively transform, that is, feminize, the space behind the Great Wall. By "feminize" I do not merely mean to point out that anecdotes about women *reduce* Mecklenburg to the domestic and private, but, oddly, rather like the turning of the land inside out described above, the recounting of the anecdotes ultimately recreates a textual Mecklenburg as the landscape not where women's desires are constrained, but rather where they are *expansively* expressed.

The appeal to contemporary readers of this textual Mecklenburg, like that of the historical novels, should not be underestimated. Mühlbach's articulation of desire in provincial dress explicitly posits the existence of a communality that transcends diversity, that is, she assumes that under the skin her readers share an interest in matters of the heart, in the intimate and everyday, in what our contemporary journalists loosely term "human interest stories." Or, to put it another way, the recollections rely on the existence of community outside of power politics. In the end quirky Mecklenburg represents not the particular, but the universal and thus stands not on the periphery but at the center of an imagined German nation. Prussia, on the other hand, which, as noted above, actually borders on Mecklenburg, has only the most tenuous of existences in these reminiscences; indeed, the word Prussia appears only once in the entire series, and then only for the purpose of identifying a guest of the Grand Duke of Mecklenburg, namely the King of Prussia ("Jugend" 45).

Mühlbach's recollections are of course nostalgic and as such must also be understood as ideological. As Stewart maintains of nostalgia in general, "...like any form of narrative, [nostalgia] is always ideological; the past it seeks has never existed except as narrative.... [N]ostalgia wears a distinctly utopian face, a face that turns toward a future-past, a past that has only ideological reality" (23). Mühlbach's remembering of the Mecklenburg of her youth expresses a longing for something akin to utopia, i.e., for a whole body that does not exist in the present. As Huyssen notes concerning the nostalgia manifest in the cultural projects of the late twentieth century, nostalgia need not in and of itself be considered morally reprehensible or dangerous. "Nostalgia itself," Huyssen writes,

> is not the opposite of utopia, but, as a form of memory, always implicated, even productive in it. After all, it is the ideology of modernization itself that has given nostalgia its bad name, and we do not need to abide by that judgment. Moreover, the desire for history and memory may also be a cunning form of defense: defense...against the attack of the present on the rest of time (88).

Indeed, after sadly reflecting upon the dispersion of her once closely knit family, Mühlbach herself, in her sentimental way, also explicitly identifies desire for the past as a defense mechanism against the obdurate present—and in the context of 1870 she presumably means by obdurate present the threat of war: "May they in the obdurate present look back and themselves say: now our skies are darkened with clouds, but we have a sunny existence behind us and we hope that one day the sun will break through the clouds again for us" ("Jugend" 65). Of course the Mecklenburg of her re-creation by no means constitutes utopia and I by no means intend to valorize it. Nevertheless, the costumed universalism of these memories of Mecklenburg offers an alternative means of binding the margin to the center, of reconnecting past and present, of weaving together disparate parts, of creating a nation of sorts. And Mühlbach is not alone in this alternative vision of nation. Precisely such combination of regionalism and universalism characterizes much of the work of liberal

Swiss, German, and Austrian fiction writers of Mühlbach's generation, those writers who have so often been misleadingly termed realists.

* * *

How did Mühlbach finally assimilate the redrawing of the German map in 1871? Was this the German nation she and her fellow liberals had imagined? At the time of writing her memories, she privately continued to identify with Prussia and, as her daughter relates, upon hearing of the victory over France at Sedan in September of 1870, she enthusiastically joined the cheering multitude before the palace of King Wilhelm I (Ebersberger xiii). Nevertheless, during the remaining three years of her public, literary life she continued her drift away from overt Prussian partisanship. Indeed, had Mühlbach reached the ripe old age of a Gottfried Keller or a Theodor Storm—her literary contemporaries—even she might have found herself increasingly estranged from a Prussian-dominated German empire that, as Keller remarked to Storm on 13 June 1880, seemed incapable of producing a "lasting unanimity of heart and mind" (qtd. in Pape 5).

From 1870 on Mühlbach began to seek inspiration elsewhere and her work began to display a marked international bent. In May of 1871, for example, on the pretext that the market was flooded with accounts of the recent war, she abandoned her plan to write a novel about the Franco-Prussian war (McClain and Kurth-Voigt 1215) only to return to it four months later, this time in international dress. The new project would play simultaneously in Rome, Paris, and Berlin (1226, 1228). Furthermore, after her first trip to Egypt in March of 1870 her work evidenced a new Orientalism;[12] in 1870 she expressed the wish that her two Egyptian novels, *Mohammed Ali und sein Haus* and *Mohammed Ali und seine Nachfolger* be published simultaneously in German, English, and French (1179).

Similarly, her report on the World Exhibition in Vienna reflects a certain public detachment from the new nation. In May 1873, four and a half months before her death, she had attended the opening of the fair. In the article she wrote for the *New York Herald,* she celebrated not the products of *Prussian* might and *German* ingenuity and work displayed there, but rather the general era of industry, which, so she thought, would peaceably unite the peoples of the world: "Outside stood a vast multitude, full of joy, comprised of all the nations of the world, united in brotherhood with a joyful smile" ("Bericht" 2).[13] What she could not know of course when she touted this international celebration of mind and labor, this liberal, universalist project, was that the financial disaster it left in its wake would produce quite the opposite effect in Austria; not only would it significantly weaken Liberalism, but also deepen the divisions among peoples by becoming the occasion for renewed Austrian nationalism and a nasty wave of anti-Semitism (Roschitz, esp. 170–78).

Even Mühlbach's last published work, the "Briefe aus Ems," addressed an international audience rather than a specifically German one, that is, once again the readers of the *New York Herald*. The newspaper had commissioned her, she explained, to report on the Kaiser in Ems ("Jugend" 254). While these four chatty letters, written in July of 1873, do talk about the Emperor in Ems, they by no means exhibit the jingoism that one might expect of a "letter from Ems" in 1873. Thus, while Mühlbach notes that an all too paltry monument has been erected on the spot where the Kaiser had his fateful encounter with the French ambassador Bendetti, she never refers to the outbreak of the Franco-Prussian war by name and instead calls it euphemistically and somewhat pathetically "the first act of the tragedy...that amazed the world and that was followed by such bloody scenes that cost so many tears, the tragedy whose last act we do not yet know" ("Jugend" 250). And while her loyalty to the subject of her article—the Kaiser—is not in doubt, she devotes no space to celebrating the new Germany; instead her descriptions of Ems take on a surprisingly melancholy tone. In fact, she observes that since the post-unification closing of the casinos, Ems has become a dull place. One guest remarks to her:

> These gentlemen in the parliament are always making speeches about freedom...and yet they want to treat people like minors and not even give them the freedom to amuse themselves at the gambling table, or even to ruin themselves if it amuses them. People are always saying the German folk has now entered its vigorous masculine majority and still they want to treat it like a minor and limit its freedom of choice about what it does or doesn't do. Was it really necessary to the happiness and success [*Glück*] of the German nation to deprive it of its casinos? ("Ems" 256)

Ems, formally the watering hole "of interesting foreigners, of genteel cavaliers from all lands who scattered around their money with both hands, of enchanting ladies, who snatched it up in proud awareness of their Grecian beauty" (257) now only has the Kaiser to break the monotony. And judging from Mühlbach's letters, which surprisingly in the end do not devote much space to him, he does not do it that well. If the new German nation, having reached its masculine majority, found its pleasure constrained, it is no wonder then if Mühlbach occasionally longed for the feminine childhood of *her* Mecklenburg, *her* Germany.

Notes

Unless otherwise indicated the translations from German are my own.

[1] In Mühlbach's *Napoleon and the Queen of Prussia* (265–66, 269–70).

[2] Mühlbach claimed that she had left Neubrandenburg in 1838 as an eighteen-year-old ("Louis Napoleon" 183). As McClain and Kurth-Voigt have noted, Mühlbach's assertions about her age do not correspond to her documented age (918).

[3] See, e.g., her self-dramatizing letter of 18 March 1866 (McClain and Kurth-Voigt 1029–34).

[4] "I'm telling you Brandenburg stories from the olden days, but I think they are German stories, for whatever Brandenburg suffered, the German Empire suffered too" (Alexis title page).

[5] This was of course hardly a revelation. Even as it reported almost daily on the "Holstein question" in 1865–66, the conservative Prussian *Kreuzzeitung*, for example, frequently noted the prevalent anti-Prussian sentiment in the South German territories (see, e.g., "Zur Stimmung in Süddeutschland").

[6] Just over four years later in the midst of the Franco-Prussian war she once again experienced the precariousness of the publishing business. She wrote to Costenoble: "Hardly had war come and you wrote me immediately and without suggesting a different arrangement that I should send the check back to you. As you know, I really couldn't, I didn't have it any more! Tell me honestly, was *I* the one who only thought of himself, only made requests on his own account? My God, *you* were the one who as soon as the horror threatened us only thought of himself and who, only worrying about himself, wanted to abandon me, to sacrifice my interests for the sake of yours" (McClain and Kurth-Voigt 1204).

[7] This letter is dated 14 June 1866; the Austro-Prussian war began officially on 15 June 1866. Nevertheless Mühlbach writes as though war has already been declared (McClain and Kurth-Voigt 1043).

[8] After the war was over, the novel appeared there in installments that ran from 2 January 1871 to 24 February 1871 (McClain and Kurth-Voigt 1165).

[9] Mühlbach was by no means alone in her recollection of Mecklenburg as the land of eccentrics. Her famous precedent was of course Fritz Reuter, but there were others. In 1867 the family magazine *Daheim* published a two-part piece, entitled "Mecklenburgische Originale," by one Eduard Hobein.

[10] We note her attempt in May 1867 to persuade her publisher and his wife to move from provincial Jena to Berlin: "You would have a richer life, richer in intellectual pleasures, and in keeping company with people, stimulating and refreshing for heart and mind.... Women very easily find their way in the freer and more genteel life style of the big city..." (McClain and Kurth-Voigt 1009–10). In fact, in the 1860s the provinces had little attraction for her. In the same letter Mühlbach leaves the impression that she seldom "went home" to

Mecklenburg; the land of her childhood had become utterly strange to her; "[In Mecklenburg] I felt as if I had been transported to another world..." (1110).

[11] I would like to thank David Barclay, whose commentary on a shorter version of this article encouraged me to make more explicit the link between the two Mecklenburg Luises, the author and the Queen of Prussia.

[12] Mühlbach's last work was for the *New York Herald,* for which she wrote the letters from Ems as well as a number of advance biographies that could be published there upon the deaths of their subjects (Ebersberger xvi). Mühlbach left for Egypt on 8 March 1870, having been invited by the khedive to write a novel about his grandfather (McClain and Kurth-Voigt 1178–79). Three works resulted from her two trips to Egypt: *Mohammed Ali und sein Haus. Historischer Roman* (1871), *Mohammed Ali's Nachfolger: Historischer Roman im Anschluß an Mohammed Ali und sein Haus* (1872), and *Reisebriefe aus Aegypten* (1871).

[13] The *Herald* published Mühlbach's articles in German with English translations; it was not a German-language publication and by no means aimed to appeal to a specifically German ethnic audience.

Works Cited

Alexis, Willibald. *Der Werwolf.* 1848. Ed. Ludwig Lorenz and Adolf Bartels. Leipzig: Hesse & Becker, n.d.

"Chinesische Mauer." *Allgemeine deutsche Real-Encyklopädie für die gebildeten Stände: Conversations-Lexikon* (Brockhaus). 1864–72.

Ebersberger, Thea. Foreword. *Erinnerungsblätter.* vii–xvii.

Fang, Weigu. *Das Chinabild in der deutschen Literatur, 1871–1933: Ein Beitrag zur komparatistischen Imagologie.* Frankfurt a.M.: Lang, 1992.

Hobein, Eduard. "Mecklenburgische Originale." *Daheim* 3 (1867): 185–87, 199–201.

Huyssen, Andreas. *Twilight Memories: Marking Time in a Culture of Amnesia.* New York: Routledge, 1995.

James, Harold. *A German Identity 1770–1990.* New York: Routledge, 1989.

McClain, William H., and Lieselotte E. Kurth-Voigt. "Clara Mundts Briefe an Hermann Costenoble: Zu L. Mühlbachs historischen Romanen." Ed. William H. McClain and Lieselotte E. Kurth-Voigt. *Archiv für Geschichte des Buchwesens* 22.4/5 (1981): cols. 917–1250.

Möhrmann, Renate. *Die andere Frau: Emanzipationsansätze deutscher Schriftstellerinnen im Vorfeld der Achtundvierziger-Revolution.* Stuttgart: Metzler, 1977.

Mühlbach, Luise. "Briefe aus Ems an den New-York Herald." *Erinnerungsblätter.* 247–82.

———. *Deutschland in Sturm und Drang.* 4 Abteilungen. Jena: Hermann Costenable, 1867–68.

———. *Erinnerungsblätter aus dem Leben Luise Mühlbach's.* Ed. Thea Ebersberger. Leipzig: H. Schmidt & C. Günther, 1902.
———. "Erinnerungen an Louis Napoleon." *Erinnerungsblätter.* 179–214.
———. "Erinnerungen aus der Jugend." *Erinnerungsblätter.* 1–178.
———. "The Historical Romance." 22 Sept. 1866. Introd. to *Old Fritz and the New Era: Mühlbach's Historical Romances in Twenty Volumes.* Trans. Peter Langley. New York: The University Society, n.d. 1–5.
———. "Louise Mühlbach's Bericht." *New York Herald* 2 May 1873: 2.
———. *Napoleon and the Queen of Prussia.* Trans. F. Jordan. *Mühlbach's Historical Romances in Twenty Volumes.* New York: The University Society, n.d.
"Our Correspondents." *New York Herald* 1 May 1873: 3.
Pape, Walter. "Cultural Change and Cultural Memory: The Principle of Hope in the Times of German Unifications." *1870/71–1989/90: German Unifications and the Change of Literary Discourse.* Ed. Walter Pape. Berlin: de Gruyter, 1993. 1–21.
Peterson, Brent O. "Luise Mühlbach (Clara Mundt) (2 January 1814–26 September 1873)." *Nineteenth-Century German Writers to 1840.* Ed. James Hardin and Siegfried Mews. *Dictionary of Literary Biography.* Vol. 133. Detroit: Bruccoli Clark Layman. 204–10. 1993.
Roschitz, Karlheinz. *Wiener Weltausstellung 1873.* Vienna: Jugend und Volk Verlagsgesellschaft, 1989.
Schuster, Ingrid. *Vorbilder und Zerrbilder: China und Japan im Spiegel der deutschen Literatur 1773–1890.* Bern: Lang, 1988.
Stewart, Susan. *On Longing: Narratives of the Miniature, the Gigantic, the Souvenir, the Collection.* Baltimore: The Johns Hopkins UP, 1984.
Waldron, Arthur. *The Great Wall of China: From History to Myth.* Cambridge: Cambridge UP, 1990.
"Zur Stimmung in Süddeutschland." *Neue Preußische (Kreuz) Zeitung.* Beilage. 12 Mar. 1865: 2.

The Whip and the Lamp: Leopold von Sacher-Masoch, the Woman Question, and the Jewish Question

Barbara Hyams

We think we know how the so-called first masochist helped to construct the fin-de-siècle's idols of perversity. Sacher-Masoch's international review *Auf der Höhe,* which claimed to raise itself above all partisan politics, reveals the extent to which he sought a more expansive drawing board for his critical imagination. Neither women nor Jews remained static idols of perversity in this imaginative forum. The inconsistencies in their representation were his own unfinished ruminations on the social emancipation of both women and Jews, on the philosophy of religion, and on sexual identity in the late nineteenth century. (BH)

We are well aware that the *femme fatale* served a particular function in European literature of the mid and later nineteenth century: "Popularizers of the theme of a connection between female sexuality and the physical decay and moral sickness of city life were legion." One of these dangerous *femmes,* i.e., "the alluring, but cruel, life-force" (Gillespie 110) was embodied in Leopold von Sacher-Masoch's figure of the Venus in Furs.

Looking back at the writer and editor Sacher-Masoch more than a century after his death, we make an automatic connection between the latter half of his name and an illness, first coined as a forensic term in 1890,[1] that has wended its way through both orthodox and unorthodox psychoanalysis to become a postmodern cultural statement about gender performativity. As modernism settles into memory and a psychoanalytically trained professor of law and psychiatry asks nostalgically at our own fin-de-siècle: "What remains of Freudianism when its scientific center crumbles?" (Stone 35), we think we know how the so-called first masochist—many would argue he had plenty of ancestors—helped to construct the last fin-de-siècle's idols of perversity, to use Bram Dijkstra's phrase.

Who was Leopold von Sacher-Masoch?[2] He was born in 1836 to a Catholic aristocratic family in Lemberg, Galicia, where his highly respected father served as Chief of Police. In the course of his life, Sacher-Masoch lived in Prague, Graz, Vienna, Bruck on the Mur, Budapest, Leipzig, Paris, and Lindheim. Having tried and rejected a career as an academic historian, he earned a living by writing numerous stories, novellas, and novels in a realist vein that also partly anticipated German naturalism. His major life's work was a cycle of novellas, *Das Vermächtnis Kains* (The Heritage of Cain), which he never finished. He became infamous for the recurring image in his 1870 "Venus im Pelz" ("Venus in Furs")—one of the novellas in the first part of the cycle—of a cruel woman in a fur jacket brandishing a dog whip while a man grovels adoringly at her feet.

The image, which Sacher-Masoch found himself obliged to repeat endlessly in popular formats in order to pay the bills, provided a model for the pathological condition named and described by Richard von Krafft-Ebing. Otherwise lauded by many literary critics for his pungent portrayals of human social interaction and vibrant Eastern landscapes—for example in the novella "Don Juan von Kolomea" (Don Juan of Kolomea)—Sacher-Masoch helped to expand the boundaries of sensual representation in German, which resulted in praise for his Slavic renewal of an overly cerebral German literature, as well as numerous charges of immorality.[3] Although Sacher-Masoch dreamed of painting a tableau of nineteenth-century life as vivid in its own way as Dante's *Divine Comedy*, one that would necessarily expose moral flaws in human character, he went to his death in 1895 still railing against Krafft-Ebing for tying *his* character to an illness.[4]

What tends to be overshadowed in our collective memory of Sacher-Masoch is that the artist and cultural critic in him attempted to communicate his positive experience of the multicultural Habsburg Empire by promoting cosmopolitanism (i.e., considering oneself a world citizen as much as a member of a specific nation) in the new German nation-state. My interest in Sacher-Masoch quickened when I learned the extent to which he participated as a writer, editor, and activist in the Austro-Hungarian and German debates about the place of emancipated secular and orthodox Jews in later nineteenth-century Central and Eastern Europe. Jews appeared frequently in the works of other writers as symbols of physical decay and moral sickness in the cities, towns, and even villages (*shtetl*) from Galicia to the Rhineland. Did Sacher-Masoch portray Jews too as another gateway to perversity? The complex answer I found to this latter question helped me to reexamine my general assumptions about Sacher-Masoch's portraits of male and female sexuality and gender roles.

Sacher-Masoch had long harbored the dream of editing a journal of high cultural content, and in 1881 he received his chance. In a bid to secure his future, he won over a young Jewish millionaire, Dr. Lionel

Baumgärtner, owner of the Leipzig publishing house Gressner & Schramm, with an idea for a new periodical to be called *Auf der Höhe* (At the Pinnacle). The international review, purportedly raising itself above all partisan politics ("Höhe" iii), proved to be anything but neutral in the climate of the first decade after the creation of the German nation-state in 1871.

There seem to be no statistics on *Auf der Höhe*'s circulation during its four brief years of existence. Sacher-Masoch's lofty aspirations did not suffice to keep his publisher happy and Baumgärtner decided to discontinue publication of *Auf der Höhe* within a few months. His discomfort with Leopold and his wife Wanda stemmed from Wanda's flirtatious behavior and Leopold's insinuation that Baumgärtner was welcome to have an affair with her. He extricated himself with the excuse that "he felt he had been mistaken in his judgment that the time was ripe for educating Germany. For the time being, he believed that he could serve the cause of cosmopolitan civilization better in Vienna" (Cleugh, *Marquis* 253). In early 1882, Sacher-Masoch's new business partner Jacques Armand rescued the venture by finding another publisher, E.L. Morgenstern, and promising to underwrite it with his (what turned out to be nonexistent) personal family fortune. Furthermore, the venture crumbled under the weight of the mutual infidelities of Wanda von Sacher-Masoch with Jacques Armand and Leopold von Sacher-Masoch with Hulda Meister. We know for certain that the periodical never had a stable base of financial support and that its run was too short-lived to have a lasting impact on German culture and society; in all likelihood it was preaching to the already converted. Its significance is best measured by the extent to which it provoked its enemies.

Auf der Höhe sought to champion tolerance in the highly charged atmosphere of Saxony. In 1869, the Deutsch-Israelitischer Gemeindebund, an association of Jewish communities that was active in charitable and educational activities throughout the German states—including the fight against antisemitism—had been founded at the behest of the Leipzig Synod. In 1879–80, shortly before the creation of Sacher-Masoch's new journal, the Gemeindebund waged a losing battle against an antisemitic publisher in Dresden, Verlag der Hof-Buchhandlung von R. V. Grumbkow. Because of the rising tide of antisemitism in Saxony, the Gemeindebund was denied legal recognition in the official registry of organizations; this led it to move its headquarters to Berlin in the beginning of 1882, i.e., just several months after *Auf der Höhe* had commenced publication (Diamant 111–16). Thus Sacher-Masoch's *Neue Judengeschichten* (New Jewish Stories), which had just been published in Leipzig by E.L. Morgenstern in 1881, must also have been regarded as a "provocation by the nationalist and arch-conservative circles that were gaining influence" (Opel 455).

Sacher-Masoch's commitment to normalizing the inclusion of Jewish culture in late nineteenth-century German-language cultural discourse was unwavering, even if many late twentieth-century readers are inclined to fault him for reinforcing stereotypes of Jews in some of his fiction.[5] Hans Otto Horch has correctly credited *Auf der Höhe* with greater objectivity and fairness than other German-language publications of the same time period (280).

Sacher-Masoch was an easy target for political antisemites of the late nineteenth century who viewed cosmopolitanism as a false banner with which to "decry German being and German *Volk* traditions" (Zimmermann, "Beitrag" 348). The writer Oswald Zimmermann—Sacher-Masoch's "literary Judas," as Sacher-Masoch's secretary Carl Schlichtegroll was to label him, was an active member of his Leipzig literary circle. Zimmermann had once hoped to join the staff of *Auf der Höhe* and had delivered the opening remarks at Sacher-Masoch's silver anniversary gala. He was the anonymous author of an antisemitic tract in the 1870s, *Die Juden im deutschen Staats- und Volksleben,* but also of a literary study published under his name in 1885 that reveals curiously deep affinities with Sacher-Masoch, *Die Wonne des Leids* (The Joy of Suffering); he subsequently pursued a career in antisemitic politics in the *Reichstag*. Zimmermann, who had become intimate with a mutual friend, Jenny Marr (the third and already ex-wife of Wilhelm Marr),[6] obtained from her highly biased, but not altogether false, compromising information about Sacher-Masoch's editorship of the review. In 1885 Zimmermann published a scathing anonymous attack in *Deutsche Reform,* in which he sought to discredit Sacher-Masoch as a Francophile, a philosemite, and a Slavophile.

Sacher-Masoch spent his waning years with his second wife, Hulda Meister, and their children in the German state of Hesse, working to counteract local antisemitism through the Oberhessischen Verein für Volksbildung (OVV), an association for adult education that he and Hulda founded in 1893.[7] Sacher-Masoch scarcely had the financial means to support himself, let alone the OVV. He had appealed for contributions to the OVV through a major German-Jewish newspaper, the *Allgemeine Zeitung des Judentums*. Some of the resulting contributors included wealthy Frankfurt Jews and the secretary of a national association to counteract antisemitism, the Verein zur Abwehr des Antisemitismus. Through his support of ostensibly non-partisan education in the form of neighborhood libraries—which included bound collections of *Auf der Höhe,* as well as his support of lectures, theater productions, concerts, and financial subsidies to young people who attended local vocational and agricultural schools, Sacher-Masoch locked horns with the Marburg librarian Otto Böckel, who had raised himself to an antisemitic "peasant king" and elected representative in the Reichstag. Perhaps the most significant aspect of the amateur theater productions and other local events was that they occasionally brought Jews and Gentiles together, which constituted an extraordinary step toward integrating Jews into Upper Hessian village life.

From the moment of the OVV's inception, Böckel led the way in attacking it in his antisemitic newspaper *Der Reichsherold*. For strategic reasons, he and his followers attempted to camouflage their antisemitism by feigning provincial affrontery at the notion that a man with Sacher-Masoch's immoral personal history and writing accomplishments would dare to think that Upper Hesse was "a dark place in need of light." Carrying the same impulse behind his journal to his subsequent role as a local activist, Sacher-Masoch declared in a pamphlet in 1893 that "enlightenment and adult education (*Volksbildung*), love of fatherland, religion, and good manners are incompatible with antisemitism" (Demandt 314, note 113). Another public controversy between Sacher-Masoch's detractors and defenders erupted in one of the local newspapers in the early months of 1895 just prior to Sacher-Masoch's death.

The majority of late nineteenth-century philosemites sought to convert their Jewish neighbors or otherwise erode their Judaism by ultimately seeking to eliminate difference (Brenner). Steven Beller has postulated that Otto Weininger's notorious turn-of-the-century bestseller *Geschlecht und Charakter* (*Sex and Character*) was an extreme consequence of this liberalism. Yet, as Robert S. Wistrich notes, "Weininger did not envisage anything approaching the sexual equality advocated by Victorian liberals like John Stuart Mill. In his view, 'moral' men and women would renounce sexual intercourse and thereby put an end to the human race—hardly a liberal or rational vision of the future" (10).

What kind of liberal, then, was Sacher-Masoch? Sacher-Masoch was a cosmopolitan; he appreciated difference. He embraced modernity as he knew it in the imperfect Habsburg Empire and had the nerve to prescribe it to the new German nation-state. He had an ethnographer's fascination with Orthodox Eastern Jewry, but he favored Jewish religious reform and thought that intermarriage was a delightful way to irritate antisemites. He totally underestimated the pressure on Jews to assimilate and never for a moment envisioned near-total eradication of Eastern and Central European Jewry in the twentieth century.

How does his innocence reconcile with our notion of the masochistic subject? There are forms of advocacy that are potentially harmful to the very social groups they are sincerely intended to benefit. While the playful inversion of social norms and cultural values, taking on subordinate roles for the pleasure of it, can be an effective strategy for social criticism, it can also become another expression of hegemony. Sacher-Masoch's antisemitic enemies understood his social criticism; hence, the viciousness of their counter-attack. But the wider, more moderate public and above all the publishers who insisted on endless repetitions of "Venus im Pelz" because they sold even long after the whip had lost its bite as a critique of present gender relations, aided and abetted the naming of an illness; that is to say, at least in the short run, hegemony triumphed.

With these aspects of Sacher-Masoch's life and reputation in mind, we can now focus on his selections as editor of the Leipzig-based monthly *Auf der Höhe: Internationale Revue,* published from October 1881 to September 1885 and collected in 16 volumes. The short-lived periodical, which attests to his faith in cultural panaceas for hatred, or what the Frankfurt School would subsequently refer to as "affirmative culture," was a literary magazine. A recent survey of the history of literary Leipzig has suggested that a plausible forerunner to *Auf der Höhe* would be a moderate Young German/*Vormärz* periodical like *Europa: Chronik der gebildeten Welt* (Europe: Chronicle of the Educated World), published in Leipzig under the editorship of August Lewald and Gustav Kühne and featuring Heinrich Heine and Heinrich Laube among its regular contributors (Herzog 218). While the readership of *Auf der Höhe* included many Jews of both genders as well as progressive gentile women of the new German nation-state and the Habsburg Empire, it was not intended to appeal solely to Jews and/or women.[8] An affirmative culture presupposed an audience engrossed in a heterogeneous world.

Auf der Höhe promoted respect for Judaism. A number of articles examine the extent to which Western philosophers have attempted to define Judaism through the lenses of various philosophical systems (Mieses), including the attempt to unite the optimism of Judaism with the pessimism of Schopenhauer (Schweinburg). Given the nineteenth century's preoccupation with and Sacher-Masoch's own leanings toward religious and philosophical pessimism, it should come as no surprise to find an article devoted to Jewish pessimists; surprisingly, however, the article confronts the negativity of pessimism head on. It posits the starting point for all pessimistic reflections in Jewish literature in the *Weltschmerz* of the two philosophical books of the Bible, Kohéleth (Ecclesiastes) and Job, as well as in the Psalms. From there, they made their way into discussions in the Mishnah, the Midrash, and the Talmud. In the course of Jewish history, hardship, treachery, and the agonies of torture and coercion tempted some Jews to focus on apathetic or melancholy aspects within Jewish thought. However, as the article has it, pessimism represents a phase, not a telos in Judaism, which is portrayed as a religion of affirmation. Typically, *Auf der Höhe* placed a high premium on the image of an idealized Jew who is no stranger to suffering, yet affirms his and her heritage, and has the forbearance to promote love and reconciliation among warring neighbors (cf. Samuely; Littrow). While clearly reformist in its views on Judaism, *Auf der Höhe* expressed disapproval of Jews who assimilated to the point of trying to erase all aspects of their Jewish identity.[9]

Auf der Höhe also addressed antisemitism by means of a variety of genres. The finest example is "Eine Wienerin in Berlin" (A Viennese Woman in Berlin), a satirical text signed only "Heinz M." and quite possibly the work of Sacher-Masoch himself. Personified as a young lady wrapped "not in furs," but in "infinite quantities of flannel and cotton wool," the Berlin feuilleton—a weekly cultural supplement carried by all the great newspapers of the era—eschews for its name the French word in favor of its dull German equivalent (*Blättchen*)—unlike its Viennese counterpart—and admits freely that it is boring because of the way it is treated by Berlin editors. In the course of the conversation between Heinz M. and the personified feuilleton, we learn that despite warnings to avoid Berlin, the feuilleton had allowed itself to be ruined by the city's philosophical pretensions.

Appearing just a few years after the public dispute between Berlin academicians Heinrich Treitschke and Theodor Mommsen, the piece is an indictment of the spread of antisemitism among the educated elite (see Boehlich). The picture is further complicated, however, by the fact that several of the Berlin feuilleton editors and shapers of cultural tastes, such as Oskar Blumenthal and Fritz Mauthner, were themselves assimilated Jews. When Heinz M. and *Blättchen* approach a "somewhat exclusive beer hall," *Blättchen* examines Heinz M.'s profile to determine whether he is Jewish. They have the following interchange:[10]

B: Guests there are very distinguished.

HM: And how does their distinction manifest itself?

B: Through their delicate antisemitism. Oh! Jews could certainly enter the premises without being censured [*stöckered*].[11] But people would simply ignore them.

HM: Ah, so these marvellous people have stolen from Fichte; just as his world exists only through our idea of it, so too, according to this newest version, do Jews exist only as our idea of them. One stops imagining them, and they cease to exist.

B: Yes, just think: wanting to deny a brutal fact like the existence of Jews by means of philosophy!

HM: May I speak frankly? I find the vulgar antisemites less stupid than this delicate sort.

B: You're quite right. The mob embodies a certain force that emerges from love of enterprise or scandal. But these would-be champions of refinement? In their case, inability is the key to everything.

Blättchen laughs and explains that it is the eighteenth-century dramatist Lessing's fault, because he was "the only one who told his fellow Germans the truth"; since then, the vain and the envious have been offered poetic or philosophical illusions with which to delude themselves, culminating in antisemitism itself, which offers the ultimate effortless identity: "You no longer need be ironic [Heine] or arrogant [Schopenhauer], you do not need to become anything, you are something: an Indo-German" (Heinz M. 134–35). The satire positions itself, then, against both Treitschke *and* overly assimilated Jewish purveyors of taste—without succumbing to the emerging cliché of the evils of the Jewish press.

The articles on women range in content from the anatomy of women's brains and mental potential, higher education for women, suffrage, comparative studies of marital rites and divorce practices in occidental and oriental cultures, and the representation of women in contemporary literature, to male and female consumers of contemporary literature. The themes are the same red threads as those running through Sacher-Masoch's entire *oeuvre*: his great fascination with and respect for natural science, his preoccupation with the war between the sexes *and* guarded support of political and social equality for women, his enthusiasm for ethnic studies beyond the narrow confines of Christian Germany, and his aspiration to educate a German-language readership to accept immorality in the literary realm.

The significance of Viennese professor of zoology Carl B. Brühl's 1883 article, "Frauenhirn, Frauenseele, Frauenrecht" (Woman's Brain, Woman's Soul, Woman's Rights), cannot be overestimated when attempting to understand the tenor of the articles Sacher-Masoch solicited for publication. The 1870s and 1880s were the breakthrough period for certification of women physicians throughout the Western world. Brühl's decisive refutation of the renowned Munich professor of anatomy and physiology Theodor Bischoff whose manifesto of 1872, *Das Studium und die Ausübung der Medicin durch Frauen* (The Study and Practice of Medicine by Women), was widely accepted as the definitive argument against women physicians, had as its goal "the anatomical rescue of the honor of woman's brain" (Brühl 68). Brühl denounced the pseudo-science of phrenology in no uncertain terms. His refutation of all scientific theories that would infer diminished intellectual capabilities in women from brain size acted as a counterforce to the rise of a popular scientific notion that posited a link between the female sex and inferior races (cf. Dijkstra 373).

Josef Beckmann's lengthy treatise in the periodical on the woman question asserts that the emancipation of women is inseparable from the emancipation of mankind. Women's dependence is not natural but historically conditioned; women's nature is the product of history and environment. The telos of history is a movement from hierarchy (*ein Übereinander*) to equality (*ein Nebeneinander*). The argument that women's procreative function has diminished their intellectual ability does not account for women having the same intellectual potential as men

(Beckmann cites Brühl in *Auf der Höhe*), but women must *develop* their brains by using them.

I have highlighted these articles because they add complexity to Sacher-Masoch's enduring reputation as the creator of "Venus in Furs" and the association of his name first with an illness and more recently with a cultural statement about submission. There are, to be sure, aspects of this Sacher-Masoch in *Auf der Höhe,* but the periodical ought to be seen as a conversation between the voices to which Sacher-Masoch lent credence, that is, as a working through of his own opinions in the guise of a non-partisan international review.[12] This explains why Sacher-Masoch wrote at times under pseudonyms, including that of a brilliant new female author Charlotte Arand, in order to set an example for his vision of a new standard in women's writing—arrogant as that may be. *Auf der Höhe* was a drawing board for his critical imagination, an intertextual discourse within his own belief system, such as his decision to applaud the affirmative aspects of Judaism while he portrayed himself in general as a cultural pessimist. Neither women nor Jews remained static idols of perversity in this imaginative forum. The inconsistencies in their representation were his own unfinished ruminations on the social emancipation of women and Jews respectively, on the philosophy of religion, and on sexual identity in the late nineteenth century.

Notes

[1] The first edition of Krafft-Ebing's *Psychopathia Sexualis* appeared in 1886, but he did not include the term "masochism" until 1890 when the text had undergone a number of revisions.

[2] In addition to steady interest since 1890 in the gender-specific psychological phenomena and cultural practices known as masochism, there has been a modest resurgence of interest in the nineteenth-century figure who inspired the term. While James Cleugh published his revised biography of Sacher-Masoch in the 1960s, the best known theoretical study by far is Gilles Deleuze's *Coldness and Cruelty,* which first appeared in French in 1967. A year later in Germany, Karl E. Demandt thoroughly documented Sacher-Masoch's local efforts in Lindheim, Hesse, to counteract antisemitism through creation of the Oberhessischen Verein für Volksbildung. In 1989 Hans Otto Horch provided the most complete account to date of Sacher-Masoch's history of positive relations with the Jewish community and offered a balanced assessment of Jewish themes and characters in Sacher-Masoch's fiction. Monika Treut has studied the image of the "cruel woman" in writings by de Sade and Sacher-Masoch. Michael Farin has worked since the mid-1980s to uncover the scope of Sacher-Masoch's publications, many of which were destroyed in the Nazi era, and to assess Sacher-Masoch's place in cultural and social history; Albrecht Koschorke's work is overtly indebted to

Farin's. John K. Noyes has published a series of major articles on Sacher-Masoch, among them one on the historical perspective in his texts. Michael T. O'Pecko has translated selected Galician tales by Sacher-Masoch into English. Robert S. Leventhal's article on Franz Kafka and theories of masochism came to my attention too late to include in the present discussion. A number of books on Sacher-Masoch and masochism, including my own, are in the works.

[3] Robert C. Holub's study of "how realism functions as a normed discourse that excludes otherness" (17) is a useful guide with which to read the views of Sacher-Masoch's contemporaries on his mixed contribution to German realism and early anticipation of naturalism. Rudolf von Gottschall, arguably Sacher-Masoch's greatest contemporary admirer, praised Sacher-Masoch in 1878 for his ability to reproduce landscapes with keen accuracy. For Gottschall there is no permissible connection, however, between nature, philosophy, and "abnormal" sensuality in realist aesthetics; his views thus underscore Holub's point that realism excludes otherness.

[4] In an autobiographical essay published in the German cultural monthly *Deutsche Monatsblätter,* Sacher-Masoch quoted Schopenhauer on the moral freedom of the poet as a justification for the scandalous elements in his writing: "...no one can prescribe to the poet that he should be noble and sublime, moral, pious, Christian, or anything else, still less reproach him for being this and not that" ("Autobiographie" 73).

[5] Dijkstra, for example, is unaware of Sacher-Masoch's *oeuvre* and therefore misreads the protagonist of "Venus im Pelz" as a self-conscious Aryan who is offended by the alien presence of "greasy-haired Jews" (373). O'Pecko, in contrast, defends certain stereotypes in Sacher-Masoch's fiction "as an attempt to ameliorate the Jews' position in Central Europe" (331). Biale and Aschheim take opposing views on the significance of Sacher-Masoch's portrayals of Jewish women in his fiction.

[6] In addition to provoking Sacher-Masoch to sue Zimmermann for libel, Zimmermann's liaison cost him the editorship of Theodor Fritsch's new antisemitic periodical, the *Antisemitische Correspondenz,* in late 1885. Zimmermann quickly recovered from Fritsch's rebuff by joining forces with other political antisemites like Otto Böckel, who took on Sacher-Masoch as an educator in the state of Hesse.

[7] On the hundredth anniversary of Sacher-Masoch's death in March 1995, an article in the *Frankfurter Rundschau* argued that, particularly in light of the Holocaust, it was time to "forget the whip" and to remember Sacher-Masoch for his contributions as an educator (Winter). However well-intentioned, this would be counter-productive, since Sacher-Masoch's sexual politics were inextricable from his cultural criticism (see Mosse; Koch).

[8] However, an advertisement on the back cover of the February 1883 issue of *Auf der Höhe* for the *Deutsche Frauenblätter*—which boasted an "elegant *Gartenlaube* format" and featured everything from *belles lettres* to articles on

fashion, cooking, and childcare—may provide some indication of its popularity among women.

[9] *Auf der Höhe* displayed particular reverence toward Rabbi Leopold Stein. As a newly appointed rabbi in Frankfurt, Stein served in 1845 as president of the second of three rabbinical assemblies held in Germany with the goal of ushering in moderate reform within Judaism. Even within the reform-minded rabbinate, Stein was a "spokesman of moderation" (Meyer 132).

[10] In order to keep the voices separate, I have added the designations "B" for *Blättchen* and "HM" for the narrator.

[11] The writer invents the verb *anstöckern* from the name of the antisemitic pastor turned politician, Adolf Stöcker.

[12] Sacher-Masoch pledged in the first issue of *Auf der Höhe* (1881) to provide a "poetic natural history of mankind" rather than "bland, inane entertainment" and to render a cultural-historical or ethnographic portrait of nations.

Works Cited

Aschheim, Steven E. *Brothers and Strangers: The East European Jew in German and German Jewish Consciousness 1800–1923*. Madison: U of Wisconsin P, 1982.

Beckmann, Josef. "Zur Frauenfrage." *Auf der Höhe* 11 (Apr.-May-June 1884): 64–81.

Beller, Steven. "Otto Weininger as Liberal?" *Jews and Gender: Responses to Otto Weininger*. Ed. Nancy A. Harrowitz and Barbara Hyams. Philadelphia: Temple UP, 1995. 91–101.

Biale, David. "Masochism and Philosemitism: The Strange Case of Leopold Sacher-Masoch." *Journal of Contemporary History* 17 (1982): 305–23.

Bischoff, Theodor L. W. von. *Das Studium und die Ausübung der Medicin durch Frauen*. München: Literarisch-artistische Anstalt (Th. Riedel), 1872.

Boehlich, Walter, ed. *Der Berliner Antisemitismusstreit*. Frankfurt a.M.: Insel, 1988.

Brenner, Michael. "'Gott schütze uns vor unseren Freunden': Zur Ambivalenz des 'Philosemitismus' im Kaiserreich." *Jahrbuch für Antisemitismusforschung* 2 (1993): 174–99.

Brühl, Carl B. "Frauenhirn, Frauenseele, Frauenrecht." *Auf der Höhe* 6 (Jan.-Feb.-Mar. 1883): 31–80.

Cleugh, James. *The First Masochist: A Biography of Sacher-Masoch*. London: Blond, 1967.

———. *The Marquis and the Chevalier: A Study in the Psychology of Sex as Illustrated by the Lives and Personalities of the Marquis de Sade, 1740–1814, and the Chevalier von Sacher-Masoch, 1836–1905*. New York: Duell, Sloan and Pearce, 1951.

Deleuze, Gilles. "Coldness and Cruelty." *Masochism*. Trans. Jean McNeil. New York: Zone Books, 1991. 7–138.

Demandt, Karl E. "Leopold von Sacher-Masoch und sein Oberhessischer Volksbildungsverein zwischen Schwarzen, Roten und Antisemiten." *Hessisches Jahrbuch für Landesgeschichte* 18 (1968): 160–208. Reprinted in Farin. 272–331.

Diamant, Adolf. *Chronik der Juden in Leipzig: Aufstieg, Vernichtung und Neuanfang*. Chemnitz: Heimatland Sachsen, 1993.

Dijkstra, Bram. *Idols of Perversity: Fantasies of Feminine Evil in Fin-de-Siècle Culture*. New York: Oxford UP, 1986.

Farin, Michael, ed. *Leopold von Sacher-Masoch: Materialien zu Leben und Werk*. Bonn: Bouvier, 1987.

Gillespie, Gerald. "The City of Wo/man: Labyrinth, Wilderness, Garden." *Comparative Criticism* 18 (1996): 107–25.

Gottschall, Rudolf von. "Sacher-Masoch als Novellist." *Allgemeine Zeitung* No. 374. 13 Dec. 1878: Beilage: 5125–126. Reprinted in Farin. 114–21.

Herzog, Andreas, ed. *Literarisches Leipzig: Kulturhistorisches Mosaik einer Buchstadt*. Leipzig: Edition Leipzig, 1995.

Holub, Robert C. *Reflections of Realism: Paradox, Norm, and Ideology in Nineteenth-Century German Prose*. Detroit: Wayne State UP, 1991.

Horch, Hans Otto. "Der Außenseiter als 'Judenraphael': Zu den Judengeschichten Leopold von Sacher-Masoch." *Conditio Judaica*. Ed. Hans Otto Horch and Horst Denkler. Tübingen: Niemeyer, 1989. 2: 258–86.

Koch, Friedrich. *Sexuelle Denunziation: Die Sexualität in der politischen Auseinandersetzung*. Frankfurt a.M.: Syndikat, 1986.

Koschorke, Albrecht. *Leopold von Sacher-Masoch: Die Inszenierung einer Perversion*. München: Piper, 1988.

Krafft-Ebing, Richard von. *Psychopathia Sexualis: Mit besonderer Berücksichtigung der conträren sexuellen Empfindungen*. 5th rev. ed. Stuttgart: Enke, 1890.

Leventhal, Robert S. "Versagen: Kafka und die masochistische Ordnung." *German Life and Letters* 48.2 (1995): 148–69.

Littrow, H. "Die Juden in Europa." *Auf der Höhe* 10 (Jan.-Feb.-Mar. 1884): 389–410.

M., Heinz. "Eine Wienerin in Berlin." *Auf der Höhe* 12 (July-Aug.-Sept. 1884): 132–36.

Meyer, Michael A. *Response to Modernity: A History of the Reform Movement in Judaism*. New York: Oxford UP, 1988.

Mieses, Fabius. "Das Judenthum der Vergangenheit." *Auf der Höhe* 15 (Apr.-May-June 1885): 291–97.

Mosse, George L. *Nationalism and Sexuality: Middle-Class Morality and Sexual Norms in Modern Europe*. Madison: U of Wisconsin P, 1985.

Noyes, John. "The Importance of the Historical Perspective in the Works of Leopold von Sacher-Masoch." *Modern Austrian Literature* 26.2 (1994): 1–20.

O'Pecko, Michael T. "Afterword." *A Light for Others & Other Jewish Tales from Galicia.* Leopold von Sacher-Masoch. Trans. Michael T. O'Pecko. Riverside, CA: Ariadne, 1994. 329–38.

Opel, Adolf. "Nachwort: Ein illustrer Unbekannter." *Der Judenraphael: Geschichten aus Galizien.* Leopold von Sacher-Masoch. Wien: Böhlau, 1989. 435–70.

Sacher-Masoch, Leopold von. "Auf der Höhe." *Auf der Höhe* 1 (Oct. 1881): iii–v.

———. "Eine Autobiographie." *Deutsche Monatsblätter* 2.3 (June 1879): 259–69. Reprinted in Sacher-Masoch. *Souvenirs: Autobiographische Prosa.* Trans. Susanne Farin. München: Belleville, 1985. 60–76.

———. *Das Vermächtniß Kains: Novellen.* I. Theil: Die Liebe. Vol. 2. Stuttgart: J.G. Cotta, 1870.

———. "Venus in Furs." *Masochism.* Trans. Jean McNeil. New York: Zone Books, 1991, 141–293.

Samuely, Nathan. "Shylock und Nathan." *Auf der Höhe* 7 (Apr.-May-June 1883): 448–456.

Schweinburg, S. "Jüdische Pessimisten." *Auf der Höhe* 10 (Jan.-Feb.-Mar. 1884): 377–402.

Stone, Alan A. "Where Will Psychoanalysis Survive?" *Harvard Magazine* (Jan.-Feb. 1997): 35–39.

Treut, Monika. *Die grausame Frau: Zum Frauenbild bei de Sade und Sacher-Masoch.* Basel: Stroemfeld / Roter Stern, 1984.

Winter, Johannes. "Vergiß die Peitsche! Sacher-Masoch und die oberhessische Volksbildung." *Frankfurter Rundschau* 11 Mar. 1995: ZB1.

Wistrich, Robert S. "Clichés of Hatred." Rev. of *Jews and Gender: Responses to Otto Weininger.* Ed. Nancy A. Harrowitz and Barbara Hyams. *Times Literary Supplement* 2 Aug. 1996: 9–10.

Zimmermann, Oswald. "Sacher-Masoch's 'Auf der Höhe': Ein Beitrag zur Charakteristik der philosemitischen Presse." *Deutsche Reform.* Dresden, 1885. Reprinted in Farin. 342–56.

———. *Die Wonne des Leids: Beiträge zur Erkenntnis des menschlichen Empfindens in Kunst und Leben.* 2nd rev. ed. Leipzig: Carl Reissner, 1885.

Her (Per)version: *The Confessions of Wanda von Sacher-Masoch*

Katharina Gerstenberger

This article on Wanda von Sacher-Masoch's 1906 autobiography *Meine Lebensbeichte* is informed by turn-of-the-century studies in its focus on constructions of sexuality and gender, as well as by feminist studies of autobiography and issues of female self-representation. With her autobiography, Wanda von Sacher-Masoch created a countertext to her husband Leopold von Sacher-Masoch's masochistic texts, in particular his "Venus in Furs," by introducing female subject positions outside the heterosexual paradigm of the male master text. The misogynist reception of Wanda von Sacher-Masoch's assertion of female authorship and self-representation illustrates the contested position of the female autobiographer around 1900. (KG)

As we approach the turn of another century, the last *fin-de-siècle* continues to attract scholars as a period during which its contemporaries were both alarmed and fascinated by the "sexual anarchy" of their time.[1] Sexologists, criminologists, and psychoanalysts confronted the perceived loss of sexual order by delimiting the boundaries between masculinity and femininity, by creating typologies designed to separate deviancy from normalcy, and by classifying forms of perversion. A contribution to feminist autobiography studies, my article suggests a reading of Wanda von Sacher-Masoch's autobiography *Meine Lebensbeichte* (*The Confessions of Wanda von Sacher-Masoch*, 1906) as a text that represents an "anarchical" female self whose identity is inscribed across the very boundaries of sexual difference that turn-of-the-century culture sought to enforce.[2]

The Confessions of Wanda von Sacher-Masoch cannot be understood without reference to the autobiographer's relationship to the person and the work of Austrian writer Leopold von Sacher-Masoch (1836–1895), her husband of ten years. It was, of course, Leopold von Sacher-Masoch's work, most importantly his 1870 novella "Venus in Furs," that inspired sexologist Richard von Krafft-Ebing (1840–1902) to borrow the Slavic component of Sacher-Masoch's name for the purpose of denoting the sexual perversion we know as "masochism."[3] "Masochism," as described by Leopold von Sacher-Masoch and defined by Krafft-Ebing, is the common referent shared by Wanda von Sacher-Masoch's contemporaries and present-day readers. I am interested in the entanglements between the male- and the female-authored text, and I therefore approach "masochism" as a textual practice rather than a lived reality, concentrating on the position and role of the female partner in the male masochistic script. In tracing Wanda von Sacher-Masoch's autobiographical response to her husband's work, I focus on the strategies she employed to assert female subjectivity and self-representation within and against his textual/sexual parameters and the gendered politics of authorship. I offer my reading of *Confessions* as a contribution to the understanding of female autobiography as a particularly rich nodal point in which notions of sexuality, writing, and gender intersect and diverge.

A feminist analysis of a female autobiography written around 1900 would be incomplete without a reference to Georg Misch's multivolume *Geschichte der Autobiographie*, 1907–1969 (*A History of Autobiography in Antiquity*, 1951) and its influence over both the production and the reception of autobiographies in the twentieth century. Misch's ideal autobiographer was by definition male, a coherent subject equipped with a unique individuality (12, 13). Beginning in the 1980s, feminist scholars of autobiography have theorized the incompatibility of male models of subjectivity with female life stories and proceeded to challenge the resulting marginalization of women autobiographers.[4] More recently, feminists have reexamined turn-of-the-century culture and diagnosed a "crisis of identity for men" (Showalter 8) triggered by the rise of urban mass society, by the pressures of feminism and the growing presence of homosexuals in the public sphere, as well as by the newly emerging science of psychoanalysis and the discovery of the unconscious. The stable male subject of autobiography with his ability to represent not only himself but his times comes under scrutiny at precisely the moment in which Georg Misch postulated his existence. Turn-of-the-century autobiography studies must therefore account for the autobiographers' desire to create stable subject positions and simultaneously tease out what Sidonie Smith calls the "instabilities of the late nineteenth and early twentieth centuries" (*Subjectivity* 54).

Wanda von Sacher-Masoch's *Confessions* were viciously attacked before both the author and her work fell into oblivion.[5] In his lengthy review article titled "Eine Ehrenrettung" ("A Vindication," 1906) cultural philosopher and literary critic Theodor Lessing denounced Wanda von Sacher-Masoch's *Confessions* as a "poisonous book" (Farin 219), and accused her of having created a "fabric of dangerous pathological lies" (Farin 205). Drawing on the century-old tradition of pathologizing women's words as well as female sexuality, Lessing condemned Wanda von Sacher-Masoch's book as a particularly unsavory example of the artistic cult of decadence, citing the countless memoirs of "lost" and "fallen" women it inspired (Farin 205).[6] Lessing, however, did not take offense at the description of female sexuality, nor did he direct his repugnance against male masochistic sexual practice. Applying the all-too-familiar double moral standards, the critic complained that Wanda von Sacher-Masoch's *Confessions* revealed both too little and too much, concealing certain facts about her own sexual history and disclosing too many aspects about her husband's. Lessing urges his readers, in particular the sexologists of his day and the executives of the publishing industry, to "forget" Sacher-Masoch's "sexual tragedy" (Farin 219) and instead to honor his work.[7] Wanda von Sacher-Masoch challenged the hierarchy that privileged the male literary work as a unique artistic achievement over the female autobiography as a secondary product of a minor subject.

Female autobiography, especially if it does not adhere to the conventions of high literature, can pose a threat to the male literary work by obscuring the truth about female sexuality while putting into words those aspects of male sexuality better left unspoken. In Theodor Lessing's eyes, Wanda von Sacher-Masoch's *Confessions* presented yet another version of the emerging genre of sensationalist female confessions that corrupted the standards of literary high culture perhaps even more than the norms of respectable sexual conduct.

Lessing's fervent rebuff of *Confessions* is of interest here because both his review and Wanda von Sacher-Masoch's autobiography identify the relationship between the female- and the male-authored text as a space in which the struggle over gender and genre hierarchies is carried out. To this day, critics label *Confessions* as at least partially "untrue" and dismiss it as the author's (unsuccessful) attempt to exonerate herself from the accusation of promiscuity and participation in sexual perversion. Holger Rudloff, for instance, rejected her autobiography as a willfully deceptive documentation of an unusual marriage (21), and Michael O'Pecko goes so far as to claim that Leopold von Sacher-Masoch's work was "almost obliterated after his death by the invective of *Meine Lebensbeichte*" (2). Fearing for Leopold von Sacher-Masoch's reputation within the tradition of high culture, turn-of-the-century as well as contemporary critics apply a gendered definition of autobiographical truth to discredit Wanda von Sacher-Masoch's narrative. The history of its reception, with its mixture of blatant misogyny, double moral standards, and class bias— critics drew on her lower-class background to dispute her ability to write, while at the same time considering her book dangerous—suggests that *Confessions* provokes anxieties that reach well beyond turn-of-the-century culture and the scope of this particular autobiography.[8] At stake are the lines of demarcation between truth and lie, the difference between masculinity and femininity, and the protection of male-defined high culture from a feminized culture of decadence.[9] The desire for discernible distinctions is propelled by the fear that these differences might not be enforceable.

Feminist scholars have argued that women's autobiographies have traditionally met with critical disbelief because their writers were not trusted to speak the truth upon which the autobiographical contract is based. Leigh Gilmore, in her recent study *Autobiographics*, has emphasized that concepts such as subject and identity, both of which are fundamental to the writing and reading of autobiographies, depend on specific cultural practices rather than universal standards. In the preface to her book she writes: "Whether and when autobiography emerges as an authoritative discourse of reality and identity, and any particular text appears to tell the truth, have less to do with that text's presumed accuracy about what really happened than with its apprehended fit into culturally prevalent discourses of truth and identity" (ix). While none of Wanda von Sacher-Masoch's critics doubt Leopold von Sacher-Masoch's masochistic disposition, they all deem it necessary to separate the "truth" about his sexuality from his identity as a serious writer. Consequently, the critical skirmish over his wife's female autobiographical truth was to a large extent driven by the desire to secure the subject position and the identity of Leopold von Sacher-Masoch, the male author. The discursive links between writing, sexuality, and the gender of the author reveal the contested position of the female autobiographer in turn-of-the-century Germany.

Ironically yet perhaps not surprisingly in light of its hostile reception, Wanda von Sacher-Masoch's autobiography has helped to obscure her biography. Her own narrative breaks off in 1898 with the death of Jakob Rosenthal, the journalist and publisher for whom she had left Leopold von Sacher-Masoch. Contemporary literary encyclopedias do not include biographical data for her beyond 1906, the year of the publication of *Confessions*. Declaring the autobiography to be the death of its author, some encyclopedists conjecture that she died "after 1906" (Kosch 2357). Her "untruthful" autobiography must have made biographical facts superfluous in the minds of those who shaped the literary canon for the turn of the century and beyond. The following biographical sketch is based on *Confessions* and the results of Adolf Opel's research.

Wanda von Sacher-Masoch was born on 14 March 1845 in Graz, Austria, as Angelika Aurora Rümelin. Her father, a military administrator and later a clerk for a railway company, left the family around 1860. Trained as a seamstress, Angelika Aurora supported herself and her mother by taking in piecework. In 1871, she made the acquaintance of the 35-year-old Leopold von Sacher-Masoch, a historian by training and a writer with an international reputation. A child born to the couple in 1872 died a few days after his birth. On 12 October 1873, Angelika Rümelin married Leopold von Sacher-Masoch. The first years of marriage were ones of financial difficulties, necessitating repeated changes of residency.

After a brief period in Vienna, the couple moved to Bruck an der Mur, a provincial center in Styria. In 1874 and 1875, two sons, Alexander and Demetrius, were born and Leopold von Sacher-Masoch's daughter from a previous relationship, Karoline, joined the family. The marriage began to dissolve in 1882 while the family was residing in Leipzig, and, after several years of separation, ended in divorce in 1886. Beginning in 1883, Wanda von Sacher-Masoch lived in Paris with her son Demetrius and the journalist Jakob Rosenthal, until Rosenthal, who had made a name for himself as Jacques Armand Saint-Cères, left her in 1888. Little is known about her life after the publication of *Confessions* in 1906 and a second autobiographical text *Masochismus und Masochisten* (Masochism and Masochists) in 1908. She did, however, continue her literary activities as translator and writer into the 1920s, publishing her stories in journals (Opel 301–02). Leopold von Sacher-Masoch's biographer Bernard Michel reports that she died in France in 1933 (287).

For the present-day reader, the sensationalism of *Confessions* might not be as evident as it certainly was for the author's contemporaries. Just like Leopold von Sacher-Masoch's stories and novels, Wanda von Sacher-Masoch's autobiography tells a story of a sexual perversion by omission of the sexual act rather than through its exposure. Subdivided into short segments of one to four pages each, *Confessions* presents itself as a conventional narrative structured by chronology, beginning with the narrator's family background and her early childhood. The style is descriptive rather than reflective, following external organizing principles such as the appearance of new characters or a change of residency. Following the tradition of nineteenth-century realism, Wanda von Sacher-Masoch did not share in the stylistic experiments of modernism. Her 500-page autobiography does, however, include characters and events who represent those abnormal sexual identities that occupied the collective fantasy of the turn of the century. The most important protagonist of these sexual plots is, of course, Leopold von Sacher-Masoch, the feminized man of masochism who relinquishes his socio-sexual dominance to a cruel woman. His typological opposites, the mannish woman, the lesbian, and the prostitute, are all embodied by the autobiographer's close friend, Kathrin Strebinger, a young woman from Switzerland who translated many of Leopold von Sacher-Masoch's works into French. Taking up a sexual subject position in contrast to both of these figures, the narrator writes herself into the culturally sanctioned female role of wife and mother. *Confessions* thus organizes the subject positions of its characters along the binary opposition of conventional and perverse sexualities. The narrator's participation in Leopold von Sacher-Masoch's sexual aberrations as well as her role as an object of lesbian desire, however, complicates this picture by placing the female subject of this autobiography on both sides of the divide. In *Confessions*, Wanda von

Sacher-Masoch thus plays off conventional femininity against transgressive female sexuality and feminized male sexuality, simultaneously "resist[ing] and produc[ing] cultural identities" (Gilmore, "Mark of Autobiography" 4). The autobiographical subject that emerges through these constellations refuses to take up an unambiguous position within the socio-sexual system of her time. Instead, through her narrator, Wanda von Sacher-Masoch probes the limits of culturally sanctioned categories of identity.

Wanda von Sacher-Masoch's use of gender as a site of autobiographical identity production deserves closer examination. In autobiographical narratives, the opening sentences are often intended to mirror the precarious beginnings of the narrator's life. Not unlike the first paragraphs of Goethe's *Poetry and Truth*, the first lines of *Confessions* suggest that this autobiography almost remained unwritten. Unlike Goethe, Wanda von Sacher-Masoch relates the precariousness of her origins to gender difference and legitimizes herself with a reference to her patriarchal lineage: "In 1845 I was born in Graz, Austria, to Wilhelm Rümelin, a military clerk" (4, translation modified). Only the name of the father possesses the power to provide the subject with the necessary legal identity. Without transition the narrator continues, avowing the physical dependency of her life on her mother's: "Several months before my birth my mother suffered an accident..." (4, translation modified). While the unnamed maternal body cannot endow the autobiographical subject with a legal status, *Confessions* privileges the mother-child relationship as a bond that precedes and outlives patriarchal social structures. Wanda von Sacher-Masoch's only lasting relationship, according to her autobiography, is that with her surviving son Demetrius.

The opening section of *Confessions* ends with the reminiscence of a proposed suicide. "I was three years old when death and despair brushed me for the first time" (4), the narrator states, recalling her father's suggestion to commit a communal suicide whose motivation remains unexplained. The autobiographical subject introduces herself to the reader as a survivor of events that contrast the figure of the weak yet life-affirming mother with a father figure who fails in his traditional function as the provider and protector of the family. Familial turmoil turns into social upheaval, and the following segment shows the narrator in a convent during the 1848 revolution, where she takes a liking to the "pale-faced nuns, with their renouncing [*entsagenden*] eyes and melancholy smiles" (4, translation modified). As wives and mothers, the narrative implies, women carry the signs of renunciation, an appearance that makes them strangely attractive to the narrator's young self. These introductory scenes set the stage for a narrative that endorses a conventional female gender role while bemoaning its unattainability as lived reality. In her assessment of gender difference Wanda von Sacher-Masoch concurs with many nineteenth-century thinkers when she focuses on male sexuality as an unpredictable force that even the institution of marriage cannot always successfully contain. Adultery, the violation of the marital contract's mandate of sexual exclusiveness, runs through the autobiography like a leitmotif. The narrator's discovery of her father's illicit relationship with a prostitute ushers in the demise of her family. Her statement, "I never saw him again" (8), signifies not only her father's disappearance from the narrative but foreshadows the ultimate break with Leopold von Sacher-Masoch. "I never saw Sacher-Masoch again" (118), the narrator comments when Leopold fails to keep his appointment with her because "there was a woman," as the maid informs her "with that discreet and so expressive smile with which French servants confide news of this sort" (118). *Confessions* attests to the failure of the institution of marriage to control male sexuality; as a paradoxical consequence, the family fails to guarantee the female role of wife and mother that it creates and sanctions in the first place. Wanda von Sacher-Masoch casts her autobiographical self within the parameters of traditional female gender roles; yet, like many women writers of her time, she uses the language of gender conservatism to tell a story of transgression. In the end, the story of her constant struggle against those private and social circumstances that prevented her from maintaining the desired position of wife and mother exposes the unreliability of the boundaries that separate normality from perversion.

Readers perusing the pages of Wanda von Sacher-Masoch's autobiography expect, of course, to find the true story of a transgressive sexuality with which they are already familiar: Leopold von Sacher-Masoch's repetitious tales of the male masochistic fantasy with its endless cycle of impending punishment, the execution of punishment, and more elaborate anticipation of more refined torture. Let me briefly recapitulate the story of the most famous male masochistic fantasy, Leopold von Sacher-Masoch's novella "Venus in Furs." In the framing story, a nameless narrator falls asleep while reading Hegel and dreams about a talking Venus statue clad in furs. He recounts his dream to his friend Severin von Kuziemski, the main protagonist of "Venus in Furs," who gives him a manuscript titled "Confessions of a Supersensualist." On its pages, Severin has chronicled the story of his masochistic relationship with a beautiful young widow named Wanda von Dunajew. In the first part of the narrative, Severin persuades Wanda to treat him like a slave. She complies, albeit reluctantly. Having grown into the role that requires her to whip and humiliate him, Wanda von Dunajew forces Severin to sign a contract in which he relinquishes his freedom and submits to whatever cruelty she pleases to engage in. In return, Wanda promises to wear furs as often as possible, especially when abusing her slave. With the appearance of a successful rival, "the Greek," the story progresses towards a triangular relationship. The final scene shows Severin being whipped by "the Greek" in front of an amused Wanda. Under the Greek's cruel blows, Severin states, he cured himself of his fantasy. Back in the framing story, Severin's despotic treatment of his current lover convinces the reader that this man will never again be whipped by a woman.

"Venus in Furs" is Leopold von Sacher-Masoch's life-text, the script that dictated the terms of his relationship with Wanda von Sacher-Masoch as a continuous "staging of a perversion."[10] Based on his affair with a baroness named Fanny von Pistor, "Venus in Furs" provides the plot that bound them together as much as it drove them apart: "[M]y husband had openly declared that he hoped to relive 'The Venus in Furs' with me 'in a more delicious fashion' than with P___, [and] spoke of nothing but that when we were alone together" (43). Wanda von Sacher-Masoch appropriated the autobiographical genre to revise the lines and the role of masochism's cruel woman. In *Confessions*, masochism's foremost female protagonist presents yet another, hitherto unwritten version of this text, challenging the master text with an act of subversive intertextuality.

Confessions traces the beginnings of the relationship between its narrator and Leopold von Sacher-Masoch to the mystery of "autobiographical truth" that obscures the boundaries between life and text. Fascinated by Leopold von Sacher-Masoch, the narrator and Frau Frischauer, her Jewish friend, read his books, closely observe the author walking in the streets of Graz, and discuss the possible connections between Sacher-Masoch's texts and his life. Are his books "true"? Do his texts represent his desire? Frau Frischauer thinks so. To prove her point, she initiates an exchange of letters with Sacher-Masoch that she signs as "Wanda von Dunajew," the heroine of "Venus in Furs." After the exposure of her true identity prevents Frau Frischauer from continuing the relationship, she dispatches the narrator to retrieve her letters from Sacher-Masoch. Instead of simply collecting the letters, the narrator yields to Sacher-Masoch's pleas to take her friend's place and continues the exchange. With his suggestion that "it would be best if I kept the name of 'Wanda von Dunajew' as an address" (14, translation modified), Sacher-Masoch conducts an act of baptism, transferring a literary identification from one female interlocutor to another. The adoption of a literary name initiates Wanda von Sacher-Masoch into a form of "masochistic" authorship. She begins to write "cruel" letters to the author of "Venus in Furs," thus bringing Leopold von Sacher-Masoch's text back to life, while at the same time transforming her self according to the script of his text.

Under the guidance of Leopold von Sacher-Masoch, Wanda von Sacher-Masoch began to publish a series of prose works, and reference works indeed list "Wanda von Dunajew" as the pseudonym she used during the 1870s. A succession of texts and countertexts coordinates Leopold and Wanda von Sacher-Masoch's life stories, expressly interweaving autobiography and bibliography. Wanda von Sacher-Masoch subtitled her *Roman einer tugendhaften Frau* (Novel of a Virtuous Woman, 1873) "A Counterpart to Sacher-Masoch's 'Divorced Woman'"; her 1879 collection *Echter Hermlin* (Genuine Ermine, 1879) echoes his 1873 volume *Falscher Hermlin* (Fake Ermine); and her *Die Damen im Pelz* (The Ladies in Furs, 1882), which went into seven editions between 1881 and 1910, recalls his "Venus in Furs." Wanda von Sacher-Masoch's autobiography, finally, responds to Leopold von Sacher-Masoch's *Die geschiedene Frau* (The Divorced Woman, 1870) and his "Venus in Furs," both of which were promoted by their author as autobiographical texts. With its allusion to the Catholic practice of confessional truth-telling and absolution, the title *Confessions* establishes a further link to the "Confessions of a Supersensualist," the title of the central narrative within "Venus in Furs," and to the "Passion [*Passionsgeschichte*] of an Idealist," the title of the male protagonist's diary in Leopold von Sacher-Masoch's *Die geschiedene Frau*. All three titles suggest that the act of confession, the telling of one's story, holds the key to redemption. Moreover, they allude to the high literary tradition of Goethe's "Confessions of a Beautiful Soul." Leopold von Sacher-Masoch's male sexual fantasy as text and Wanda von Sacher-Masoch's female counter-narrative, her *Confessions*, constitute a sequence of autobiographical acts that negotiate the transformation of sexuality into textual identity. Decades before the eruption of the controversy between Wanda von Sacher-Masoch and her critics over her "true" life story, Leopold and Wanda von Sacher-Masoch engaged in a project of inventing multiple versions of the masochistic tale of the cruel woman and her male slave.[11] In *Confessions* the narrator told this story, yoking together his and her life/writing; but this time, Wanda von Sacher-Masoch wrote beyond the narrative boundaries of Leopold von Sacher-Masoch's master text.

The cover and title page of *Confessions* feature the words "Wanda von Sacher-Masoch" in the position reserved for the name of the author. In contrast to this prominent display of authorship, the narrator abstains from any further acts of self-naming throughout her entire text. "Angelika Aurora Rümelin," which the literary encyclopedias insist is her "real" name, does not enter into the pages of this autobiography. "Wanda" remains the only first name used in *Confessions*, yet, in keeping with Leopold's suggestion, only as an "address" used by other characters in the autobiography. "Wanda von Sacher-Masoch," then, not only signifies the narrator's legal status as a married woman who has adopted her husband's last name, it also blurs the boundaries between literature and life. In coupling "Wanda," the first name of the infamous literary figure of the cruel woman, with "von Sacher-Masoch," the surname of a literary author from a respected aristocratic Galician family, *Confessions* circumscribes an identity rooted in both literature and reality, in patriarchy as much as in its subversion.

Women's complex relationship to self-representation, their implication in the "male gaze" and, subsequently, the "feminist reappropriation of the mirror" (Brodzki 7) are motivating factors in many female autobiographies and continue to be of concern to feminist scholars.[12] Wanda von Sacher-Masoch introduces her desire for self-representation in a short scene that involves the erotic attraction between women. Walking with her father in a park in Graz as a little girl, the narrator feels strangely drawn to an elegant woman named Frau von K. whose "singular beauty acted on me like a spell—unnerving, ravishing, almost painful" (4). Unbeknownst to the narrator at this early moment in her life, both of them were to fall victim to the same "occult power" (*Gewalt*) (4). This power, however, is not simply Leopold von Sacher-Masoch, the man who was to become both women's lover, but the experience of encountering one's self as a work of art. Frau von K. suffered this violence twice in her life: first, at the hands of an artist, whose painting failed to convey her beauty, and a second time through Leopold von Sacher-Masoch, whose 1870 novel *Die geschiedene Frau*, the narrator concedes, does justice to Frau von K.'s beauty but casts her in a "false light" (6).

The scene in the park might well not be "true." Its inclusion in the autobiography, however, suggests that Wanda von Sacher-Masoch viewed the transformation of life into art as a process reflective of the gendered distribution of discursive power. Contrasting her memories of this meeting with the artistic renditions of Frau von K., the narrator assigns a higher truth value to her recollection and rejects the male artistic works as either inadequate or unsympathetic portrayals of Frau von K. In *Confessions*, Wanda von Sacher-Masoch challenges the "false" representation of female life in male art and confronts it with her own version. Whereas Frau von K. remained an object of art, Wanda von Sacher-Masoch reversed the process of objectification and became author and subject of her story.[13] In *Confessions*, the narrator joins her desire for self-representation with her desire for the other woman, "reappropriating the mirror" by juxtaposing male models of sexuality and writing with female homoeroticism and female self-representation.

Before I pursue my argument that Wanda von Sacher-Masoch achieves female self-representation by relating to women, I would like to turn to the kind of female representation that she protested in her autobiography. In a letter from 18 May 1868, Leopold von Sacher-Masoch noted that he felt compelled to turn his "dramatic" relationship with Anna von Kottowitz into literature (*Geschiedene Frau* 183). The resulting novel, *Die geschiedene Frau*, introduces the narrative elements of the masochistic plot and traces its inception to the juncture between "life" and text. While the novel is primarily narrated by its female protagonist, Frau von

Kossow, it is presumably written down by a figure named Sacher-Masoch, to whom Frau von Kossow relates the tale of her affair with a young man named Julian von Romaschkan, a successful writer who breaks off a prior engagement in favor of the female protagonist. It is Julian von Romaschkan who invents the masochistic fantasy of female domination and male submission, and he conveys it to Frau von Kossow in the form of a novella-in-progress entitled "Wanda" (71).[14] Reading the as-yet-unfinished novella, Frau von Kossow understands that Julian desires her to be "Wanda," and she proceeds to model herself according to his literary instructions. "I was incapable of *being Wanda*, but he had disclosed to me through his novella what I had to do to *appear to be Wanda* [*Wanda zu scheinen*]" (71). Consequently, Anna von Kossow turns herself into the masculinized woman who smokes, shoots pistols, and, most importantly, at the next ball appears in a lavish fur coat (*Geschiedene Frau* 72). While Julian von Romaschkan's completed novella becomes a literary success, Frau von Kossow's love affair with Julian ends in a tragic breakup. In the final scene of *Die geschiedene Frau*, the character Sacher-Masoch admires a copy of Frau von Kossow's portrait; its original is, of course, the flawed painting Wanda von Sacher-Masoch criticizes in *Confessions*. In response to the question of whether she owned a picture of Julian, the female protagonist replies that she possesses the "Passion of an Idealist," Julian's diary. While there is no mention of any artifacts produced by Frau von Kossow that Julian might have kept, Frau von Kossow finds her own "fate" (181) inscribed in Julian's words, to be read time and again by the rich yet socially isolated woman. Julian, by contrast, continues to be a creative and prolific writer. "He works, he creates, he is useful. *His life will not be wasted*" (182) are the final words of the novel.

The literary birthplace of the masochistic plot, *Die geschiedene Frau* provides the model for the transformation of the female protagonist into "Wanda." The male fantasy becomes the master text for teaching Frau von Kossow the role of the mannish woman. The scenes most commonly associated with male masochism, the torturing of the male protagonist by the cruel woman, take place only in Frau von Kossow's imagination, inspired by her perusal of "Wanda." She confesses her domination fantasies to the character Sacher-Masoch and they thus enter into the body of the text but are not (yet) acted out on the body of the male protagonist. A year later, on the pages of "Venus in Furs," "Wanda von Dunajew" executes the torture Frau von Kossow had fantasized in becoming "Wanda." The written text initiates the staging of the masochistic plot in the interplay between the male protagonist, who transforms his fantasy of the cruel woman into a narrative, and his female counterpart, whose function it is to adapt to the prescribed role and to implement the masochistic acts inspired by his invention. The narrative principles of the masochistic plot place the female protagonist at the threshold between literary imagination and lived fantasy, constricting her existence to the parameters of the male text.

As if to assure themselves of their identity and subject positions, the male heroes of both *Die geschiedene Frau* and "Venus in Furs" write autobiographical texts. "Passion of an Idealist," Julian von Romaschkan's diary, and "Confessions of a Supersensualist," Severin von Kuziemski's life story, define the position of the male protagonist in terms of his authorship and his ability to write beyond the masochistic plot. Whereas "Wanda," in her various appearances, remains bound by literary invention, Julian and Severin are "useful" (*nützlich*) as her creator.

In *Die geschiedene Frau*, Leopold von Sacher-Masoch portrayed himself as both Julian von Romaschkan, the wronged lover and successful writer of the novella that taught Frau von Kossow to become "Wanda," and the figure of Sacher-Masoch, the author's namesake and first-person narrator who transforms Frau von Kossow's story into a literary text. Doubling himself in these two characters, Leopold von Sacher-Masoch maintains an authorial presence both within the narrative itself and as the novelist whose name on the front page asserts his authorship. Anna von Kottowitz, the woman on whom Leopold von Sacher-Masoch modeled his "Frau von Kossow" and who entered into Wanda von Sacher-Masoch's autobiography as "Frau von K.," did not leave behind a literary work. In *Confessions*, however, Wanda von Sacher-Masoch liberates the female subject position from the pre-script of the male text and becomes herself the author.

With her critical reference to Frau von K.'s fate—"the writer...[had put her] in a false light"—Wanda von Sacher-Masoch identifies *Die geschiedene Frau* as the *Urtext* from which the female position in masochism originates. "Venus in Furs," the masochistic master text that Leopold von Sacher-Masoch desired to relive, and *Confessions*, Wanda von Sacher-Masoch's countertext, thus present two versions of the masochistic plot that offer competing interpretations of the female role. In his well-known essay "Coldness and Cruelty" (1967), Gilles Deleuze defended Wanda von Sacher-Masoch's book against the critics who cast her in the role of the sadist by simply describing it as "excellent" (9). In his efforts to uncouple sadism from masochism and to establish them as two distinct perversions, Deleuze argues that the "woman torturer of masochism [is]...a realization of the masochistic fantasy" (41), and continues that the male masochist "definitely has no need of another subject, i.e., the sadistic subject" (43). The masochistic plot depends on the woman's renunciation of her subjectivity; she must, in other words, become "Wanda." The autobiographer Wanda von Sacher-Masoch appropriates the figure of "Wanda" and turns her into the subject for which the heterosexual masochistic plot had no need. The last part of this essay discusses a sequence of "reversed" sexual constellations for which "Venus in Furs" did not allow.

Framed by a section on Leopold's correspondence with another woman and a discussion of the family pets, *Confessions* relates the first of several episodes of lesbian desire. Frau X stimulates the narrator's interest "as for a long time she had seemed mysterious to me" (39). Pretending not to know what she knows, the narrator continues: "Under this surface, which was always cold and calm, I felt an ardent vitality—a mystery which those two eyes guarded and also betrayed" (39). The lesbian's gaze bespeaks her desire for the narrator. "Finally I realized that she loved me passionately." The relationship between the two women comes to a climax in the intimate atmosphere of an "overheated" dressing room, whose temperature induces in the narrator a passive state between waking and sleeping. In the heat of the female space of the boudoir, Frau X covers the shoulders and arms of the semiconscious narrator with kisses. "Was that you?" the narrator asks, feigning ignorance. Frau X answers by describing the innocent beauty of the narrator as "so white and delicate" and continues to kiss her. Her conventional femininity makes the narrator, who passively receives the other woman's gaze and touch, an object of lesbian desire. The sexual exchange in the dressing room restores the narrator to the traditional female position denied her in the masochistic relationship with her husband. More importantly, Frau X's passion is not pre-scripted by Leopold von Sacher-Masoch's text. The arrival of both women's husbands interrupts the "alarming" situation (*böser Spuk*) (40), yet the experience with Frau X does not remain singular.

The next encounter involves the narrator's French teacher, a Parisian refugee who fled France after the defeat of the Commune. The narrator introduces Madame Marie as "bathed in mystery," with "warmth in her voice" that immediately identifies her as a lesbian. The narrator ensures the continued "relations" with her French teacher by insisting on "certain barriers" (57). Positioning herself as an object of lesbian desire, the narrator asserts the traditional female privilege to control the degree of intimacy in her relationship with Madame Marie, which comes to an end only after the French teacher's jealous lover threatens suicide. As the passive recipient of lesbian sexual desire, the narrator breaks away completely from her contractual role as the cruel woman, with its mandate to dominate her husband and to yield to the heterosexual requests of "the Greek." In her autobiographical counternarrative to Leopold von Sacher-Masoch's masochistic scripts, Wanda von Sacher-Masoch thus reinstates the possibility of traditional gender roles within nontraditional constellations. Her role as the object of a gaze that is not male allows Wanda von Sacher-Masoch to become the subject of her own plot.

The figure of Kathrin Strebinger, the young woman from Switzerland who translated Leopold von Sacher-Masoch's texts into French, presents the autobiographer's most significant challenge to Leopold's fantasy, and Kathrin Strebinger's biography becomes an extensive part of Wanda von Sacher-Masoch's autobiography. The narrator's close friend and counterpart, Kathrin represents the "mannish" woman who insists on acting out her own plots, declining to play the part prescribed by the masochistic male. Unlike the narrator, who reluctantly performs the part of the heterosexual cruel woman and reclaims her female passivity in lesbian relationships, Kathrin actively pursues sexual relationships with both men and women, and, as she relates one evening at the dinner table, has even worked as a prostitute.[15] Kathrin enters the text of the autobiography just after the narrator accepted the role of the cruel woman (34). Kathrin's presence, however, prevents the implementation of Wanda's affair with "the Greek," the last act prescribed by "Venus in Furs." The narrator comments on her husband's insistence on the reenactment of his text: "The 'Venus in Furs' was the most important matter in his life, and Kathrin had blithely [*mit ihrem Leichtsinn*] destroyed, blow by blow, his best-founded hopes" (80, translation modified). Her "blitheness" even motivates Kathrin to appropriate the narrator's place in "the Greek's" bed. Wanda's affair with "the Greek" will occur only after the translator's departure. Kathrin thus not only refuses to participate in the enactment of Leopold's script, she also prevents the narrator from fulfilling her role. Her disparaging remarks about fur coats mark the end of Kathrin's relationship with the Sacher-Masoch family. She leaves, never to return (80).

Kathrin restores the narrator to the female subject position that Leopold von Sacher-Masoch's script denies her. Suggesting an attraction between the two women whose intensity exceeds Wanda's prior encounters with lesbians, the narrator acknowledges: "Kathrin certainly exercised a physical influence on me, but for a long time I was not conscious of it. When she entered my room I felt brighter inside, and darker when she exited" (69, translation modified). After a near fatal river-crossing that the two women had undertaken upon Kathrin's insistence, the narrator finds comfort in Kathrin's strong arms, and during a trip "Kathrin slept with me, in the bed meant for my husband" (78, translation modified). Kathrin physically occupies the male space, allowing the narrator to reclaim a female subject position. During that same evening—the purpose of the trip being yet another attempt to find "the Greek"—Kathrin accidentally steps on a large needle. Instead of removing it immediately, as the narrator urges her to do, she leaves the pointed metal in her toe for an hour, blissfully anticipating the pain of its extraction (79). The scene characterizes Kathrin as a woman who refuses to do what Deleuze describes as fundamental to the masochistic situation, to renounce "her own subjective masochism" (Deleuze 43). Kathrin declines to enter into any kind of an agreement, be it a conventional marriage or a masochistic contract. Deleuze insists that Wanda von Sacher-Masoch should not have expected Kathrin and her husband to get along (41). The narrator, however, reveals an astute understanding of why the two masochists do not complement each other: "They did not like each other. To interest Leopold, women had to excite his imagination; he had to be able to impart to them everything he desired to find" (64). The autobiographer recognizes the need of the male partner to orchestrate the exchange according to his fantasy as essential to the masochistic plot. *Confessions* continues beyond Kathrin's disappearance from its pages. The ultimate reenactment of "Venus in Furs," Wanda's affair with "the Greek," marks the beginning of the breakup of Wanda and Leopold von Sacher-Masoch's marriage, and the appearance of Jakob Rosenthal, the narrator's lover with whom she states she did not have "physical relations" (110), leads to separation and subsequently divorce. In the figure of Kathrin, however, *Confessions* takes its most radical departure from Leopold von Sacher-Masoch's text, whose master plot provides no role for the female masochist. Through her relationship with Kathrin, Wanda von Sacher-Masoch carries out a fundamental break with the role of the cruel woman prescribed to her by the masochistic master text. If only transiently, she writes herself into a female subject position outside the heterosexual paradigm and its patriarchal system of representation.

Leopold von Sacher-Masoch's heroes know that they must retain control over their stories in order to remain the masochistic subjects of their narratives. Provoked by Frau von K.'s "false" portrayal as the result of male representational power, the autobiographer Wanda von Sacher-Masoch inserted herself into the male master text and subverted its already unconventional gender relationships one more time. With *Confessions*, Wanda von Sacher-Masoch slipped into the literary existence of "Wanda" and transformed the character into a narrator whose purpose it is to get the story "right." Wanda von Sacher-Masoch's autobiography does not, as Theodor Lessing feared, diminish Leopold von Sacher-Masoch's achievements as a writer. Yet her counter-narrative challenges the authority of the master text by introducing female subjects for whom masochism has no use: the mother, the lesbian, and the masochistic woman. For this, it seems, the critics cannot forgive her.

Notes

I thank the Taft Memorial Fund at the University of Cincinnati for supporting this project with a Summer Research Grant.

[1] Recent works on turn-of-the-century culture and sexuality include Showalter's *Sexual Anarchy*, Apter's *Feminizing the Fetish*, Dijkstra's *Idols of Perversity*, Finney's *Women in Modern Drama*, and Felski's *Gender of Modernity*.

[2] All references are to the English translation. The blurb on the back of *The Confessions of Wanda von Sacher-Masoch* states incorrectly that the autobiography was "originally published in French in 1907." *Lebensbeichte* was first published in Geman in 1906; Michael Farin's 1986 reedition of Wanda von Sacher-Masoch's autobiography, which he titled *Die Beichte der Dame im Pelz*, is unfortunately out of print. The original German edition counted more than 500 pages; with its modern typeface, the English version is much shorter yet its content largely corresponds to the German original.

[3] Krafft-Ebing, in his somewhat repetitive style, defines masochism as follows: "By masochism I understand a peculiar perversion of the psychical *vita sexualis* in which the individual affected, in sexual feeling and thought, is controlled by the idea of being completely and unconditionally subject to the will of a person of the opposite sex; of being treated by this person as by a master, humiliated and abused" (131). Despite the gender-neutral language of this definition, only two out of thirty-three of Krafft-Ebing's case studies refer to female masochists.

[4] See Smith for an insightful critique of Misch (*Poetics*); see also Stanton's seminal article and Smith's *Subjectivity, Identity, and the Body*, especially the chapter "Turning the Century on the Subject."

[5] The only edition currently in print is Gürtler's collection of Wanda von Sacher-Masoch's short prose, *Damen mit Pelz und Peitsche*. For critical literature that focuses substantially on Wanda von Sacher-Masoch, see Gürtler and Schackmann.

[6] Lessing must have had in mind publications such as Böhme's fictious *Tagebuch einer Verlorenen* (1905) and Salten's anonymously published "diary" of *Josephine Mutzenbacher* (1906).

[7] Theodor Lessing had personal ties to Sacher-Masoch's family. After the writer's death, he was the private teacher of Sacher-Masoch's children from his marriage to his second wife, Hulda Meister.

[8] To this day, there is no comprehensive feminist analysis of *Confessions*. In her afterward to *Damen mit Pelz und Peitsche*, Gürtler uses the autobiography as a documentary source without suggesting a critical analysis of the text. Similarly, Treut quotes extensively from *Lebensbeichte* as the "most important source of information about life with the poet [Leopold von Sacher-Masoch,

KG]" (203) to support her analysis of Leopold von Sacher-Masoch's "Venus in Furs."

[9] Lessing explicitly takes offense at the front page of *Confessions*, for which Wanda von Sacher-Masoch had chosen an epigram from Goethe's *Faust*: "Mich faßt ein längst entwohnter Schauer / Der Menschheit ganzer Jammer faßt mich an."

[10] Koschorke's subtitle, "Die Inszenierung einer Perversion," emphasizes the theatricality of Leopold von Sacher-Masoch's life and work.

[11] A discussion of Wanda von Sacher-Masoch's literary works would go beyond the scope of this essay; see the articles of Gürtler and Schackmann.

[12] The discussion of the "male gaze," which originates from feminist film studies, has become an important issue also in autobiography studies. See Smith (*Poetics*); Gilmore; also Weigel.

[13] The abbreviation "Frau von K." evokes Freud's famous "Dora" case. The similarity in name, "Frau von K." and "Frau K." is coincidence. In both instances, however, lesbian desire signifies female resistance against male-dominated heterosexuality and male-dominated systems of representation.

[14] Originally, the novella within the novel was titled "Valeska." Michael Farin, the editor of the Greno-edition of *Die geschiedene Frau*, speculates that Sacher-Masoch might have changed it after he had written "Venus in Furs" (216), thus interconnecting and conjoining the different creative stages of his sexual/textual fantasy.

[15] In the German original Kathrin states that she "has given herself to very poor men...soldiers...out of pity" (270). In the English translation, this account is characterized as fantasy (67).

Works Cited

Apter, Emily. *Feminizing the Fetish: Psychoanalysis and Narrative Obsession in Turn-of-the-Century France*. Ithaca: Cornell UP, 1991.

Böhme, Margarete. *Tagebuch einer Verlorenen: Von einer Toten*. Ed. Hanne Kulessa. Frankfurt a.M.: Suhrkamp, 1989.

Brodzki, Bella, and Celeste Schenk, eds. *Life/Lines: Theorizing Women's Autobiography*. Ithaca: Cornell UP, 1988.

Deleuze, Gilles. "Coldness and Cruelty." *Masochism*. 1967. Deleuze and Leopold von Sacher-Masoch. New York: Zone Books, 1991. 9–138.

Dijkstra, Bram. *Idols of Perversity: Fantasies of Feminine Evil in Fin-de-Siècle Culture*. New York: Oxford UP, 1986.

Farin, Michael, ed. *Leopold von Sacher-Masoch: Materialien zu Leben und Werk*. Bonn: Bouvier, 1987.

Felski, Rita. *Gender of Modernity*. Cambridge: Harvard UP, 1995.

Finney, Gail. *Women in Modern Drama: Freud, Feminism, and European Theater of the Turn of the Century*. Ithaca: Cornell UP, 1989.

Gilmore, Leigh. *Autobiographics: A Feminist Theory of Women's Self-Representation*. Ithaca: Cornell UP, 1994.

———. "The Mark of Autobiography: Postmodernism, Autobiography, and Genre." *Autobiography and Postmodernism*. Ed. Kathleen Ashley, Leigh Gilmore, and Gerald Peters. 3–18.

Gürtler, Christa. "Damen mit Pelz und Peitsche: Zu Texten von Wanda von Sacher-Masoch." *Schwierige Verhältnisse: Liebe und Sexualität in der Frauenliteratur um 1900*. Ed. Theresia Klugsberger. Stuttgarter Arbeiten zur Germanistik Nr. 262. Stuttgart: Heinz, 1992. 71–82.

Kosch, Wilhelm. *Deutsches Literatur-Lexikon: Biographisches und bibliographisches Handbuch*. 2nd ed. Vol. 3. Bern: Francke, 1956.

Koschorke, Albrecht. *Leopold von Sacher-Masoch: Die Inszenierung einer Perversion*. München: Piper, 1988.

Krafft-Ebing, Richard von. *Psychopathia Sexualis with Especial Reference to the Antipathic Sexual Instinct: A Medico-Forensic Study*. Trans. F.J. Rebman. New York: Physicians and Surgeons Book Company, 1929.

Michel, Bernard. *Sacher-Masoch: 1836–1895*. Paris: Laffont, 1989.

Misch, Georg. *A History of Autobiography in Antiquity*. Trans. E.W. Dickes. Cambridge: Harvard UP, 1951.

O'Pecko, Michael T. "Comedy and Didactic in Leopold von Sacher-Masoch's 'Venus im Pelz.'" *Modern Austrian Literature* 25.2 (1992): 1–13.

Opel, Adolf, ed. *Wanda und Leopold von Sacher-Masoch: Szenen einer Ehe. Eine kontroversielle Biographie*. Wien: Wiener Frauenverlag, 1996.

Rudloff, Holger. *Pelzdamen: Weiblichkeitsbilder bei Thomas Mann und Leopold von Sacher-Masoch*. Frankfurt a.M.: Fischer, 1994.

Sacher-Masoch, Leopold von. *Die geschiedene Frau: Passionsgeschichte eines Idealisten*. 1870. Ed. Michael Farin. Nördlingen: Greno, 1989.

———. "Venus in Furs." *Masochism*. 1967. Gilles Deleuze and Leopold von Sacher-Masoch. New York: Zone Books, 1991. 142–271.

Sacher-Masoch, Wanda von. *Die Beichte der Dame im Pelz*. Ed. Michael Farin. München: Moewig, 1986.

———. *The Confessions of Wanda von Sacher-Masoch*. Trans. Marian Phillips, Caroline Hébert, and V. Vale. San Francisco: Re/Search, 1990.

———. *Die Damen im Pelz: Geschichten*. Leipzig: Morgenstern, 1882.

———. *Damen mit Pelz und Peitsche*. Ed. Christa Gürtler. Frankfurt a.M.: Ullstein, 1995.

———. *Echter Hermlin: Geschichten aus der vornehmen Welt*. Bern: Frobeen, 1879.

———. *Masochismus und Masochisten: Nachtrag zur Lebensbeichte*. Berlin: Schuster & Loeffler [1908].

———. *Meine Lebensbeichte: Memoiren*. Berlin: Schuster & Loeffler, 1906.

———. *Der Roman einer tugendhaften Frau: Ein Gegenstück zur "geschiedenen Frau" von Sacher-Masoch*. Prague: Bohemia, 1873.

Salten, Felix. *Josephine Mutzenbacher: Die Lebensgeschichte einer wienerischen Dirne, von ihr selbst erzählt*. 1906. München: Rogner & Bernard, 1970.

Schackmann, Isolde. "Das Bild der 'Emanzipierten': Herrin und/oder Gefährtin. Zu zwei Novellen von Wanda von Sacher-Masoch und Irma von Troll-Borostyáni." *Schwierige Verhältnisse: Liebe und Sexualität in der Frauenliteratur um 1900*. Ed. Theresia Klugsberger. Stuttgarter Arbeiten zur Germanistik Nr. 262. Stuttgart: Heinz, 1992. 83–102.

Showalter, Elaine. *Sexual Anarchy: Gender and Culture at the Fin de Siècle*. New York: Viking, 1990.

Smith, Sidonie. *A Poetics of Women's Autobiography: Marginality and the Fictions of Self-Representation*. Bloomington: Indiana UP, 1987.

———. *Subjectivity, Identity, and the Body: Women's Autobiographical Practices in the Twentieth Century*. Bloomington: Indiana UP, 1993.

Stanton, Domna C. "Autogynography: Is the Subject Different?" *The Female Autograph: Theory and Practice of Autobiography from the Tenth to the Twentieth Century*. Ed. Domna C. Stanton. Chicago: Chicago UP, 1984. 3–20.

Treut, Monika. *Die grausame Frau: Zum Frauenbild bei de Sade und Sacher-Masoch*. Basel: Stroemfeld / Roter Stern, 1984.

Weigel, Sigrid. "Double Focus: On the History of Women's Writing." *Feminist Aesthetics*. Ed. Gisela Ecker. Trans. Harriet Anderson. London: Women's Press, 1985. 59–80.

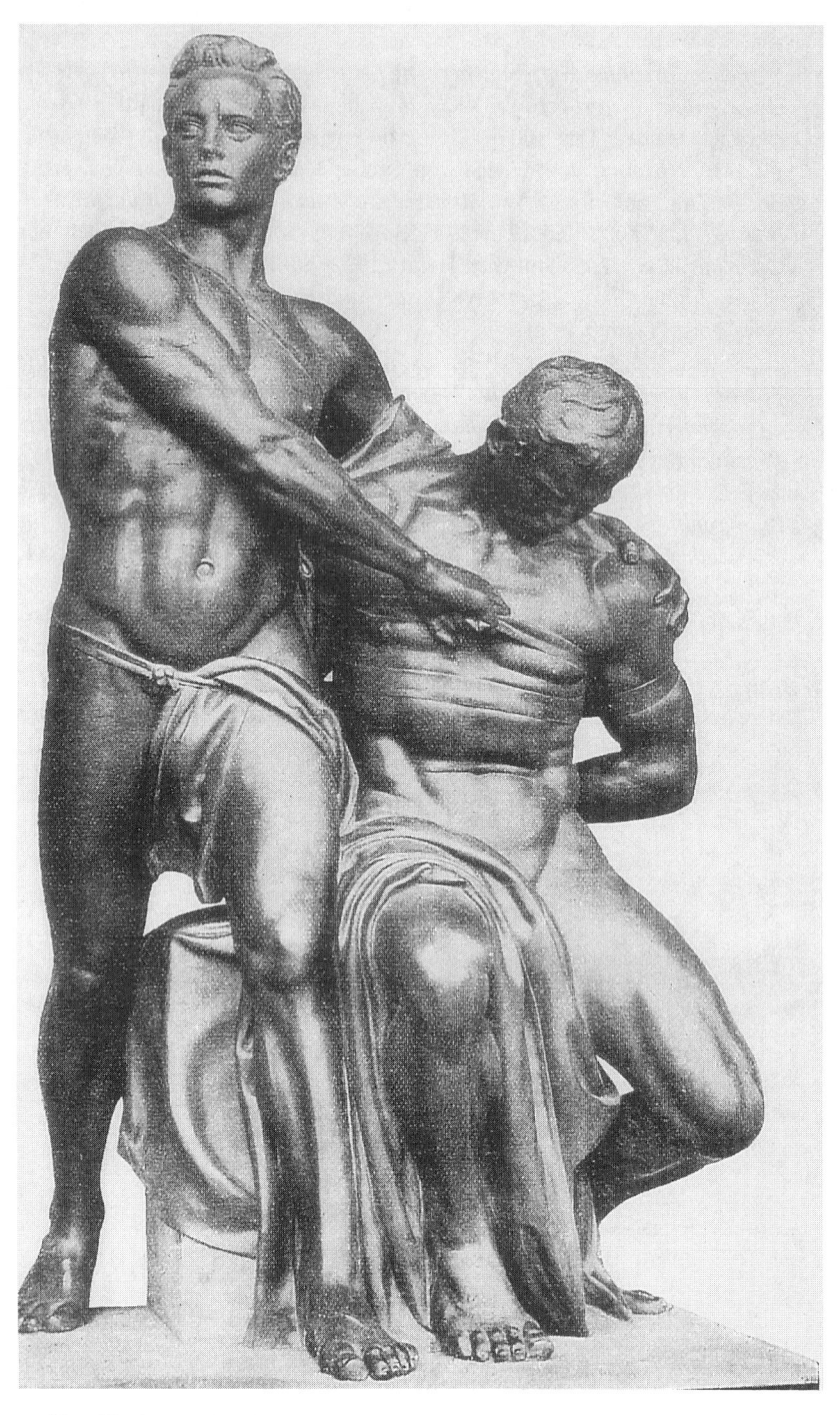

Hugo Kaufmann, "Freedom," a section of the "Unity Monument" (*Einheitsdenkmal*), in Frankfurt am Main. *Ost und West* (Feb. 1911): 139–40.

Neglected "Women's" Texts and Contexts: Vicki Baum's Jewish Ghetto Stories

David A. Brenner

Better known for her novels and Weimar-era celebrity, Vicki Baum was also of Jewish ancestry and authored two ghetto novellas (*Ghettogeschichten*) that appeared in 1910-11 in *Ost und West*, the first Jewish magazine. "Rafael Gutmann" depicts the attempt of an effeminate teenage ghetto singer, a traditional *Ostjude*, to break into the world of German opera represented by Beethoven and Wagner. Baum's own career parallels this narrative of social and cultural legitimization, yet the story's ambivalent attitudes toward Jews and *Judentum* are mediated through a discursive framework resembling that of Otto Weininger. At the same time, certain connotations are disputed by surrounding (inter)texts of *Ost und West*, a process challenging a simplistic "ideology of mass culture." (DAB)

Much of the published research on the life and work of Vicki Baum (1888-1960), author of *Grand Hotel* (*Menschen im Hotel*, 1929) and arguably the first female literary celebrity of twentieth-century Germany, omits any discussion of her Jewish background. Indeed, Baum herself was eager to disown her Jewishness, as the ambivalent attitudes toward Jews in her posthumously published autobiography *Es war alles ganz anders* (It Was All Quite Different, 1962) make abundantly clear.[1] Such attitudes were not atypical for a person raised in *fin de siècle* Vienna, yet Baum's father—the parent of Jewish descent—is primarily described in negative terms, as "shabby," "ugly," "humped over," "uncouth," and a "schlemiel," not to speak of associations with homosexuality, spying, and megalomania (90-99, 105-09). The widespread anxiety of mixed-ancestry Jews in this epoch concerning their creativity, virtue, and intelligence may illuminate Baum's love-hate relationship with her Jewish parent, as chronicled in a chapter of the autobiography entitled "My Father, My Enemy."[2]

But by following such leads, scholars have overlooked not only the contexts of Baum's early fiction, but some of that fiction itself.[3] Imagine then my surprise when I first came across her two-part serial fiction "Rafael Gutmann" in the January and February 1911 issues of *Ost und West,* the first Jewish *Illustrierte* and first "ethnic magazine" ever.[4] I was further surprised that this story, one of Baum's earliest publications, represented a significant intervention in the history of the Jewish ghetto story (*Ghettogeschichte*), a genre instantly recognizable to Jewish (and non-Jewish) readers of the time. Recently, another critic has written about this story, maintaining that it "was conceived and written under those very same material circumstances that lead [sic] to Rathenau's *Fememord,* a period of (often) right-wing terror that culminated in the Beer-Hall Putsch of 1923" (Petersen 164). The facts are different: the story (with minor differences) was conceived and written at least twelve years earlier, and it was published for a (primarily) Jewish audience. Most researchers of Baum, understandably focused on her Weimar-era fame and her best-selling novels, have not examined the vast periodical literature directed at pre-Hitler German-speaking Jewry.

I too was misled by what I knew of Vicki Baum. When I first encountered her fictional portrayal of a young ghetto singer in *Ost und West,* I located in it what I thought was an ideological contradiction between the positive attitudes of the magazine's editors to so-called *Ghettojuden,* i.e., Yiddish-speaking Jews of East European culture, and Baum's negative stereotyping of such *Ghettojuden* in "Rafael Gutmann." Yet I soon determined that Baum and *Ost und West,* for all their ideological variance, had a larger project in common: to make the openly Jewish culture of Eastern Europe—considered "low" culture—*respectable* in Imperial Germany, that is, in a culture that at the close of the nineteenth century was busily legitimating *itself* (Mosse). To render openly Jewish culture legitimate in the *Kaiserreich* meant making it more "Western" and less "East European." The ultimate goal of the Eastern-born and -raised editors of *Ost und West* was to sell magazines by attracting a Westernized, acculturated Jewish audience to their East European agenda of Jewish ethnicity and public, "open" Jewishness. In the process of legitimizing their cultural capital (Bourdieu), both *Ost und West* and Vicki Baum made themselves respectable on four levels:

1) In "Rafael Gutmann" we find the attempt of an effeminate teenage ghetto singer, an Eastern Jew, to break into the world of German middle-to-highbrow music. Vicki Baum's own career and acculturation parallel this narrative of social transformation.

2) In *Ost und West*'s literary contributions of the time, we find a re-evaluation of Jewish women's writing—"low" culture—and a legitimation of the female (and male) addressees of "Rafael Gutmann." Baum's double-edged attitudes toward Jews from the East in this novella reflect the attempt of Central European Jewish women to secure their own class status vis-à-vis such Jews as well as an attempt to break out of their own

domestic confinements or "ghettos." This move, as we shall see, is mediated through Wagner and Weininger.

3) In *Ost und West*'s critical contributions, we find a Jewish particularism (tempered by a more universalist outlook) that stresses the Jewish "nuance" or "piece of the mosaic" within German and European high culture. The magazine's proto-"multicultural" agenda, embodied in text and illustration, suggested that Eastern Jewish culture was compatible with—and as respectable as—Western Jewish culture (Brenner, *Marketing*). It further suggests that middlebrow German-Jewish culture, as exemplified by Heinrich Heine and Hugo Kaufmann, was compatible with—and as respectable as—German middle-class culture embodied by Wagner, Beethoven, and Goethe.

4) Finally, the drive to achieve legitimacy also applied to the status of *Ost und West* as a medium. The periodical medium was perceived to need "uplifting," like the poor ghetto Jew Rafael and like the Eastern Jewish editors of *Ost und West*. No "low," cheap amusement, the magazine pretended to carry only high art and high culture. It expressly dissociated itself from "sensationalist" fiction, the "self-hating Jewish comedy" of the theater, and the "popular, non-Wagnerian music" of other venues (Kellner). Each of these was imagined to be the site of possible cultural contagion.

Between 1901 and 1923 the Berlin-based magazine *Ost und West* promoted European Jewish culture to Jewish audiences in the German cultural sphere. The common goal of the magazine's editors was to reverse Jewish "assimilation"[5] in Western and Central Europe by constructing an ethnic identity that included East European or "Eastern" forms of Jewishness.[6] What most observers have failed to note is that *Ost und West* pioneered the advocacy of East European Jewry in the West long before the emergence during World War I of what Gershom Scholem dubbed the "cult of the *Ostjuden*" (47). Within a few years, the magazine's promotion of Jewish ethnicity had become highly sophisticated. By integrating essays with fiction, folklore, art, and photographs, it became something that *Hashiloah* (Berlin and Warsaw, 1896–1914), *Voskhod* (Saint Petersburg, 1881–1906), and other Jewish periodicals were not: it became a "middlebrow" magazine. This meant two things: first, that the magazine was directed at a German-Jewish public that was by and large middle-class; and second, that it tried to present content of a challenging, but not highly intellectual nature to this audience.

By making *Ost und West* a middlebrow magazine, its founders showed how skillful they were at marketing Jewish ethnicity. The magazine's mix of "high" and "low" culture appealed to all of German Jewry, male and female, intellectual and nonintellectual, upper- and lower-middle class. Women, as suggested by the cover art and other evidence, formed a significant target audience for *Ost und West* (Brenner, *Marketing*). A typical issue began with a few pages of advertisements. Then came an editorial or review essay, followed almost without fail by an illustrated arts feature. The mid-section included articles and essays on Jewish literature, culture, history, current events, and religion; these, too, were sprinkled with illustrations. The final pages were the most varied: a given issue could include poetry, literature, folklore, music, a summary of the press, short literary reviews, aphorisms, quotes, and chess. To close, there were more advertisements.

Despite its emphasis on reeducation, then, *Ost und West* did not simply advance the interests of a Jewish nationalist avant-garde. Instead, its founders knew that they would have to reflect the presuppositions of the broader Jewish audience if they were to attract more readers. To influence Jewish readers in Germany (and Austria) who knew little about Eastern Jewry, the editors of *Ost und West* appealed specifically to three main audiences: Jewish intellectuals, middle-class Jewish women, and middle-class Jewish men. And judging by its wide circulation—*Ost und West* reached at least ten percent of the 625,000 Jews in the *Kaiserreich* at its height[7]—the magazine was a success. At least in the public sphere, it brought *Westjuden* closer to *Ostjuden*.

This task was well-suited for Leo Winz (1876–1952), the transplanted Ukrainian Jew and public relations adept who published the magazine.[8] Winz was a savvy entrepreneur, "image-maker," and sponsor of the arts, music, boxing, and film until he permanently left the *Reich* in 1935. In his capacity as editor-in-chief of *Ost und West* and other periodicals, he was keenly aware of the need to conduct market and audience research. Ever astute, he correctly anticipated that Baum would be a hit, featuring her stories in the popular January issues of the magazine.

Vicki Baum also had an understanding of mass market appeal, and it is no accident that she herself became a pop icon at the end of the "Golden Twenties." She was already a talent in the making when Winz decided to publish her "Im alten Haus" (January 1910) and "Rafael Gutmann" (January and February 1911). Both stories show glimpses of her style of the 1920s, which is marked by suspense, tension, foreshadowing, and the interplay of desire and fear. Although she was a mere twenty-two years old in 1910, her skillful command of popular narrative points to her later success in the Weimar Republic as a creator of middlebrow fiction for the blockbuster Ullstein Verlag, where she was offered a lucrative contract to become a staff writer and edit a glossy women's magazine.[9]

Prior to Baum, women writers rarely appeared in *Ost und West*, not even under male pseudonyms. Many female-sounding names disguised the identity of a male author. In the early years, the poet Dolorosa was the exception along with several women painters.[10] Until Baum's "Im alten Haus," then, there had been very little writing by women in *Ost und*

West—all the more reason why regular readers would have taken note of her stories.[11] To point out the magazine's new commitment to contributions by women, Baum's second work in *Ost und West*, "Rafael Gutmann," was preceded by a feature on the textile designs of a Berlin Jewish woman ("Eine interessante Handarbeit"). This gesture may also have been a nod in the direction of the Jewish women's movement, which had evolved rapidly after the 1908 legalization of women's associations in Germany.

A fine preview of Baum's later works, "Im alten Haus" equivocates on Jewish as well as women's issues. As a critique of a prototypical Jewish ghetto and its inhabitants, its point of view is neither discernibly Western nor Eastern Jewish; in addition, it reveals nothing to identify its locale as Baum's native Vienna. The main character is a decrepit, elderly Jewish woman who runs a ritual bath (*mikva*).[12] Serving as a metaphor for the assimilation process, she eventually goes blind after allowing herself to be operated upon by a doctor. When her children decide to sell the house and leave the Jewish quarter, she drowns herself in the basement *mikva*. On the one hand, the spectacle of sick Jews living and working underground anticipated Nazi calumnies directed against Jews; on the other hand, the story's critique of the ghetto, while harsh, appeared to be directed at all European Jewish locales in the Diaspora (*galut* [Hebrew] or *goles* [Yiddish]).

Yet from the Eastern Jewish nationalist standpoint of *Ost und West*, the Diaspora of Western—not of Eastern—Europe was in need of renewal (Brenner, *Marketing*; Berkowitz). To underscore its anti-Western, non-Zionist bias, *Ost und West* framed "Im alten Haus" with a photograph of proud-looking Oriental Jews.[13] In addition, the editors juxtaposed the story with an obituary for the Berlin-based social activist, Lina Morgenstern (N.O.).[14] While praising Morgenstern's work on behalf of all Jews, the writer responsible ascribed to her the following roles: mother and wife first, philanthropist second, activist third. This negative understanding of Western Jewish women's roles tacitly belittled Baum's protagonist as well as Baum's own accomplishments as a Western Jewish female writer.

Baum's second story in *Ost und West*, "Rafael Gutmann," has few women characters. Yet its fifteen-year-old Eastern Jewish male protagonist, Rafael Gutmann, is depicted as feminized or even "queer." Through Western culture, Rafael hopes to break out of his stifling milieu, not unlike other Eastern Jewish artists—and not unlike the readers of *Ost und West* who may have identified with them. Materially and spiritually impoverished, weak and unmanly, this musically gifted ghetto boy virtually cries out for rescue from the ghetto.

As a typical narrative of philanthropy, "Rafael Gutmann" excoriates the Jewish ghetto and parodies the Yiddish language as *Mauscheln*. Rafael is a traditional (or "orthodox") Eastern Jew who longs to be westernized.[15] Although the son of a second-hand clothes dealer, he discovers his love of song, becoming a choir boy and soloist at an elegant Liberal Jewish synagogue. He also sings magnificently and speaks flawless German, in stark contrast to his Yiddish-speaking family. Yet his father Lazar, bent on making a retailer out of him, compels him to leave music and liberal Judaism behind. Weak-willed, Rafael accedes to his father's wishes in the second half of the novella.[16] He becomes a caftan-wearing clerk in a dingy store in the Jewish quarter. To make matters worse, his blind ex-mentor Menkis betrays him by marrying the non-Jewish soprano Corinna with whom he is infatuated. The "Russian" folk song Rafael composes for her functions as a cipher for the many Yiddish folk songs collected by Winz and published in *Ost und West*.[17] To lend these "low" cultural products a degree of legitimacy, one segment of "Rafael Gutmann" is juxtaposed with a *Lied* based on Heine's poem, "Das gold'ne Kalb."

Ultimately, the young man's desire to make it in the West remains unfulfilled. Typecast as a degenerate, he can resist neither the familiar ghetto milieu nor the allure of Wagner's music; indeed, he knows both *Tristan und Isolde* and *Die Meistersinger von Nürnberg* by heart. After escaping the ghetto to attend the opera one final time, Rafael commits suicide, literally divided between the two worlds of East and West, tradition and modernity. Baum's own childhood was not unlike Rafael's. A musical prodigy, she studied harp at the Vienna *Konservatorium* and appeared with various orchestras in her teens and twenties. Her family life was also troubled, despite comfortable middle-class surroundings: she depicts herself in her memoirs as having been traumatized not only by her father—who at times called her "son"—but also by her mentally disturbed mother whom she was compelled to nurse for several years.[18]

At first glance, it is surprising that Winz and his colleagues would publish "Rafael Gutmann," indeed, that they would publish any images of Eastern Jews that were even slightly negative. But as I have argued elsewhere (Brenner, *Marketing*), *Ost und West* did not always object to negative representations of Jewish ghettos or their inhabitants. Instead, the critique of the traditional Jewish milieu became a way to promote ethnic ideals of the new Jew, a Jew liberated from centuries of mental and physical stagnation. In fact, Baum's ambivalent portrayal of Yiddish-speaking *Ostjuden* reflected competing receptions of the ghetto story (*Ghettogeschichte*). One school expressed longing for the old world; the other, disdain.[19] At the turn of the century the critique of Diaspora life was a flourishing industry among Jewish intellectuals, whether East European or Western, socialist or Zionist.[20] According to Scholem, Eastern Jewish discourse about the Jews, particularly in elitist Hebrew-language forums, could be even harsher than German-Jewish stereotyping of Jews (see Gelber, "Judendeutsch" 174). Micha Joseph Berdichevsky (1865–1921), representing the Nietzschean fringe, found no redeeming value in the Diaspora era (Aschheim 123–24). Ahad Ha'am (1858–1927), in contrast, argued for tolerance: If someone declares "our entire people is 'degenerate'—why not, if he loves that people in his soul?" (quoted in Acher 537).[21] Both the ghetto and the *goles* were backwards and deplorable, but to judge them required an insider's sensibility. Such a view suggested that Jewish self-criticism was necessarily of a different tenor from non-Jewish criticism of the Jews.[22]

The ambivalence of *Ost und West* toward the Diaspora was influenced by Ahad Ha'am and cultural Zionism at least as much as by anti-capitalism or anti-modernism. But its Eastern Jewish empathy for the ghetto did not stop the presses when Baum's stories came along. In short, *Ost und West* promoted Eastern Jewish nationalism in more than one way, further revealing Winz's public relations savvy. Double-edged messages, in fact, could only work to the magazine's benefit and enable it to reach several audiences.[23] Baum's ghetto stories were no less polysemic in both their range of discourses and their suggestive, elliptical style. Furthermore, the criticism of the ghetto in Baum's "Rafael Gutmann" did not contradict the pro-Eastern Jewish discourse of *Ost und West* as German Jews had come to know it. Within the broad framework of Diaspora criticism, it was permissible to portray the figure of Rafael as a powerless but talented victim in need of Western philanthropy and *Bildung*.

The editors of *Ost und West* allowed these associations to resonate in their choice of illustrations to accompany "Rafael Gutmann." The interplay of text and image was meant to encourage German Jews to act philanthropically toward East European Jews.[24] The commemorative medal designed by Hugo Kaufmann and titled "Den Helfern in der Not," pictured in juxtaposition with Rafael's final attempt at leaving the ghetto, thematizes the uplifting of the enslaved to freedom. One page later, we find a reproduction of Kaufmann's "Die Freiheit" ("Freedom"), a section of the "Unity Monument" (*Einheitsdenkmal*) in Frankfurt am Main (see page 100). This sculpture of a semi-nude Herculean male epitomizes Western respectability—a stark contrast to Rafael's weak and dependent nature. To drive the point home, a long article on Kaufmann directly precedes the final installment of Baum's story. In this piece, Kaufmann serves as an icon of the successful and established Western Jewish artist. The reference to his spacious atelier in the Western suburbs of Berlin returns us full circle to the Western Jewish audience of *Ost und West*.

Savvy promotion, as public relations people know, does not always function as intended. Despite bringing Baum's ghetto singer fiction to a largely German-Jewish audience, the magazine's tolerance towards Jewish ghetto fictions was stretched to its limits by "Rafael Gutmann." When written from an Eastern Jewish perspective, a typical ghetto story excoriated the Diaspora "ghetto," a milieu perceived as the breeding grounds for Western Jewish parvenus (Brenner, "Out"). But when written from a Western Jewish perspective, as in the case of "Rafael Gutmann," the stereotypes were potentially more detrimental to Jews. On the sensory level, for instance, Baum associates the smell of onions and chicken fat with "ghetto Jews" (*Ghettojuden*). In addition, synagogue scenes in "Rafael Gutmann" are exotic and depict the worshippers as near-hysterics.[25] And for any reader the most conspicuous feature of the story is that many Jewish characters do not speak standard German. The stereotyping of *Mauscheln* (Yiddish-accented German) had a long history. Both Western- and Eastern-based writers employed the myth of the corrupt language of the Jews (Gilman, *Self-Hatred*) when looking at the ghetto, but it was not difficult to discern an anti-*Ostjuden* bias in "Rafael Gutmann."[26]

Baum's analysis of the Jewish Diaspora was likely more influenced by "enlightened" Western (Jewish) thought than by Eastern Jewish traditionalism. Taken to its logical extreme, Baum's thinking equated Rafael's Judaism with femininity, madness, and a counterfeit creativity. Such an equation had become a centerpiece of turn-of-the-century science, in particular in the theories of Baum's Viennese contemporary, Otto Weininger (1880–1903). Known today as the paragon of Jewish self-hatred, Weininger's views on race and gender mirrored those of his time and place; hence, the popular appeal of his revised dissertation *Sex and Character* (*Geschlecht und Charakter*, 1904), which was praised by Freud, Karl Kraus, and others.[27] It is not surprising that Vicki Baum, like many other Central European Jews, came under the spell of this young philosopher. In fact, Baum was an adolescent and a student in Vienna when the influence of Weininger was at its summit (between 1903 and 1910), and she explicitly refers to him in her autobiography (*Es war* 196).

Weininger's contribution to the debate on racial degeneracy rests upon a strict dichotomy between the categories of "Jew" and "Aryan." This corresponds in turn to a dichotomy between "masculine" and "feminine." By extending the category of the feminine to the Jews (a move that gave Arthur Schopenhauer's misogyny a "scientific" grounding), Weininger attempted to link them with psychopathology. The protagonist in "Rafael Gutmann" can be read as an exemplar of such "Jewish" symptoms. In his impotent attempts to assimilate to "Aryan" culture, Rafael resembles Weininger himself: a baptized Jew, repressed homosexual, and young suicide. In fact, the circumstances of Weininger's self-destruction at age twenty-three may have influenced Baum's novella. Weininger's suicide became a *cause célèbre* and helped to publicize his ideas. That he killed himself in the house where Beethoven died suggests a desire to identify with a German-Gentile "masculine" genius. Similar patterns can be found in "Rafael Gutmann." Not only is Rafael stereotyped as an inferior, feminized Jew, but his suicide is also linked to Beethoven. This episode thus merits closer examination.

In the first half of "Rafael Gutmann," Rafael's only escape from the darkness of the squalid Jewish quarter (*Judengasse*) has been music: he is infatuated with the opera and with the singer Corinna. The second installment of the novella (in February 1911) relates Rafael's atrophy in the ghetto environment. Prevailed upon by his father to abandon his musical aspirations, he gives up his starring role in the choir and his confidence diminishes. Meanwhile, the ghetto continually "works on" Rafael, destroying his "fine, dreamy nature." Externally and internally, he is transformed back into a "typical" ghetto Jew, and this retrograde Jewishness is variously described in terms suggesting impotence: Rafael is "unaware," "without will," "full of horror," and "helpless."

By the second half of "Rafael Gutmann" a full year has passed without song and without visits to the opera.[28] Deprived of Corinna, and therefore of music, Rafael is rendered a neurotic dreamer and hysteric. As if secretly aware of Rafael's defiant unconscious, his father and his employer keep him under steady watch. Yet one February night while sleeping in the stifling kitchen of his parents' flat, Rafael dreams of melodies and awakens in tears. This is a prelude to his final attempt at breaking out. As the store where he works is closing for the Sabbath, Rafael randomly glimpses a newspaper. There he sees a (dated) advertisement for Beethoven's *Fidelio* and, shedding his restraint, he decides to attend the opera one last time. This new resolve reiterates a dynamic that defines the novella as a whole: a movement between desire and repression—and correspondingly—between assimilation and dissimilation. In perfect analogy, the play of desired and repressed dominates Beethoven's *Fidelio*. The opera's plot reflects Rafael's wish to be rescued from ghetto imprisonment: the rescue of Don Fernando Florestan by his wife Leonora—disguised as a male prison guard—points to Rafael's passive hope that the Christian Corinna will rescue him from the scourge of the ghetto. Fidelio, as a politicized feminine body, calls male operatic roles into question; in the context of *Rafael Gutmann*, the opera's cross-dressing motif evokes Weininger's feminizing of the (male) Jew.

In deciding to attend the opera, Rafael's pathology reaches its summit. Proceeding with his plan to attend *Fidelio*, Rafael takes his week's wages and heads into town. But having just descended happily into the colorful, inviting city, his desire is met with resistance when he bumps into Moritz Belft, the son of his employer. The caricature of an Eastern Jew, Belft wonders out loud where Rafael might be going on the Sabbath. Rafael, undaunted by Belft's "tricky questions," emerges into the illuminated, sensual metropolis and, arriving at the opera, is taken in by the seductive smells of silk, perfume, and women's hair.[29] His red ticket underlines the dream atmosphere, suddenly punctuated by the appearance of Corinna, "leaning against the wall, slender, pale, and blond" (140–41). Presumably leaning away from Menkis, who is seated, she has extended her hand down to him. This ultimate condescending gesture is reinforced by her gently affected smile. Her entire habitus suggests the condescension of the bourgeois philanthropist for the ghetto Jew.[30] The suspense is heightened when the lights go down before she can return Rafael's glance. To his surprise, the opera is *Tristan und Isolde* rather than *Fidelio*. As a devoted Wagnerian—like many other European Jews, especially women[31]—he soon grows receptive to *Tristan* and its theme of forbidden, decadent love. With head in hands, he trembles and sobs. At this point, Corinna lays her "free" hand on his head, a gesture elucidated by the accompanying illustration of Hugo Kaufmann's "Unity" ("Einheit"). Kaufmann's sculpture of an Athena-like female suggests not only the fatal unity of Tristan and Isolde; it also reinforces the symbolism of Corinna as assimilation, as the Enlightenment way out of the ghetto. In extending the succor of philanthropy, she may function in this text as a cipher for the middle-class Western Jewish (female) reader.

Demoralized after *Tristan*, Rafael reverts to his effete, excitable Jewishness. In addition, he becomes aware of the rift between himself and his would-be benefactors. Menkis admonishes him in patronizing fashion: "Come again, Rafael.... Only, you can't be so weak—a little backbone, and keep your head up!" (141). Here, Rafael's inner lack of resolve is explicitly linked to his inferior Jewish body, suggesting that his future attempts to assimilate himself are condemned to failure. Listening to Rafael's steps as he takes his leave, Menkis is apprehensive that he will not find the right path [*Weg*] for himself. Corinna—at a greater "racial" distance, as it were—articulates Menkis's pessimism more fully: "Maybe—there is no right way [*Weg*] for his kind [*Art*]" (143). Both are convinced that this prisoner of the ghetto is doomed and that he does not have the power or will to save himself. Though still not conscious of his own decision to die (he returns briefly to gaze at his parents' window), Rafael accepts it as a *fait accompli*. He is content to be leaving the corrupt ghetto; when he kills himself, he will be killing off one more incarnation of its "Platonic form" (a favorite term of Weininger). In his last moments, Rafael is not sad. Engulfed in reverie, he feels a "strange, happy intoxication." He acknowledges, as Menkis suspected earlier, that he is "without direction" (*ohne Weg*) (144). (The repeated references to Rafael's having lost his *Weg* may allude to Arthur Schnitzler's comprehensive *Zeitroman, Der Weg ins Freie* [1908], which treats similar themes of Jewishness and aestheticism.) Oblivious to the snow and the biting cold, he reprises "Todessehnsucht," the introduction to *Tristan*, while waiting on the tracks for the approaching train.

How are we to interpret the allusions to Wagner in "Rafael Gutmann"? In Jewish nationalist (and Zionist) literature of the time, the encounter with Wagner and his music is overshadowed by the maestro's anti-Semitic pamphlet "Das Judenthum in der Musik" (1850).[32] One of

Ost und West's other serial novellas, Heinrich York-Steiner's "Koriander, der Chasan" (1904), is typical of such a reading of Wagner. In this proto-*Jazz Singer* narrative, the protagonist's Hungarian *shtetl* roots enable him to overcome the negative Wagnerian influence and become a successful (but proudly Jewish) opera star.[33] Yet in "Rafael Gutmann," the role played by Wagner is different. Because Rafael is inherently unworthy of the great Beethoven's legacy, he shares a kinship with the modern decadent Wagner and, by extension, Weininger. What is more, in Weininger's eyes, even the great anti-Semite Wagner was polluted because of a reputed accretion of "Jewishness" in his art (404). In his regression to ghetto Jewishness, Rafael thus shares Wagner's proclivity for death and the Dionysian.[34]

It matters little for the present interpretation of "Rafael Gutmann" that Wagner was not a genius by Weininger's standards. More important are Weininger's judgments of Jewish notables like Spinoza and Heine: they, like women, possess either superficial genius or no genius at all. Weininger's conjectures here are linked with music and language.[35] For him, women's language is lies, as is the Jew's deformed language (*Mauscheln*), and Weininger's insistence on this point illuminates Baum's focus on Yiddish, song, and Wagner in "Rafael Gutmann." Rafael becomes the classic Jew of Weininger's schema. In fact, he returns so rapidly to ghetto traditionalism as to suggest that his golden choirboy days had been a lie all along. A key passage from *Sex and Character* sheds light on Rafael's flightiness, oversensitivity, and radical shifts between assimilation and dissimilation: "The impulse to lie is stronger in woman because, unlike that of man, her memory is not continuous, whereas her life is discrete, unconnected, discontinuous, swayed by the sensations and perceptions of the moment instead of dominating them" (Weininger 181). Rafael too has degenerated back into a mendacious "ghetto-ness": he thinks like a Jew and like a woman. He lacks the capacity for dominance necessary to be a Nietzschean creator who "wills" his life.[36]

Baum's protagonist Rafael is thus a distillate of "feminine" and "Jewish" characteristics. In his impotent attempts to assimilate to "Aryan" culture, Rafael directly resembles Weininger. Through allusions to him as well as to Oscar Wilde and *Jugendstil*, Baum also created an emasculated Jewish "queer." For while Rafael is depicted as a fan of a cross-dressing opera (Beethoven's *Fidelio*) and a decadent, self-mortifying one (Wagner's *Tristan*), he is a failure at assimilation, indeed at "passing."[37] On the one hand, he is a sympathetic teenage singer (not unlike Baum had been), struggling to escape his Eastern Jewish ghetto milieu.[38] On the other hand, he bears the classic symptoms of degeneracy: *Ostjudentum*, unmanliness, hysteria, and pseudo-genius (Gilman, *Self-Hatred*).

In the end "Rafael Gutmann" proved too multivalent for any single interpretive framework.[39] The magazine's German-Jewish male and female readers were thus free to identify with and then dissociate themselves from the Eastern Jewish boy-artist. In effect, Baum's novella invited these readers to graft negative self-images onto a perceived "Other": a non-threatening ghetto *Ostjude*. A negative, feminized West European Jewish self might be projected onto the East European Jewish subgroup, exemplified by Rafael. At the same time, the publication of "Rafael Gutmann" revealed how flexible the editors of *Ost und West* could be in their choice of contributions, even when those contributions appeared to attack Eastern Jewry, as in the case of Baum's anti-ghetto fictions. These fictions ironically empowered Western Jewish women (and men?) to escape their own inner ghettos by means of Jewish anti-Semitism.

Yet such self-hatred was ultimately at cross-purposes with the agenda of *Ost und West* and became the occasion for redefining editorial policy. Even if an effete Eastern Jew like Rafael was granted some sympathy by Western Jewish women, he was likely to be rejected by Western Jewish and Eastern Jewish men whose "manliness" he called into question. To be sure, a degree of anti-Eastern sentiment was permissible in *Ost und West*, as shown by the decision to publish Baum's stories. For a long time the editors had been using such sentiments—recast positively—to appeal to Western Jewish readers. But while this kind of nonpartisanship was a guiding principle of *Ost und West*, some of the magazine's producers felt that fictions like "Rafael Gutmann" went too far in their anti-Eastern sentiment.

Although there is no record of a direct editorial response to "Rafael Gutmann," Baum's double-edged attitudes towards Eastern Jews required some "damage control" so that *Ost und West* could protect its reputation as *the* advocate of East European Jewry. In order to counteract the ambiguities of "Rafael Gutmann," the magazine subtly addressed the same issues in a number of contributions in 1911. Some responses even appeared in the same issues as the installments of the novella.[40] These attempts to steer the reception in a particular direction suggest that an effeminate pathological character like Rafael was a dubious role model for Jewish males, thus revealing the boundaries of what European Jews considered respectable on the eve of World War I.

The argument I have mapped out should alert us to the ways in which unnuanced ideological analyses can lead to misinterpretation, even in the most overtly political of forums like *Ost und West*. Multivalent stories like Baum's "Rafael Gutmann" contest notions of intrinsic textual meaning and remind us that all cultural products can be selectively appropriated for very different ends than those imagined by their producers. Here the idea of middlebrow culture for a middle-class audience—the specialty of Winz and *Ost und West*—offers a challenge to the "ideology of mass culture" propagated most memorably by Adorno and Horkheimer in *Dialektik der Aufklärung*.

A number of books, magazines, films, and dramas have influenced German-Jewish audiences since the mid-nineteenth century. Yet historians of Central Europe have tended to neglect popular culture as well as minority cultures. Researchers in ethnic history, for their part, are based largely in the Americas and lack a more global perspective. The field of Jewish studies continues to be focused on intellectual and political history at the expense of the history of mass culture, studies of which have been almost entirely limited to the United States. Equally unencouraging is the sub-discipline of German-Jewish history, where battles between liberals and Zionists guided my own early steps as a scholar. Finally, the notion that Jews knew how to, and actually *did*, "sell" culture appears still to be taboo, fifty years after the Holocaust.

Also at stake in this essay and other work on popular culture in Imperial and Weimar Germany is the notion that cultural studies can be applied to the past. Historians, confronted with a paucity of source materials, have often focused on the production of culture instead of spotlighting its circulation and consumption. Although the publisher/editor of *Ost und West* was a cultural producer, it may have been his social position as an East European Jew that brought him both insight and success, suggesting comparison with his more famous contemporaries, the Jewish movie moguls of Hollywood. Vicki Baum also had an unerring eye for the popular, despite her wish to be taken more seriously; hence, her self-characterization in her memoirs as "a first-class second-rank writer" ("eine erstklassige Schriftstellerin zweiter Güte," *Es war* 377). The three main areas of cultural studies scholarship today—audience/fan studies, semiotics and textual analysis, and institutional and/or theoretical approaches—correspond neatly to the old "communication model" known from reader-response and reception theory, i.e., the triad of producer, text, and reader. With respect to Jewish (cultural) history in Central Europe, while we know about Jewish cultural producers and institutions, and about texts intended for Jews or texts with Jewish content, *one* part of the picture is still missing. Exactly what specific German-Jewish readers *did* with texts like Baum's "Rafael Gutmann" or the magazine *Ost und West* is difficult to ascertain. More research needs to be done on how different groups and individuals have interpreted popular entertainment. Yet such potentially fertile ground has its price, requiring a return to a place often eschewed by those "professing literature": the archives. In addition, such a project presupposes more than a passing acquaintance with the relevant intertexts. But it is only in this manner that we can determine historically possible, if not historically *certain*, readings. *Ost und West*, Vicki Baum, and their readers were—and are still—the result of a complicated dialectic between intertextual and social factors, an interaction with the common goal of achieving legitimacy for "low" Jewish cultures and for themselves.

Notes

I would like to thank the anonymous readers of my original manuscript for their helpful comments as well as John Hoberman, Janet Swaffar, and Katherine Arens for their comments on an earlier draft. All translations from the German texts are my own.

[1] At one point in her memoir, which was posthumously edited by her daughter-in-law (Ruth Lert), Baum claims that her father's ancestors may have been (non-Jewish?) Swabians (*Es war* 137).

[2] Gilman sees Baum's native Vienna as the paradigmatic site for mixed-raced Jewish anxiety: "Vienna is where the problematic nature of Jewish response to the meaning of Jewish superior intelligence can best be seen. The image of the 'smart Jew' at the end of the nineteenth and beginning of the twentieth century is so poisoned and so contested that Jewish intellectuals—no matter how defined—come to understand themselves as 'spoiled.'...In Vienna at the *fin de siècle*, the normal self-doubt every individual has about his or her abilities became tied to discourses about race" (*Smart Jews* 142–43).

[3] For an example, see the bibliography of Baum's *oeuvre* in King's *Best-Sellers*, an excellent study that goes to great lengths to contextualize Baum's fiction.

[4] On *Ost und West,* ethnic magazines, and the concept of "ethnicity," see Brenner (*Marketing*).

[5] On the terms "acculturation" and "assimilation," see Sorkin (27–33). Recent researchers prefer "acculturation," owing to the negative connotations of "assimilation" (which many Zionists used as a term of opprobrium). According to the sociologist Milton Gordon, assimilation is a continuum. Beginning with what he calls "acculturation," a type of "cultural assimilation," an ethnic group adopts the dress, recreational tastes, economic patterns, language, cultural baggage, and political views of the general society without necessarily losing its sense of group identity. Total assimilation and group disappearance, however, do not take place unless primary contacts—friendships, associations, marriage, and family ties—have disappeared. This "structural assimilation" and the final stage of "marital assimilation" render the minority indistinguishable from the culture at large.

[6] "Identity" or "self-understanding" is properly understood as a system of allegiances one assigns to oneself or to others.

[7] Until 1906 *Ost und West* was subtitled *Illustrierte Monatsschrift für modernes Judentum* and after that time *Illustrierte Monatsschrift für das gesamte Judentum*. According to Winz's and independent estimates, the journal had

anywhere from 16,000 to 23,000 subscribers in the period between 1906 and 1914. Allowing for families, cafés, reading rooms, and libraries, these figures should be multiplied by a factor of three or more. The result: a broad resonance in the Jewish population of German-speaking Europe (Winz).

[8] Winz was a veteran image-maker who had served from 1906 to 1908 as the head of public relations (*Chef der Propaganda*) for the oldest major German advertising firm, Haasenstein and Vogler. To date, there exists no biography of Winz, nor of his main associates at *Ost und West*. Besides owning and investing in a range of businesses, Winz was the publisher of the largest Jewish newspaper in Germany (the *Gemeindeblatt der jüdischen Gemeinde zu Berlin*) from 1927 to 1934 as well as the founder of *Der Schlemiel: Ein illustriertes jüdisches Witzblatt* (1904–23).

[9] On Baum's later career, see King (*Best-Sellers*).

[10] Rachel Mundlak (1887–?), a Polish Jew and the in-house artist after Lilien moved on, was the most visible artist in the magazine, of equal profile with Leopold Pilichowsky (1869–1933) and Samuel Hirshenberg (1863–1908). Other women artists featured were Marie Dillon (1858–?), in May 1904; Helene von Mises, in December 1905; Marie Cohen, in March 1905; Helene Darmesteter, in February 1907; Käthe Münzer, in January 1908; Sophie Blum-Lazarus, in June 1908; Julie Wolfthorn, in December 1911; and Margot Lipmann, in November 1912.

[11] In *Ost und West*, Jewish women artists were frequently characterized in the terms reserved for male colleagues: "restrained melancholy" and full of "deep inner feeling (*Innerlichkeit*)." But usually they are marginalized. Heinz Schnabel asks "why...great German women talents act masculine?" and notes that Käthe Kollwitz (1864–1945) "does work impossible for a female" (359). The best example for the eroticization of the Jewish woman, especially the Eastern Jewish woman, is the art of Leo Bakst, featured in the September 1912 and March 1913 issues. More traditional Jewish women would have objected to images of unclothed women in the magazine.

[12] Managing a *mikva* suggests that the protagonist is "Eastern Jewish" in background, though not necessarily an immigrant from Eastern Europe.

[13] The advent of photography may have made it more difficult to contest images of the ghetto in Baum's terms. See, for instance, Forchheimer.

[14] The article is signed "N.O." Its author was possibly Karl M[artha] Baer, the author of an autobiographical memoir of a Jewish boy raised as a girl; see N.O. Body.

[15] The *Judengasse* where Rafael lives resembles the Jewish quarter of Vienna.

[16] Rafael's namesake in Herman Heijermans's (1864–1924) socialist drama *Ghetto* (1899), set in the Amsterdam *Judenviertel*, does not give in to his father. In addition, the character of Menkis is related to that of the blind father in Heijermans's *Ghetto*.

[17] Baum's attitudes toward Yiddish are somewhat more nuanced in her autobiography: "Jiddisch—eine größere Schande war nicht möglich für die verfeinerten und ihrer Umgebung sorgsam angepaßten österreichischen und deutschen Juden" (*Es war* 86).

[18] Music was not the only means Baum used to escape her repressive family environment. As a teenager, she entered and won a literary contest after having been forbidden to read by her father. At eighteen she left home to marry Max Prels, a writer. Baum continued to write during their marriage, so well that Prels sold several of her early stories under his name (!) to the German magazine *Velhagen und Klasings Monatshefte*. Prels may also have brought about the decisive contact with *Ost und West*.

[19] Hans Otto Horch maintains that there is a basic ambivalence inherent in ghetto fictions (165-68). I would only add that this ambivalence is conditioned by competing receptions of the *Ghettogeschichte*.

[20] A recent example of criticism of the Diaspora was the government-sanctioned disdain for most expressions of Diaspora culture in Israel—including Yiddish culture—that dominated until the 1970s.

[21] Ahad Ha'am and Micha Josef Berdichevsky were arguably the two leading ideologues of *Kulturzionismus* at the turn of the century. Although both wrote primarily in Hebrew, Berdichevsky is also known for his publications in German under the name of "Bin Gurion." "Cultural Zionism" (or "spiritual Zionism") varied mainly in its Palestinocentrism from the "diaspora nationalism" of Simon Dubnow (1860-1941) and related forms of Jewish nationalism and cultural autonomy. Ahad Ha'am felt that a spiritual renewal had to precede any restoration of a Jewish state. Despite being a former *maskil* (or Jewish "Enlightener"), he represented a cultural Zionism that did not break with Enlightenment ideals but which was distinctly Eastern European. Not surprisingly, he was a formative influence on Winz and the main contributors to *Ost und West* (on Ahad Ha'am, see Zipperstein). Also a former *maskil,* Berdichevsky preferred the Israelite prophecy of the Bible over the "fossilized" law of the Diasporic age. Influenced by Nietzsche, he also sought to liberate Eastern Jewry from its "ghetto" lethargy; see Aschheim (123-24).

[22] Baum's fiction was influenced not only by the colonializing narratives published in *Ost und West* but also by the tradition of the *Dorf- und Ghettogeschichte* set in Europe. There is no canonical Jewish "ghetto story," and most attempts to define the genre have been haphazard and oversimplified. Most of all, the diversity of Jewish populations in Europe and their modes of expression renders illusory any attempt to adequately characterize the ghetto story. Nearly every size of settlement is depicted (village, town, city), and nearly every region where Jews settled brought forth its own ghetto poets (Germany, Bohemia, Poland, Galicia, Ukraine, Russia, etc.). From Posen to Moscow and from Prague to Odessa, the Jewish ghetto was part of the landscape—not to speak of areas beyond Eastern Europe. The *Ghettogeschichte* shows correspondences with the vogue of regionality in German and other literatures, beginning with Realism

of 1848 and extending to Naturalism and the *Heimatkunstbewegung* (e.g., Liliencron, Viebig, Thoma, Hauptmann). The last obstacle to a binding definition is that the literary genres employed (sketch, novella, novel) and the type of authorial intent (idealization, lament, satire) vary greatly; see especially Horch (165–66). One of the best examples of the multivalence possible in the interpretation of the ghetto fiction is the reception of Stefan Zweig's 1902 novella "Im Schnee." Gelber writes: "Es ist möglich, daß Buber und Feiwel die Geschichte 'Im Schnee' anders auslegten als Zweig. Sie sahen darin vielleicht einen Versuch zur Wiederaufrichtung des jüdischen Selbstbewußtseins, eine Warnung und einen verzweifelten Aufruf zur 'Verjüngung' des jüdischen Lebens, eine Richtung, die in ihr kulturell-zionistisches Schema paßte.... Buber's Ansicht, daß die jüdische Ghettoexistenz in Osteuropa einer der wahren inneren Feinde des jüdischen Volkes sei, entsprach Franzos' eigener Ablehnung des Ghettos. Für beide war die Judenfrage eine Kulturfrage, obwohl ihre Vorschläge zur Lösung des Problems äußerst verschieden waren" ("Franzos" 43).

[23] Instead of judging *Ost und West* by a rigid standard of consistency, we might rather see its publishing policies as a set of coexisting compatibilities. This explanation accounts for the fact that the magazine attracted opposing audiences (Brenner, *Marketing*).

[24] Western Jewish *women* readers, such as Winz's assistant (and later wife) Else Jacoby, were especially targeted to support young male Eastern Jewish artists. In Berlin and beyond, Winz himself was something of a ladies' man.

[25] Exotic descriptions of Jews praying have a long history in European culture. Goethe describes a rabbi in the Frankfurt ghetto as praying with "fanatic zeal...repulsive enthusiasm, wild gesticulations...confused murmurings... piercing outcries...effeminate movements...the queerness of an ancient nonsense" (quoted in Aschheim 7).

[26] For Baum, language is intimately connected with cultural difference. The holy language of the Jews, like their vernacular Yiddish, is marked by corrupting influence and is described as "a strange sing-song...distorted by an excessive number of screeching sounds (*Quetschlauten*)." This causes Rafael to slowly "unlearn" the "language of the city" (Baum, "Rafael Gutmann" 135). The caricature of Jewish speech in German culture, especially of Yiddish, goes back to Sessa, but it is not present in all ghetto stories. Unlike *Mauscheln,* which parodies a native Yiddish speaker's attempts to speak "proper" German, the typologizing of the "improper" Jewish characters in "Rafael Gutmann" is a fairly neutral reproduction of how one dialect of Yiddish may have sounded in the Viennese milieu where Baum grew up. Nevertheless, Yiddish retains the markings of degeneracy in the story, participating in the centuries-old discourse of the corrupt language of the Jew (Gilman, *Self-Hatred*). In the 1922 version of the story, which appeared in a rather different context (the [Leipziger] *Illustrirte Zeitung*), the Yiddish was completely Germanized (Baum, "Raffael").

[27] *Ost und West*'s reviewer was ambivalent regarding Weininger, agreeing on his view of women, but defending Judaism as a great religion (Münz).

[28] Rafael's situation in this year parallels closely aspects of Baum's life during the period when her mother was dying (e.g., *Es war* 113), yet no mention is made of "Rafael Gutmann" in her autobiography.

[29] The reader is implicitly asked to compare the pleasant odors of the Gentile city with the stereotypical Eastern Jewish smell of garlic and onions. Similar olfactory prejudices are discussed in Marc A. Weiner's *Richard Wagner and the Anti-Semitic Imagination* (24–25). According to Weiner, *Tristan und Isolde* (a favorite of Rafael Gutmann) "came to be viewed by Wagner's contemporary audiences as an explicitly erotic work, shocking to bourgeois sensibilities of the time.... If such a response seems all too literal to listeners today, it may serve to underscore the distance between Wagner's world and our own; in Wagner's time, his music—like his texts and stage directions—was both intended and perceived to convey physiological states" (24–25). Isolde's orgasmic apotheosis and union with her lover at the conclusion to the drama is accompanied by unparalleled aromas, for *Tristan und Isolde* is "the most synesthetic of Wagner's synesthetic works, and the highly charged Oedipal nature of its suggestive psychological content is enhanced by the aesthetic merging of elements in the text. In *Tristan und Isolde* the borders are sexual, social, and olfactory; a sexual union is implied in the union of sense perceptions, and the union is, in terms of the society depicted in the drama, a *forbidden* one" (my emphasis, 201–02).

[30] The *femme fatale* Corinna is not the first non-Jewish women to disappoint a Jewish male in *Ost und West*. See also the character of Elsa in Hartmann and the diva character in York-Steiner.

[31] Jewish women, in particular, attended opera and theater in numbers far exceeding their proportion within the German population. If the multiple references to it in her memoirs are any indication, *Tristan und Isolde* was Vicki Baum's favorite opera in Wagner's repertoire (Baum, *Es war* 62, 137, 191).

[32] Wagner's "Das Judenthum in der Musik" appeared anonymously in its early editions.

[33] On Baum's identification and friendship with Samuel Raphaelson, author of *The Jazz Singer* (the basis for the 1927 film starring Al Jolson), see Baum (*Es war* 125).

[34] Compare Thomas Mann's early stories, where Wagner functions as a destructive decadent and threat to bourgeois stability. In her autobiography, Baum relates her knowledge and admiration of Mann as well as her identification with the dark artist figures over the *Bürger* (e.g., *Es war* 100, 191, 458).

[35] Weininger was doubtless familiar with Wagner's "Das Judenthum in der Musik."

[36] Baum claimed "[w]ie meine gesamte Generation wuchs ich geradezu berauscht von Wagner und Nietzsche auf" (*Es war* 62).

[37] On stereotypes of opera, degeneracy, and Jews in Richard Strauss's *Salome*, see Gilman (*Disease* 55–81).

[38] Rafael may have functioned as the cast-off skin of Vicki Baum, as her image of social failure. According to Lynda King, "Baum was proud that she was able to accomplish things 'lesser' people couldn't, like emancipate herself without any help" (King, "E-mail").

[39] It would be valuable to compare the reception of "Rafael Gutmann" when it appeared elsewhere, for instance, in the [Leipziger] *Illustrirte Zeitung*.

[40] For example, Binjamin Segel—Winz's main associate by 1911—offered a mainstream Jewish nationalist response to Baum in *Ost und West*. This series of strongly worded editorials on Galician Jewry depicted Eastern Jewish men not as emasculated boys, but as independent and strong. At the same time, it showed that the editors of *Ost und West* did not accept the definition of Jewishness implicit in Baum's fiction. Even though Segel strove to be neutral in his writings, he became vehement in attempting to defend Eastern Jewish masculinity.

Works Cited

Acher, Mathias [Nathan Birnbaum]. "Ghetto." *Ost und West* (Mar. 1903): 533-40.

Adorno, Theodor W., and Max Horkheimer. *Dialektik der Aufklärung: Philosophische Fragmente*. Amsterdam: Querido, 1944.

Aschheim, Steven E. *Brothers and Strangers: The East European Jew in German and German Jewish Consciousness, 1800-1923*. Madison: U of Wisconsin P, 1982.

"Aus dem New Yorker Judenviertel." *Ost und West* (July 1909): 461-66.

Baum, Vicki. *Es war alles ganz anders*. 1962. Köln: Kiepenheuer & Witsch, 1987.

———. "Im alten Haus." *Ost und West* (Jan. 1910): 15-32.

———. "Rafael Gutmann." *Ost und West* (Jan. 1911): 37-50; (Feb. 1911): 131-44.

———. "Raffael Gutmann." [Leipziger] *Illustrirte Zeitung* 12 Oct. 1922; 19 Oct. 1922; 2 Nov. 1922.

Bennett, Tony, and Joanne Woollacott. *Bond and Beyond: The Political Career of a Popular Hero*. London: Macmillan, 1987.

Berkowitz, Michael. *Zionist Culture and West European Jewry before the First World War*. Cambridge: Cambridge UP, 1993.

Body, N.O. [Martha Baer]. *Aus eines Mannes Mädchenjahren*. 1909. Berlin: Edition Hentrich, 1993.

Bourdieu, Pierre. *Distinction: A Social Critique of the Judgement of Taste*. Trans. Richard Nice. Cambridge, Mass: Harvard UP, 1984.

Brenner, David. *Marketing Identities: The Invention of Jewish Ethnicity*. Detroit: Wayne State UP, forthcoming 1998.

———. "Out of the Ghetto and into the Tiergarten: Redefining the Jewish Parvenu in *Ost und West*, 1901-1906." *German Quarterly* 66.2 (Spring 1993): 176-94.

Forchheimer, Stephanie. "Ein Gang durch das Judenviertel in Amsterdam." *Ost und West* (Nov. 1913): 889-96.

Gelber, Mark H. "Das Judendeutsch in der deutschen Literatur: Einige Beispiele von den frühesten Lexika bis zu Gustav Freytag und Thomas Mann." *Juden in der deutschen Literatur: Ein deutsch-israelisches Symposion*. Ed. Stéphane Moses and Albrecht Schöne. Frankfurt a.M.: Suhrkamp, 1986. 162-78.

———. "K.E. Franzos, Achad Ha'am und S. Zweig." *Bulletin des Leo Baeck Instituts* 27 (1982): 19-43.

Gilman, Sander L. *Disease and Representation: Images of Illness from Madness to AIDs*. Ithaca: Cornell UP, 1988.

———. *Jewish Self-Hatred: Anti-Semitism and the Hidden Language of the Jews*. Baltimore: Johns Hopkins UP, 1986.

———. *Smart Jews: The Construction of the Image of Jewish Superior Intelligence*. Lincoln: U of Nebraska P, 1996.

Gordon, Milton M. *Assimilation in American Life: The Role of Race, Religion and National Origins*. New York: Oxford UP, 1964.

Hartmann, Moritz. "Bei Kunstreitern." *Ost und West* (Mar. 1901): 211-22.

Horch, Hans Otto. *Auf der Suche nach der jüdischen Erzählliteratur: Die Literaturkritik der "Allgemeinen Zeitung des Judentums" (1837-1922)*. Literaturhistorische Untersuchungen 1. Bern: Lang, 1985.

Kaufmann, Hugo. "Die Einheit." *Ost und West* (Feb. 1911): 141-42.

———. "Die Freiheit." *Ost und West* (Feb. 1911): 137-38.

———. "Den Helfern in der Not" (commemorative medal in a series of Goethe medallions). *Ost und West* (Feb. 1911): 133-34.

Kellner, Leon. "Eine jüdische Toynbee-Halle in Wien." *Ost und West* (Apr. 1901): 291-98.

King, Lynda. *Best-Sellers by Design: Vicki Baum and the House of Ullstein*. Detroit: Wayne State UP, 1988.

———. E-mail to the author. 21 Apr. 1995.

Lilien, Ephraim Moses. Cover of *Ost und West* from 1901 to 1906 (drawing).

Mosse, George L. *Nationalism and Sexuality: Middle-Class Morality and Sexual Norms in Modern Europe*. 1985. Madison: U of Wisconsin P, 1986.

Münz, Bernhard. "Das Judentum in der Beleuchtung eines jungen Philosophen." *Ost und West* (Dec. 1903): 823-26.

N.O. "Lina Morgenstern." *Ost und West* (Jan. 1910): 33-34.

Petersen, Vibeke Rützou. "The Best of Both Worlds? Jewish Representations of Assimilation, Self, and Other in Weimar Popular Fiction." *German Quarterly* 68 (Spring 1995): 160-73.

Schnabel, Heinz. "Sophie Blum-Lazarus." *Ost und West* (June 1908): 357-60.

Scholem, Gershom. *Miberlin liyerushalayim* (From Berlin to Jerusalem). Expanded Hebrew ed. Tel Aviv: Am Oved, 1982.

Segel, Binjamin . "Das Judenelend in Galizien." *Ost und West* (Feb. 1911): 101–08; Mar. 1911: 197–206.

———. "Volkswohlstand und Volksaufklärung." *Ost und West* (July 1911): 593–600.

[Sessa, Karl B.A.]. *Unser Verkehr: Eine Posse in Einem Aufzuge. Nach der Handschrift des Verfassers*. Leipzig: In Commission der Dykschen Buchhandlung, 1815.

Sorkin, David. "Emancipation and Assimilation—Two Concepts and Their Application to German-Jewish History." *Leo Baeck Institute Yearbook* 35 (1990): 17–33.

[Wagner, Richard.] Freigedank, K. *Das Judenthum in der Musik*. Leipzig: J.J. Weber, 1850.

Weiner, Marc A. *Richard Wagner and the Anti-Semitic Imagination*. Lincoln: U of Nebraska P, 1995.

Weininger, Otto. *Geschlecht und Charakter: Eine prinzipielle Untersuchung*. Wien: Braumüller, 1904.

Winz, Leo. Papers. Central Zionist Archives, Jerusalem. File A136/108.

York-Steiner, Heinrich. "Koriander, der Chasan." *Ost und West* (Oct. 1904): 687–92; Nov. 1904: 783–90; Dec. 1904: 859–72.

Zipperstein, Steven. *Elusive Prophet: Ahad Ha'am and the Origins of Zionism*. Berkeley: U of California P, 1993.

Zweig, Stefan. "Im Schnee." *Jüdischer Almanach*. Ed. Berthold Feiwel. Berlin: Jüdischer Verlag, 1902.

Avant-gardist, Mediator, and...Mentor? Elke Erb

Birgit Dahlke

This examination of Elke's Erb's texts and the interview that follows it seek an answer to the question of why most GDR women writers vehemently rejected the label "feminist author," even when they explicitly deal with gender issues in their texts. As poet and theoretician, but also as mediator between different generations and literatures, Elke Erb continues to receive much attention, particularly from young authors. Her way of dealing with gender questions, on the one hand, and with a politically understood feminism, on the other, exemplifies her own ambivalence about the issue of gender-specific writing. At the same time, she displaces some of the familiar feminist questions, rejects them, breaks them down, and appropriates them for herself in original ways. (BD)

The Mediator

An early interview with Christa Wolf provides insight into Elke Erb's developing self-awareness as a writer in GDR society. In response to Wolf's question as to whether she feels "something would be missing in the world" without her poetic contribution, Erb answers: "I live, therefore I think. I wouldn't need the awareness that something would be missing if I myself were missing" (Wolf 188). Both question and answer point to a considerable difference in the way the two women see themselves as artists. Erb makes a distinction between Wolf's generation and her own. She states that she herself was raised with the "promises of dogma" (*Dogmenverheissungen*) against which her generation reacted by "insisting on the concrete" in poetry (187). The term "promises of dogma" underlines a difference between the two generations: What Wolf's generation still experienced as a new beginning was already considered to be purely the "promise of dogma" by Erb's. Differences are also evident in terms of basic aesthetic and poetological questions: While reflection on the process of poetic production is, for Erb, a natural component of her poetry, it is for Wolf "a breaking of the spell" (*ein Entzaubern*). In Wolf's opinion, the metalevel does not belong in the text and, in fact, even counteracts the lyrical impulse. Unlike Erb, whose aesthetic concept is based on self-reflexivity, Wolf does not consider an analysis of the mental preconditions for writing to be worthy of poetic representation. As the thematic focus of her writing, Erb explicity chooses to analyze society's formation of its subjects and the liberation from "wanting to obey, being seduced, wanting and having to believe" (186). By no means does this apply only to the level of ideology, but also to the danger of being "led astray" on the level of everyday thoughts. She repeatedly seeks to thwart her own perceptions and interpretations, and tries to break out of the "horizon of heteronomy" (*Fremdbestimmung*) (*Winkelzüge* 317). She is continuously intent on keeping herself from sinking into "the sleep of assumed authority" (315).

When the conversation with Wolf took place in 1977, such a concept and understanding of a text were unique in GDR literature. Also decisive was Erb's relationship to language; in the years following Wolf's observation that Erb used "language material" as a sign "in place of *real material,*" Erb would yield more and more to this "language material" and not, to be sure, because of its specific referents. Her interest was drawn to the medium of language itself—to its resistance and internal rules. It is this "non-instrumentalized relationship to language" (Köhler) in particular that would later appeal to younger authors. Writing for Erb is not "describing, but changing. Bringing oneself to the world. Bringing the world to oneself" ("Zwölf Jahre" 136).

Especially in the context of literature published unofficially during the last decade of the GDR, there was a marked affinity of authors born between 1950 and 1965 for Erb's poetics—for her treatment of language and her poetic form. In addition to her poetological positions, it is first and foremost Erb's distanced and analytical view of GDR society, as well as her recognition that individual creative endeavors have their own inherent worth and do not have to gain legitimation through their "social usefulness," that connects Erb to the younger poets.

Because of such points of shared interest, Erb could become mentor, mediator, and advisor to the "alternative scene" of Prenzlauer Berg (East Berlin), although she refused such a role and even now, in retrospect, does not claim it for herself. Her openness, readiness to talk, and role as a mediator, as well as her impeccable eye for innovation, are particularly evident in her preface to the 1985 anthology *Berührung ist nur eine Randerscheinung* (Touch is Merely of Peripheral Importance) that she published with Sascha Anderson. Erb wrote sympathetically and insistently about the young poets. She depicted their social environment, explained their intellectual horizon, lifestyle, and background, and thereby became the defender of the younger generation. It is important to note here that in her preface she draws attention not only to literary concepts that were innovative for GDR literature, but also places them within a social context. In 1985, the GDR had not yet officially acknowledged the rejectionist posture among those (predominately male) individuals who chose to drop out from society and whose attitude was no longer an isolated phenomenon in the young generation. Both national security and cultural-political institutions tried to criminalize the conscious opposition to the "normal" GDR socialization processes, describing it as a crazy idea among the "asocial elements" of society. Erb insisted that these unusual, unconventional texts revealed a "new (corrective and responsible) way of thinking," a "new social consciousness" ("Vorwort" 12, 15).

Not a Feminist?

In all of her observations, Erb expresses an interest in both the writers and the works of the older generation. Yet one issue remains untouched in her analysis, namely, the relationship between aesthetics and the life experiences of a female poet. An important reason for this lies in Erb's disinterest in feminist questions. Central to her critical analysis of handed-down, rigidified thought and behavior patterns are the categories of power and hierarchy, not the battle of the sexes. Only recently has Erb commented on the relationship between the sexes, particularly in response to questions from others. While the GDR still existed, the category of gender seems not to have played a role in Erb's thinking and writing.

This is evident, for example, in her preface to *Berührung ist nur eine Randerscheinung*. To point out the innovative nature of the anthology, she cites texts almost exclusively by male authors, without taking the least notice of the absence of female poets. Only once does she refer to one of the four female authors represented in the anthology, and even then her comment remains strangely nebulous: "Gabi Kachold surrenders herself to the homelessness of clichés and platitudes" (12). Gabriele Stötzer-Kachold's texts, in particular, did not seem accessible to Erb. The relationship between the peculiarities of the texts and the author's gender went beyond the scope of Erb's analysis, even though female roles and masks in the prose selections that represent Stötzer-Kachold's work in the anthology were so obviously problematized that a discussion of gender-specific questions would have seemed almost inevitable.

In the few remarks she has made on feminist questions, all of them dating from the 1990s, Erb has expressed a growing attentiveness to the connections between poetry and feminist commitment, as well as her own careful distance from feminism. In a women's magazine in 1992 she writes: "Dear women, you will neither recognize yourself in me as oppressed copies, nor as the poor Mary" ("Frauen und Kunst"). She clearly rejects for herself the role of the artist as designated spokesperson for her sex. Towards the end of the same text she does, however, make an observation indicating that she cannot simply exclude questions of gender from her own thinking and behavior. Almost with amazement she describes her recognition that "when it gets serious, you turn towards women.... In a world not dominated by men such a discovery could not surprise me, could it?" What irritates Erb? Does it bother her that she, who puts so much effort into the analysis of her own, even unconscious presuppositions, only now seems to have become aware of her own gender determinedness? Is her disinterest in her own gender related to the male-dominated Prenzlauer Berg scene? Did this male-centeredness perhaps make it easier for her to succeed as a woman writer in this group? Erb is, after all, the only woman of the group who was and continues to be regarded as an undisputed authority by both female and male authors.

While Erb's earlier position towards gender issues can be understood for the most part in terms of how she (like many other women) perceived conditions in the GDR, one can, in my opinion, see her present-day distance towards the feminist movement and its literature primarily as a rejection of confrontational thinking. From the very beginning, a consistent element in Erb's texts and commentaries has been the renunciation of confrontational structures. In a conversation with Kerstin Hensel published in 1993, she places both feminism and confrontational thinking in closer context: "You know, it is very sad the way women work towards self-determination, aiming at the social and only in a political-confrontational way. If it were real liberation—I just happen to know this now—then the male of the species would also be enlightened by it" (22).

Her position seems strangely self-assured and definitive, and is particularly surprising in view of the discursive and open character of her responses to other questions. In her opinion, female emancipation often results in confrontation and a dualism between man and woman, male and female art. In her writing she tries to undo such dualistic and causal thinking. She sees her own discomfort with the confrontational attitude and aggressiveness of the women's movement in the West as representative of the reservations many GDR women had. The way she views gender relationships today is interesting not only for these reasons: Seeing herself as a professional woman with an emancipated lifestyle, she does not disassociate herself from the other sex as much as show an interest in the "other" for its different qualities. She also questions the ignorance and limitations of her own perceptions of the other sex. Her self-criticism is, however, more provocative and confrontational than that of many other GDR women. For Erb, the disassociation and liberation from alien, male norms is self-evident because she does not consider these norms to be merely male, but rather hierarchical. She demands of herself, as of other women, that traditional gender roles be dismantled, yet she treats this predominately as an individual rather than a structural problem. To describe the way in which she herself functions in a male-dominated realm of literature, she evokes an image of androgyny[1] that allows her to play with accepted forms.

There are at first glance few references to the author's gender in her poetic texts, unlike those of Stötzer-Kachold. Quite often Erb even refers to herself with the masculine form (*Winkelzüge* 308 ff.).[2] Despite the seeming thematic absence of "the woman," Erb's style nevertheless reveals surprising features that cannot be found to such a degree in any male author of either her generation or the next.

Defining Features of Erb's Poetic Development

In her 1991 volume *Winkelzüge* (Tricks), the question "But will I then still love?" is both the starting point and the goal of her "process-oriented writing." Because of its intimacy, the question can be described as traditionally "feminine." As a syntactical figuration, this question becomes the text's "heroine," capable of "triggering its novella-like qualities" (*Winkelzüge* 8). Erb lets this "heroine" become the personified subject, the agent of her text. She sets it apart from the authorial "I" that comments on, follows or evades, precedes or maintains pace with the "heroine." The grammatical trick allows for a direct analysis of language that itself has become a character. As catalyst for a text that was written over a period of years, this seemingly private diary notation that aims to understand its own evolution is somewhat unusual. Through its almost 450 pages, Erb by no means limits the question to the individual dimension, but rather shifts her analysis to a more general level of questions about happiness, love, and inner harmony.

The "tricks" (*Winkelzüge*), whereby the "I" acts on the suggestion of the "heroine," lead to "unsuspected, informative relationships" (the volume's subtitle). Language has not only symbolically taken on a life of its own; sentences and questions become figures that act independently in ways that are not always foreseeable, even by the author:

Die Namen der Umstände waren Begriffe.
Die Umstände blieben nicht stehen. Es zeigte sich,
dass sie zu Themen wurden, Themen, die handelten,
ein Schicksal hatten, eine Rolle spielten: Figuren (338).[3]

In a manner similar to the question "But will I then still love?," concepts such as rupture (*Entzweiung*) and conceptual pairs such as "right-wrong," "effect-cause," or "heart-paper" are abstracted ad infinitum. Erb's "tricks" originate in the pleasure of a "gymnastics of logical operations" (244). Even in earlier volumes, words or letters that had "preserved their own mentality" (Simpson 271) had been the springboard for associations, such as in "Meine Letteratur" (My Letterature) (*Der Faden* 27 f.).

Language for Erb has a life of its own. In a manner of speaking, it even participates in the writing of the text. Thus "the author" (*der Autor*) as supposed creator of the text is relieved of the role of authority figure. Erb allows herself to be surprised as much by ideas and associations as by the "needs" of the text, its "maturation" and "growth" (*Winkelzüge* 20, 168): "The text said it without my knowledge" (394). This receptive model for writing is indebted to intuition, to the creative mechanisms of the unconscious. The author also waives her control in the process of writing. She strives for an open relationship vis-à-vis the text.

An important feature of Erb's texts is the significance she ascribes to everyday life. The author directs her attention to the small, seemingly irrelevant, external reasons for emotional outbursts, moods, and social behavior. Here, too, her vision extends beyond emotional conditions to lay bare their premises. She depicts everyday details in an almost naturalist manner: walking along Kastanienallee (a street in East Berlin), waking up in an unfamiliar hotel room, experiencing the mood around the kitchen table, shopping. She succeeds in dissolving the distinction between "big" existential questions (happiness, death, love, aging) and profane everyday life. Her desire to "bring the claim to self-realization [*Selbstwerdung*]...down from the level of ideas and bind it to everyday existence" has been described by Ursula Heukenkamp as "anti-utopian" (364). The everyday situations Erb describes are almost always tied to traditionally female roles: those of housewife, mother, wife, lover. The "I" in the texts continuously identifies herself as a vehicle for presenting role conflicts, without placing these in the foreground. Elsewhere Erb observes that women fail to impress upon men that they should be more willing to take responsibility for other people, or even become familiar with the perspective of the victim (*Gutachten* 71-77). In some passages in *Winkelzüge,* the author describes how the mundane sphere of shopping, cooking, washing, and childcare pushes its way into the writing process. In such places, she continues, the text begins to resemble a diary. The notes remain more or less private, but they have a plaintive tone that, through the process of reflection, is again brought under control and finally overcome. The act of writing itself is seen as having a therapeutic effect. By writing of profane, everyday events, the author pushes this sphere and its related distractions away from herself. Erb resolves the creative crisis, brought on by repeated interruptions of the writing process, by making it a component of the text—a technique reminiscent of Irmtraud Morgner's montage novels.

The attempt to record her own perceptions and images as precisely as possible has thematic and aesthetic consequences for all of Erb's work: More and more, the "I" moves to the center of the texts. In her work on the volume *Kastanienallee,* Erb observes: "I don't have to take the 'I' for granted...but rather I must scout it out from place to place" (29). In the "idea...of being present in my texts and present to myself" (7), she looks for a way to keep the distance between "lived" reality and its representation in language as small as possible. Therein also lies the challenge for the reader: The "representation from an unconventional, shortened perspective...completely without descriptive additions or epic-explanatory ambitions" (Gerhard Wolf 104) demands that readers get fully involved in Erb's way of thinking.

This concept of "immediacy" borders on the limits of written representation. One of its consequences is the attempt to dissolve the linearity of thought. Already by the beginning of the 1980s, in the volume *Vexierbild* (written 1977–81, published 1983), Erb had developed a new manner of representation—the "process-oriented discussion of the subject matter" (*prozessuale Felderörterung*). In her opinion, the linear arrangement of the written line only insufficiently represents the intended simultaneity and complexity of different impressions. The author gets caught in the "difficulty of phrasing" (*Vexierbild* 105). In order to break up this linearity, she first uses spaces in the lines, paragraphs, and insertions, and finally experiments with the spatial arrangement of the entire text, something she also explains theoretically.

In the volume *Kastanienallee* (written 1981–84, published 1987), her interest shifts to looking behind the text. Her thinking process increasingly originates from the poetic text itself. Even textual weaknesses are used in order to change mental directions suddenly and to venture out into open civility/civil openness (*offene Verbindlichkeit/verbindliche Offenheit*) (*Kastanienallee* 225; *Winkelzüge* 326). Irritation becomes a principle. The author does not reject deviating from the norm (be it only a typo), but rather responds to it positively with astonishment. She transforms "a lack into a gain" (*Winkelzüge* 223). Similar to *écriture automatique,* her text unfolds between the poles of "automatic" and "strictly directed" development.

If at first Erb sets off this reflexive level from the poetic text with a level of commentary in which the author remains present in her texts, in *Winkelzüge* (written in 1983–89, published in 1991) these both become integral to the text. The confrontation between the "I" and the written text is, in fact, just as important as the text itself. The focus of the poetic act shifts from the result to the process. Using rhetorical forms such as proclamations, curses, and scoldings, Erb undertakes an analysis of obstacles to thought between anger and pleasure. Thus a new textual form comes into being where boundaries between text and essay merge: a form in which the texts can "no longer be contained within the usual unity" (41). The information about writing offered by the author has become part of the text; it expresses the search for communicative possibilities and also helps to introduce the reader to the text. The reflexive "I" moves closer to the authorial "I" that conveys information about the preconditions for and the process of writing. The goal of such an analysis of one's own texts is a "gain for the 'I'" in writing. This, though, refers to the "I" as textual authority and must be distinguished from the writing of an identity. Erb's "I" "narrates" from the moment of writing; it not only reflects and comments on the process of writing in the past, but also in the present.

Erb's justification for placing the "I" in the central position in *Winkelzüge* differs from that of other writers who explicitly reflect on the process of writing as women. Unlike most women who write first-person texts, Erb does not first gain assurance in the process of writing her "I." Her interest is not directed towards the constitution and the consolidation of the "I." Therefore, the texts in *Winkelzüge* are not inner monologues, but rather discussions, as Erb understands them, "a going from place to place, a recognizing, a looking for, a walking all over and through a place" (45).

Her comments in the following interview on the texts of younger women writers clearly show that Erb distances herself from the first-person narration of other writers. In these comments, such as one about Heike Willingham, she claims to recognize a metaphoric movement around an "integral 'I'" that she describes as having some "sustaining quality" and against which she sets her own interest. At the same time, Erb recognizes the danger of positing and presupposing the "I" in such an unproblematic manner.

Towards the end of *Winkelzüge,* life and writing are one. The process of finding oneself and the story of one's own writing are no longer separable. There is no difference between autonomy in everyday life and in writing. The connection between the "lived" and the written poem, between "life in the text" and "the text of life" (*Kastanienallee* 30), can no longer be suspended.

Regardless of her distance towards feminist positions, Erb's style has features that can be found in various texts by women: an intense self-awareness and openness in the text, the renunciation of linear language and thought, a mistrust of traditional structures in language, associative thought, the presence of the everyday in the text, and a refusal of authorial authority. All of these features can certainly be found in texts by male authors, particularly in modernist literary works. However, the presence of all of these features together is conspicuous here.

The experimental texts of Erb (as well as those of some younger women writers including Gabriele Stötzer-Kachold, Barbara Köhler, and Katja Lange-Müller) challenge the thesis of a "pre-modernist" East German literature. As an important part of the unofficially published GDR literature of the 1980s, they are "not a substitute for but an integral part of social issues such as gender and power relations," as Friederike Eigler asserts (145).

Translated by Karein Goertz

Notes

I wish to thank Karein Goertz, Sieglinde Geisel, and the editors of this volume for their intense support and enormous help.

[1] Erb uses a feminine neologism "Die Zwitterung" rather than the neuter term "das Zwittertum" to describe this state of androgyny or hermaphroditism.

[2] "Der Autor" is a male author, "Die Autorin" is a female author. Erb indicates in the interview that at the time she had not thought about the "-in" ending.

[3] The names of circumstances were concepts. / The circumstances did not stand still. It happened / that they became themes; themes that acted, / that had a destiny and played a role: figures.

Works Cited

Eigler, Friederike. "At the Margin of East Berlin's 'Counter-Culture': Elke Erb's *Winkelzüge* and Gabriele Kachold's *zügellos*." *Women in German Yearbook 9*. Ed. Jeanette Clausen and Sara Friedrichsmeyer. Lincoln: U of Nebraska P, 1993. 145–61.

Erb, Elke. *Der Faden der Geduld: Kurze Prosa, Mit einem Gespräch zwischen Christa Wolf und Elke Erb*. Berlin: Aufbau, 1978.

———. "Frauen und Kunst." *Weibblick 2* (1992): 5.

———. *Gutachten: Poesie und Prosa*. Berlin: Aufbau, 1975.

———. *Kastanienallee: Texte und Kommentare*. Berlin: Aufbau, 1987.

———. *Vexierbild*. Berlin: Aufbau, 1983.

———. "Vorwort." *Berührung ist nur eine Randerscheinung: Neue Literatur aus der DDR*. Ed. Sascha Anderson and Elke Erb. Köln: Kiepenheuer & Witsch, 1985. 11–16.

———. *Winkelzüge oder nicht vermutete, aufschlußreiche Verhältnisse*. Mit Zeichnungen von Angela Hampel. Berlin: Galrev, 1991.

———, ed. "Zwölf Jahre später: Zweites Nachwort." Sarah Kirsch. *Musik auf dem Wasser: Gedichte*. 2nd ed. Leipzig: Reclam, 1989. 136–40.

Erb, Elke, and Kerstin Hensel. *DIANA: Gespräch im Februar*. Mit Zeichnungen von Karla Woisnitza. Berlin: Kontext, 1993.

Hensel, Kerstin. *Im Schlauch: Erzählung*. Frankfurt a.M.: Suhrkamp, 1993.

Heukenkamp, Ursula. "Poetisches Subjekt und weibliche Perspektive: Zur Lyrik." *Frauen Literatur Geschichte: Schreibende Frauen vom Mittelalter bis zur Gegenwart*. Ed. Hiltrud Gnüg and Renate Möhrmann. Stuttgart: Metzler, 1985. 354–66.

Köhler, Barbara. Interview with Birgit Dahlke. 11 May 1993.

Simpson, Patricia Anne. "Die Sprache der Geduld: Produzierendes Denken bei Elke Erb." *Zwischen gestern und morgen: Schriftstellerinnen der DDR aus amerikanischer Sicht.* Ed. Ute Brandes. Berlin: Lang, 1992. 263-76.

Wolf, Christa. "Gespräch mit Elke Erb." *Die Dimension des Autors: Essays und Aufsätze, Reden und Gespräche 1959-85.* Berlin: Aufbau, 1986. 1: 175-95.

Wolf, Gerhard. "Elke Erb's Vexierblick: Ein Gutachten." *Sprachblätter: Wortwechsel. Im Dialog mit Dichtern.* Leipzig: Reclam, 1991. 104-08.

Not "Man or Woman," But Rather "What Kind of Power Structure Is This?"

Elke Erb in Conversation with Birgit Dahlke[1]

Birgit Dahlke: *I'm interested in your perspective on the role of women writers in the unofficial journal scene.*

Elke Erb: There were almost no women, but then again I can't really say anything about it because I wasn't with them. Ask Bert Papenfuß or others why they think women in the scene didn't write.

Men's opinions on this are not part of my topic. Nor is it only the "Prenzlauer Berg." There were women who wrote, maybe more on the periphery of the "scene" in Berlin, for instance, in Karl-Marx-Stadt, Leipzig, Erfurt...

What do you mean by "on the periphery"? Kerstin Hensel, for example, is herself a center. I wouldn't talk about the periphery there. Barbara Köhler's tongue only loosened up later on. Then there's one, Heike Willingham. Recently, at a reading on Gerhard Wolf's birthday, I thought how amazing it is that one of us could already have been so successful in the West. It's a kind of further development of conventional literature.... With Kerstin Hensel it's not possible to say such a thing, neither theoretically nor directly, although she does ask: So, what was going on there in the Prenzlauer Berg anyway? What did I miss there? She tends to stick with Karl Mickel's poetic structure. Then there are a lot of tricks... It's strange that in some of the texts one feels that a bit of the old codes are "scrubbed away," and in others not. That's strange.

How do you pin down these differences?

That's hard to describe. What first comes to mind is an inadequate word, democratization, a word that will have to do. Heike uses metaphorical fish, forms that fly in the air, doesn't she? "I" metaphors. The goal is not to improve or correct the given circumstances. That is basically parasitic. She makes use of what she puts in. It's very difficult for me to pinpoint the transitions.

For many of the women writers I have asked, you are the only older poet they mention as an important point of reference and as a mentor of sorts.

Mentor—that's going too far: It's written in all of the articles. Not to be taken seriously. Nothing is true about that! Were you a part of it? How would you know about it?

Wait a minute, I simply asked the younger ones about traditions and important writers, and almost all of them mentioned your name exclusively.

It's not uncommon that someone makes you out to be an ideal so that they can secure their own shrine. And that with me, who never had a shrine anywhere for myself.

I do understand what you're resisting: this cliché of being the mother of the "scene." At first, I did not in the least intend to include your texts in my work. I just wanted to focus on my own generation. However, at some point, all of the conversations turned to your texts....

If it's like that, then I'll have to concede a bit.

It certainly has to do with the fact that your texts represent a particular inspiration for writers...

Are you sure?

The women writers talk about the texts and not about the person.

Until now, I haven't come across any writers who would have said that, except for the Swiss writer Ilma Rakusa, whom I simply have to believe when she says that she was inspired. Just as Friederike Mayröcker constantly inspires me because she always changes, varies, entices. I actually have more the feeling that I have readers than that people are inspired by me in their writing. When people tell me that they like to read my work, then I immediately understand it. While writing, I have never considered the other perspective (that readers might be inspired by me when they write), but obviously such a perspective exists. The way I write is also to confirm the existence of another level of being. Particularly, by the way, in early texts until 1980. It's interesting, isn't it? Where I believe I've made a lasting impression in communicating contexts is in the texts before the reforms, that is, in *Gutachten* and *Faden der Geduld*. This effect was often long-lasting. So when a woman tells me after seventeen years that she is still haunted by a text from my earlier work... That's already pretty good. Such an effect can't necessarily be multiplied, but I do have such readers, men and women, in both parts of Germany.

Since you just made a distinction between male and female readers, I do have to ask another question: I'm curious why you always refer to "the author" as male in Winkelzüge. *Is it an intentional rejection of the feminist insistence on the use of the feminine form? Or do you mean both sexes?*

No. At that time, I hadn't thought about this feminine ("-in") ending, I didn't pay any attention to it. Too bad that it doesn't work the other way around, that you begin with the feminine ending. If it's so that the masculine form is applied to everything, then men no longer have it at their disposal as a masculine form. There's no agreement about this. We're told to go back now, as if there were no third form. In any case, I believe that the decisive question in the GDR was not man or woman, but rather: What kind of power structure is this? What is wrong with the body politic? Then you are more likely to come up against a hierarchical order, and it subjugates both sexes.

Yet I do recognize a distinctly female "I" in Winkelzüge...

Yes, of course. Even earlier. Naturally. But that doesn't mean that... I did, incidentally, discover something and even wrote it down in a text that begins with the form of address "Dear women"...

It was published in Weibblick. *I'm familiar with it.*

I discovered that, when it comes to important issues in certain areas, women have always been the only ones who counted for me. I'm not only referring to events among writers, but, in general, whenever something was going on, I oriented myself towards women. For example, I had only a short time to get to know the Georgian Soviet Socialist Republic. Later, in Berlin, I realized that on the buses, for example, I had only been looking into the eyes of women in order to get a feeling for the country...

What I mean is that you want to love and be loved. Then when you realize that you aren't really concerned with the men... What is essentially going on here is precisely what women complain about: that men always count only on each other. Perhaps one could give some thought to the following: Is it really so difficult to understand that people quite naturally orient themselves by association with others like themselves?

Do you really think it's like that?

In any case, it's an aspect that is not taken into consideration. Just the burdens everyone has to deal with. For example, a generational conflict can't last when parents are so preoccupied with themselves. I saw it in the publishing houses in the 1980s among editors and mid-level cultural functionaries in connection with the introduction of the literature of the younger generation. For the following reason I told myself that this was not a generational conflict: What should these editors do? They have to defend their manuscripts against some bigwigs who are dumber than they are, who are their superiors, and whose heads are filled with cultural politics, the phrases, the directives—that is quite enough. Anything beyond that was simply not understood, it was outside of any area of conflict, no one would touch it, so consequently no conflict could begin.

On top of all that, the literary or artistic avant-garde wasn't very aggressive. A change took place. At first, in the beginning of the 80s, the young generation followed a code of opposition but later gave it up. I remember it precisely. First, they talked about "cops," but later that kind of talk completely disppeared. It happened intentionally.

In your preface to the Berührung *anthology you found yourself in the position of mediator between the generations. You were trying to explain the social and political context of these unfamiliar texts.*

Of course. I categorized them, but that didn't cause a conflict. By the way, that was also quite controversial.

What?

The lack of conflict. For us, that was an unsuitable concept.

Who is meant by "us"?

The GDR.

In this precise and insistent preface I notice that you hardly make reference to any of the women.

Really? There are three... For Conny Schleime, it's not the main issue; she deflects any close examination of her artistic works. Then Gabriele Stötzer-Kachold and...Katja Lange. No, there are four of them. They are not pivotal. There are others who handle the working motifs in a better way.

Gabriele Stötzer-Kachold's text is conspicuous in its own way...

I'm not keeping statistics on how often a particular topic comes up.

I'm not referring to the themes of her work.

If you mean stylistically, then she is quite conservative. She makes no innovative movements, she doesn't dare to, she goes backwards...

In what way does she go backwards?

She presents some kind of harsh contradictions and then goes backwards. She doesn't draw any conclusion. It's as if she wanted to preserve the conflicts.

She conducts herself differently, not like a traditional author... However, what she brings to her text in terms of expression and tone is, in my opinion, quite original. Okay, she discusses all aspects of gender identity, and that is something original and something I consider important in this anthology, particularly for the GDR.

Yes, well then you have a kind of existential catalogue and not one that emphasizes a way of seeing. That is something else.

Why, then, did you include her in the anthology?

Because she belongs to it. I have to refresh my memory a bit now. She did contribute some innovative texts to the anthology. She broke them up. They had a better chance... There are also texts that show her to be one who doesn't constantly talk about orgasm. The way I represent her, she is a working writer, not a guru.

The texts by Gabriele Stötzer-Kachhold that are printed in the anthology have been incorrectly condensed. They are actually three separate...

Don't tell me you have the edition with the many printing errors! It happened twenty-seven times that texts that don't belong together were printed together. What a brilliant performance! And we believed that everything was okay in the West, that we could depend on everything. The know-it-alls even threw out some texts without asking us, amateurishly, since they confused typos with innovative poetry.

In some texts, however, it is hard to tell...

No, absolutely not. Even in the case of Tohm di Roes. You just have to get it. Unfortunately we didn't include reading instructions. I even had inhibitions myself, inherited from the intimidating presence of the avant-garde movement in the 60s.

Was the Prenzlauer Berg, as you see it, the Eastern version of Western avant-garde poetry?

No, not at all. I would always challenge that view. There is no resemblance between the attitudes of Franz Mon, for example, and the language-transforming texts of the "princes" of the Prenzlauer-Berg. I don't know how they're even related. It's very hard to find a link. To constantly claim that they are making up for something, that's a claim that can only be made by people who have never undertaken such a step, who have never grasped what it means, who say "Jandl" to anything that is even slightly different. They never understood it, but have long since put it behind themselves with "cool."

Let's return again to the younger women writers. Could you describe your reservations more precisely?

I'm still very careful.... You know, I often see how such a vase or fish form comes into being. A kind of integral "I"... Yet it's not only about conserving. It's about living, also about destroying, undermining, doing something for the good of something else. It's about ringing bells, not about sustaining. It seems to me that Heike Willingham, for example, has no idea about these things.

Whereas Heike Willingham posits an "I" with ease, you can't say that about Stötzer-Kachold. She problematizes the "I." So does Barbara Köhler...

That's not what I mean, rather, what kind of image is evoked, what is interesting about this image, and how the words sound. A kind of vase form emerges, but now I'm only talking about Heike. It was that way with Barbara in the beginning. I know it has something to do with amateurism... In any case, it's easier to begin that way.

It is striking that it's precisely women who can't easily say "I" in their texts...

That concurs with what I'm saying. Always these vase forms, streamlined...

Also in your work, in Winkelzüge, *I notice this proximity between the textual "I," the reflexive "I," and the writing "I."*

I use this "I" ruthlessly. When I say "I," then no one can contest the fact that *I* saw that, that *I* believe that, etc. This "I" is indisputable, just like that stone lying there is indisputable... Yet I don't know if that is always the case.

Would you agree that there is a great proximity between the author and the "I" in the text?

It is, of course, considered a social weakness if one doesn't depict the "I" as a figure with several layers...that is asocial: an "I" is not a stone. I am the witness to the things I say. I am the black box. I can use myself for any purpose. It is a kind of "I" without an "I." It is rendered functional, but not elaborated on. The "I" is not the main issue.

You use the "I," but it is not the main issue. Is it taken for granted? Could it have something to do with the fact that hardly anyone asks you about your gender as a writer? Or do people ask you that? Kerstin Hensel, for example, often gets asked. She reacts with frustration because the question doesn't interest her...

No, I don't get asked. But then again I don't shred (*rumfetzen*) things like Kerstin does. Otherwise people would rightfully ask me about my connection to the big shredder, namely feminism. For example, her book about moving into an apartment (*Im Schlauch*) gets very close to this feminist shredding.

What do you mean by that?

Shredding? When you push aside what's right in front of you and plunk down truths like: "It was getting moldy," "it stank," "then I first did that"... It is Kerstin's latest volume and it's very interesting. One should analyze its attitude towards feminism. One should compare how feminist texts open up a subject and how she does it. What I mean by "shredding" is to open up a text, to read it against the grain—that is what I call shredding.

What makes that feminist?

Women writers do this also, Stötzer-Kachold, for example. They relate something completely different from the official text. Also in terms of content, they often talk about "shreds." Shredding (*fetzen*) does have two meanings: to tear something apart and rags or ragged... By the way, I never do that. For example, I never write "the Truth." I never get myself involved in adventures of that sort where reality shines through, as one so nicely puts it.

There are passages in Winkelzüge, *however, where you describe precisely what you are doing, almost like a diary: "I go down to the greengrocer's and shop..."*

That's different. Whenever people present their own text, they shred something off. Women often adopt child-talk when they are describing childhood, even if they are over fifty. This baby-talk is really hard to take. It's a form that eases and cushions this shredding. Hold on, it's so difficult to talk about these things because they are impressions... It always makes me angry when I encounter this tone.

But there's also something liberating about it.

It doesn't happen to me that I free myself from something, let go of something, get something off my chest.

But you do! There are passages like that in Winkelzüge.

But that's not true for the text in general!

You're right. But there are such passages in it and that is interesting. There's a completely different attitude there.

What determines the text in *Winkelzüge* is that different elements are brought together. It is not driven by an inner monologue or such. It doesn't have that. Its character is really that of an orderly discussion, moving from one point to the next.

But it also has something of liberation and anger...

Yes, anger. But the anger is very contained within a theme. *Winkelzüge* has a theme, doesn't it? It really deals with the following: What aspects of culture already existed in my subconscious? What exists in a human being of the willingness to achieve, of culture, goodwill, ability, sweetness, grace, and also intelligence? What gets obscured by the surface level at which society engages the individual as a human being? Below this surface there is still anger and unrest. I can spontaneously say one sentence that bears with it a realization. Months later I can utter a second one. Why couldn't I immediately continue on to the second one when I said the first one? Put differently, it would be a complaint about my inability to move forward. That could have become a genuine lament.

Then there are occasional discoveries that literally lead the text onward. Now and then there is always the question: What? How did I move from one discovery to the next? What is this? What are we doing? Again and again there is a series of curses and scoldings. Why am I so eager whenever it comes to something negative? Why don't I finally move on to something other than that?

Have you made it a ritual?

No. I use rhetorical forms, if that's what you mean. I haven't ritualized it, but I use ritual forms. The grand exclamation, for example, as a rhetorical form also used in poems, is something I did not make use of earlier on, before *Winkelzüge*. Of course, it also has to do with my desire to get back at this "they," this enemy, this invisible entity, to do a number on them with a text. That is true revenge. I'll give it to them over and over again. When I think about this book, then I remember these outbursts of anger. Exclamations like "Bewußtsein," rather than "Bewußtsein."[2] Or "the dragon of the public at large demands of you..."

Is that directed or undirected?

Undirected? Undirected anger? That's a bit tricky. We don't speak about liberation for nothing. I wouldn't even know where such undirected anger could go, there can hardly be such a thing as undirected anger. A real undirected anger would be one that is completely off the subject. Such lack of restraint doesn't exist. You're surrounded by inhibitions. With these rhetorical forms I raise myself to a level of power and control, don't I?

And then you play with them, too.

I play with them in the sense that they don't necessarily have this backdrop rhetoric of power and control. I play with the other side, with "O" proclamations, with Dionysian torrents of words... Then again the punishing father, the act of defining: "That is so, that is so," "you sinner." But this confrontational aspect did come to an end. It happened quite automatically, without my having done it consciously. In *Winkelzüge* the points of opposition resolve themselves. It is quite obvious.

Is it the confrontational attitude that bothers you in the texts of the younger women?

No. It is, rather, their lack of attention to what is confrontational, an unexamined ignorance of the different fronts... To some degree, it is intentional. Gabriele Stötzer-Kachold, for example, deliberately sets herself apart. And continuously writes clever things.

In connection with the Berührung *anthology, you often explained and made the male authors aware of their own poetics...*

No, no, I asked them and took what they told me...

But it was the question that first got them to reflect on the process of writing.

This is how it was: They were unfamiliar texts and somewhat of a mystery to me. At one point I began to poke around with my questions and then it all came out. I was downright amazed. There were many explanations behind their texts. I remember that I once reproached Leonard Lorek that his rows of the word "and" and his babytalk lacked form, as if he knew nothing about structure. Horse-trading. In response to my reproach he came up with such an excellent explanation that I agreed with him and no longer knew what I had actually wanted from him. That is typical for me, by the way: I let stand whatever comes up, there is no hierarchy. It is also a weakness that I then forget my own objection.

Could your lesser interest in women writers have something to do with the fact that they do not offer such explanations of their work?

Lesser interest? Hm... It is true that I never heard such poetic explanations from them. They are not as aggressive in that respect. It's impossible that a woman would begin speaking like Sascha Anderson. And I also mean that as a reproach. Where have they been, why don't they get started? The only one, really, is Conny Schleime with her directive statements. The others...therefore: Ask the men who were with them what those women who didn't write were doing. I don't know what they were doing.

At one point in the journal Schaden *there were the beginnings of a discussion on female writing. Heike Willingham said you wrote a text for it that was never completed.*

I also can't remember it. I was surprised that Sarah Kirsch and others reacted in such a way, but then again I thought it was quite okay. I didn't know what to do with it, others obviously did. It's comforting to know that a text can branch out elsewhere and develop, even when I don't see how.

Did you actually approach the authors in the "scene" or did they come to you?

It was really easy. It started with the anthology. Within half a year I had thirty people here, try to image that... That meant, every time a bottle of wine and so on.

Who initiated it? Sascha or someone else?

No, the publishing house. The editor was here. He was first at Martin Hoffmann's, and then Hoffmann sent him over to me. I thought to myself that I already had a publishing house, but then there were also these young people. All of this was going on after the anthology had been rejected by the Akademie der Künste. Then I began to talk about it. The editor said they would only publish prose. So I thought, well okay, then we have to shape it all so that it has a kind of framework. Sascha had accumulated manuscripts, and so it went on from there. If I had had more time, I would have gone right ahead and put together a second volume. That was from August to February. For many of the young people at the time, it was quite new to be speaking with someone like me. I noticed that. They were amazed by the response they were suddenly getting. When they were among themselves, of course, it wasn't that way. That had something to do with the mixture of acceptance and a school logic they had left behind that wasn't worth anything anymore. It must've been fascinating since they hadn't always been so conscious of the fact that they wanted to abandon logic.

When you speak of linguistic criticism in this period, you often use "we." Did your own thinking and that of the younger generation come closer to each other at the time?

Of course there were major differences, but not on critical points. That was the crazy thing. For example, I started thinking about symbols—the number two, the number one. Then someone appeared on the scene, his name was Karsten Behlert, he was 21, and he used the number seven as the heroine of the text, as the big thing in the text. There you can already refer to a "we." It's just that for me it came from a completely different source. It was as if life was bringing forth the very things that had taken place inside of me through thought... For me, however, thought had to overcome obstacles. For them, this was obviously not the case.

That was also a generational difference.

Yes. I still remember that certain old figures and old ways of thinking in new texts made me sick. That has let up now, but when you go off and start up a tiny new thing, then you get extremely sensitive. The old is like poison, really.

Only you always remained willing to engage in conversation with the "old" side, for example, in the interview with Christa Wolf...

The innovative phase came later...

But for GDR standards, what you were doing at the time was also something completely new and unfamiliar.

I was equally willing to converse with the old and with the young. There were certain laws according to which one had to operate. At the time, it had to do with the afterword in a new volume of mine. There had been a meeting of authors at Erich Arendt's earlier on where I had read a text by Marina Tsvetaeva. Christa Wolf asked me when the text was going to be published, with such a sparkle in her eye that I believed there was something that connected us and so I asked where we could meet. That's how the discussion got to be the afterword to the book. The reception of this discussion was very lively; perhaps not lively, but rather quiet, yet thorough. It was interpreted in two ways; some thought that I was providing the answers, others thought that Christa was prevailing. Strange.

From today's perspective, it seems to me rather that Christa Wolf did not have much of a grasp on the material. She was receptive, but the discussion actually resulted in a major misunderstanding.

Now you have to explain to me why so many people saw this as "Well, finally we have a discussion." You say, "They're talking past each other." You have to explain to me what that means....

Did you feel closer to the younger generation than to your own?

If you want to put it that way, I never felt close to anyone. What do you mean by closer? What the older generation didn't give me in terms of the human, personal, etc., the younger one didn't give me either. Yet among them there was at least an answer to this misunderstanding among the living. You could say that there was at least one step in the right direction. I don't know; it is very, very difficult to say. I do have the impression that the older generation was and still is more "up-tight," but that could be my own failure to see things correctly. I had a certain criterion in *Winkelzüge*: our images of puberty, again, of course, those of women. For myself and also for others of my generation, there is always a phase of "self-obscuration" roughly between the ages of fourteen and seventeen. Later, the younger ones were more free, they no longer imitated the adults. You can see that on photos, unbelievable. This whole aspect of feeling embarrassed, awkward, and, at the same time, trying to make a big impression, that was still my generation....

Why do you say "again, of course, those of women." Did I understand that correctly?

Because, actually, I paid no attention to it in men and don't have a clue about it. Isn't that horrible? That was what I discovered that time in the Georgian Republic: that I seem to orient myself towards women, that I do exactly what women reproach men for doing. Although that's probably not the case at all. Perhaps men think much more in terms of women than women do in terms of men. What do you think?

I do think that men always serve as a model for me, even though I want to avoid it.

When they become politicians, then they don't have a bit of woman left in them. They completely adapt themselves to the man-to-man routine.

But we as women do that too.

How so? You can feel what you are as a living being: your background, what you've seen in life, your own response, your field of perception—these are all things you can't even know about in a man! So naturally you start out from your own gender. I can't image anyone being so clever as to observe and find out something about the other. I haven't yet been so clever in my life. I would like to be.

Not really. We adopt standards without realizing that they are male standards and that there is very little of us in them.

All right, but I don't consider this standard to be masculine, but rather hierarchical....

Didn't many of the women writers of "Prenzlauer Berg" need the recognition of men to consider their work good and worthy of publication? Whereas, the other way around, the opinion of women was hardly of any significance?

That is true. Women probably write in a less self-congratulatory way. There might even be something slightly parasitic about that on the part of women, when they demand that their texts be approved. Writers like Gabriele Stötzer-Kachold wanted someone from the outside to show them what was missing in their texts. That is a parasitic relationship that certainly corresponds to gender roles. Women are raised that way: the helpless one, incomplete without the man. That's one side of it, not all of it.

Whereby, of course, most of the male writers in the "scene" won your support by explaining their work. Gabi Stötzer-Kachold never attempted to do so in such a manner... To this day, she has not gained your recognition.

She should first have her own opinions on her texts. It's not going to work *that* way. Another victory for male self-confidence, to the point of obnoxiousness (*Großkotzigkeit*).

Gabi's mistake is not her lack of obstreperousness. And to your comment about the explanations—that they won me over with their explanations—that is false.

Gabi is not independent. But it is precisely the struggle for independence that women in a male-dominated society must continually wage. Male self-confidence and female insecurity are two sides of the same coin. Obnoxiousness is not a very charming term, but apparently quite a few men have simply and without question taken themselves as great poets, regardless of their actual poetic originality...

Perhaps women have to do that, too.

Perhaps women can't do it as often. And it is not only an issue of individual personality.

The conditions for it vary. I once saw it in Droste-Hülshoff. She had a weak father, a strong mother, and next to that a large extended family headed by a grandmother. In my case, my father was in the war and, on top of that, we lived in the country without any relatives around. I did not experience all of the infrastructure conflicts, the way they subjugate and conquer each other, so I can freely go anywhere.

You don't have a brother, do you? Sisters?

Two sisters. It also suits me, not to be spoiled by ignorance. By spoiled I mean not being subservient. Of course, otherwise I am...but concealed. I once discovered that I am afraid of stating my own opinions. All at once it became clear to me. I would never have thought so.

When was that?

It began with Hans Arp. Sometime in the 80s there was a call for submissions for an anniversary volume. From the very beginning, in the new study of Arp, I thought, no, they're not seeing it right.... When it came to an important text in the cycle, I thought to myself, if they read this now, it'll knock them out. And that's precisely the one I took out, without noticing it, although I renumbered everything. That was complicated and irritating.

Who were "they?"

Those who held the majority opinion about Arp. That was perhaps the first time that my standing up against something had such a direct effect. When you're working on something you don't just attain a level that extends into other dimensions and also touches on the social sphere. You're working from down low, with the responses of an animal-like sense of orientation. Who knows what's even produced in old age in direct opposition to fear and subjugation.

When I read the preface to your 1985 anthology, I had the impression you wanted to explain what was going on in the country. You wanted to call out, "Stop!"

Well, yes, I did bring out a few things about the communal system. When you wake up and say, "This is how things fit together," you're not talking with the society at large, but rather with the being inside of yourself that had not yet become aware of it. Somehow, the human being is always a kind of age-old over-cooked egg (*so ein abgekochtes Ei aus Jahrhunderten*) and has no clue, or thinks everything is quite normal;

that's very strange. It is difficult to accept the structures in oneself. I wasn't able to talk about the conditions underlying GDR thought before. When you're the object, you can't simultaneously be the subject....

You also mention your own separation from the structures of "GDR thought."

Until the very end, in *Winkelzüge,* I still discovered some of these old structures in me. There are several phases. I try to get a handle on them whenever I get to the word "consciousness." It is actually marginal, not central, but in this book the peripheral actually fosters the main idea. The theme of rupture and reconciliation, for example, surfaces only on the margins. It can only appear where it is not itself the theme. That's where it asserts itself and that is how consciousness continues to surface at certain points. It has to be at the end, where I ask, "When will I finally begin to understand consciousness as a matter of temperament?" I realize with horror that I'm still comparing consciousness with the way the state forms society, the state as consciousness. Although that frightens me, I tell myself that this is not surprising, where else should it come from? Many things in life are dependent upon what you encounter. That was in 1988-89.

That is why Winkelzüge *is not only meaningful for writers, but also for people who have experienced and are experiencing a similar separation process from their own encrusted structures of thought. The fascinating aspect of your texts is precisely that you undergo this separation process in such a conscious manner....*

Well, I do insist that I arrive with no less than elephants and trumpets, that at least! With hoopla. With much ado (*Gedöhns*), as they say in the Rheinland. After a while...I gained more of a voice, even more rhetorical language.

Tell me, the question "But will I then still love?" as the point of departure for Winkelzüge *is a very female question, isn't it? I can't imagine a man beginning his poetic enterprise with such a "personal" question.*

That's true, it's really hard to imagine that. For women, this question is a very existential one—very close, unspeakably close, underneath that which is spoken. It is still only under the skin, but there it is widespread. "Is that still even possible? Will I ever again, once more...?" There is, of course, also something nicely rebellious about adding this delicate element.

For me, there's an interesting contradiction: On the one hand, hardly anyone would at first glance classify your writing as "feminine writing"—

you yourself irritably reject such a label; on the other hand, it is precisely in your texts that I discover several aspects that I would describe as characteristic of feminine writing.

It's got to be that way if, indeed, I do orient myself to women when it gets serious. Perhaps I deal with men as if they were women. I'm not sure. It's not as if I exclude them. Yet perhaps I do in terms of the specifically masculine... That's not very clever! And I don't do it with those who are able to understand us as female beings. That's stupid! It's socialization.

How could you understand them as male beings?

Well, cannibalistically, guzzling and nibbling, like they do! But that's the first thing that comes to mind with that question. Why doesn't one go any further?

Some of the passages in Winkelzüge *reveal very traditional images of women, though. In the diary-like parts, when you talk about pillow covers, for example.*

I am the father. What would be an untraditional role? If you remember the household passages, that's where I think my kingdom is, that's where I'm free. It is completely woman's traditional role: I am now what my mother was then. Of course it also means taking control: I am the master in my kingdom. No father exists.

The intensity of self-awareness in your texts is probably also feminine, isn't it?

Maybe not feminine, but rather a form that came into being through androgyny. I do it with the existing, therefore probably male-determined forms. I use the forms provocatively, teasingly, playfully.

Does that mean you use them as if you were a man?

It's like the second level of working through something. The first level would be: you are a man, you are someone who counts. (Sociologically speaking, these are almost the same thing for me.) The second level is: you aren't a man, so you can play freely with the forms, you can be as open as you wish. This shredding that I mentioned earlier acts as if it, the shredding itself, knew that it were so open. I don't know exactly, but one must treat the subject at one's leisure and let things build up. There's a lot of rebellious spirit in it, that I know.

Hm. I've often wondered, how you could manage, for over a decade, as the only recognized woman writer in the "scene." It probably also has something to do with the generational difference, but...

The only recognized woman? Wait a minute, where were the others? Sarah Kirsch wasn't there... It was also the case that they drew a person in. Some of them addressed the older generation and went over to Volker Braun, to Heiner Müller.

Do you see women writers today who play with (male) language in the way you describe it?

You know, I actually don't like to hear language described as male. I just described it that way, too, but... I really prefer to say the "traditional," "existing," or "dominant" language, in order to bring in the element of power and control. There are many women who are struggling intensely with this, Ilma Rakusa and Elfriede Czurda, for example. In fact, all of the women who are writing. The most conscious, unconsciously the most conscious, examine language critically. But one would have to say the same for men, wouldn't one?

Don't you think there are differences?

I always had the impression that there was a big difference between Friederike Mayröcker and Ernst Jandl, for example. But, you know, it's very difficult to explain. It's not easy to compare them. She undertakes something completely new and follows through with great consistency, one thing is the result of another. When she reads, she doesn't force me in any way. I like that. Also, the whole thing that she creates doesn't fit into any kind of theory. More features of different ways of being are included, though without leaving the "keyboard."[3] That's opposition.

Maybe it's impossible to leave this "keyboard," as you put it.

It's not necessary. Where else should she go? On the other hand, people criticize her poems for being "made texts" (*Poesilien*).[4] I don't think it's so. I think she uses collective symbols in a truly radical way. Collective directives or a collective inventory of symbols have accumulated in the subconscious. This is evident, for example, in the fairly similar ways people behave when they gesticulate. What she does there is incredible. I've learned to read it somewhat, always tentatively. It makes no sense to start somewhere in her work and to break it down, because everything is always immediately there. There she's really a queen, she masters it all. I don't know how it happens. Why is she so strong? Maybe she thought it had to be that way and so then she did it, uninhibited, uninhibited as a woman. A totality, something encompassing, is also present in women. I discovered that in relation to the word "completeness" (*Lückenlosigkeit*) since it's connected to totality, the total taking over of everything. When you raise a child, you have to raise it completely, you can't skip any part.

That is something men don't have to do, they don't have any real experience with it.

Do you think women carry more totalitarian aspects within them than men?

I don't know if you can call them "totalitarian," but I enjoy making this unconventional connection... Moving towards something total, which also means losing inhibitions. In Friederike Mayröcker's work, for example, any kind of inhibition is like a key on the keyboard, it is everything you run into. There, where she grasps, steals, and takes something for herself, I think you could say she exhibits a trait one might call masculine. It's strange what happens to me when I read her work, how I react: "But she can't do that, that's none of her business. Why does she talk about flowers, they're none of her business, they're not hers." That's how I discover my own restraint towards taking possession of things. Perhaps there's a difference between appropriating the masculine form and having reservations vis-à-vis this form... I can't describe it precisely. It's annoying always referring to it as masculine.

Translated by Karein Goertz

Notes

[1] The interview was conducted in Berlin on 25 October 1993.

[2] Erb takes the word "*Bewußtsein*" (consciousness) and creates a neologism "*Bewußtstein*" (conscious+stone) that might translate as "the consciousness of a stone."

[3] Erb used the word "*Klaviatur,*" meaning "the totality of all keys that are used for playing."

[4] Erb's neologism "*Poesilien*" from the word "*Poesie*" brings to mind the word "*Textilien*" (textile) from "*Text*" (text). Thus perhaps "*Poesilien*" might translate as "having the quality of something made" as "*Textilien*" means "having the quality of something woven."

Erotic Provocations:
Gabriele Stötzer-Kachold's Reclaiming of the Female Body?

Beth Linklater

The article examines constructions of the sexual in some writings by Gabriele Stötzer-Kachold, specifically through an analysis of the author's attempt to reclaim the derogatory term *Votze*. This aspect of Stötzer-Kachold's art is contextualized with reference to the general reception of her work as authentic autobiography, the notion of the sexual as taboo in GDR literature, and more general issues of feminism and feminist theories. Such a contextualization recognizes the importance of this author's feminist writing, while also evidencing the difficulties involved in such a project of revision and redefinition. (BL)

wenn wir frauen uns nun lauter unanständige sachen sagen und das unanständige ganz normal also fast moral wird wozu ist die anständigkeit da?—Gabriele Stötzer-Kachold (*grenzen* 79)[1]

"My cunt energy" (*votzenenergie*), writes Gabriele Stötzer-Kachold "is my starting point" (*tag sonnentag*). This emphatic statement is representative of much of the young artist's work: it not only draws attention to the female body, it also provokes, challenges, and shocks. Stötzer-Kachold defies cultural stereotypes of benign, passive femininity, while questioning the associations between female sexual language and the language of patriarchal insult. Erotic ideas and images are not simply a means of titillation in her work. Nor can they be neatly categorized as GDR critique; for Stötzer-Kachold, in the words of Ricarda Schmidt, "the antagonism between *Volk* and *Macht* is a given of GDR reality" (160). One cannot, as Thomas Jung does, blithely equate her "drive for artistic production"—which he regards as a result of her experiences of state repression—with "sexual drives," repressed in the Freudian sense (18). Stötzer-Kachold's eroticism has a much wider political purpose—a feminist purpose. She uses her art to condemn patriarchy, wherever it may occur, and to suggest utopian alternatives.

In this article I shall explore Stötzer-Kachold's literary reclaiming of the female body, whereby I concentrate upon her appropriation of the term *Votze,* which she uses both positively as a source of energy and negatively as a reflection of the male voice that she condemns. At the same time, she is well aware that the attempt to invest such an "offensive" concept with aesthetic value is an extremely provocative gesture. In order to contextualize this aspect of the author's work, I begin with a description of the general reception of her writing. I will then offer a short analysis of the role of the sexual in her prose, both as subject matter and in terms of form. In particular, I shall relate this utilization of sexuality to Stötzer-Kachold's feminism.

Authentic Autobiography? Readings of Stötzer-Kachold's Work

Gabriele Stötzer-Kachold is the young woman who appears in Christa Wolf's *Was bleibt* (Paul 127, note 21). Wolf describes the poetry of the less well-known writer as "true" (76). Gerhard Wolf, Christa Wolf's husband and Stötzer-Kachold's editor, similarly praises the "frankness" of the latter's texts, which he characterizes as "authentic portraits" (157). Following this lead, many critics have noted the *genuine* nature of Stötzer-Kachold's ostensibly transparent writing. "Since the publication of *zügel los* no discussion of authenticity can avoid mention of the name Gabriele Stötzer-Kachold," claims, for example, Dorothea von Törne (14). The word "honest" features in Elisabeth Wesuls's title, and Annette Meusinger similarly talks of "uncompromising authenticity and truthfulness" (372). Stötzer-Kachold's art is thus generally labelled as "authentic," a label that is often justified with reference to her biography. She is, for many, first and foremost a GDR author, and her writing is therefore, seemingly automatically, "GDR literature *par excellence*" (Böck 156). Some critics ignore the author's work altogether, concentrating instead on her experiences in the GDR, notably that of imprisonment, or even her appearance. As Stötzer-Kachold herself laments, "they marginalize me as something exotic, and that means I'm out of the literary scene" (Dahlke, "Ich-Figur" 258).

The process of effectively ignoring a writer's work by concentrating instead on his or her life is one with which students of GDR literature are familiar. We need look no further than the defamation of Christa Wolf after the revelations surrounding her *Stasi* connections for confirmation of this. Indeed the entire *Literaturstreit* had more to do with artists than with their art, as Wolfgang Emmerich contends: "Paradoxically, literature itself is rarely mentioned (its producers, on the other hand, are discussed correspondingly more frequently). The debate was hardly ever about the texts as texts, that is, as 'aesthetic representations'" (8). This exemplifies to an extreme degree a more widespread tendency in literary reception. In asking "What is an Author?" Michel Foucault shows how modern

Western society has created a cult figure, whose name is not just another element in cultural discourse, but has a specific function in modern society, as guarantor of authenticity, of status, of classification, of limitation, and of publicity value. Despite Roland Barthes's announcements of "the death of the author," the business of recreating him or her would seem to be very much alive. As Sigrid Weigel writes of the West German literary industry: "When, for once, a female author was accepted into the canon, curiosity about her personality (and about her private life) dominated interest in her literature" (314).

The emphasis Weigel places upon the way in which the issue is gendered is important. Focusing upon their personal lives creates an image that keeps female artists within the supposedly private sphere that is traditionally women's own. Anna Kuhn, for example, has made a strong case for seeing the Christa Wolf controversy in similarly gendered terms. She argues that the journalists' aggression is directed both against "the East's pre-eminent *writer,*" and against "the writer as *woman*" (215). In her opinion the media attacks against Wolf functioned "*ad feminam*" (207). Media constructions of Stötzer-Kachold similarly concentrate on her person and on her identity as female, a construction that is then elided with her art.

The use of labels such as "honest" and "true" to describe Stötzer-Kachold's writing can, in part, be justified. Many of her texts are intense, intimate, and emotional, thematizing pain, anger, fear, hatred, and love. However, terms such as "authentic" have to be treated with skepticism, for they are not unequivocally applicable to fiction, which, of course, has been edited, reworked, or simply invented. In particular, to equate the female body with "authenticity" is to ignore the discursive creation of what Birgit Dahlke terms the "facile formula woman = sensuality" (*Bilder* 176). Foucault's demonstration of how the body is constructed in modern society began a radical questioning of the assumption that anatomy is "natural." The female form cannot enjoy an unmediated relationship to nature and neither can literature simply reflect a given "reality." Statements that glibly unite fiction with reality fail to take proper account of the system within which literature is produced and received.

Relating Stötzer-Kachold's texts to her biography is also one obvious way to approach writing that is so intricately bound up with the body, writing in which the word "ich" dominates, writing that we are told by the editor comes from a diary, writing that does indeed thematize prison experiences, *Stasi* experiences, and so on. Particularly in *grenzen los fremd gehen*, the author states openly and constantly that she is writing her self: "ich habe nur eine geschichte aufzuschreiben / und die bin ich" (*grenzen* 94).[2] However, characterization of Stötzer-Kachold's work as pure autobiography is again too simplistic. In terms of content such a label ignores the wider appeal of her work, the "fundamental issues of so-called modern civilisation" (Althammer). This more general relevance is what is important if texts from the former GDR are to survive, their *Ersatzfunktion* now an anachronism.

Stylistically, the category autobiography suggests a linear narrative involving development of a character to a point from which he or she can recount personal history. In Stötzer-Kachold's prose there is on the whole no telos of a chronological story, no development of character, no one narrator, no one addressee. Her best texts refuse to situate meaning and instead remain open, deliberately exploiting the "lack of aesthetic closure" with which Dahlke credits many of the "unofficial" texts written by women ("Im Brunnen" 180). In texts such as "der wecker ist geklungen" (*zügel los* 7-9), "an treiben" (*zügel los* 17-19), or "die sexfigur" (*roulette* 106-07), the word "ich," the foundation of any autobiography, is open and fragmented, the self is split and becomes ambiguous. Much of Stötzer-Kachold's prose is concerned with "this splitting of my inwardness" (*zügel los* 30), a search for a subject or subjects, a self or selves, rather than discovery or certainty. This search takes place through language, through analysis of personal experiences, through deconstruction of social and cultural images, and within the body. As Eigler contends: "The identity of the writing subject is not fixed or stable, but rather part of the subject matter of these texts, that is, part of the writing process itself" (150).

Thus, if we are to take Stötzer-Kachold's writing seriously as an aesthetic product, the parameters of much of the available criticism need to be widened. For labels such as "authentic autobiography" deny that side of her work which is deliberately polemic, deliberately orchestrated, and which is designed, as are her performance-style readings, to shock and to disturb as well as to turn her own experiences into art. As she says of her role as artist: "I came to art for very selfish reasons...with my search for originality, for individuality, and with a considerable amount of desire, I'm in exactly the right place. Art looks for, or even demands, these qualities for success and that's what I wanted to achieve" ("Die Frauen" 7-8).

The programmatic titles of Stötzer-Kachold's books clearly convey that her prose aims to break barriers, barriers of both form and content. Michael Braun, for example, dramatically commends *zügel los*, which, he states: "strives towards literary freedom, the shattering of ideological conventions, the subversion of grammar, and towards the dissolution of boundaries between literary genres." The author experiments with genre, punctuation, spelling, form, stereotypes, and clichés. This radical, if occasionally forced, playing with language and image is decisive in Stötzer-Kachold's use of the sexual.

Literary *Her*story: Stötzer-Kachold and "No Taboos"

Stötzer-Kachold's first texts were published unofficially in the magazines, journals, and poetry collections of the underground literary "scene."[3] By this time the erotic was also an accepted dimension of "official" East German literature, no longer regarded as pornography and associated with formalism, as it had been in the 1950s and early 1960s.[4] Honecker's famous speech of 1971, by sanctioning a new cultural era of "no taboos," was understood to imply a redefinition of the boundaries of sexual writing. Of course one cannot assume an automatic correlation between texts that address taboo subjects and art. To do so would be to ignore issues of form and style. Neither can one presume that Honecker's speech ushered in a homogenous linear and teleological literary history. The speech was as much an endorsement of aesthetic developments that had begun in the 1960s as the signal of a new direction. The fact remains, however, that none of the former East German publishing houses I have contacted was aware of any "concrete rules that were to be adhered to when describing the erotic."[5] As Rudolf Chowanetz from the publishing house Neues Leben contends: "Authors could write freely about such things, if they wanted to—or were able to." Indeed, my research has revealed great diversity and discontinuity in literary constructions of sexuality from the late 1960s onwards.

Yet, despite these variations, a specific paradigm remained within all mainstream East German discourses of sexuality, namely that of a loving, heterosexual relationship. Descriptions that departed from accepted, and so-called "normal," erotic behavior, were generally underrepresented in literature, as they were in medical and social text books such as Siegfried Schnabl's *Mann und Frau intim* (Man and Woman in Intimacy) and Kurt Starke's popular *Liebe und Sexualität bis 30* (Love and Sexuality before 30). On the other hand, fictional writing also provided a space in which alternative sexual themes could be pursued. Regarding the issues of, for example, prostitution, pornography, rape, and homosexuality, the status of art in GDR society meant that it could fulfill an important role as substitute forum for discussion. Authors who introduce these, and other, sexual topics into their art are, for example, Irmtraud Morgner, Volker Braun, Uwe Saeger, Helga Königsdorf, Annette Gröschner, and Christoph Hein—successful writers who for the most part published through officially endorsed channels in the GDR. It is within this critical, although not necessarily marginal, context that Stötzer-Kachold's concentration upon the themes of lesbianism, orgasm, masturbation, sexual fantasy, rape, genital mutilation, and sexual drives must be set. Her use of the erotic represents, even in the 1980s, a breaking of taboos that goes well beyond Honecker's pronouncements; its radicalism is, as Thomas Jung recognizes, "singular in GDR literature" (23). It goes beyond sexual writings by authors such as those mentioned above in that the sexual becomes the primary artistic theme. Stötzer-Kachold is not alone in challenging prejudice by introducing formerly taboo themes into her work, but in her choice of theme she does stand out as a notable iconoclast. Where noted at all then, Stötzer-Kachold's sexual poetry is most frequently described in terms of taboo flaunting. Her writing is not only unrestrained (*zügellos*) and unbounded (*grenzenlos*), but also shameless (*schamlos*) (Heim).

Stötzer-Kachold's "sexperimentation" is, however, not merely concerned with breaking taboos, adding to the list of subjects covered in East German literatures, and building upon the achievements of other artists. Neither is it simply a question of "the public staging of one's own sexuality" (Jung 20), an assertion made by many critics. Stötzer-Kachold represents an unusually woman-centered feminism, which can be viewed as radical when compared with other women's writing from the GDR. Prose by Kirsch, Morgner, or Wolf, for example, emphasizes "humankind" rather than "womankind." Morgner's utopian future, for example, is a "a third order, which should be neither patriarchal nor matriarchal, but human" (20). Emancipation, for Morgner and others of her generation, is "not a women's problem, but a problem concerning all humanity, and can only be solved by the whole of society" (Neumann 98).

Morgner's writing is "feminist" because it represents the ideology of women's liberation, demonstrating that women suffer injustice because of the specific forms in which their sexuality is gendered. Stötzer-Kachold's work too is concerned with the status of women in patriarchal societies, whether socialist or capitalist. In the attempt to portray the oppression of the female, however, her writing often appears as anti-male, rather than anti-patriarchy. It inveighs against men "as concrete individuals, as a sex, as a symbol of power" (Meusinger 369). The text "rap 2," for example, is dedicated "to all the men who have ever betrayed and deceived me":

> eines tages wird es euch kostenlos geben
> wenn eure 1000 jährigen reiche zerbrochen sind
> wenn niemand mehr eure uniformen bügelt
> und die spucke auf stiefeln realitäten sind (*grenzen* 75).[6]

Individual male figures become embodiments of power, and masculinity is reduced to a negative stereotype. The association of men with fascism is provocatively unambiguous.

In the face of male domination, Stötzer-Kachold seeks utopia in the context of the female body, the female orgasm, or female sexual drives, and it is this unequivocal gendering that upsets her critics, just as it aroused the hatred and suspicion of the men who wrote the reports for her police files.[7] More serious critics have written of the "anti-male gesture" (Kleinschmidt) of Stötzer-Kachold's texts. Wesuls detects a "female self-consciousness...closely associated with rage and with a powerful contempt for men" (339), while Schmidt contends that the texts evidence the "war of the sexes" (159). Such reactions appear justified when one reads vehement statements such as "die männer sind von ihrer grundsubstanz her barbaren" (*zügel los* 40).[8] The force of these assertions overshadows any poetic, lyrical content they may have. Expressive hatred of, and anger towards, men themselves appears largely personal rather than historical, didactic, moral, or indeed artistic.

Another aspect of Stötzer-Kachold's feminism that makes it woman-centered is the fact that the lyrical subject in many of the texts, particularly those in *grenzen los fremd gehen* and *erfurter roulette*, is clearly situated in the female position. Texts ask, for example, "meine frauenfragen" (*grenzen* 106)[9] and search for "fraueneigene inhalte, energien und kräfte" (*grenzen* 138).[10] Stötzer-Kachold has, or so she claims, not only attempted to create "a genuine female identity" (Dahlke, "Ich-Figur" 248), but also a language in which this figure can express *her* self. Many texts are, however, more ambiguous. "der wecker" for example, about a man's suicide attempt, can also be read as the poetic description of a failed abortion or of female self-mutilation.

The directly and radically female text represents, then, only one aspect of Stötzer-Kachold's feminism. As Eigler recognizes, this prose also "provides challenging perspectives on gender identity and the question of individual responsibility" (150). The author's concern is not merely to criticize men and glorify women, but also to effect change in the constructions and images of femininity that form female subjectivity. Through her art Stötzer-Kachold becomes "die böse frau, die sich gegen das bild zur wehr setzende frau, die um das bild, gegen das bild kämpfende frau" (*zügel l*os 50).[11] The text "eine rede," for example, provides evidence:

> gegen die führungsrolle des mannes
> gegen die führer
> gegen die rollen
> gegen die bilder
> gegen die frauenbilder der letzten 40 jahre (*grenzen* 101).[12]

Furthermore, Stötzer-Kachold does not only aim to criticize and deconstruct gendered mainstream cultural images. She also puts forward her own canon of utopian alternatives. It is only where this alternative canon becomes as prescriptive as that which it aims to replace that problems arise. At times the author fails to recognize that the categories to which she accords positive meanings are themselves elements of existing discourse, rather than essential "female" qualities. The more successful pieces show an awareness that "aus der permanenten wiederholung der frau ergibt sich nicht der beweis der frau" (*grenzen* 111).[13]

Stötzer-Kachold's feminism thus challenges conventional conceptions of GDR literature, appealing to Western feminist discourses and extending the meanings of the author's art beyond the boundaries of its site of production. Sexuality, in terms of erotic imagery and diction, is central to this debate. The images of women the author rejects are sexual in both the wide and narrow senses. The personal is made political and sexuality is regarded as an arena of struggle. The author aims to give women a sexual identity and a sexual voice, while critiquing patriarchal relations that deprive them of these rights. If, as Carol Vance suggests, "feminism's best fantasy" is one where women can realize erotic desire and pleasure (xvi), then the desire for this freedom is expressed even in the titles of Stötzer-Kachold's prose: it is a desire that lies at the heart of her work.

The individual locutions that Stötzer-Kachold forms into poetry are themselves physical, including bodies, bodily parts, and bodily fluids; her art is characterized by "ein anderes stück leibverantwortung" (*grenzen* 89).[14] Sensual contact, in whatever form, acts as a means of liberation from isolation, from bodily oppression, and from a situation where identity is threatened. As Schmidt states: "What characterizes the experiences of this subject is above all their physicality" (159). Dahlke writes of a "poetics of the corporeal" (*Leibverantwortung* 149), which, she argues, "is based directly upon bodily experience, but which cannot be reduced to writing about the body" (*Bilder* 157). Against the "castrated" German language (*grenzen* 38), Stötzer-Kachold sets a body language representing the moment "wenn die stimme im körper spricht und tanzt und händelaute hat und füßelaute daß körpersprache nicht röcheln oder schreie nur trauer gebiert" (*grenzen* 45).[15]

While she dispenses with standard means of punctuation, Stötzer-Kachold's language is structured by both physical shape[16] and by physical rhyme and rhythm. It is as if her writing is to ebb and flow, explicitly driven forward by sexual drives. There are countless examples of this rhythm practice (*rhythmusübung*) (*zügel los* 141) in her work; especially notable is the author's reliance on, and experimentation with, certain sets of words: *liebe, triebe, treibe, abtreiben, antreiben,* and *schreiben*.[17] Stötzer's *liebe* is one dominated by *triebe,* her *schreiben* is a form of *treiben*. Indeed she describes writing as if it were a sexual act, the energy of which is expressed in repeated "ei" sounds:

> das schreiben ist wie mein sexueller trieb
> bis zum letzten steigern sich beide und dann gehts los (*grenzen* 157).[18]

Stötzer's performance art, too, is reliant not only upon the spoken word, but also upon the body. On stage her poetry is almost danced, and this will certainly affect the way in which the erotic elements of the work are understood. As Dahlke notes: "The author sings and dances, whispers and screams, shouts for joy and wails, stutters and drawls" (*Bilder* 163). The anatomy is actively brought into the art, the text moves from the page and into physical and vocal expression. Stötzer-Kachold's work depends, then, upon establishing a specific relationship between the body and language in order to extend linguistic boundaries. The author works with and through the body, using it as poetic material and striving to reclaim it for her own purposes.

Votzenenergie—"What's the point of decency?"

One especially notable example of the author's bid to reclaim the female body is the concept of cunt energy. It is a neologism that remains nebulous and utopian rather than realistic. The foundation of the term, and, as I have shown, of much of the strength of Stötzer-Kachold's writing, is the female anatomy. In this case it is that part of a woman's body which Freud connected with absence and lack, and which patriarchal society designates in derogatory terms. Here, emptiness is filled with life, with truth, and with creative energy in the form of words:

> da wo der schwanz sich in die votze schiebt ist es nacht und im dunkel wartet
> die wahrheit
> wer redet schon von der votzenenergie und deren strahlung
> und den worten einer lebendigen unterwelt (*tag sonnentag*).[19]

Gabriele Stötzer-Kachold "speaks of it" (*redet davon*), and seemingly without hesitation. She, for this is very clearly a female voice, further describes

> diese unentdeckten kontinente der sinne
> meine votzensignale meine votzenwärme meine energie die wir als geilheit spüren dieses reservat an strahlung wenn du es mir zurückgibst am tag was du nachts genommen hast wenn wir das behalten und nicht der statisten zahlen gehören
> komm mund küß mich leck dem [sic] schmerz von den lidern (*tag sonnentag*).[20]

The text *tag sonnentag* is a questioning of the feminine ideal that postulates motherhood as natural, as normality. Here, Stötzer-Kachold's *votzenenergie* offers a radical alternative to the gynecological energy of conception, the ability to give birth. The stomach pains that run through her description are artistically productive and are a different form of labor pains. In this text they represent a longing, a longing for "the dark thoughts of the night." It is the night, particularly the "night's genitalia," that is connected with both the female and with truth: "nie hörte ich von den kräften der frau es sind die kräfte der nacht" (*tag sonnentag*).[21] These "powers" are autoerotic and solipsistic, the "you" addressed by the lyrical subject could represent a lover, but could equally well refer to a part of the self.

However, the parallels constructed in this text between the female genitalia and a natural, powerful entity detract attention from very real problems of rejecting such strong feminine role models as the mother figure. Similar mis/constructions occur in other texts. In "rap 2" genital satisfaction becomes a cipher for a utopian future:

> eines tages wird es euch kostenlos geben
> wenn das schwanzsein nicht die weltmacht bedeutet
> und die votze nicht mit geld befriedigt wird
> und die verachtung aus dem bett geworfen ist (*grenzen* 75).[22]

In this reverie, orgasms hang freely on trees, words dance, and love is "boundless." The lack of punctuation in the text "ich möchte dir etwas sagen" (I would like to tell you something) (*zügel los* 148–50) further suggests that the lyrical subject *is* her vagina:

> der neue körper weich zum harten halten der umklammerung sag mir
> meine größe und wer ich bin vagina in jeder festen form abgetastet
> geliebt geleibt berührt geführt getrügt getragen gesagt ich hab dich lieb
> und wenn ich wachse dann wächst du einfach mit (*zügel los* 150).[23]

Elsewhere the female anatomy is clearly part of nature, a realm that is romantically regarded as positive and indeed inspirational:

> meine votze der flüssige spalt der die erde auffängt zum
> aussenden von fruchtbarkeit
> da versackt nichts im gedächtnis meiner rinden
> alle überdeckten figuren sind auffindbar
> ich vergaß kassandra mein ich anzubieten (*grenzen* 204).[24]

Such an unquestioning association of the female body and romantically invested nature is, as has been argued, problematic. In this text the feminist icon Kassandra appears as a figure who can be discovered through communion with the vagina. It would seem as if the female genitalia too can see, even if their message goes unheard.

The idealist conceptions described rely upon a discredited notion of the essentialized, female body, invested with an undefined inner power. In much of her work Stötzer-Kachold similarly places her faith in a system of the senses (*zügel los* 86), whereby the sensual is primary, no longer suppressed, but rather celebrated, liberated, lived. Her utopia is one where "wir frei ficken frei gehen frei sprechen können ohne opfer zu sein" (*grenzen* 198).[25] Her prose is dedicated to the "anerkennung der sinne...sinne für sich, nicht als anbiederung an die außenwelt, sondern als schutz, kampf, spiel mit der außenwelt" (*zügel los* 41–42).[26] Where this "game" is successful it accords her work its momentum. At its best

Stötzer-Kachold's relationship with both the world around her and that inside allows various interpretations, and her most successful visions arise out of this openness. At its worst the sensual offers only a visceral truth, located in the female genitalia, or in the writer's own self. It is a truth that relies upon the immediacy of orgasm, masturbation, lust, love, fundamental sexual drives, or, as in this case, the vagina. That the body itself is mediated through cultural representations is an argument that often remains unacknowledged by the author.

Although Stötzer-Kachold denies any knowledge of French feminism (Dahlke "Ich-Figur"), the stylization of the body and, more specifically, of the vagina as a source of truth and self-knowledge does suggest ideas of *écriture féminine*. In all of Stötzer-Kachold's work one is constantly reminded of Hélène Cixous's entreaty to "write your self. Your body must be heard" (250). For Stötzer-Kachold, language is not only something alive and something to develop (*grenzen* 185), but also a woman, a sexual woman with whom the author can identify, to the point where they enjoy a physically sexual relationship:

> die sprache ist eine frau
> ich streiche an den beinen der frau lang
> bis ich ihren spalt berühren kann...
> ich geh in die frau rein die sprache ist
> sage ich zu der frau die gespalten ist...
> ich bin eine frau mit diesem spalt zwischen den beinen (*grenzen* 140).[27]

As Thomas Jung correctly notes, the female narrator, the female body, and language are here merged into one. However, his assertion that the result is the confirmation of an individual, unified identity (22) appears inappropriate, idealizing Stötzer-Kachold's own ideal. The choice of the terms *Spalt, Spaltung,* and *gespalten* surely suggests a *split* identity, which is reflected, but not transcended, in her vaginal imagery.

The "spalt" of the vagina also echoes the early psychofeminism of Irigaray, where she accords positive significance to woman's "two lips which embrace continually" and writes: "in her statements—at least when she dares to speak out—woman retouches herself constantly" (100). Stötzer-Kachold too makes language both female and tactile. She does not, however, problematize this connection in the same way as does Irigaray, but rather reduces, thematically and stylistically, the notions of a female aesthetic theorized by French feminist psychoanalytical thought. Her poetry is circular and open-ended. It is constructed as if to flow with the bodily fluids, in particular blood and milk, as a *brustmilchmeer* ("sea of breast milk") (*zügel los* 132). Circularity and open-endedness are also implied in the deliberate experimentation with punctuation, rhyme, and repetition that characterizes much of the poet's work.

Cixous encourages a specifically female form of writing, "because so few women have as yet won back their body" (256). "For far too long," writes Barbara Sichtermann, "the female body was misused as a field for patriarchal projections and politics" (60). The efforts of feminists have led to general recognition of this fact and women everywhere have begun to create their own politics and language. A form of prose too close to biological *écriture féminine* can, however, become, as in the use of *Votze*, mystical and essentialist. This essentialism may be construed as strategic, but in my opinion references to "ancient female powers and knowledge" ("Die Frauen" 9)—recalling an innate matriarchal core—serve rather to mystify than to strengthen the feminist message.

It is the dominant female physicality of Stötzer-Kachold's art that also invites comparisons with the West German *Frauenliteratur* of the 1970s, in particular with Verena Stefan's *Häutungen* (*Shedding*). Schmidt writes: "To a degree unprecedented in GDR writing, but reminiscent of Western feminist writing in the 1970s, Kachold explores the reactions of the body to loneliness, oppression, hope, desire, etc." (159), and Dahlke notes that "Stötzer-Kachold's texts were often associated with Verena Stefan's *Häutungen*, most commonly in the context of the term *authenticity*" (*Bilder* 120). There are certainly some important similarities in the two writers' discovery of the erotic, although I would maintain that these similarities can easily be exaggerated.

Stefan too recognizes, for example, the importance of sexual vocabulary. She contends, however, that "[w]hen a woman starts to talk about her *pussy* she has simply adopted the jargon of left-wing men. The path to her vagina, to her body and to her self remains as closed as ever" (33). Stefan's response to this dilemma is to use the cold, clinical jargon of medicine when depicting heterosexual love, and a flowery, nature-bound diction of "lakes," "rivers," "sparkling moss," and "sun rays" (122) to raise her homosexual experiences into the mystical. Thus statements such as "the penis searches blindly in the vagina" (101), are contrasted with "I flow and sink with Fenna through fields of lip blossoms" (130). Whereas Stötzer-Kachold accords positive meaning to the word *Votze*, Stefan does not reclaim terms such as *Möse*. Again Stefan's answer lies primarily in nature. She asks, for instance: "The vagina—a dark pipe? What came then? Were there pearls in the depths of the body? Coral reefs?" (47). Examples akin to this abound in the text, and it is this aspect of her writing that has brought Stefan the most criticism.

The style of certain references to *votzenenergie* in Stötzer-Kachold's work opens it to similar censure. On the whole though, Stötzer-Kachold does not place the same stress on the natural. Although she does appear, in some texts, essentialist, elsewhere this charge is refuted. In her description of "silvester 92," *Votze* is used to comment ironically upon the relations of German reunification: "ach wir kuscheligen ostmäuschen.

meine freundinnen die sich mit meinen freunden trafen und dort am liebsten gleich die erste nacht ihre votzen unter die schwänze hielten um vom köstlichen westsperma etwas abzubekommen" (*roulette* 58).[28] Elsewhere the vagina is just one in a long list of parts of the body; it appears almost normalized: "deine schultern an meinem mund dein arsch zwischen meinen fingern dein schwanz in meiner votze" (*roulette* 9).[29] In examples such as this, Stötzer-Kachold's use of the word *Votze* is harsher and more demanding on the reader than any of Stefan's proposed alternatives. It is also more liberating and more openly political; it can even be more humorous. As Dahlke argues: "Where Stötzer-Kachold's energetic text is successful and her joy in experimental formulations are convincing, Stefan's obvious acts are too forced" (*Bilder* 168). Stötzer-Kachold is, then, more aware of the textuality of her prose. The work of the East German is not just a repetition, ten years later, of what West German women achieved in the 1970s.

Other texts in Gabriele Stötzer-Kachold's work thus use the concept of *Votze* as a vehicle of critical comment rather than as an essential force of liberation. One of the most successful pieces in *zügel los* is "die rose ist keine rose ist keine rose ist keine rose" (the rose is not a rose is not a rose is not a rose) (110–13), in which the constant repetition of the negative article powerfully hammers home the hatred that can dominate in relationships between the sexes and the denial of the female that takes place in phallocentric communities. Competing speakers create a strangely rhythmic cacophony of clichés, quotations, insults and, almost buried, answers. The term *Votze* is here used in its more common context and the links with violence are clear:

> die sau gibt es
> die alte votze gibt es...
> eine in die fresse gibt es
> ich hau dir eine in die fresse gibt es
> stell dich nicht so an gibt es
> laß mich mal lecken gibt es
> hol mir einen runter gibt es (*zügel los* 112–13).[30]

If this voice is "male," the reply is seemingly genderless and detaches the violence evoked from its roots in gender identity: there is nothing to prove; there are no women, no men" (*zügel los* 113). In a much more direct and less ambiguous text Stötzer-Kachold opens, "es kotzt mich an in einer männerwelt voller lieben mädels und bräuten zu leben," a world she goes on to describe:

> du alte votze jeden tag wenn ich nach bahnhof nord gehe
> dieses hetzende atmen bevor sie mir an die schulter greifen

> sie wissen es doch
> sie erlauben es sich
> wir erlauben es ihnen (*grenzen* 98).[31]

When she describes the vagina as "the mirror of all insults" (*zügel los* 131), it is perhaps this type of insult that she has in mind. In these examples, Stötzer-Kachold acknowledges and demonstrates that the foundation of her utopia is also a word full of negative connotations.

The poetic usage of the term *Votze* is thus finely balanced on that "tightrope between subversion and reappropriation" (140) that Griselda Pollock claims is walked by feminists who attempt to "decolonize the female body" from existing male forms of signification. The feminist potential of radical sexual imagery can, for example, easily be subsumed within direct and violent pornographic representations of the vagina. Jane Flax, as one among many, criticizes the emphasis on the female anatomy as a "reduction," which "precludes considering the many other ways in which we experience our embodiedness" and "replicates the equating of women with the body" (53).

In an interview with Birgit Dahlke, Stötzer-Kachold summarizes her own aims in using the expression:

> Women sometimes react aggressively to concepts such as *cunt energy*...you notice it at readings.... At first the word shocked me too, but then I began to use it, not to shock back but to try to work out why it had shocked me. It's so difficult to use this male German language. That's what I'm trying to do, to change the language—as a woman—until I can live with it. That's what the adjective "feminist" has meant for me, I've penetrated the male world ("Ich-Figur" 249–50).

Thus, if we are to take her at her word, she is attempting to find a way of positively constructing the female body and, in particular, the female sexual organs; Dahlke writes of "emancipatory work with sexual semantics" (*Bilder* 164). As part of this work, Stötzer-Kachold also widens the range of terms available as alternatives to *Votze*. She writes of *votzeleien* and uses the adjective *votzig*. Synonyms for *Votze* include: *ritze, schoß, scheide, möse, spalt, vagina,* and even *schmetterlingslippen,* whereby this last is unusual in its more conventionally romantic associations. Pictorial images of the vagina reinforce this message. Avoided, however, are any of the more traditional alternatives connected with *Scham*.

The choice of names for the male sexual organ is less wide, reversing the existing linguistic situation. It includes *schwanz, stock, waffe,* and *pimmel*. The traditional Freudian theory that defines woman according to absence, her lack of a penis, is subverted into an ironically phallocentric joke and applied to the ultimate male figure, God himself: "wenn gott an sich heruntersah hatte er nur einen makel ∞ in seiner mitte war ein loch und das hieß o ∞ gott war unglücklich er war sich schon des männlichen bewußt ∞...herr gott brauchte einen schwanz ∞ also drehte er den pferdeleib um und hatte nun einen schwanz vor sich" (*grenzen* 76).[32] Indeed, when a woman is given a penis there are no signs of envy. As in Morgner's "Gute Botschaft der Valeska" (Valeska's Good Tidings) (421–44), the sex swap is simply not taken seriously: "etwa so war ihr schwanz dick und biegsam und führungslos sie hatte keine kontrolle darüber oder wollte es gar nicht ernsthaft" (*grenzen* 139).[33]

In its endeavor to reclaim one of the most fundamental aspects of the female body, Stötzer-Kachold's writing represents an important contribution to feminist debate, particularly in the GDR of the 1980s. Whether or not she is seen as, against her professed aim, merely provocative, or whether her work really is liberating in its use of language is a question to which there is no objective answer. There are certainly difficulties associated with so great an emphasis on an ostensibly biological feature that has been so greatly invested with cultural meanings. Postmodern feminism has successfully questioned the very notion that the body can be encountered outside discursive frames of reference. Such critiques, situated within a chain of signification where nothing is essential, make clear that a feminist construction of the self can become problematic if given cross-cultural values. Judith Butler, for example, has convincingly asserted that "the regulatory norms of 'sex' work in a performative fashion to constitute the materiality of bodies" (*Bodies* 2). She understands sexual identities as permanent copies, as performance. Thus she strongly maintains the need to deconstruct not only *gendered* images, but also *sex* itself. She deems the division between sex and gender irrelevant and misleading: "If the immutable character of sex is contested, perhaps this construct called 'sex' is as culturally constructed as gender; indeed, perhaps it was always already gender, with the consequence that the distinction between sex and gender turns out to be no distinction at all" (*Gender* 7). If sex cannot remain outside of discursive production, then neither can bodies. The vagina, therefore, can never exist except where it is materially embodied through discourse.

To define women in terms of their sexual attributes may thus simply add to the list of affronts for which there are no readily available male equivalents. Adverse associations do not simply disappear if a term generally considered abusive is combined with positive "energy." Language is not an independent entity, devoid of social context. Words such as *Votze* cannot simply be "reclaimed." As Deborah Cameron has argued, such a process "can make meanings (and thus cultural beliefs) less monolithic, but it is a continuing struggle" (110). Stötzer-Kachold's writing can be seen to form part of this struggle. Her "indecent things" raise, at the very least, basic issues of sexual morality, a morality that, in both socialist and capitalist countries, has been used to oppress women, and a morality that should be challenged. However, "indecent" presupposes, and is reliant upon, "decency"; thus the challenge can pose questions, but will not necessarily provide answers.

Notes

The translations are my own, unless otherwise noted. I am indebted to Stuart Taberner and Margaret Littler for their careful reading of my work.

[1] "if we women tell each other nothing but indecent things and the indecent becomes quite normal, almost decent in fact, what's the point of decency?"

[2] "I only have one story to tell / and that is myself"

[3] See, for example, *UND* 5 (1982), 8 (1983), 12 (1983); *Mikado* 2 and 3 (1984); *Ariadnefabrik* 2 (1986) and 1 (1988); *Koma-Kino* 2 (1987) and 4 (1988); *Kontext* 5 (1989).

[4] E.g., "Mysticism and a passion for pornography are characteristic of the decay and the degradation of bourgeois culture" (Ždanov 46).

[5] The citation is from a letter to me from Frau Matschie, an editor for Domina Verlag.

[6] "one day you'll cost nothing / when your thousand year empires have come crashing down / when nobody irons your uniforms / and the spit on your boots are reality"

[7] See comments by Sasha Anderson, who denounced Stötzer-Kachold as a "mental anarchist, who would leave the GDR sooner or later" and her literature as "literary feminism" and "psychic occult" (*grenzen* 157). See also Stötzer-Kachold's "Frauenszene."

[8] "men are, at heart, barbarians"

[9] "my woman questions"

[10] "women's contents, energies, and powers"

[11] "the angry woman, the woman defending herself against the image, attacking around the image and against the image"

[12] "against the leading role of the man / against the leaders / against the roles / against the images / against the female images of the last 40 years"

[13] "the proof of woman does not result from the constant repetition of woman"

[14] "a different piece of bodily responsibility"

[15] "when the voice in the body talks and dances and has hand tones and feet tones, so that the body language gives birth to more than just gurgling or screams or mourning"

[16] See, for example, "anpassungsorgasmus" (*grenzen* 79), where both shape on the page and meaning express the theme of orgasm.

[17] The base meanings of the words are "love," "desires," "drive," and "to abort," "to urge on," and "to write."

[18] "writing is like my sexual drives / both rise to a climax and then we're off"

[19] "there, where the prick penetrates the cunt, it is night and in the dark truth waits / but who speaks of cunt energy and of radiation, / of the text of an underground full of life"

[20] "these undiscovered continents of the senses / my cunt signals my cunt warmth my energy / which we feel as lust, this radiation when you / give me back in the day what you took at night if only we could / hold on to that, and not give in to statistics or numbers / come mouth kiss me lick the pain from my eyelids"

[21] "I never heard of the powers of the woman they are the powers of the night"

[22] "one day you will cost nothing / when a prick does not mean world power / and the cunt cannot be satisfied with money / and hatred is thrown out of bed"

[23] "the new body soft to hold hard in an embrace / tell me my size and who I am vagina in every form felt loved embodied / touched led betrayed carried said I love you and when I grow / then you just grow too"

[24] "my cunt the fluid split which takes in the earth / and gives out fertility / nothing is forgotten in the memory of my bark / every lost figure can be rediscovered / I forgot to offer Cassandra myself"

[25] "we can fuck freely walk freely and speak freely without becoming victims"

[26] "recognition of the senses, the senses for themselves, not as conformity to the outside world but as protection as fight as a game with the outside world"

[27] "language is a woman / I stroke her legs / until I can touch her split / I enter the woman who is language / say 'I' to the woman who is split / I am a woman with this split between my legs"

[28] "oh we cuddly eastern mice. my girlfriends who met my boyfriends and spent the first night with their cunts under pricks, just so that they could benefit from some valuable western sperm"

[29] "your shoulders on my mouth, your backside between my fingers your prick in my cunt"

[30] "there is the sow / there is the old cunt / there is a punch in the mouth / there is I'll punch you in the mouth / there is don't be so awkward / there is let me have a lick / there is jerk me off"

[31] "it makes me sick to live in a man's world full of nice girls and brides... / you old cunt every day when I go to the station / this provocative breath before they grab my shoulder / they know it / they allow it / we allow it"

[32] "when God looked down at himself he had only one problem ∞ there was a gap in his middle and that was called o ∞ god was unhappy, for he was aware of his masculinity ∞ Mr. God needed a penis ∞ so he took a horse and turned it around, and there in front of him was a penis"

[33] "her penis was fat and bendy and undirected / she had no control over it or rather she didn't really want to"

Works Cited

Althammer, René. "Postmoderne Prosa als Mitteilungsform. *zügel los* von Gabriele Kachold." *Berliner Zeitung* 24 Apr. 1990: 9.

Böck, Dorothea. "Fixierte Realität: Gabriele Kacholds *zügel los.*" *Neue Deutsche Literatur* 38.11 (1990): 154–56.

Braun, Michael. "Entfesselungsversuche: Gabriele Kacholds Prosadebüt *zügel los.*" *Frankfurter Rundschau* 4 Oct. 1990: 7.

Butler, Judith. *Bodies That Matter: On the Discursive Limits of "Sex."* London: Routledge, 1993.

———. *Gender Trouble: Feminism and the Subversion of Identity.* London: Routledge, 1990.

Cameron, Deborah. *Feminism and Linguistic Theory.* Hampshire: Macmillan, 1992.

Chowanetz, Rudolf. Letter to the author. 18 Dec. 1992.

Cixous, Hélène. "The Laugh of the Medusa." *New French Feminisms.* 245–64.

Dahlke, Birgit. "'Im Brunnen vor dem Tore': Autorinnen in inoffiziellen Zeitschriften der DDR 1979–90." *Neue Generation—Neues Erzählen. Deutsche Prosa-Literatur der achtziger Jahre.* Ed. W. Delabar et al. Opladen: Westdeutscher Verlag, 1993. 177–93.

———. "Eine glaubhafte weibliche Ich-Figur kommt von einer glaubhaften weiblichen Identität: Gespräch mit Gabriele Stötzer-Kachold." *Deutsche Bücher* 23.4 (1993): 243–58.

———. *Die romantischen Bilder blättern ab: Produktionsbedingungen, Schreibweisen und Traditionen von Autorinnen in inoffiziell publizierten Zeitschriften der DDR 1979–90.* Diss. Humboldt University (Berlin), 1994.

———. "'ein stück leibverantwortung.' Gabriele Stötzer-Kachold: *grenzen los fremd gehen.*" *Neue Deutsche Literatur* 41.6 (1993): 148–50.

Eigler, Friederike. "At the Margins of East Berlin's 'Counter-Culture': Elke Erb's *Winkelzüge* and Gabriele Kachold's *zügel los.*" *Women in German Yearbook* 9. Ed. Jeanette Clausen and Sara Friedrichsmeyer. Lincoln: U of Nebraska P, 1993. 145–61.

Emmerich, Wolfgang. *Die andere deutsche Literatur: Aufsätze zur Literatur aus der DDR.* Opladen: Westdeutscher Verlag, 1994.

Flax, Jane. "Postmodernism and Gender Relations in Feminist Theory." *Feminism/Postmodernism.* Ed. Linda Nicholson. New York: Routledge, 1990. 39–62.

Foucault, Michel. "What is an Author?" *The Foucault Reader.* Ed. Paul Rabinow. London: Penguin, 1991. 101–20.

Geist und Macht: Writers and the State in the GDR. Ed. Axel Goodbody and Dennis Tate. Amsterdam: Rodopi, 1992.

Heim, Uta-Maria. "Mißtrauen gegen deutsche Ordnung: Gabriele Kachold liest im Stuttgarter Schriftstellerhaus." *Stuttgarter Zeitung* 7 Sept. 1991: 41.

Irigaray, Luce. "Ce sexe qui n'en est pas un." *New French Feminisms.* 99–106.

Jung, Thomas. "Grenzenlos und lustvoll: Über das Politische und das Private in Gabriele Stötzer-Kacholds Lyrik in Zeiten der Wende." *Focus on Literature* 1 (1995): 11–30.

Kleinschmidt, Claudia. "Spannungszustände: Porträt Gabriele Kachold." *Sonntag* 2 (1990): 4.

Kuhn, Anna. "Eine Königin köpfen ist effektiver als einen König köpfen: The Gender Politics of the Christa Wolf Controversy." *Women and the Wende: Social Effects and Cultural Reflections of the German Unification Process. German Monitor 31.* Ed. Elizabeth Boa and Janet Wharton. Amsterdam: Rodopi, 1994. 200–15.

Matschie, Frau. Letter to the author. 1 Dec. 1992.

Meusinger, Annette. "Von der Notwendigkeit ständiger Grenzüberschreitung: Gespräch mit Gabriele Kachold." *Lebensweise und gesellschaftlicher Umbruch in Ostdeutschland.* Ed. G. Meyer, G. Riege, and D. Strützel. Erlangen: Palm und Enke, 1992. 371–78.

Morgner, Irmtraud. *Leben und Abenteuer der Trobadora Beatriz nach Zeugnissen ihrer Spielfrau Laura.* 1973. Frankfurt a.M.: Luchterhand, 1990.

Neumann, Oskar. "Weltspitze sein und sich wundern, was noch nicht ist." *Kürbiskern* 1 (1978): 95–99.

New French Feminisms: An Anthology. Ed. Elaine Marks and Isabelle de Courtivron. Amherst: U of Massachusetts P, 1980.

Paul, Georgina. "Text und Kontext—*Was bleibt* 1979–89." *Geist und Macht.* 117–28.

Pollock, Griselda. "What's Wrong with Images of Women?" *The Sexual Subject: A Screen Reader in Sexuality.* London: Routledge, 1992. 135–45.

Schmidt, Ricarda. "Im Schatten der Titanen: Minor GDR Women Writers—Justly Neglected, Unrecognised or Repressed?" *Geist und Macht.* 151–62.

Schnabl, Siegfried. *Mann und Frau intim: Fragen des gesunden und des gestörten Geschlechtslebens.* Berlin: Volk und Gesundheit, 1969.

Sichtermann, Barbara. *Weiblichkeit: Texte aus dem zweiten Jahrzehnt der Frauenbewegung.* Frankfurt a.M.: Büchergilde Gutenberg, 1989.

Starke, Kurt. *Liebe und Sexualität bis 30.* Berlin: VEB Verlag der Wissenschaften, 1984.

Stefan, Verena. *Häutungen.* 1975. Frankfurt a.M.: Fischer, 1994.

Stötzer-Kachold, Gabriele. *erfurter roulette.* München: Peter Kirchheim, 1995.

———. "Die Frauen und die Kunst." *Weibblick* 9 (1992): 7–9.

———. "Frauenszene und Frauen in der Szene." *Nachtspiele: Literatur und Staatssicherheit.* Ed. Peter Böthig and Klaus Michael. Leipzig: Reclam, 1993. 129–37.

———. *grenzen los fremd gehen*. Mit Zeichnungen der Autorin. Berlin: janus, 1992.
———. *tag sonnentag*, as yet unpublished. Personal copy.
———. *zügel los*. Frankfurt a.M: Luchterhand, 1990.
Törne, Dorothea von. "Eine Obduktion der Verhältnisse: Gabriele Stötzer-Kachold schreibt gegen die Zerstörung der Persönlichkeit." *Neue Zeit* 15 Dec. 1992: 14.
Vance, Carol. "More Danger, More Pleasure: A Decade after the Barnard Sexuality Conference." *Pleasure and Danger: Exploring Female Sexuality*. Ed. Carol Vance. London: Pandora, 1992. xvi–xxxv.
Weigel, Sigrid. *Die Stimme der Medusa: Schreibweisen in der Gegenwartsliteratur von Frauen*. Dülmen-Hiddingsel: tende, 1987.
Wesuls, Elisabeth. "zügellos, ehrlich und radikal." *Die Weltbühne* 12 Mar. 1991. 337–39.
Wolf, Christa. *Was bleibt*. 1990. Hamburg: Luchterhand, 1992.
Wolf, Gerhard. *Sprachblätter: Wortwechsel. Im Dialog mit Dichtern*. Leipzig: Reclam, 1992.
Ždanov, Andrej. "Die Sowjetliteratur, die ideenreichste und fortschrittlichste Literatur der Welt." *Sozialistische Realismuskonzeptionen: Dokumente zum 1. Allunionskongreß der Sowjetschriftsteller*. Ed. Hans Jürgen Schmitt and Gerhard Schramm. Frankfurt a.M: Suhrkamp, 1974. 43–50.

Jigsaw Puzzles: Female Perception and Self in Brigitte Kronauer's "A Day That Didn't End Hopelessly after All"

Jutta Ittner

This essay analyzes one of Brigitte Kronauer's early stories, which magically draw readers into a fragmented, ambiguous reality and then challenge them to question their everyday experience. Their highly sophisticated structures, their "furor of precision," and simple, yet blindingly clear language illustrate the author's redefinition of literary reality. In "Ein Tag, der zuletzt doch nicht im Sande verlief" we accompany an increasingly anxious narrator in her effort to perceive the vertiginous world and herself. When the last episode ends with her "complete satisfaction," we are nevertheless required to create a full picture out of seemingly unrelated pieces—the odyssey of female maturation. (JI)

The stories of Brigitte Kronauer, one of Germany's most highly acclaimed contemporary women writers, are an oddity in the landscape of fiction. They will not easily captivate the kind of reader who expects to be drawn into a plot or engrossed in a character's emotional dilemmas. Instead, they seem written for readers who become oblivious to the world around them in their effort to conquer a complex jigsaw puzzle. Sensuous yet far from emotional, they do not reproduce reality or reflect an imagined world. Kronauer's prose is of blinding clarity, simple and at the same time artificial and highly constructed—to the point where the mind behind it seems more calculating than poetic. Although these stories are told by first-person narrators, they are strangely objective and so impersonal that not even the most naive reader would mistake them for autobiographical narratives. In short, Kronauer writes fiction that seems to defy most of the generalizations of *écriture féminine*.

It may not be a coincidence that German feminist critics have neglected Kronauer who, while not ignoring feminist issues, is far from embracing them uncritically. Although she may say that "when I sit down to write, it doesn't cross my mind whether I am a woman or a man" ("Zehn Jahre" 14), this is anything but a naive position. She contends that to

Virginia Woolf, who is "forever being quoted on the issue of women's literature, it would have been unthinkable to confuse the subjects of 'woman' and 'self-realization' with aesthetics," and she issues a general warning against an exchange of aesthetic criteria for feminist ones, asserting that a "skeptical attitude towards a generalizing feminism increases... the artistic quality of a work that strives not to narrow reality but to widen it" ("Literatur" 19).

In the gallery of Kronauer's characters, fragile, insecure, disembodied women who struggle for a sense of self are contrasted and complemented by frighteningly active women who have a grip on the real world. Starting with the early stories collected in *Die Gemusterte Nacht* (The Patterned Night, 1981) and culminating in her first novel *Frau Mühlenbeck im Gehäus* (Mrs. Mühlenbeck in Her House, 1980), the narrating voices almost invariably belong to the first group, and the active "Frau Mühlenbecks" are the objects of their scrutinizing eyes and minds.[1] As the author's "eye, ear, and pen," they are mediums of perception and observation, creatures of the mind (Jung 48). How much do these nameless narrators have in common with the author? Nothing, Kronauer contends; the narrative is pure fiction: "Let's call these narrating individuals who experience various perceptions, emotions, and insights, the 'I'-in that customary and misleading fashion" ("Revolution" 5). And she warns her readers against jumping to autobiographical conclusions.

What about their gender? Unlike Jeannette Winterston in *Sexing the Cherry,* for example, Kronauer does not use gender ambiguity as a central device. The ungendered narrative voices of Kronauer's early stories almost programmatically show the author's unique way of gaining her readers' trust. In fact, readers will not find their initial presumption of a female voice challenged. Yet if pressed to find solid evidence for the gendered voice, a reader will have to read closely.

Some stories offer direct clues. In "Eine erfolgreiche Bemühung um Fräulein Block" (A Successful Effort for Miss Block), the narrator, confronted with an aging woman, remembers how in the gray morning light "I'd still be afloat under my pillows, bodiless, still free of obligations, of weight, of figure, and size, trying to avoid or at least postpone the effort to adopt shape and gender.... As to gender, it's female—just a word at this point, no feelings. But not for very much longer: I sit up, and I am—what are my choices?—a woman" (*Nacht* 60). Other texts offer indirect evidence such as a woman's housebound existence. She may feel a surge of anxiety at the sound of steps invading the safe space created by her well-trimmed hedge ("Der entscheidende Augenblick," *Nacht* 63), overcome the protective yet imprisoning walls by looking from the dormer window onto a fascinating outside ("Das Wunder einer Hypothese," *Nacht* 114), or she may escape a sterile life amidst "furniture and plants existing side by side peacefully and without purpose" by magically transforming her home space into a meaningful, living organism ("Wunder" 114). In the world of these narrators, man is a negligible quantity. For example:

> The light from the kitchen window shines on the upturned branches, and the perfume of lilac is all over the garden, almost uncanny, lurking out there in the dark. After I've used the bathroom, washed my hands, supper, conversation with my husband, I go back into the conservatory ("Eine Art Leistung nach der Natur," *Nacht* 77).

Their place is in the house—a haven, prison, or vantage point—as they perceive the world through a window, from their backyards, on their way to work or the supermarket.

Other stories lack direct clues, but as one critic has suggested, Kronauer's narrators seem to be part of one female essence (Baumgart). Others adopt Kronauer's own "Ichperson" or use such terms as "Ichfigur," "Sprechfigur"—all gendered feminine in German—or simply "Erzählerin." But even a neuter term will serve to illustrate how a gender-less, anonymous subject is granted contour and—climactically—an identity of its own: "Ich, Rita Münster" (*Rita Münster* 153).[2] In translating "Ein Tag, der zuletzt doch nicht im Sande verlief" (A Day That Didn't End Hopelessly after All) for another project, I have become painfully aware of what Hélène Cixous calls "those fearful imperatives of language which force us to construct sentences with grammatical correctness, attributing genders properly; those who write are called into account" (14). A gender-neutral sentence like "von *einer Person* betrachtet, die jetzt sehr schnell *den* Kopf hin und her schleudert" (watched by a person shaking her head very quickly from side to side; "Ein Tag" 9, my italics) forces the translator to choose between using the awkward all-embracing "his or her head" or avoiding gender determination altogether. The example illustrates, however, that a noun with feminine grammatical gender can contribute to shifting subtly the weight from gender neutral to female. Instead of using "ein Mensch" (a person) or "ein Kind" (a child), the author frequently chooses the feminine noun "eine Person," or—in the "Narcissus/Narcissa" episode—repeatedly uses "die Gestalt" and "die Figur." I have therefore decided to attribute gender. Even though the narrative voice in the first episodes of "Ein Tag" seems ungendered, the "I" of this text is not different from the other stories in Kronauer's collection or from that of her novels.

For Kronauer, literature reflects the way the mind constructs a chaotic reality by arranging it according to internalized, traditional patterns. Her fiction tries to escape this "dictatorship of literature" ("Gang" 3), which pretends to offer a valid perspective and interpretation. In "A Day That Didn't End Hopelessly after All," the most programmatic of her early stories, there is no place for the reader's empathy, for narration in the traditional sense, for plot, or for characters. It is a world of stills, frozen into a series of pictures, perceived by the narrating self as a fluid system of tectonic movements, of differences, of discontinuities (Cramer 21). What we encounter is the "terror of reality" ("Gang" 3), the confusion of one day—the pattern of a life.

The text begins:

> At the very beginning, early in the morning, I saw a colorful object run across a green surface. Sometimes it stood still, and the colors—yellow, red, blue—were distinctive, got mixed up, hardly perceptible, and became clearer after a while, until separate fields of color emerged that no longer mixed. A ball rolling across grass, light, a beach ball, so light that the wind spins it. Or a circle lying on the grass watched by a person shaking her head very quickly from side to side (9).

What makes this world move is the observer's eye and the observer's mind. If we feel magically drawn into this text, it may be because we are intrigued by the description of something as banal as a beach ball in the grass. Or by the "furor of precision" of the "I," by its obsessiveness in observing and questioning an everyday experience (Dormagen 17). Where will the text lead us as we patiently follow in its small, cautious footsteps when we are accustomed to taking big strides? What will we see once we have assembled this heap of disconnected bits and pieces? Will our effort to make sense of a fragmented world eventually result in a complete, perfect picture? In this essay I undertake to see that fragmented world through the eyes of Kronauer's narrator in "A Day"—assuming a female "Ichperson," even though this is the most "un-gendered" of her narrative voices—to sift through her tentative interpretations, and to help the reader arrange the thousands of pieces by suggesting one possible reading, a vision of the complete picture as it would appear on an imaginary jigsaw puzzle box—the picture of a woman's world.

"A Day That Didn't End Hopelessly after All." An auspicious title—in fact, this title could be read as a final assessment rather than as a beginning. It does not seem to serve its purpose visually, since it is really the first line of the first paragraph, and stylistically it is much too rambling and uncertain, requiring a slow, attentive reading. A typical Kronauer sentence, it is filled with adverbials and flavoring particles. Unlike English syntax, which tends to keep the core of a sentence free from distracting ballast, German syntax heaps any additional information between the subject "a day" and the final verb "end," thus inflating the sentence and blurring its structure: "*Ein Tag*, der zuletzt doch nicht im Sande *verlief*" (my italics). Kronauer's style mimetically reflects the author's odyssey of perception and an emerging self. In her fiction the simultaneity and ambiguity of perception and the narrator's failure to arrange events in a hierarchy or order by putting them in their proper perspective are mirrored in coordinating structures that pile up relentlessly without relief from subordinating elements.

Where other German masters of the convoluted sentence like Kleist and Mann start, Kronauer has already finished. Her readers find themselves entrapped not in Kleistian syntactic intricacies that reflect the psychological entanglement of human nature nor in the complex gestures of Thomas Mann's omniscient narrator, but in a paratactical maze. Her writing "slows down, then stops to display single pictures, until everything comes to a simultaneous standstill" (Dormagen 18). Once again the pieces of a puzzle come to mind as an image for the "spatial form" of modernist prose by Proust, Joyce, or the authors of the *nouveau roman*. Like Uwe Johnson, whose influence she acknowledges, Kronauer's early work requires readers to construct a meaning out of seemingly loose elements. And yet, "the time for academic games of demolishing narrative sequence is over!" proclaims Kronauer in her essay "Die Revolution der Nachahmung" (The Revolution of Imitation), using her customary exclamation marks even in critical comments. "Now we're dealing with more serious issues. We need to bring back the magic of a beginning and an end, where the units, though at times contradictory, indicate the possibility of development when seen from a different perspective" (4). She even offers a direct clue on how to read this story when she advises the reader to "construct a process—the possible development of the self" (5).

It will be helpful to outline the structural components of "A Day That Didn't End Hopelessly after All," a text that reveals a calculated arrangement and an increasingly complex structure. The narrator leads us through five episodes of roughly equal length. They are linked by her comments, which steadily increase in length from one to four lines. Halfway through each scene an additional agent enters—a gust of wind, a change of mind, a twist of interpretation—thereby complicating an already puzzling situation. With Kronauer's narrator our day begins early in the morning when a colorful object runs across a green surface. The day passes, and our senses experience jolt after jolt. As the narrator moves from one experience to the next—first playfully, then restlessly, then nervously, even frantically—the reader wonders what this is all about. There seems to be a direction, but what could it be? The narrator's efforts to find whatever she is after seem to fail one after the other.

The reader, first intrigued by the narrator's curiosity and then puzzled—even infected—by her increasing anxiety, tries to discover the underlying idea and to visualize the complete picture. At the end of the day the narrator finally arrives at the vantage point where everything falls into place. She looks down on the landscape of her life and remembers all the individual steps that brought her there. Her personal growth has been an uphill struggle where each new effort started with excitement and optimism and ended in frustration or failure, just as a student stretches her limits until she is ready for the next, more advanced task. These five episodes mark the stages of growth from early childhood to maturity when the narrator sees her endeavour as having "resulted at last in my complete satisfaction" (13).

Kronauer, however, does not offer a total vision. Instead, she challenges the readers to complete their own picture. They are left to go over every expression, every word, and every subtle change as they would sort the pieces of a puzzle according to minute nuances of color, and as in a puzzle the missing pieces are no less important than the ones already in place. The readers' day will end successfully only if they pick up the fragmented pieces, find the imaginary gestalt, and recreate the whole picture for themselves.

"At the very beginning early in the morning I saw a colorful object run across a green surface"—this first paragraph starts a little abruptly, and deceptively simply. It has all the trappings of a traditional beginning: time, place, and narrator; a story unfolds. What might make the reader a little uneasy is the verb "run," as if this object had a life of its own. The next sentence confirms our suspicion. Although there is a narrating "I," it has no control over this seemingly unidentifiable thing that runs: "sometimes it stood still, the colors got mixed up." The "I" can only relate in minute detail what it sees, using the traditional past tense of storytelling. As the third sentence switches to the present tense, however, we participate in the observer's thought process. In a straightforward and definitive way an explanation is offered, simple enough. It is a ball, a beach ball, what else could it be? But the next sentence deflates our complacency and takes us back to a new beginning: "Or a circle lying on the grass watched by a person tossing her head very quickly back and forth."

What happened? Seeing a picture and understanding what it is that we see requires us to solve a rather complicated problem. In a very fast and altogether unconscious mental process we move through several steps of an "inferential model"—classification, identification, and the attribution of meaning—in order to define reality (Kanisza 3). Because inferring the obvious—some answer already stored in our minds—usually works well, we do not even realize how successful we have been in processing visual information. The narrator, however, tries to understand what is happening without any experience to draw on. She seems to have a child's mind, although she speaks with the voice of an adult. It is thus not surprising that her guess about the identity of the moving object before her eyes is unsuccessful. In Faulkner's *The Sound and the Fury,* Benjy is similarly intrigued by details, yet unable to read any meaning into them. Faulkner's character, a thirty-three-year-old man with the mind of a three-year-old, loves to watch people playing golf, but all he sees are people waving flags and hitting balls. The idea of the game is lost on him.

Both of these narrators' adult voices with children's minds experience the ambiguities of "reading" the world and show us how truly disconcerting our seemingly safe, everyday world is. But a comparison between Kronauer's child and Faulkner's childlike male illustrates a fundamental difference between their worlds. The action unfolding before Benjy's eyes has a logical structure that he is unable to grasp, whereas for Kronauer's child the world consists of coexisting shapes, colors, and movements—details that the adult would see as an organic whole.

Kronauer's narrator grows even more confused when a new protagonist enters the scene in the second paragraph: "A fat, red spot approached the balloon. When it reached it, the balloon jumped away, and the spot, the circle, the shape rolled after it, slower than the first spot, circle, shape, and reached it only because the fugitive reduced his speed and finally lay still" (9).

Of course, additional action only complicates an already puzzling issue. What is it? A red spot, a round shape, a balloon, or a circle? Discriminating between two-dimensional and three-dimensional shapes can be difficult unless we can somehow establish or eliminate the third dimension. E.H. Gombrich illuminates the narrator's experience when he explains that our "confidence in the stability of things in a changeable world is deeply ingrained in the structure of language but we cannot tell whether what we see, in the absence of other clues, is a sphere approaching or a balloon being blown up" (270). To make matters worse, the unknown object in Kronauer's story moves rather like a human being. A child playing with the beach ball could approach, follow, circle—but either one of two red spots moving in the grass could be a balloon or a toddler. Does language provide assistance? Could the "fugitive" be the beach ball that, as we remember, did the "running" before? Words may be deceptive. Used to describe a deceptive reality, they may prove revealing.

The odyssey continues as the most likely explanation—"A child, I said, a child has shoved the ball away and now recaptures it"—is rejected, "or a red balloon helped by the wind is following a child in colorful pants until it falls down." Then the ball jumps—or is it a person jerking her head up and down? And then another, even more disconcerting perception: "I saw the ball replicated. The new little balls lay close together and rolled around a little. Many balls, I said, were now being tossed onto the grass." This is happening, this is real, the narrating voice describes it —or is this yet another illusion? Could the red spot have rolled behind some bush so that the foliage "that allows only a limited view is dissecting the big ball so quickly and irregularly because it is being shaken violently?" (9) Instead of producing an integrated, coherent, stable, and sharply detailed image of the world, the exhilarating experiment only increases the narrator's confusion.

Gombrich describes a situation in which the protagonist is confronted with the same puzzling perception. His adult observer can, however, draw on more life experience and knows that all he needs are a few hints to infer the shape from the position of an object that is hidden. So he can afford to experiment consciously with his "mind's eye" and its efforts to complete the "subjective contour" (Kaufman 174):

> I was looking out of the window, and I saw through the shrubs by the fence the brilliant red slats of the familiar truck; just patches of red, brilliant scarlet. As I looked, it occurred to me that what I was really seeing were dead leaves on a tree; instantly the scarlet changed to a dull chocolate brown. I tried to recover the red by imagining the truck, and found that I could redden the leaves somewhat; then I made them leaves again, and found that I could brown them somewhat... (Gombrich 226).

Finally Gombrich's protagonist goes out to see what the color "really" is, so even though this observer is enjoying a game he has just found, he still feels the need to certify reality. Our narrator does not have that option. Her reality is too complex for her to define, and she fails in her effort to understand it.

Yet unfazed by the negative outcome and less like an adult logically pursuing a plan than a child following a whim, the narrator moves on to some new project. "I turned to something else" (9). This inconspicuous little sentence marks a new beginning and a new stage. The narrative subject now tackles something that cannot be seen or touched—a very different venture that takes place on a much higher level of self-awareness and self-confidence; consequently, the goals are set much higher. How can the air be made to reveal itself? Not only is the new goal more consciously set and far more ambitious, attaining it also requires new and more sophisticated strategies. The narrator uses both her sensitivity and her intellect—an experiment in bodily sensations rather than physics:

> Air was everywhere. I could look through it and not feel it at all. But I knew for certain—it was filled in between all things and adapted to them so smoothly that no one was hindered by it or even aware of it. Only when I whizzed my hand very quickly by my face did it reveal itself. It reacted too slowly, it didn't follow the hand fast enough; you could outsmart it and recognize it as it tried to accompany what had escaped from it. You felt it near your skin and heard it swish (10).

In an almost sassy tone the narrator deals with the most elusive of elements. She knows how to "outsmart the air" and gets absorbed in the pleasure of physical sensations. But soon the air seems to develop an uncanny life of its own, and it starts playing tricks on her. By making "a much stronger sound above" than her hands ever could, it draws her attention away into the sky. She looks up, leaving her safe, contained, "hands-on" space. Inevitably, what at first glance looked like birds moving in the invisible, elusive element becomes utterly confusing. Didn't it look as if the air were blowing the birds around? She is back in the ambiguous universe.

Her dilemma reminds us of the giddy world of the Dutch artist M. C. Escher in which perspective and spatial arrangements deceive the viewer. As long as we can focus on his birds or fish, we are on safe ground. But as soon as the spaces in between attract our attention, we become confused, until the spaces become the new carriers of meaning and recognizable shapes. On either end of Escher's spectrum there is order and stability, but moving from one interpretation to the other creates chaos. This confusion is exactly what our observer experiences. First she notices "a flock of birds with beautiful shining wings. There was air between them." Then she focuses on the air: It "fluttered; it was heated by [the birds], or had taken and thrown them up and now blew them around, or the birds stood still, and it was just the air that shook and did flips; I could see it trembling." And then an even more upsetting thought occurs to the observer, whose initial confidence is by now totally shattered. How do we know that there is air at all? What if the air has withdrawn? If it cannot be heard, seen, or felt anymore, is it still there? This passage also illustrates how Kronauer's narrative technique moves almost imperceptibly from the perceptual to the conceptual point of view. "There was a much stronger sound above me" is a statement about the external world. We hear the narrative "I"—a voice recording an event, informing us, and conveying certain emotions directly related to its experience. We visualize what the narrator witnesses; her eyes function like the eye of a camera to create an illusion of mimesis. The voice continues: "The air fluttered, it was heated by them, or the birds stood still, and it was just the air that did flips" (10). In a tone of recording business as usual and as though the point of view were still *perceptual*, it confronts the guileless reader with a *conceptual* point of view—a consciousness mediated through the "I." This narrator is totally unreliable, or consciously leads us into her world of doubts and guesses. We depend on her to extricate herself—and us—from this confusion. This is not stream of consciousness in the traditional sense. We are trapped within a compulsively focused mind from which we can be released only if it turns back to the safe ground of narration. But this passage draws us deeper and deeper into ambiguity. The sustained inside view leads into chaos—and finally even the grammatical structure lets us down by almost imperceptibly changing from a statement to a question:

> [The air] trembled and circled like mad, and then the birds circled and shot wherever they wanted, and got ahead of the air which had perhaps withdrawn after all; or was it because I didn't feel it and heard only the

birds and saw the whirl of their flapping wings and not the whirls of the air? (10).

What starts as a statement ends with a question mark, revealing that we have been lured into a mental game. Of course, by now it is too late. The narrator's confusion mounts and remains unresolved, and so does ours.

But we are given another chance. "I became restless and went to a place that had more to offer" (10). Like a *deus ex machina*, the safe voice from the outside world reappears, releasing us and announcing that a new experiment is about to begin. Clearly, however, the narrator is slowly becoming unnerved in her quest. Initially, when she "turned to something else," it had seemed casual, even quirky, as if due to a child's short attention span. Now she decides to move on "to a place that has more to offer." She seems to be looking for something, although the reader can only guess what her objective might be.

For her third adventure, she carefully chooses just the right rock in the water to stand on. Is this another effort to *feel and see* simultaneously, hoping that by submerging her feet in the water she will get a foothold in the world? Will she be more successful with water than with air? A place on a rock seems a safe bet, and this time she will not play games with the element; she will stay focused on her feet below in the water. But far from being reassuring, the water test is even more disturbing. Her toes flicker around, although she keeps them perfectly still. As she tries to reestablish contact by touching them with her hand, they disappear, and on reappearing, they are fragmented. The water "washes away the watery bits and pieces" of her feet and even her "searching arm" and "carries them to the wrong places." Worse, the fragmented self she sees and the one she feels are in different places. By now she is totally involved in the process of locating her disassembled self, slyly but unsuccessfully sliding her other arm down into the water to retrieve her lost feet. This adventure could quickly develop into a real identity crisis: "Down there, that was not me any more" (10).

Yet by now she has learned to distinguish between the deceptive appearance of things and their true nature. Although her visual sense may still fail her, her sense of self is stronger, and she no longer falls prey to illusion—she pulls her legs out of the water and gets them back whole, "as if nothing had ever happened" (11). But her encounter with the wet element is not yet over. Looking at the water, she discovers that it is not empty—a figure is in it. Everybody is familiar with the sudden realization that the person in the watery mirror is oneself. Yet, far from quietly reflecting the figure, the water in this story attacks it. This element is a force with a life of its own, just like the air, yet more aggressive. It seems determined to keep what it has captured and destroy it:

———. "Zehn Jahre lang auf den Erfolg gewartet." *Brigitte.* Sonderheft Bücher, 1982. 12–15.

Ovid. *Metamorphoses.* Trans. Rolfe Humphries. Bloomington: Indiana UP, 1955.

Sill, Oliver. "Wirklichkeitsauffassung und Literaturverständnis: Zum programmatischen Charakter der frühen Erzählungen." *Text+Kritik* 122 (Oct. 1991): 6–12.

The Wired Mouth: On the Positionality of Perception in Anne Duden's *Opening of the Mouth* and *Das Judasschaf*

Annette Meusinger

This study is part of a comprehensive book project on concepts of identity and body in both feminist theories and modern literature by women in Germany and the USA. Referring to the dispute between Leslie Adelson and Sigrid Weigel (1988) about racist elements in feminist aesthetics, the article examines Anne Duden's *Opening of the Mouth* and *Das Judasschaf*. Both are seen to reproduce the idea of a universality of woman and the female body and exclude issues of race, nationality, ethnicity, and class from the concept of identity. My analysis presents a traumatic structure of the protagonist in *Das Judasschaf* and questions her imago as a surviving memory-body and the position of "responsible sufferer." (AM)

"To the extent that political and ideological certainties and utopias diminish, the reading of images and characters from the cultural memory, of dreams, symptoms, and expressions of body language gains increasing significance in contemporary literature," Sigrid Weigel writes in a post-*Wende* volume of rereadings of contemporary literature (*Bilder* 10). Contemporary authors also react to the complex unmasking of the autonomous, homogeneous, rational male subject as a construct of power structures of the symbolic order by resorting to traditional myths, by rewriting "archival material," and by exploring memory structures and their permanent traces (Freud). Within the discourse of feminist theory, this has led to extremely contradictory arguments about the feminist subject's desire, about the relationship between postmodernism and feminism, and to a continuing search for adequate writing strategies (the debate about Judith Butler's *Gender Trouble* is indicative of these conflicts).[1]

Essential for my project here is the observation that in feminist theories the understanding of the subject as fragmented, unhomogeneous, and unstable is always closely tied to the concept of positionality as well as to a rejection of the unambiguous nature of identity, gender, sexuality, and body. Positionality here signifies (following Adelson and de Lauretis) an individual's specific relationship to power and knowledge, in the sense of individual participation in or exclusion from authority. This relationship results from a complex mesh of personal factors such as race, biological gender, class, religion, cultural differences, and sexual preferences, as well as the significance assigned to these factors by the concrete cultural order. The individual's positionality creates specific ideological, political, aesthetic, and epistemological systems of norms and values, as well as a specific perception of the structures of cultural memory. Positionality shapes the inscription of permanent traces (Freud) in the body as well as the reading of the traces. The concept of positionality expressly contradicts an additive idea of identity and the inequalities of sexism-racism (de Lauretis, *Alice* and *Technologies*; Adelson, "Racism" and *Bodies*; Butler; Hagemann-White).

Memory-Body

Weigel considers Anne Duden's writings as paradigmatic for innovative and avant-gardistic aspects of contemporary literature. Weigel comes to the conclusion that literary criticism "has trouble" with Duden's writings and takes the side of the author. As early as *Die Stimme der Medusa* (1987), Weigel had singled out Duden's *Opening of the Mouth* because the text specifically "pays attention to the modus of the protagonist, which is excluded from the narrateable existence, [as] movements and perceptions that contain what Luce Irigaray calls woman's being-elsewhere, outside of the identity ascribed to her and outside of language" (128). According to Weigel, the body in the text serves as an organ of perception that recovers "what had already existed but had been invisible, and thus revives that which had been suppressed into the unconscious" (125). The ravaged body of the woman as a symbol for her "raging speechlessness" and the experience of the dismembered body show (with Lacan and Freud) the female protagonist in *Opening of the Mouth* as an excellent critic of the misjudgment inherent in the process of ego development (124). Weigel recognizes the central topics of Duden's second text, *Das Judasschaf*, to be "survival as structural participation in guilt and the question of how going on or surviving is even possible with the knowledge of continuing violence" (129). It is necessary to explore the premises of Weigel's theses, as well as the problems resulting from them.

"My memory is my body. My body is honeycombed with holes. The only thing that doesn't fall through its mesh is love and torment" (*Opening* 128). If, following Walter Benjamin, memory is seen as a medium, with "memories simultaneously providing an image of the person who remembers," then the (political) present of the artist is not a neutral place but rather a "particular moment," an experienced moment, charged with all the tensions and contradictions of its concrete, individual, historical constellation ("Ausgraben" 400). An individual's/society's memory, therefore, can be compared to a staging, in which memories are fragmentarily assembled into images[2] according to the momentary needs of the concrete historical situation. I consider these premises enormously important for the discussion of Duden's writing.

It is symptomatic that the protagonist both in *Opening of the Mouth* and in *Das Judasschaf* perceives/represents life as a "slaughterhouse," a "strangling angel," a permanent ordeal leading into the depths of (cultural) memory, which is meant to be preserved and reconstructed through the recording of its traces on the woman's ravaged body. These traces can be read as evidence of complex processes and contexts of violence in which the protagonists in both texts find and define themselves. This is demonstrated in the brutal assault on the protagonist by a group of black GIs in *Opening of the Mouth*. She is literally made speechless (*entmündigt,* also the legal term for "declared incompetent") when a rock smashes her jaw. For her, the physical loss of her voice seems appropriate because now the "body could begin to catch up on what had until then been reserved only for my brainhead...the limitless chaos of the world...let it break into me then, and rage in me" (63).

As a concrete act within the continuum of violence in history, as a multi-layered metaphor for female experience as well as the German past, the assault and its consequences for the protagonist embody central thematic and structural aspects of Duden's prose. In this sense, the assault is also experienced by the protagonist in *Das Judasschaf*. For instance, the manner of existence of the "brainhead" mentioned in *Opening of the Mouth* is described in *Das Judasschaf*: "It was her raw brain that had been living in a slaughterhouse for twenty years now. To be more precise, it was stuck on the ceiling there" (38–39).

In her essay "Racism and Feminist Aesthetics," Leslie Adelson shows conclusively that in *Opening of the Mouth* Duden (in keeping with Irigaray's and Cixous's theories) creates a model for the presumed exclusion of woman from the dominant language, for the inscription of this exclusion into woman's body, and for the attempt to overcome speechlessness with a "different syntax of woman" (Irigaray). "What had been eaten inwards became the grammar of a...language that would not come to its senses...beyond the threshold of meaning and form," Duden writes (*Opening* 65). The procedure of wiring the mouth can also be read as a (failed) attempt at reconstructing woman (in a dual sense) by removing the visible traces of violence from her body through violent reconstruction of this body. The assault is the outer expression of the destruction of a "[female] existence, thrust completely inwards" (87) that began a long time ago. An additive concept of identity is obviously inscribed into Duden's writings and frequently into the critical analyses of the texts as well (by Weigel, for instance); in both texts, the gender of the protagonist is assumed to be the primary creator of identity. Adelson correctly points out that femininity and the exclusion of woman from power and language are always experienced as historically, socially, or racially specific ("Racism" 236). However, as she has shown, both Duden's text and Weigel's analysis ignore the fact that the protagonist in *Opening of the Mouth* is not "Everywoman" (242).

The protagonist in *Das Judasschaf* then experiences as well as executes a shift to an image-body space that appears to be outside of concrete time and history. She imagines herself into an "uninhabitable layer between heaven and earth" (33). This location within a practically transcendent sphere separates her from almost all others anchored in everyday life whom she sees as "survivors without memory" because of their indifference toward remembering. This is demonstrated radically in the description of Vittore Carpaccio's painting *St. Peter the Martyr,* seen as one who will continue fighting, eternally carrying out orders, even with a split skull and pierced heart. "He stopped at nothing; everything was carried out, however, by God's hand. He didn't dirty his own hands." The description of the painting follows a Waffen-SS major general's report on the minutely organized use of prisoners' shorn hair. Juxtaposed to both passages is the protagonist's self-ordained passion: "My heart is not pierced, but smashed. My skull not split, but distended...under the sun of torture" (32–33).

The protagonist finds models for the passion in Renaissance paintings, especially Carpaccio's *Meditation on the Passion of Christ.* With extraordinary aesthetic originality, Duden reconstructs from these paintings spaces of experience that the protagonist enters, coming to herself. Here, she encounters a "knowledge that cannot be shared, towards which she rushed uninterrupted" until she "would become congruent with it" (*Judasschaf* 40).

Weigel sees the symbolism of this passion in the fact that "in the midst of a culture of tracelessness, the protagonist takes on the function of memory by recording the traces on her body" (*Bilder* 29), becoming a "surviving memory-body" into which "traces of a German history after the Shoah are inscribed" (*Bilder* 11). Despite debates about the racial, social, and cultural specification of body inscriptions and perceptions, Weigel sees the body of woman as the place of truth, as memory. This presumption of the universality of woman's body corresponds with a nonhistorical understanding of the body posited by Barbara Duden.

The Black Box of Factuality

> Only the piled-up memories were bad, which never decompose and all of which I had to endure day and night. An arsenal of unbelievable size...from the darkest corner of the torment of the ten thousand I want

to sneak away, still spared against all odds, and not arrive at the torment of the present (*Judasschaf* 43).

Although some passages seem to lead to such a conclusion, *Das Judasschaf* is not about remembering the Shoah, not about "memory-work" (Brügmann 266), not about being unable to forget. Remembering as the subjective re-creation of the world is a process in the realm of the imaginary, where past events return as imagination and are captured in aesthetic form—inseparably linking art and the work of mourning. In this context, remembering is a mental act of situating the self within the continuum of time (Koch).

The protagonist in *Das Judasschaf* does situate herself within a historically concrete context by associating her date of birth with the Wannsee Conference (where the Final Solution was agreed upon in January 1942), thus placing herself as born into a context of guilt and mourning (Weigel, *Bilder* 24). But her location as "surviving memory-body" in a transcendent sphere effectively revokes this so that her imago is that of someone "informed alive" (*Judasschaf* 38) who moves restlessly between the poles of going insane and wanting to die and for whom there is no salvation because all exits appear to be blocked: "Pit or heaven, past or future reject me because they are as congested as my skull" (33).

Das Judasschaf embodies a shock of realization set off by knowledge about the factuality of the Shoah that the protagonist can no longer repress. Although the Shoah as event is part of the past, it refuses to be historicized, forgotten, and thus part of the aesthetic ritual of mourning. In "Der Engel des Vergessens und die Black Box der Faktizität," Gertrud Koch refers to the metronymic independence of historical documentary images in Claude Lanzmann's film *Shoah*: piles of hair, shoes, and other objects have replaced the dead whom they represent within the system of cultural signifiers, thus historicizing them as concluded past. For Lanzmann, the Shoah therefore cannot be remembered or represented within the historicity of semantic signifiers (Koch). To Anne Duden (and Weigel), the language of the dominant discourse appears similarly unsuited as a medium; it is used in "speeches about...history that have become common knowledge" in which "the traces of a German history...are at risk of getting lost" (Weigel, *Bilder* 11). Weigel applies the reversal of Bachmann's statement "When one has survived, survival stands in the way of realization" (*Malina* 211) to *Das Judasschaf* and states as Duden's central concern the question of "how it can be possible to go on living with the knowledge of the Shoah" (*Bilder* 25). Both Duden's text and Weigel's analysis completely avoid a question that to me seems obvious in this context, namely how the knowledge about the Shoah should be perceived in present-day Germany as active, responsible anchoredness.

My examination of Duden's *Das Judasschaf* has led to the thesis that the text obviously follows a traumatic structure. In this context, trauma signifies a rupture in the continuum of time, where chronological time is "pulled back into a mental state as if on a rubber band" (Koch 76). As a break in the structuring of time, the trauma is a sort of "black box," i.e., a space that destroys time and makes self-reconfirmation and action impossible for the individual.

This is the context for the thesis that the trauma of the protagonist in *Das Judasschaf* is not merely the result of knowledge about the factuality of the Shoah. It is also based on her realization that, in the "petrified memory" of the dominant German culture, this knowledge only leaves traces as inscriptions in the female body. Obviously, Duden's text considers culture and cultural memory in terms of a "homogeneous space" (*Memoria*) and presumes memory and truth as definite and constant. It ignores the fact that the idea of truth and the mechanisms of the alternating inclusion and exclusion of cultural meaning are legitimized and directed by a culture's model of self-description that is actuated by hierarchical interests of culture-sustaining groups.

The presumption of culture as a "non-homogeneous space" would thus have to include both the question of which cultural signs memoria value would be assigned to in order to establish a current model of self-description of a concrete culture. This would also entail the analysis of the mechanisms of selection and the hierarchical structures and interests connected with them (*Memoria*).

The protagonist in Duden's *Das Judasschaf* states:

> Germany, [which] exhaled (itself) above one...this completely used-up air.... A point of saturation had been reached, a deadly quiet moment where the threads that came together in it continuously neutralized each other.... Whatever had been newly brought up disappeared immediately, was silenced, invisible, no longer to be probed (41).

The protagonist sees herself within a "general lack of events and traces" (57); Berlin or New York, it does not make any difference to her.

This perspective causes a radical intensification of the protagonist's body experience. At the same time, this perspective distorts any perception "outside" of this body. Perceived is only that which she already knows. The result is an increased reproduction of clichés, especially in the chapter "New York, with a Scream." It also illuminates the chasm between her (traumatic) knowledge and "the foreign," the "life outside": "Once again, she ultimately arrived in a place, lay down on the bed assigned to her, and immediately fell asleep...as if in the abyss of all times that ever passed. And she awoke exactly into this abyss. Numerous miles away from New York" (55). The "tiny breakthrough time" (57) that she once experiences in New York is not enough to truly open the mind's eye to the "outside," to perceive, for instance, New York as the center for European Jewish emigrants whose "traces" in everyday political life are difficult to overlook.

However, several passages in the text suggest that the protagonist in *Das Judasschaf* senses that she preserves from inside a traumatically sealed space of knowledge, a "black box": "a woman...unlocked a door to the contents of a black cube. The protagonist entered it, smiling.... That was it" (13). "Thus, the (black) cube that sheltered her now was only a small darkened cell, and in front of it, expanding and stretching in all directions, were the events, overextended and boundless" (16); or: "The woman stands in the air, immobile, or in the sea, or in the branches of the shoreless times, perhaps also in a tear" (116). With noticeable frequency, inclusion and exclusion, rupture and incision mark the impossible or severed connection between her and the "other."

In parable-like parallelism to an understanding of history that considers the year 1945 a turning point and the period from 1933 to 1945 "a rupture in civilization" (Briegleb 145),[3] the protagonist in *Opening of the Mouth* was already separated "from what was" with a "bloodless, precise incision" (62). In *Das Judasschaf* the idea of history becomes dubious:

> I, running along inside the mechanism, continuously jumping over the meshing cogwheels at their highest point in order not to get caught in them...can't go in any direction...can only turn back. "Repent my love and come away." But she has already regretted everything and that didn't help her or anyone else. In reality she can't turn back anymore anyway. Perhaps, if the wooden sandals have a chance to find a grip, she can turn around quickly. Turned around..., she sees what lay behind her now ahead of her, so she is now stepping backward. It is difficult to run into the moving stillness like this...and surely she will soon fall, face and front of her body first, into the past that was crushed without a trace (108–09).

Not only does Benjamin's "angel of history" get turned around metaphorically (Weigel, *Bilder* 28), but the "moving stillness" can also be read as a sort of establishment of the trauma, a renunciation in principle of a possible intervention by the subject. The human being (of integrity) now only seems imaginable as a "responsible sufferer" (Briegleb 147).

E guerra e morte

In *Opening of the Mouth* and in *Das Judasschaf*, the woman is primarily inscribed as victim. The assault in *Opening of the Mouth* is verbalized as an act of sexual violence, to which women often are exposed without power and legal rights. The protagonist experiences the act of physical "silencing" as a "rape of the head. By means of an iron pipe. Painted red and white.... Flakes and crumbs of rust mingle with the contents of my head. Penetration and violent ejaculation have caused increased mucus secretion" (42). This also implies the sexual act as an element of the violence within a structural power system. Using the image-space of Piero della Francesca's painting *St. Michael,* the text "Der Auftrag die Liebe" (The Mission the Love) in *Das Judasschaf* (107–17) impressively shows that the conditioning of man to become an autonomous, (self)-disciplining, controlling subject who kills love and erases memory is an "assignment" with a tradition in cultural history. Interestingly enough, it is still the male lover (female friends or lovers do not appear) who can reach the protagonist for moments while she is in a state of absolute "isolation and balanced suspension" (38): "His voice said: This is really crazy. Come out here right away. I still hear myself asking: But where to?" (39). These passages can be read as indications that she is in a sort of traumatic state. The assault and its physical consequences for the protagonist illustrate a trauma, i.e., they incorporate what had already existed inside her.

At the same time, Duden suggests that "the mission the love" is inscribed into the female body like the lost traces of cultural memory. The protagonist in *Opening of the Mouth* is obsessed with "incurable love" (109), a "shameless...crazy" (110) love that takes hold of her as a personified force.

The protagonist in *Das Judasschaf* also ties the few, tenuous threads that connect her to "the life outside," through a man, because he is anchored in pragmatically functioning everyday life.[4] In contrast to *Opening of the Mouth,* the protagonist in *Das Judasschaf* has buried as an illusion all hope for the saving power of love. Within the context of knowledge about the factuality of the Shoah, love becomes an emotion "no living being can afford" (53). She states:

> Something completely unharmed, not even slightly singed, rose all the way to the ceiling. Love. Very impersonal and untouchable. You have to be cold to be born again, to be resurrected or not to be charred in the ashes.... In contrast, the parched skins of the protagonist, her scabby features, for which there was no turning back and no resurrection. Still, her lips had involuntarily contorted into a smile when she looked up to the ceiling. As if something imaginary of this kind still had anything to do with her (41).

This constellation is almost unbearable for the protagonist: "I would like to entomb my head and no longer be" (42), she complains. She sees herself as a "trunk person tortured into shape, wreckage leftover of the living" after an "overly long female life" (48). The textual strategy in *Das Judasschaf* pushes her farther and farther into the role of the "responsible sufferer."

The passion for writing against the forgetting of knowledge in cultural memory is inherent in the text (Weigel, *Bilder* 1994). *Judasschaf* hypothesizes forgetting as an immoral, irresponsible, male behavior of the "others." At the same time, however, forgetting her knowledge in the sense of total amnesia is an extraordinary temptation for the protagonist (in the sense of a salvation). She is aware of this. She rejects this possibility and finally imagines herself as a self-sacrificing victim: this woman, "smoke...rain of ashes...black snow" (37), "crashed, drowned, burned, smashed, worn out" (116), has, after many *Ways of Dying* (*Todesarten,* an allusion to Ingeborg Bachmann's uncompleted trilogy), finally "arrived and she doesn't count anymore. Ave verum corpus. Finally the knowledge can spread all over the body" (117).

In Bachmann's *Malina,* the "I" (readable as an unliveable manner of existence) disappears into the wall. In *Das Judasschaf,* the protagonist (probably) merges into the image-space of Carpaccio's painting *Preparation of the Grave of Christ* that embodies her knowledge. Thus she (as woman) sketches herself as memory-body.

It seems problematic to me to see this position as the only one of moral integrity and to denounce social and political engagement (anchoring) in everyday life as cold (male) lack of memory.

Threshold Existence and Dark Spots

In both of Duden's texts, the central figure exists primarily in border realms of perception. She is frequently in the zones between sleep, dream, delusion, and awareness. In *Opening of the Mouth* she also has an apparent affinity for transcendent spheres. All boundaries between these forms of existence appear lifted, as well as those between physical and psychological processes and (especially in *Opening of the Mouth*) between animal, plant, and human forms of existence. Past, present, and future merge in her traumatic knowledge; its most concrete expression is in *Das Judasschaf,* in knowledge about the factuality of the Shoah. Inscribed into both texts is the concept of sensually and physically fragmented perception. The physically smashed body in *Opening of the Mouth* and the fragmentarily perceived body in *Das Judasschaf* express her placement in time and history and are thus an element of her positionality. Both the specificity and the limits of her perception are conditioned by this positionality. Nevertheless, her perception in (especially) *Das Judasschaf* is charged with the authoritarian demand for truth of an autonomous, homogeneous subject: "Somebody should come and revolt with sudden rage into this extended stillness.... It's high time that the tongues loosened here and there.... There is boundless silence" (89–90). This is the protagonist's complaint in front of Carpaccio's *Meditation on the Passion of Christ* in New York, as if no civil rights movement, no multicultural women's movement had ever revolted loudly and with sudden rage and actually caused a social and cultural movement.

Another problem in *Das Judasschaf* corresponds to this gap in perception. Although the protagonist situates herself as someone guiltily tangled up in history—"I am from Germany" (52)—this description of her position is preceded by "I am a woman, a girl, a female child" (52). She sees herself as someone marked since birth (106), someone condemned (107).

Das Judasschaf ties identity and gender of the protagonist as well as of "woman," victim, and memory inseparably and fatefully together. The protagonist feels

> as if the whole inside of her body were violated from the beginning and as if all her brain cells had to inspect the terrain individually, one after the other and continuously, so that no memory would ever be lost as long as she lived and long after that. An individual human being, a woman, a female child, beyond love and with all the murdered as provisions, "street-wise," up to the moment where the sounds, noises, dissonances, the laughter, and the screams turn into music. Ave Maria Stella (56).

The core of the protagonist's identity doubtlessly seems to be her woman-ness. This corresponds with the theory of a natural binary gender difference, which Renate Gildemeister and Angelika Wetterer confirmed as still prevalent within the German women's movement in 1992. Inherent in the theory is a "conservatism in the basic structures of political concepts," theoretical aporias, and a "naturalizing of authority relations" (Knapp and Wetterer 202). The theory indirectly promotes non-intervention in political structures as well as a victim-perpetrator relationship that places an undifferentiated "woman" on the victim's side of history.[5]

In this context, it is necessary to refer to a specific aspect of Duden's writings. The physical experience of femininity, the participation in or exclusion from power and language as well as their traces in the body differ greatly for women from different cultures (or within one culture) because of their individual positionality. The assumption of the universality of woman ignores this, thus inscribing racist elements into Duden's *Opening of the Mouth* (Adelson). Furthermore, *Opening of the Mouth* and *Das Judasschaf* contain aspects of the sort of supercilious arrogance that Sara Lennox has found in some feminist impulses. On the other hand, the gaps in perception as well as the harshness and specificity of the suffering of Duden's protagonists are in fact determined by their entanglement in a concrete historical constellation, by their nationality, race, and color, precisely their positionality. In a certain sense, the texts therefore undermine the assumption of woman's universality.

Adelson discussed this in her paper "Racism and Feminist Aesthetics in Anne Duden's *Opening of the Mouth*" in Hamburg in 1986; in a 1988 article she asked about the protagonist: "How much of her experience is German, how much of it female, how much of it white?" Adelson also emphasized that "it is to Duden's great credit that she does not allow us to isolate surgically one from the other, for it is only historically, in the context of these other factors, that gender can be experienced" (243). Adelson clearly names the connection between the gaps in perception caused by positionality, feminist strategies of writing, and racism in *Opening of the Mouth*:

> Duden's tendentially positive appropriation of blackness on behalf of a female subjectivity evidences, on the one hand, a close affinity to generally held premises about écriture féminine. On the other hand, however, the racist core-image of this text underscores this issue of positionality vis-à-vis the dominant order for author, character, and reader alike.... The racism in Duden's aesthetic, once it is named, forces us to acknowledge that the experience of femaleness is historically, socially, and racially specific (236).

Adelson's paper caused a fierce debate. The focal point of the argument was the fact that the perpetrators in *Opening of the Mouth* were faceless black GIs—a fact that had not played a role in the German criticism before Adelson's discussion of the text. This led to an argument about the representation of "blackness," "darkness," "the blacks," and "black perpetrators" in Duden's text. As Adelson emphasizes:

> This highly questionable equation of a group of faceless blacks with what functions implicitly in the text as indiscriminate evil is rendered all the more problematic by the consequences of this attack for the female narrator.... What we have here, one might contend, is the affirmation of the racist stereotype that black men pose an inherent danger to white people and to white women in particular (236).

In her article "Die Schwelle des Körpers: Geschlecht und Rasse" (The Body's Threshhold: Gender and Race), Theresa Wobbe refers to similarities in the production modes of gender and race that run along signs of attribution of affiliations. She considers the unprotectedness of women of various nationalities as the mark of a specific position in the social space, connected "with a special stock of knowledge" and "habitual organization." According to Wobbe, this implies

> that through the vulnerability of the female gender, the whole group can possibly be threatened. The presence of those who are constructed as foreign can be interpreted as a threat to the female gender. By this process of shutting off, the community marks its borders and creates the group "we."

Wobbe sees the phrase "The Turk rapes the German woman" as the colloquial expression of this construction (111).

In my opinion, the scenario of the assault in *Opening of the Mouth* also has to be read within this context. Adelson also interprets the inherent sexual connotation of the assault as an unconscious redoubling of male violence that falls back on the racist stereotype of the "black man." Elaborating on her Hamburg paper, Adelson shows in a later article how attributes that the history of civilization often ascribes to women as the "others," the "foreign," are projected onto another group in *Opening of the Mouth*, other "foreigners"—blacks. The scenario ultimately refers to the femaleness as well as the whiteness of the victim ("Racism" 242).

Weigel strongly rejected Adelson's argumentation, reasoning that Adelson saw "the representation of the assault as racist because, among other reasons, the perpetrators aren't presented as individuals." Weigel had pointed out that

> the representation comes from the perspective of the victim, but the perpetrator-victim relationship de-individualizes those involved. If, however, one wanted to establish the norm that black perpetrators could not be described as perpetrators, this would then resemble helpless anti-racism or even reverse racism (*Stimme* 128-29).

Weigel emphasizes that in her manner of writing Duden actually breaks through the structures of eurocentrism and returns "the ambiguity to the darkness contained in her text," but that it does not talk about symbols but "about concrete blacks" (128-29).

In *Making Bodies, Making History,* Adelson correctly doubts "that the perpetrator-victim relationship necessitates such abstractions." Adelson agrees with Weigel's evaluation of Duden's ambiguous representation of darkness, but emphasizes that "it is decidedly not true of her treatment of dark-skinned persons. She does not portray, as Weigel contends, 'concrete' blacks" (145).

This manner of perception of persons of color is basically also decisive for *Das Judasschaf*, where the persons are differentiated as men, women, and blacks ("a group of young blacks" [59]; "a black man" [111], etc.). Weigel is right in that in *Das Judasschaf*, Duden by no means "analogizes woman as victim and black man as victim" (129). The self-concept of the protagonist excludes such an analogy in principle. The blacks are part of the "life outside," an incorporation of the foreign. They are inevitably perceived through the grid of the protagonist's cultural knowledge and the blanks conditioned by her positionality.

To read *Das Judasschaf* as a reflection of "survival as structural participation in guilt" (Weigel, *Stimme* 129) is therefore first of all an intellectual statement. It becomes consequential when the protagonist's identity is understood as a (variable) process within historically concrete power structures, in which the protagonist is responsibly anchored on the basis of her positionality.

The discussions of Anne Duden's *Opening of the Mouth* and *Das Judasschaf* provoke very different ways of reading; they are determined in part by feminist scholars' own positionality. The debate about *Opening of the Mouth* between Adelson and Weigel is symptomatic. It is therefore important to become aware of the positional differences between women in order to be able to develop productive, positionality-specific feminist theories, political strategies, and literary aesthetics.

Translated by Sabine Schmidt

Notes

[1] An exemplary discussion takes place in *Feminist Contentions* and in *Feministische Studien* 2 (cf. de Lauretis; B. Duden; Wobbe).

[2] In the context of his critique of a positivist understanding of history and the idea of progress as going through a homogeneous, empty time, Benjamin sees the relationship between present and past not as a continuous chronological connection but as an image, a jump: "Every present is determined by those images which are synchronic with it: every Now is the Now of a certain recognizability.... It is not that the past casts its light on the present, or that the present casts its light on the past, but image is that wherein what has been comes together like a flash with the Now and creates a constellation. In other words: image is dialectic in stillness" (*Allegorien* 147).

[3] To me, an understanding of history appears to be more adequate which (also!) considers Auschwitz as the most extreme expression of western European modernism's implementation of its ideas "of plenitude, purity, centrality, totality, unity and mastery...in their various narrative performances, whether cast in the rhetoric of totalization or of liberation"—"a sort of modern industrial apparatus for the elimination of differences" (Santner 9).

[4] Compared with texts by writers from the German Democratic Republic, it is striking how naturally "the life outside" is linked here to a job and has primarily male connotations.

[5] In my opinion, this harmonizes perfectly with the dominant "male" interests in the Federal Republic of Germany than some German feminists are willing to realize to this day.

Works Cited

Adelson, Leslie A. *Making Bodies, Making History: Feminism and German Identity*. Lincoln: U of Nebraska P, 1993.

———. "Racism and Feminist Aesthetics: The Provocation of Anne Duden's *Opening of the Mouth*." *Signs* 13.2 (1988): 234–52.

———. "Rassismus und feministische Ästhetik in Anne Dudens Übergang." *Eurozentrismus: Zum Verhältnis von sexueller und kultureller Differenz.* Reader der Sektion II bei der dritten Tagung von Frauen in der Literaturwissenschaft Frauen-Literatur-Politik. Hamburg, 1986.

Bachmann, Ingeborg. *Malina. Ausgewählte Werke in drei Bänden.* Vol. 3. Berlin: Aufbau, 1987.

Benhabib, Seyla. "Feminismus und Postmoderne: Ein prekäres Bündnis." *Feminist Contentions: A Philosophical Exchange.* 9–30.

Benjamin, Walter. *Allegorien kultureller Erfahrung: Ausgewählte Schriften 1920–1940.* Ed. Sebastian Kleinschmidt. Leipzig: Reclam, 1984.

———. "Ausgraben und Erinnern." *Gesammelte Schriften.* Ed. Rolf Tiedemann, Hermann Schweppenhäuser, Theodor W. Adorno, and Gershom Scholem. Vol. 4. Frankfurt a.M.: Suhrkamp, 1974–1983. 400–01.

Briegleb, Klaus. "Der Weg in die absolute Prosa: Peter Weiss und Anne Duden." *Gegenwartsliteratur seit 1968.* 140–50.

Briegleb, Klaus, and Sigrid Weigel. *Gegenwartsliteratur seit 1968.* München: Hanser, 1992.

Brügmann, Margret. "Das gläserne Ich: Überlegungen zum Verhältnis von Frauenliteratur und Postmoderne am Beispiel von Anne Dudens *Das Judasschaf.*" *Amsterdamer Beiträge zur neueren Germanistik 29: Frauen-Fragen in der deutschsprachigen Literatur seit 1945.* Ed. Mona Knapp and Gerd Labroisse. Amsterdam: Rodopi, 1989. 253–74.

Butler, Judith. *Gender Trouble: Feminism and the Subversion of Identity.* New York: Routledge, 1990.

Cixous, Hélène. *Die unendliche Zirkulation des Begehrens: Weiblichkeit in der Schrift.* Trans. Eva Meyer and Jutta Kranz. Berlin: Merve, 1977.

de Lauretis, Teresa. *Alice Doesn't: Feminism, Semiotics, Cinema.* Bloomington: Indiana UP, 1984.

———. "Der Feminismus und seine Differenzen." *Feministische Studien 2* (1993): 96-102.

———. *Technologies of Gender: Essays on Theory, Film, and Fiction.* Bloomington: Indiana UP, 1987.

Duden, Anne. *Das Judasschaf.* Berlin: Rotbuch, 1985.

———. *Opening of the Mouth.* Trans. Della Couling. London: Pluto, 1985.

Duden, Barbara. "Die Frau ohne Unterleib: Zu Judith Butlers Entkörperung." *Feministische Studien 2* (1993): 24-34.

Feminist Contentions: A Philosophical Exchange. Ed. Seyla Benhabib, Judith Butler, Drucilla Cornell, and Nancy Fraser. New York: Routledge, 1995.

Gildemeister, Renate, and Angelika Wetterer. "Wie Geschlechter gemacht werden." *Traditionen Brüche: Entwicklungen feministischer Theorie.* Ed. Gudrun-Axeli Knapp and Angelika Wetterer. Freiburg: Kore, 1992. 201–54.

Hagemann-White, Carol, and Maria S. Reerich. *FrauenMännerBilder.* Bielefeld: AJZ, 1988.

Irigaray, Luce. *Das Geschlecht, das nicht eins ist.* Trans. Eva Meyer and Heidi Paris. Berlin: Merve, 1979.

Koch, Gertrud. "Der Engel des Vergessens und die Black Box der Faktizität." *Memoria: Vergessen und Erinnern.* 67–77.

Knapp, Gudrun-Axeli, and Angelika Wetterer. *Traditionen Brüche: Entwicklungen feministischer Theorie.* Freiburg: Kore, 1992.

Lennox, Sara. "Impulse aus den USA und Frankreich." *Frauen Literatur Geschichte: Schreibende Frauen vom Mittelalter bis zur Gegenwart.* Ed. Hiltrud Gnüg and Renate Möhrmann. Stuttgart: Metzler, 1985. 380–94.

Memoria: Vergessen und Erinnern. Ed. Anselm Haverkamp and Renate Lachmann. München: Fink, 1993.

Santner, Eric. *Stranded Objects: Mourning, Memory, and Film in Postwar Germany.* Ithaca: Cornell UP, 1990.

Weigel, Sigrid. *Bilder des kulturellen Gedächtnisses: Beiträge zur Gegenwartsliteratur.* Dülmen-Hiddingsel: tende, 1994.

———. *Die Stimme der Medusa: Schreibweisen in der Gegenwartsliteratur von Frauen.* Dülmen-Hiddingsel: tende, 1987.

Wobbe, Teresa. "Die Schwelle des Körpers: Geschlecht und Rasse." *Feministische Studien* 2 (1993): 110-16.

"Between Worlds": Reading Jeannette Lander's *Jahrhundert der Herren* as a Postcolonial Novel

Monika Shafi

This article examines Jeannette Lander's novel *Jahrhundert der Herren* in the context of postcolonial and travel literature. It offers a close reading of the text and traces the conflicting discourses the main protagonist, a young German woman, confronts in settling down in Sri Lanka. It argues that the protagonist is on the one hand able to critique the (neo)colonial masters' discourse, alluded to in the title of the novel, but that she also remains deeply implicated in it through her identification with the concepts of bourgeois subjectivity and progress, which ultimately hinder her from developing a dialogic, reciprocal relationship with Sri Lankan culture. (MS)

In 1993 Jeannette Lander published the novel *Jahrhundert der Herren* (Century of the Masters), the enticing story of a German woman's struggles establishing a new home and business in contemporary Sri Lanka. The issues Lander addresses in this text, the relationship between displacement and identity, exile and home, as well as the legacy of colonial rule, mark the novel as engaged in the contemporay interrogation of the colonial relationship. The process of decolonization depicted in postcolonial literature has been defined as a way "of unlearning historically determined habits of privilege and privation, of ruling and dependency" (Mohanty 110). In *Jahrhundert der Herren* Lander investigates these shifts from the perspective of a Western, female figure who is caught in the often opposing discourses that these two components of her identity entail. The concept of an existence "between worlds," as the protagonist Juliane repeatedly describes her situation, thus refers on the one hand to the geographical and cultural contrasts between Germany and Sri Lanka. On the other hand, it also describes the contrasts between the discourses of femininity and the (neo)colonialism Juliane confronts in her life in Sri Lanka.

I would like to trace here the conflicts, contradictions, and complexities of this existence between worlds and examine how Juliane, the "daughter of the masters" (315), negotiates and alternates between the two discursive sites alluded to in her self-description. My argument is that she is able to recognize and critique the hegemonic rule of the "masters"—highlighted in the novel's title and in numerous references throughout the text—but that she also remains deeply implicated in it through her identification with the concepts of bourgeois subjectivity and progress. The crucial marker in the encounter between West and East, as it is staged in this novel, lies precisely in the different notions of time and self represented by Juliane and the Asian characters. The meditative stasis Juliane perceives in Sri Lanka contrasts with her dynamic, teleological concept of time, and she privileges autonomy and individuality over the non-selfhood she ascribes to the people of Sri Lanka. Juliane's ambivalence toward patriarchal, colonial rule, which she both detests and practices, also reveals itself—as the following analysis will show—at the level of narrative and genre.

The process of political decolonization has, in the realm of literature and culture, been accompanied by forms of cultural and textual decolonization, which Bill Ashcroft et al. succinctly summarized as *The Empire Writes Back*. The title of their influential introduction to "theory and practice in post-colonial literatures" and the textualization it alludes to express, however, not only the defining features but also the inherent contradictions of postcolonial literature and theory. The title refers on one hand to the extensive interrogation and critique of the imperial process as expressed in the texts of authors from former colonies. Salman Rushdie, Michael Ondaatje, Anita Desai, and Derek Walcott, to name a few, explore how the identity of their societies and their cultures has been shaped by colonial regimes and continues to be influenced by neocolonialism. Despite the many differences among these writers, their countries of origins, and the distinct forms of colonial oppression imposed upon them, the imperial experience nevertheless produced similar forms of alienation and identity conflicts, among them the postcolonial writers' concern with positionality. This concern circumscribes not only the relationship between Third World margin and First World center, but also the loss of language and self caused by centuries of colonial hegemony and exploitation (Ashcroft et al. 8–11).

Yet, both the term *post*colonial as well as the movement of writing *back* to the *Empire* indicate the continuation and dependency of this process in relation to the former and current centers of power and control. The prefix "post" implies not only modes of reference and response, but more importantly that the term "postcolonial," as Anne McClintock has pointed out, "is haunted by the very figure of linear development that it sets out to dismantle" (10), and therefore continues to define itself by a "subordinate, retrospective relation to linear, European time" (11). In similar fashion, *Empire* remains the normative focus against which the postcolonial writer directs his/her attempts at self-definition, seemingly forever caught in the epistemic and discursive control of the (former) master's voice and power.

This double-bind of identities has not only been explored in former and current postcolonial narratives, it also has influenced the biographies of postcolonial writers themselves. Pico Iyer in his brief survey of contemporary postcolonial authors focuses on their "hyphenated" existence between cultures. According to Iyer, the aforementioned authors are representative of a postwar generation of writers born and raised in former colonial countries who now reside in the metropolitan centers of the West, and who decided at one point to write in English. Iyer calls them "amphibians" (13), for they have neither lost nor found a home but live instead in two "half-way homes" (*Halbwegsheimaten*) (13), where they straddle several spaces and languages, a position these authors describe for the most part as stimulating rather than stifling. The origin of postcolonial writing is thus firmly rooted in the experience of the colonized subject, but postcolonialism has come to entail all discursive practices engaged in questioning and dismantling the colonial legacy and therefore also includes the responses of First World writers to Third World realities.

Within the German literary context of the 1980s and 1990s, postcolonial discourse has been rather slow in taking root.[1] According to the German author Hans Christoph Buch, the Third World has deteriorated into a cliché, for both sides of the political and cultural spectrum claim already to know the reasons for the rampant poverty and underdevelopment in Third World countries, which subsequently do not warrant their critical attention (213). An awareness and interest in postcolonial matters would also require a form of multicultural thinking and behavior that, as Paul Michael Lützeler has pointed out, is "underdeveloped in Germany" ("Multiculturalism" 453). German writers' responses to postcolonialism have mainly taken the form of travel reports about visits to Third World countries. These travel accounts as well as novels set in Third World countries have remained, however, for the reasons outlined above, a somewhat marginal element in contemporary German literature. *Jahrhundert der Herren*, too, has been largely ignored by both the *Feuilleton* and literary critics, and the few reviews it received were rather mixed.[2]

Jahrhundert der Herren is Jeannette Lander's first novel exploring the colonial condition, yet in the context of her biography and literary development, the topic appears neither unusual nor strange. Lander has consistently explored conditions of foreignness and displacement, and she herself has been exposed to numerous locations and languages. Born in New York in 1931 as the daughter of Polish-Jewish immigrants, Lander grew up in Atlanta, Georgia, and moved to West Berlin in the 1960s.

Since 1966, Lander, who first published short stories and essays in English, has been writing novels, radio plays, and television screenplays in German. In a 1979 interview she referred to her own position between cultures as an enriching rather than a limiting experience: "I feel at home abroad. Only as a stranger do I feel at ease. I enjoy the advantages of someone who cannot quite be categorized.... The uncertainty is freedom" ("Unsicherheit" 258). This statement suggests an affinity to the previously mentioned postcolonial writers with whom Lander shares the precarious status of being one of the "not quites," as the Indian author Bharati Mukherjee called the decentered personality formed by a life between languages and cultures (Iyer 13). Like the authors of English postcolonial literature, Lander draws on her own multicultural background as material for her texts.[3] Like them she writes in a language that is not her native one, and she has experienced—albeit in a different way—the multilingualism that characterizes the lives and works of postcolonial authors.

Already at the beginning of her literary career, Lander examined issues of positionality and displacement in novels such as *Ein Sommer in der Woche der Itke K.* (A Summer in the Week of Itke K., 1971), *Auf dem Boden der Fremde* (On Strange Ground, 1972), and *Die Töchter* (The Daughters, 1976). Although noticed by the major German newspapers, these texts often received rather unfavorable reviews. Literary scholars, too, were slow to engage with Lander's oeuvre, which so far has caught only the attention of feminist literary critics.[4] Sabine Schilling explains this lack of interest by the novels' unusual poetic strategies and by Lander's profoundly unsettling demystifications of female, Jewish, and German identities (2). In a sophisticated analysis of *Ein Sommer in der Woche der Itke K.*, Leslie Adelson has argued that

> Lander's particular representation of Jews and other "Others"...unhinge[s] an allegedly homogeneous "German" center against which minorities...have been defined. If this center no longer holds—this center that has provided the basis for long-standing concepts of German national identity—then neither do the margins to which any number of minorities have been banished (*Bodies* 91).

While *Jahrhundert der Herren* is no longer primarily concerned with questions of German-Jewish identity and history, it continues this process of challenging established perceptions of center and margin. It also continues the geographical expansion that Lander began in her earlier works. Moving from the American South (*Ein Sommer*), Germany (*Auf dem Boden der Fremde*), France, Poland, and Israel (*Die Töchter*) to the island of Sri Lanka, off the southern coast of India, takes the process of decentering to the international, postcolonial scene.

Interestingly, the novel's new theme and location are accompanied by changes in style and narrative structure. The experimental, fragmented, and multiperspectival mode of Lander's earlier novels is replaced by a realistic form. This return to realism is a result, I believe, of the novel's locale and Lander's intention to portray a country and society unknown to most German readers, which thus requires detailed description of customs, landscapes, characters, and events. Since the story takes place in the mid-1980s, during the first years of the armed confrontations between the Sinhala government forces and the Tamil separatists, Lander has to provide some background information.[5] Emphasizing such historical specificity and lacking self-reflexive comments about the preliminary nature of signification and representation, the novel shows little affinity to postmodern narratives. It is narrated in an unusual style that combines matter-of-fact description, including the familiar sights of Third World reporting (i.e., hopelessly overcrowded buses, slums, lack of European-type sanitation and hygiene), with a dense metaphorical, almost lyrical manner of expression. Eager not to fall into the trap of European exotic discourse, Lander seems at times to lapse into rhetorical overkill and sententiousness in order to stress the protagonist's awareness of the colonial legacy. Adelson correctly points out that the "apparent focus on the protagonist's cultural and historical positioning exists at odds...with the narrative's simultaneous appeal to generalizations and repetitions" ("Imagining" 22). It comes as a surprise to the reader that the novel reveals itself in the end to be the story of a murder.

Jahrhundert der Herren is narrated retrospectively by the main character, Juliane Brabant, who fled to Sri Lanka with her six-month-old daughter. Her husband Alexander, portrayed as an extremely abusive character, does not believe he is the child's father and accuses his wife of infidelity. Having inherited an estate (Greystones) in the tea highlands from her brother, an eccentric loner who devoted his life to studying the bird species of the island, Juliane escapes to Sri Lanka. There she uses her training as a weaver and founds *spider*, a textile co-operative that eventually becomes a highly successful enterprise. Much of the novel's plot is devoted to the extraordinary difficulties and obstacles Juliane Brabant faces in creating the co-operative, as well as in maintaining her new home, Greystones. She remains fearful of being tracked down by Alexander, a highly successful and powerful business consultant who would not tolerate a decision made independently by his wife, let alone acknowledge a failed marriage. After several years, Alexander visits Colombo on a business trip, finds his wife, and demands the return of his daughter. Knowing that he has the means to achieve this goal, Juliane has him killed by a Tamil terrorist. The crime, though undetected, haunts her from then on.

As this short synopsis indicates, the novel contains two different narrative strands: the story of Juliane's failed marriage and that of her encounter with Sri Lanka. Alexander's murder links these two strands and points to the omnipresence of violence, not only as manifested in Sri Lanka's colonial legacy and its brutal civil war, but also in the private realm of intimate relationships.[6] Violence, be it directed at a different gender, race, religion, or ethnicity, thus intersects with and connects the novel's various histories and geographies. This omnipresent violence is also referred to in a quote from Walter Benjamin introducing the novel: "The current amazement that the things we are experiencing are 'still' possible in the twentieth century is not philosophical" (*Illuminations* 257).[7] Here Benjamin's shock about Nazi brutality and terror causes him to question and reconsider the prevalent concept of history from the perspective of the oppressed. His analysis of violence as a *constituting* factor of history is confirmed by what Juliane sees in Sri Lankan politics. The killings, committed both by Sinhala government troops and Tamil terrorists, seem irrational and pointless to her, since they do not solve but rather aggravate the conflicts. Alexander's murder, furthermore, implicates Juliane herself in the practice of violence and thus highlights her own ambivalence toward the exercise of power and terror. Though capable of planning and ordering the killing, Juliane is unable to excuse or forget the act that destroyed not only Alexander's but ultimately also her own life:

> I believe that injustice will be avenged. No matter when or in what form. A lie is unjust, a murder.... It was years ago. Years like ice caves. Years like flaming oceans.... All around me, the garden is in lush bloom. Through all the colors of its splendor speaks delightfulness, speaks violence (319).

This final comment reveals that the novel is constructed as one long, uninterrupted monologue, a continuous apostrophe to Alexander that Juliane seems unable to terminate. She also ends her confession in almost exactly the same way in which she began, thus creating the impression of a non-linear, circular, endless movement of time and narrative. Comparing years to "ice-caves" and to "flaming oceans" suggests both a passionate as well as a terrifying experience of time. A similar opposition is evoked in the view of the garden reminding her of the coexistence of beauty and violence. These images, rendered particularly powerful due to their prominent position at the beginning and at the end of the text, express metaphorically that Juliane's life in Sri Lanka was marked by extremes, by contradictions and paradoxes that refer to the simultaneity of different discourses and voices within her.

In looking at the main signposts of Juliane's sojourn, one could read her tale as a contemporary reenactment of the colonial drama, i.e., a story in which the explorer sets out to overcome a hostile nature, along with bizarre and unintelligible natives in order to exploit the land and its people for his own (business) interests. This narrative paradigm is after all evoked in the *spider* venture, which would never have been successful without Juliane's highly skillful use of foreign investment loans, local resources, Buddhist monks, and corrupt politicians. Juliane also readily admits that her very presence contributes to the exploitation and subjugation of the people in Sri Lanka. At the same time, she would like to overcome the ideological tenets of the colonial pursuit and text, which have been identified as "the myths of power, the race classifications, the imagery of subordination" (Boehmer 3). Lander is of course fully aware that Sri Lanka does not offer a blank page onto which a non-colonialist reinterpretation could be inscribed. Any such reinterpretation, as Boehmer reminds us, has "to be predicated on the previously interpreted" (170). *Jahrhundert der Herren* thus uses the colonial framework in order to attempt a different drama, in which the protagonist tries to respect and understand cultural alterity. The most crucial difference concerns, however, the change from a male to a female protagonist, which accounts for some of these changes in attitude.

Quest, travel, exploration, in fact all forms of voyages, have traditionally been the almost exclusive domain of male activity and desire. The absent woman was reinscribed in metaphors of space, signifying the 'foreign' that was both feared and desired.[8] *Jahrhundert der Herren* reverses this gendered travel paradigm by replacing the male adventurer and the masculine qualities he is expected to demonstrate with a young woman, a mother moreover, whose first concern after landing in Colombo is to find milk for her baby daughter. In this way, the focus shifts from grandiose deeds and extraordinary enterprises to ordinary tasks and responsibilities, from the heroic individual to communal work and support. Neither Greystones nor *spider* could have been (re)built without extensive group efforts. The exotic quest is taken over by the very mundane concerns of caretaking and day-to-day existence, which do not allow for the hegemonic stance so typical of male adventurers.

This relationship between gender and travel has in recent years been thoroughly examined by a number of feminist critics.[9] For the purpose of this investigation Karen Lawrence's study is particularly useful. Lawrence based her insightful analysis of female travelers on the figure of Penelope, the enduring model of female stasis, and asked: "What happens when Penelope voyages? What discourse, what figures, what maps do we use? Can Penelope, the weaver and teller of the story of male absence, trace her own itinerary instead?" (x). As a weaver Juliane certainly evokes the figure of Penelope and can be examined within the mythological paradigm. One could thus answer Lawrence by pointing to Juliane's newfound independence and autonomy, which do not rely on the rhetoric of mastery and quest. But I would like to ask within the context of the novel: What happens to *Ulysses* when Penelope voyages? or What does the change of gender in the travel plot entail for the presence of the male both in its discursive and its concrete manifestations? Where and how is the male reinscribed? Does it—in a reverse movement—appear as a "place on the itinerary" (Lawrence 2), the way the female did for the male journey, or does it retain its agency?

Throughout the novel Juliane remembers her past life predominantly in reference to Alexander and their marriage. Since the entire narrative is directed at Alexander, he, despite his absence, is continually present. What Roland Barthes has called a "lover's discourse", i.e., the silent presence of the absent lover, structures also—albeit in an inverted way—Juliane's communication with Alexander (Lawrence ix). Barthes defines the lover's discourse as "a discursive site: the site of someone speaking within himself, *amorously*, confronting the other (the loved object), who does not speak" (3). This is precisely the framework in which Juliane operates, but she confronts the unloved partner, the object of her fear and scorn. The "ordeal of abandonment" (Barthes 13) thus becomes for her the ordeal of retrieval. Waiting, the passive act of hoping to turn the lover's absence into presence, is thus replaced by Juliane's urge to escape Alexander. While in a lover's discourse all efforts are directed at reducing the distance, Juliane proceeds in the opposite direction, maximizing the divide, while remaining at the same time inextricably linked to her point of departure: Alexander. Like his namesake the grandiose conqueror, Alexander seems to be the true explorer of the story, for he is the driving force behind all of Juliane's efforts. She functions as the "reluctant heroine" (Lawrence 28), propelled into action, into travel and displacement by the deeds of her husband, who even from a distant Europe inscribes himself into the fabric of her life. Indicative of his control is the fact that Juliane never knew that the store in which she sells and showcases her products in Colombo stood on property that had already been sold to the consortium whose business interests Alexander represents. Even a dead Alexander retains his powerful presence, forcing his memory upon her. He acts as the continuing reminder that she cannot really escape the master's control.

Seen within the context of the Penelope figure, Juliane appears to be a Penelope who both voyages and weaves. She is able to narrate and weave her own story, but while abroad she also remains at home, for she cannot escape Ulysses' concrete and discursive control. Juliane's statement, "I design my life like a tapestry, only to realize it through my body" (183), shows her to be a *spider*, an Arachne caught in the web of patriarchal narrative that she is simultaneously weaving and critiquing. Being caught between agency and dependency also describes Juliane's position between cultures. In this sense the history of her marriage and the history of her cultural displacement are mutually dependent and mirror each other.

Critical self-awareness, precise observation, and a desire to understand the country characterize Juliane's attitude toward Sri Lanka from the first moment on. This approach prevents her from employing what has been termed in postcolonial studies the "imperial gaze," a binary mode of perceiving other cultures, particularly former colonies, that privileges the position of the Western observer.[10] Arriving in Sri Lanka, she realizes that it is she, not the Sri Lankans, who is strange and unfamiliar:

> I walked across the runway with the other passengers, followed their lead, suddenly small like a speck among specks in the flickering dust. Suddenly large, suddenly white, suddenly Western, European, out of place (10).

Juliane perceives herself, and not the Sri Lankans, as foreign and she does not project her own difference onto them, the strategy employed by most travelers. This traveler directs her gaze not at the Asian people, which would have been the classical response of both the colonial and the postcolonial traveler (Pratt 216–19), but at herself, suddenly bewildered by the foreignness of her physique outside a Western context. Contrary to her expectations, Juliane recognizes that she is not the spectator, but the spectacle, and that she, not the Sri Lankans, represents the only exotic element at the Colombo airport. At the same time, she cannot conceal how shocking this discovery is. The anaphoric repetition of "suddenly" and the parallel word sequences, void of both subject and verb, suggest a sudden inability to act, arresting Juliane in a state of (self-)observation. This passage vibrates with drama and fear, signaling the extent of Juliane's insecurity, but it also shows her ability to recognize and be astonished at her own otherness.

In this context it is important to note that Juliane has not just come to visit, but to stay in Sri Lanka. She defies, as she herself observes, the standard modes of contemporary travel ("neither tourist...nor 'helper,' nor merchant" 18). Subsequently, the corresponding versions of the native as exotic, needy, or consumer Other also do not figure in her encounter. Juliane designates Sri Lanka as the country of her expatriation, a country chosen because of circumstances, not because of desire or knowledge. *The Oxford English Dictionary* defines expatriation as "banishing a person from his own country...the action of leaving one's country for another" (422–23). In contrast to exile, however, expatriation does not entail the *forced* removal from the native home. Despite this crucial difference, expatriation and exile overlap in numerous ways, since both deal with the loss of the patria and the challenges that the new location entails. In both cases, "a force that drives one away from one's native soil" (Benstock 24) compels the person to relocate, to travel. In this sense, one can argue that the discourse of journey as exile dominates and fuels the novel. Whereas the exotic quest and exploration are geared toward adventure, surprise, and discovery and contain the hope for a triumphant return once the journey's goals have been achieved, exile denotes the voyage that has not been undertaken deliberately and that will not end in the return home. Not desire and longing, but "a decree or enactment" (*The Oxford English Dictionary* 412) causes the departure and the original home remains forever lost. To be sure, Juliane has the privilege and luxury of a "voluntary exile" (Ingram 5). She is not a victim of the political, religious, or economic persecution that drives people away from their homes and countries. At the same time she too fled from persecution, for she fled from an abusive husband and his verbal assaults. The very first words Alexander utters in the novel are: "You whore, you are lying" (10). Though he fulfilled his financial obligations, Alexander was bent on destroying her dignity, self-worth, and integrity. Juliane's situation certainly differs in scope and intensity when compared to the sufferings of people persecuted by brutal state agencies, but it is characterized by structurally similar forms of oppression.

Speaking of literature written by exiled writers, Elisabeth Bronfen has described the specifics of the exile situation as follows:

> Against this uprooting and dislocation, which bring about a worldlessness, one must react with a new invention of the Self, or, to be more exact, with an attempt to mend the broken pieces of one's life in the form of a narrative (71).

This process of displacement and of recreating self and home in a new country also describes Juliane's situation in Sri Lanka. Her adaptation to a new life is symbolically enacted by a name change: "I would give both of us new names to disguise, to strengthen ourselves. Maybe we would really become different beings, people from this place" (15). By replacing her original name, Ilse, and that of her daughter, Vera, with Juliane and Viorica, Juliane invents new protagonists for the story that can now begin to unfold. More importantly, since naming is an act indicating authority, she also signals her authorship over this narrative, which should finally bear only her imprint. Yet Juliane cannot free herself from the Brabant surname and the paradigm it evokes.[11] This name change provides yet another example for the opposing narratives Juliane is trying to combine. As Juliane she is the new woman, intent on creating an independent self-directed existence, as Brabant she remains tied to hegemonic control, which—and this is the real paradox of her situation—she herself needs to exercise in order for *spider* to be successful.

Through her choice of these particular names—Juliane was the name of her maternal grandmother and Viorica the name of a school friend who suddenly died at age sixteen—Juliane also confirms her rootedness in German (personal) history. By not choosing Sinhala or Tamil names, Juliane signals that she does not intend to discard her former self entirely in an artificial attempt to "go native." Yet, as the above quotation suggests, Juliane had in the beginning hoped for a more or less complete integration, a hope she quickly abandons. The novel traces this process of rapprochement and distance, of attraction and repulsion through a series of encounters with the island's "repertoire of signifiers," a term describing a culture's dress codes, food habits, religion, forms of address, etc. (Smith 297). Juliane's first exposure to Asian food offers a particularly revealing example of her double-pronged approach.

> The old couple ate with their hands.... I had a hard time learning that. Yes, I believe, I did not want to learn it. The tines of a fork tasted unpleasant with the spice of the curries, and yet it was important for me to use cutlery. As important as walking upright through the streets of the small neighborhood, as important as wearing my Western clothes, my white skin (18).

Implied in her reluctance to touch the food directly is a comment on different notions of cleanliness and correct table manners. While Juliane obviously upholds the German standards she has learned, she does not negate the other mode. In fact, she views the Sri Lankan way as more appropriate for the spicy food, but she needs nevertheless to act according to her own upbringing. Again her sense of insecurity is palpable in the repetition of words and sentences. By reminding herself of who she is and where she came from, she tries to ward off the anxiety that arises from being the only one who is different, the only one who is white and tall and wears a dress. Juliane is able to endure this de-familiarization, but she also learns that it cannot be overcome: "I thought that if I overcome the fear, I can overcome the strangeness. But the thought that I would be assimilated or accepted by people, that I would become part of society...did not occur to me" (88). Juliane recognizes that fear is one of the crucial elements in constructing and maintaining difference as otherness, and that it could only be overcome at the expense of giving up her *difference*, an equally frightening thought since this would entail negating her identity.

This fear, which reveals the extent of her displacement, is played out through Juliane's body, which becomes the site where the two cultures clash. In contrast to her ongoing encounter with Alexander, which manifests itself primarily discursively, her encounter with Sri Lanka manifests itself physically. The island materializes and inscribes itself in her body, for Juliane responds literally, not just symbolically, with her body when confronted with Asian customs that are both frightening and attractive. When discussing, for example, the custom of arranged marriages, Juliane feels both envious and terrified, for she longs for the security they provide and abhors the lack of independence they imply. These contradictions express themselves physically with equal strength:

"My skin became numb with desire and defense" (25). Not only does Juliane in this instance acknowledge both her desire and her fear, she also is able to sustain both emotions without either dismissing the custom as 'primitive' or switching sides. Another example concerns the type of behavior required from her in setting up *spider*. Though she needs to act like a prototypical Alexander—"I live like a man: I give orders, I evaluate, decide, and take risks" (141)—her body is unable to maintain this male self. It responds with weakness ("limp to the point of weakness" 57) or "paralysis" (319), indicating that Juliane endangers and perhaps even erases her body through her masculine habits. It seems that for Juliane the female and the male self cannot coexist, or put differently, that she cannot reconcile the discourse of femininity and the discourse of entrepreneurial neocolonialism embodied by Alexander and other male characters whom she meets in Sri Lanka. Though she functions according to these business rules, she does not feel legitimized by them. Caught between two contrasting discursive sites, Juliane fears losing her femininity and her sexuality. Though she feels strongly attracted to a young Tamil rebel, she never enters an amorous liaison. Avoiding such a relationship could also indicate a distance Juliane ultimately wishes to maintain, for an intercultural intimacy would draw her into a fusion and closeness she is otherwise trying to avoid.

A juxtaposition of different discourses can also be seen in Juliane's attitude towards the women of Sri Lanka. On the one hand she pays particularly close attention to women, frequently observing and describing them in a way that suggests that she seeks access to and understanding of their culture through the commonality of gender. On the other hand, she describes only poor women who for the most part live in rural settings. Never once does she meet a woman who equals her in education and professionalism. Instead, Juliane details village life and domestic activities and consequently sees the women as fundamentally different from herself. Both in the detailed portraits of the women she comes to know as well as in observations of them as a group, Juliane comments on what distinguishes them from her: "I don't envy them. I enjoy the finiteness. I exercise self-discipline. I sing praises to the increase of what has been accomplished. I want" (121). The ironic tone of this comment in its familiar use of anaphers, parallels, and repetition points, however, to anxiety rather than to confidence, and it appears to question Juliane's belief in her mission. Though one could interpret her focus on domesticity and rural life as a critique of women's continuing oppression—and the portrait of the wife of a resthouse manager in Badulla would particularly support such a reading—Juliane tends to universalize women. To her, they are "sisters in silence" (197), poor, rural, and domestic, who stand no chance of partaking in her world. Sympathy towards their lot goes hand in hand with maintaining her own singularity.

In another instance, Juliane characterizes the (male and female) participants in a Hindu festival: "They are without distance. Without a sense of privacy. Without the desire to be alone" (254). She thereby indirectly describes her own position as that of the unique, distinct bourgeois subject. Such comments are intended to be comparative, not derogatory in nature, and one cannot reproach Juliane for privileging her own cultural identity or judging a different way of life. Yet the contrasts she establishes between a communal and an individual approach to life seem to grant only the latter exclusiveness and importance, thus marking it ultimately as superior. This tension between Juliane's autonomous self and the non-selfhood she tends to attribute to Sri Lankans is also enacted in the linguistic representation of their voices.

One of the major challenges in representing members of another culture is how to adequately portray their language without subjugating it to the control of one's own necessarily foreign idiom and culture. Crossing the discursive and epistemic divide is particularly difficult when the cross-cultural encounter involves former colonizers and colonized, since "the modes of representing the language of the colonized have always reflected the structural monologism of the colonizer, and in each case they have served to consolidate the respective image of the self" (Streese 291). Juliane becomes acutely aware of this problem in a conversation with her maid Chandra: "Again and again I made the mistake of translating her words into my realm of thinking right when I heard them, the mistake of judging her experiences from my vantage point" (283). In addition to such self-reflexive comments, the novel displays a number of strategies in order to avoid the structural monologism Streese refers to. On the simplest level, Juliane uses Sinhalese words, particularly for food, which remain either untranslated or paraphrased, but not glossed in the German text: "We ate kiribat, the rice pudding served on holidays...we ate it with the hottest of the sambols, hot green peppers with mint, hot red peppers with salt" (22). Words like *seeni-sambol, dahl, roti, pittu, thosai, iddili, vesak, sangha, sarong, rupee,* names of places, towns, and sights as well as the English vocabulary of colonial and postcolonial times ("first houseboy," "joint-venture") assert in the German sentence the particularity and difference of Sri Lankan culture.[12] Furthermore, Juliane frequently inserts English sentences in order to denote direct speech by Sinhalese or Tamil speakers who are thus at least partially marked as non-German characters. In this way the use of English appears as the normal and not as a foreign idiom.

Lander is of course unable to use the same technique for sentences in Sinhala or Tamil. The continuous use of English and the occasional use of Sinhala or Tamil words both indicate, however, linguistically and culturally different subjects as well as the multilingualism of this society, which the exclusive use of German would have obscured. Differences are thus to some degree maintained and not completely homogenized into the speech of Juliane. Supaya, "the first houseboy" (38), and other characters speak to the extent possible in their "own" voices. At the same time, these voices remain completely under Juliane's (narrative) control, for they are always presented from her perspective. Not surprisingly, Juliane also never learns Tamil or Sinhala. This exclusive focus on Juliane privileges her self and her view at the expense of a mutual exploration of otherness. In her narrative stance Juliane reveals a hegemonic perspective that contrasts with the integration she is otherwise seeking. Since her monologue is furthermore directed at the absent German master, it doubly confirms Western dominance. Both discursively and economically Juliane participates in the upkeep of the Western influence and power she wishes simultaneously to deconstruct and decenter through her work in Sri Lanka. This double-bind becomes particularly visible in her position as landlady, which she describes as "Mistress...of Greystones, proprietor" (38).

The construction or demolition of homes is one of the principal themes of postcolonial literature (Ashcroft et al. 28). In recreating Greystones, Juliane is thus engaged in the quintessential postcolonial activity, which again mirrors her stance between worlds. She literally and symbolically occupies the space of the master as the expatriate, the European who controls and gives orders. As ruler of the estate, Juliane reenacts the colonial role complete with sweeping vistas and servants, down to the last detail of wearing clothes fitting for the Victorian lady of the colonial mansion. But Greystones is also a rundown mansion in dire need of repair, where both master and servants have to go for weeks without running water. The restoration transforms it into a beautiful and lively communal home, where young women weavers and an ever-growing number of people live and work together. This transformation also symbolizes the change from a male-dominated colonial past to a communal and woman-centered postcolonial present.[13] Greystones' utopian potential, as seen in the peaceful coexistence of Sinhalese and Tamils, is shattered, however, by the ongoing civil war.

In repairing Greystones and particularly in establishing *spider*, Juliane had to apply the values of Western capitalism and bourgeois subjectivity rigorously. She clings to her ideas of work, responsibility, and progress, but increasingly questions the validity of her efforts and the idea of autonomous selfhood they entail:

> How angry I was.... The lack of a guilty conscience irritated me even more than the lack of responsibility. But what are such values to these people? Maybe these values are generally questionable, and I should...reconsider my own value system (279–80).

Though Juliane continues to operate according to Western ideas of autonomy, work ethic, and progress, she no longer accepts their ideological legitimation, as can be seen in her rejection of the ideas of the Enlightenment with its futile efforts to suppress the murderous human instincts. "Nevertheless, we, I, hold high that ludicrous lantern, rationality, and command with a shudder: Let there be light!" (191) Instead, she begins to appreciate Buddhism, which she considers to be a superior world view. At times, she seems to idealize Buddhism and particularly the German-born Buddhist monk Nyanaponika, who plays a key role in helping her to establish *spider*. Yet, she also acknowledges the very worldly influence of the monks on behalf of the Sinhalese majority and recognizes that neither Buddhism nor Hinduism are excluded from the omnipresence of violence.

Ultimately, the exposure to Buddhism and to life in Sri Lanka teaches Juliane to see her own mental conditioning and the contradictions it produces. After having successfully established *spider*, she confesses: "I know it is paradoxical to feel like a puppet on a string, incapable of moving autonomously, and at the same time to be proud of one's own achievement, of success" (280). This questioning of her own agency and autonomy distances Juliane from the notion of the bourgeois subject she had upheld for so many years. In the end, Juliane conforms only outwardly to this model, playing the role of the independent, entrepreneurial Westerner, but she has lost faith in linear progress and the future-oriented pace of the European self. At the same time, she cannot replace this loss, for as much as she admires people who radiate "inner peace" (246) or the tenets of Buddhism, she is unable to follow this path: "I am not a believer. I am one of the the usual busy fools, and I become probably more foolish the more success I have. And poorer" (294).

Despite the novel's almost exclusive focus on Juliane's encounter with Sri Lanka, the text does provide some alternate models for the life between worlds. The most important one is represented by Harry Silberzweig, Juliane's German friend and business partner. Harry, a German Jew who fled from Nazi persecution, and thus an expatriate and exile like Juliane, shares few of her scruples and sentiments. He defines himself and his life in Asia in business terms, and differences are consequently based on financial, not cultural contrasts. When discussing Juliane's *spider* project, he dismisses her insistence on selfhood and autonomy as ideological rhetoric: "Forget being 'determined,' forget that you 'have' to do things, that you have to 'lose yourself' in your work. Not even the Hindus in Sri Lanka rave like this, and, after all, they have a god with eight arms and an elephant's head" (153). This flippant, ironic tone, which Harry uses regardless of subject matter, subsumes all contrasts in the undisputed rule of global capitalism. Harry insists on the sameness of economic interests that overrules all cultural differences. With this belief he feels much more rooted in Sri Lanka than Juliane; furthermore he does not have to balance opposing discursive demands. Harry represents the neocolonial merchant, who seldom questions the ethics of his business ventures.[14]

Yet another stance is embodied by Juliane's brother, a nameless and faceless character of whom she has little memory. The only reminders of him in Greystones are atlases, and reference and history books, as well as an incomplete manuscript, entitled "The Woodpecker of Ceylon: Its Instinctive and Intelligent Behaviour" (51). These books, particularly the title of his manuscript with its reference to "Ceylon," the colonial name given to the island by British rulers, show him engaged in the classical colonial pursuit of scientifically classifying, measuring, and thereby distancing the unknown. At the same time, the only book he ever sent his sister was a publication by the German-born monk Nyanaponika, indicating a rupture in his own scientific-colonial perception. Both brother and sister are in one way or another unable to balance their German and their Sri Lanka experiences. Whereas the brother could deal with Sri Lanka only by distancing and isolating himself, Juliane seeks closeness and integration, only to find her own position as outsider reaffirmed. Juliane hopes, however, that Viorica, who moves happily and effortlessly between the members of the cross-cultural and multilingual community of Greystones, will become a true "daughter between worlds" (32), but the novel never develops this theme.

Creating an existence between cultures based on different notions of self and time is, as *Jahrhundert der Herren* shows, an inherently paradoxical enterprise. Juliane is no longer rooted in the ideas and concepts that formed her self in Germany, but precisely this origin and heritage prevents her integration into Asian society. Neither at home nor abroad, neither Western nor Oriental subject, and equally insecure in her gendered self-perception, Juliane lives in a permanent liminal stage. Arrested at this threshold, she can neither return to a European subjectivity nor embark on a Buddhist path. Worst of all, this condition cannot be resolved or overcome through the passage of time. In this particular case time does not heal, as is also stressed by the numerous references to time interspersed throughout the novel. On the contrary, the longer Juliane lives in Sri Lanka, the more she is aware that she will remain an outsider. The instability of the political situation to which she could easily fall victim acts as an external reminder of her inner turmoil and lack of center. Since both modes of organizing life, the European and the Asian, are presented as mutually exclusive, an intercultural hybridity that could bridge the two worlds is equally impossible:

> The strangeness of the culture, of the language, also of skin color influences me less and less. But the difference in being (*Wesensfremdheit*) is a defense from inside, something that protects and separates me,

also because I am aware of it, aware of the fact that it cannot be reduced or even overcome (254–55).

We can read Juliane's observation, made after years of living in Sri Lanka, as a kind of final summary of what can be achieved in this intercultural rapprochement. Juliane is on the whole able to respect, tolerate, and understand difference without the need to subjugate and homogenize it, and she has also learned to accept the coexistence of a separate "repertoire of signifiers" (Smith 297), even though it remains fundamentally foreign to her. Does this imply that Juliane distinguishes herself from the masters and their sons only by a more self-reflexive and self-critical consciousness? Does the discourse of the "masters" ultimately prevail over that of the "daughter"? Viewing Juliane's position this way misses out on the ambiguities and contradictions of her life in Sri Lanka, where several discourses intersect and overlap. But if the goal of postcolonial literature is to provide models of noncolonizing relationships, then *Jahrhundert der Herren* participates in this effort, for the novel illustrates the struggles, achievements, and failures of pursuing this goal.

Notes

I wish to thank Manuel Kraus for his translations of the primary and secondary sources.

[1] For an overview of postcolonial discourse and German literature, see Paul Michael Lützeler ("Der postkoloniale Blick").

[2] The novel was reviewed by Eva-Elisabeth Fischer, Jürgen Jacobs, Eva Kaufmann, and Sabine Schilling. Leslie Adelson ("Imagining") offers an in-depth analysis.

[3] Lander knew the political situation in Sri Lanka from an extended stay in 1984–85 on the island.

[4] In addition to Schilling, see Sigrid Weigel (156–58) and Adelson (*Bodies* 87–105), who offers the most comprehensive analysis of Lander's early novels.

[5] Since independence, politics in Sri Lanka has been marked by ongoing conflict between the Buddhist, Sinhalese-speaking Sinhala majority and the Tamil-speaking minority. The Sinhala-dominated government has been unable (or unwilling) to settle the grievances of the Tamils, who felt they were continually and systematically discriminated against. Of the armed militant groups that sprang up in the mid-1970s, the *Liberation Tigers of Tamil Eelam* (LTTE or Tigers) became the most well-known. They demanded the creation of an independent Tamil homeland (*Eelam*) in the northern and eastern provinces, which they saw as the 'traditional homelands' of the Tamils. The situation escalated after 1983 when "thousands of Tamils were killed in rioting in the Sinhala-dominated south after a massacre of government soldiers in the north"

(Spencer 2). See also Little, Hellmann-Rajanayagam, O'Balance, and Pfaffenberger for Tamil history and present politics. Juliane by and large supports the position of the Tamils even though she condemns their acts of terror.

[6] Lander's drawing of these parallels between political and personal violence is reminiscent of Ingeborg Bachmann's narrative *Der Fall Franza* in which Bachmann explored fascism in intimate relationships.

[7] "Das Staunen über das, was in diesem Jahrhundert noch möglich ist, ist kein philosophisches mehr." The exact quotation from Bejamin's essay "Über den Begriff der Geschichte" reads: "Das Staunen darüber, daß die Dinge, die wir erleben, im zwanzigsten Jahrhundert 'noch' möglich sind, ist *kein* philosophisches" (697).

[8] For a summary of this point see Lawrence (1–17).

[9] For a discussion of women and travel in the British literary context, see Mills, Lawrence. For German literature, see Frederiksen and Archibald, Felden, Pelz.

[10] For a theoretical discussion of perceiving, scrutinizing, and distancing colonial realities, see Pratt (15–37).

[11] Juliane explicitly refers to the Genoveva legend and the parallels between Genoveva and her own destiny (164). See Adelson ("Imagining") for a detailed analysis of the function of this legend in the novel.

[12] On the use of untranslated words, see Ashcroft et al. (65).

[13] Ruby, the wife of Juliane's driver, is also instrumental in this change. Ruby's organization of the large household seems like the beginning of a new era (222).

[14] Adelson's observation that Lander's portrayal of Jewish characters and the German-Jewish relationship "illuminates... some of the ways in which historical experience does not disappear but is *refracted* under shifting historical circumstances" (89) also applies to Harry Silberzweig.

Works Cited

Adelson, Leslie A. "Imagining Migrants' Literature: Intercultural Alterity in Jeannette Lander's *Jahrhundert der Herren*." *The Imperialist Imagination*. Ed. Sara Friedrichsmeyer, Sara Lennox, and Susanne Zantop. Forthcoming.

———. *Making Bodies. Making History: Feminism and German Identity*. Lincoln: U of Nebraska P, 1993.

Ashcroft, Bill, Gareth Griffiths, and Helen Tiffin, eds. *The Empire Writes Back: Theory and Practice in Post-Colonial Literatures*. London: Routledge, 1989.

Bachmann, Ingeborg. *Der Fall Franza. Werke*. Vol. 3. Ed. Christine Koschel, Inge von Weidenbaum, and Clemens Münster. München: Piper, 1978. 339–474.

Barthes, Roland. *A Lover's Discourse: Fragments*. Trans. Richard Howard. New York: Hill and Wang, 1978.

Benjamin, Walter. *Illuminations*. Ed. Hannah Arendt. Trans. Harry Zahn. New York: Schocken, 1969.

―――――. "Über den Begriff der Geschichte." *Gesammelte Schriften*. Ed. Rolf Tiedemann und Hermann Schweppenhäuser. I.2. Frankfurt a.M.: Suhrkamp, 1974. 691–704.

Benstock, Shari. "Expatriate Modernism: Writing on the Cultural Rim." *Women's Writing in Exile*. 19–40.

Boehmer, Elleke. *Colonial and Postcolonial Literature: Migrant Metaphors*. Oxford: Oxford UP, 1995.

Bronfen, Elisabeth. "Entortung und Identität: Ein Thema der modernen Exilliteratur." *The Germanic Review* 69 (Spring 1994): 70–78.

Buch, Hans Christoph. "Nachwort." *Tropische Früchte: Afro-amerikanische Impressionen*. Frankfurt a.M.: Suhrkamp, 1993. 213–19.

Encountering the Other(s): Studies in Literature, History, and Culture. Ed. Gisela Brinker-Gabler. New York: State U of New York P, 1995.

Felden, Tamara. *Frauen Reisen: Zur literarischen Repräsentation weiblicher Geschlechterrollenerfahrung im 19. Jahrhundert*. New York: Lang, 1993.

Fischer, Eva-Elisabeth. "Eine Frau webt ihr Leben." *Süddeutsche Zeitung* 14 July 1993.

Frederiksen, Elke, and Tamara Archibald. "Der Blick in die Ferne: Zur Reiseliteratur von Frauen." *Frauen Literatur Geschichte: Schreibende Frauen vom Mittelalter bis zur Gegenwart*. Ed. Hiltrud Gnüg und Renate Möhrmann. Stuttgart: Metzler, 1985. 104–22.

Hellmann-Rajanayagam, Dagmar. "The Politics of the Tamil Past." *Sri Lanka: History and the Roots of Conflict*. Ed. Jonathan Spencer. London: Routledge, 1990. 107–22.

Ingram, Angela. "Introduction: On the Contrary, Outside of It." *Women's Writing in Exile*. 1–15.

Iyer, Pico. "The Empire Writes Back: Am Beginn einer neuen Weltliteratur?" *Neue Rundschau* 107.1 (1996): 9–19.

Jacobs, Jürgen. "Ein Instrument der Herren." *Frankfurter Allgemeine Zeitung* 24 June 1993.

Kaufmann, Eva. "Im Bann der Widersprüche. Jeannette Lander: 'Jahrhundert der Herren.'" *Neue Deutsche Literatur* 41.7 (1993): 152–54.

Lander, Jeannette. *Jahrhundert der Herren*. Berlin: Aufbau, 1993.

―――――. "Unsicherheit ist Freiheit." *Fremd im eigenen Land: Juden in der Bundesrepublik*. Ed. Henryk M. Broder and Michel R. Lang. Frankfurt a.M.: Fischer, 1979. 258–64.

Lawrence, Karen R. *Penelope Voyages: Women and Travel in the British Literary Tradition*. Ithaca: Cornell UP, 1994.

Little, David. *Sri Lanka: The Invention of Enmity*. Washington, DC: United States Institute of Peace Press, 1994.

Lützeler, Paul Michael. "Multiculturalism in Contemporary German Literature: Introduction." *World Literature Today* 69.3 (Summer 1995): 453–58.

———. "Der postkoloniale Blick: Deutschsprachige Autoren berichten aus der Dritten Welt." *Neue Rundschau* 107.1 (1996): 54–69.

McClintock, Anne. *Imperial Leather: Race, Gender and Sexuality in the Colonial Context.* New York: Routledge, 1995.

Mills, Sara. *Discourses of Difference: An Analysis of Women's Travel Writing and Colonialism.* London: Routledge, 1992.

Mohanty, Satya P. "Epilogue. Colonial Legacies, Multicultural Futures: Relativism, Objectivity, and the Challenge of Otherness." *PMLA* 110.1 (1995): 108–18.

O'Ballance, Edgar. *The Cyanide War: Tamil Insurrection in Sri Lanka 1973–88.* London: Brassey's, 1989.

The Oxford English Dictionary. Vol. 3. Oxford: Clarendon, 1978.

Pelz, Annegret. *Reisen durch die eigene Fremde: Reiseliteratur von Frauen als autogeographische Schriften.* Köln: Böhlau, 1993.

Pfaffenberger, Bryan. "Introduction: The Sri Lankan Tamils." *The Sri Lankan Tamils: Ethnicity and Identity.* Ed. Chelvadurai Manogaran and Bryan Pfaffenberger. Boulder: Westview, 1994. 1–27.

Pratt, Mary Louise. *Imperial Eyes: Travel Writing and Transculturation.* London: Routledge, 1992.

Schilling, Sabine. "Jeannette Lander." *Kritisches Lexikon zur deutschsprachigen Gegenwartsliteratur.* Ed. Heinz Ludwig Arnold. München: edition text und kritik, 1994.

Smith, Sidonie. "Isabelle Eberhardt Traveling 'Other'/wise: The 'European' Subject in 'Oriental' Identity." *Encountering the Other(s).* 295–318.

Spencer, Jonathan. "Introduction." *Sri Lanka: History and Roots of Conflict.* Ed. Jonathan Spencer. London: Routledge, 1990. 1–16.

Streese, Konstanze: "Writing the Other's Language: Modes of Linguistic Representation in German Colonial and Anti-Colonial Literature." *Encountering the Other(s).* 285–94.

Weigel, Sigrid. *Die Stimme der Medusa: Schreibweisen in der Gegenwartsliteratur von Frauen.* Dülmen: tende, 1987.

Women's Writing in Exile. Ed. Mary Lynn Broe and Angela Ingram. Chapel Hill: U of North Carolina P, 1989.

Re-Thinking and Re-Writing *Heimat*: Turkish Women Writers in Germany

Heike Henderson

Since German unification, questions of *Heimat* and belonging have been discussed with renewed urgency. The definition of who is allowed to claim Germany as their home, and what its characteristics are supposed to be, has been at the center of many political, cultural, and literary debates. Examining literary texts by four Turkish women in Germany, I analyze how these writers challenge narrow and exclusive concepts of *Heimat*. They investigate home on the national as well as the family level, thereby pointing to the racist and sexist implications of traditional definitions. Ultimately arguing for a redefinition of *Heimat* that allows for cultural differences, their texts open up new possibilities of belonging. (HH)

Fragt man mich nach meiner Heimat / Antworte ich: / Meine Großmutter (Aysel Özakin, *Zart erhob sie sich, bis sie flog*)[1]

In a postmodern era of world-wide migration, shifting identities, and re-definitions of culture, the concept of a homeland is emotionally charged and contested. Despite the fact that a considerable number of foreigners claim Germany as their home, they are neither granted the same basic rights as German citizens nor are they perceived as a legitimate part of German society. By virtue of their culture and religion, the Turks, the largest group of foreigners in Germany, are often viewed as the embodiment of an imaginary otherness and confront even more prejudices than most other foreigners.[2] Particularly interesting is the situation of Turkish women writers in Germany, who have produced some of the finest works of contemporary literature and whose literary texts have helped call into question and broaden our notion of what constitutes "German" literature. Their writing represents their historical and personal conflicts as ethnic and gendered subjects and their positioning between different traditions. They question the ideologies implicated in representations of women both in their own cultural tradition and in the popular culture of their host country. By creating counter-images to stereotypical constructions of Turkish womanhood, they interrogate the legitimacy of the representations of otherness perpetuated by the dominant ideologies of the host culture.

With the exception of Aysel Özakin, whose prose writings have been translated into German from Turkish, or, most recently, from English, the other Turkish women writers whose texts I discuss—Alev Tekinay, Saliha Scheinhardt, and Zehra Çirak—all write in German.[3] They reflect on the possibility or impossibility for Turkish women to find a home in Germany, thus analyzing home on a national level, and they also investigate the most privatized and feminized of all spaces, the home in the sense of house or family. Analogous to Biddy Martin and Chandra Talpade Mohanty's investigation of the "tension between the desire for home, for synchrony, for sameness, and the realization of the repressions and violence that make home, harmony, sameness imaginable, and that enforce it" (208), these women vividly describe how their Turkish home also represents forms of containment that men do not suffer. Because of the violence associated with the enforcement of home, on the personal as well as on the national level, these women writers do not give in to nostalgia for the lost homeland as easily as do some of their male counterparts. However, given the legal and social constraints they encounter, it is also difficult for them to perceive of Germany as their home.

Before I analyze how these authors participate in the process of re-thinking and re-writing *Heimat*, I would like to present the arguments and concepts with which these literary texts enter into a dialogue. This is especially important because of the contradictory multiplicity of meanings clustered around the concept of *Heimat*. Associations that easily come to mind are community and belonging, family, shared traditions, memories, and identity. For most people *Heimat* is linked to strong feelings; it can refer to the place where one lives now, to the place where one grew up, or to the mythic homeland of parents or ancestors that one may never have actually seen. As Angelika Bammer points out, it is this very indeterminacy of home that "has lent itself to the continual *mythification* of 'home' as an almost universal site of utopian (be)longing" (vii).

In her study of *Heimat* and German identity, Celia Applegate states that "[f]or almost two centuries, Heimat has been at the center of a German moral—and by extension political—discourse about place, belonging, and identity" (4). In the Nazi era, *Heimat* was a synonym for race and territory, a deadly combination that led to the exile or murder of anyone who, according to this logic, did not belong to the homeland. Under the National Socialists, *Heimat* meant the murderous exclusion of everything "un-German" (Kaes 166). For Germans themselves, this overdetermination of the concept of *Heimat* led to homelessness and displacement after World War II on a larger scale than ever before. As

Michael Geisler, among others, has pointed out, "National Socialism was the greatest movement towards the destruction of 'Heimat' in German history" (59). Thus, in the first years after the war, for many Germans *Heimat* evoked above all experiences of loss and nostalgic memories of the past.

Heimat has been the theme of so many films, novels, sentimental songs, and radio and television talk shows that it has become an inextricable part of postwar German culture.[4] Like no other word, "Heimat encompasses at once kitsch sentiment, false consciousness, and genuine emotional needs" (Kaes 166). Many Germans continue to regard the *Heimat* they live in or come from as an essential part of their social identity. Telling proof is the phenomenal success of Edgar Reitz's sixteen-hour film *Heimat*, which aired in eleven episodes on West-German television in the fall of 1984.[5] Recent developments indicate that German provincial identities and consciousness of *Heimat* have been reasserting themselves in East Germany since the opening of the Berlin Wall in November 1989. There has been a recent revival of old GDR rock groups as well as numerous GDR consumer products. For example, the old East German champagne "Rotkäppchen" has experienced a remarkable comeback ("Sehnsucht"). Two articles in a recent issue of *Der Spiegel*, significantly entitled "Stolz aufs eigene Leben" (Proud of One's Own Life) and "Wir lieben die Heimat" (We Love the Homeland), discuss this increasing consciousness of *Heimat* and identification with the GDR.[6]

It is also striking that a unification that moved so quickly to include all Germans denied *Heimat* to so many others. More recently, the impact of race on the definition of who can claim a *Heimat* in Germany has again emerged as a central issue. Among others, Jeffrey Peck examines the impact of race on the definition of Germanness. Based on the observation that Germans perceive people according to how they look, and not according to their nationality or their asylum or immigration status, he concludes that the debate about asylum seekers and immigration is misdirected. After all, it is not only the law, but also an unofficial, though forceful, set of criteria that determines who finds a home and social acceptance in Germany. In his view, to be able to participate in the German *Heimat* "requires an identification that is at least ethnic, if not racial" (78). He thus introduces race and differentations according to skin color as dominant criteria. Telling proof for the validity of this classification is, in his opinion, the acceptance of "ethnic Germans" not as foreigners, but as *Aussiedler*.

Since personal as well as national identities are always relationally constructed through processes of boundary-drawing and exclusion, it can be argued that it is necessary for a state to define itself in relation to an Other from which it is distinguished. West Germany, like most other Western European countries, defined its postwar national identity in opposition to the Communist countries of the Eastern bloc. Deep-seated anxieties about European identity, and the centrality of Christianity to this definition, were driven underground by the Cold War, during which the Communist East provided Europe with a *de facto* eastern frontier. Since the "fall of communism," Europe has had to reestablish its boundaries anew. In this process of re-definition, questions of who is included and who is excluded, as well as against whom or what European identity is to be defined, have moved to the center of the contemporary political stage. David Morley and Kevin Robins describe the situation as follows:

> Our common European home remains to be built: but the stories we tell ourselves about our common (and uncommon) past are already shaping our understanding of how it should be constructed, how many floors it should have (a basement for the servants?), which way it should face (what price a south-facing garden?) and who should have the keys to the door (16).

An analysis of current European discourses shows that the Eastern boundary once occupied by Stalin's regime has been replaced by Islam. Of course, Islam has served as the Other in Europe's self determination before. Morley and Robins, for example, ponder the question whether an Islamic state like Turkey can be fully accepted as part of Europe, given that "historically (through the Crusades, and the Moorish and Ottoman empires' invasions of Southern Europe) 'The Turk' and 'The Moor' have always provided key figures of difference, or 'threat' (and indeed, dread) *against* which 'Europe' has defined itself" (15). They further contend that implicit in much recent debate is, in fact, a rather ancient definition of Europe as what used to be referred to as Christendom, to which Islam supplies the boundary.

In light of recent developments, I would argue that it is not only undesirable but also quite impossible to sustain impermeable boundaries at the end of the twentieth century—no matter what some politicians in their quest for votes try to make the public believe. In the context of a global economy, Western imperialism, and worldwide migration, Europe has had to come to terms with its Muslim minorities. Racial hostility toward Islamic people has manifested itself in complex ways as violence and hostility to Turks in Germany, North Africans in France and Italy, and Southeast Asians in Great Britain, where the Rushdie affair has complicated matters even more. Many of these conflicts have been portrayed as a standoff between Islam and Christianity. Sefyi Tashan, director of the Turkish Foreign Policy Institute in Ankara, puts it as follows: "In Europe, many people see us as a new version of the Ottoman empire, attacking this time in the form of guest workers and terrorists" (qtd. in Morley and Robins 16).

Morley and Robins conclude by stating that "[i]n this world, there is no longer any place like Heimat" (20). While I agree that there can be no recovery of an authentic cultural homeland, nor is there any place for absolutisms of the pure and authentic, I would like to point out that *Heimat* does not necessarily have to be stable and absolute. Because of the genuine emotional need that most people experience for some form of *Heimat*, it may be more fruitful to re-think and re-write *Heimat* rather than to abandon the concept totally. This view is supported by Doreen Massey who argues that it is not "home" itself that has been destroyed, but rather the aura of its uniqueness (24–29). Instead of lamenting the loss of a concept of home, she suggests we reconceptualize home in relational terms as the place or places we inhabit with others in the shifting geography of social relations.

To this end, I would argue that literature by migrant writers fulfills a valuable and necessary function. Bammer reminds us that "what 'home' means to us is shaped at once by the material circumstances of our experience and by the various narratives that attempt to define and interpret that experience for us" (ix). Therefore it is especially important, in a time marked by racist hostilities and tirades of ethnic purity, that these racist narratives are not the only ones we hear. Because of their particular situation at the center of these debates and contestations, Turkish women in Germany are especially able to challenge narrow and exclusive interpretations of home, and to develop a concept of *Heimat* that allows a diverse population of people to feel at home, regardless of citizenship and skin color. What is at stake, after all, is not only an individual's sense of (not) belonging, but rather the political landscape of Germany, the question of whether Germans are willing to include minorities and migrants in their understanding of *Heimat* or not. For this reason I would like to discuss how these Turkish-German women writers engage in the necessary task of re-thinking and re-writing *Heimat* in German culture and politics today.

Aysel Özakin, who was born in 1942 in Urfa, near the Syrian border, is probably the most well-known Turkish woman writer published in Germany. She was already a renowned author before she left Turkey in 1981, after the military assumption of power.[7] Most of her work can be classified as semi-autobiographical. Her first collection of short stories to be published in Germany, *Soll ich hier alt werden?* (Shall I Grow Old Here?), describes the feeling of *Fremdheit* many Turks experience in Germany.[8] Key themes of these stories, as of many other early texts by migrant writers, are loneliness, homesickness, and coldness. The protagonists of her stories have not (yet) found a home in Germany, and therefore do not want to grow old there. At this stage in Özakin's writing, her concept of *Heimat* still refers exclusively to Turkey. Only later will it become more complex and also more problematic.

In Özakin's semi-autobiographical novel *Die Leidenschaft der Anderen* (The Passion of the Other[s]), the search for *Heimat* figures prominently. While this story of a reading tour can be understood as yet another document informed by and at the same time celebrating her unsettledness, it also eloquently ponders the (im)possibility of finding a home in Germany or Turkey. On the very first page, the narrator recalls the pledge of allegiance, a habitual and obligatory performance by all Turkish students: "It is my ideal to move forward and to love my homeland more than myself. My life shall be dedicated to my Turkish homeland" (7). Like many children in many countries, the protagonist is told that the nation state is the equivalent of *Heimat*, which is to be loved, and to which one's life is to be devoted. It is of course ironic that the Turkish state, like most nationalistic states, tries to enforce this love with the help of violence, thereby making *Heimat* an inhospitable and not very home-like place for many people. It is this nationalistic state, after all, that forces the narrator of *Die Leidenschaft der Anderen*, as well as the author herself, to leave her original *Heimat* and to emigrate to Germany—a decision that she later on describes as being like a suicide or a birth (112).

Once in Germany, the protagonist experiences a strong feeling of belonging with people from what she calls "the other Germany," the less formal, more tolerant Germany of leftist and feminist circles. Despite the fact that she repeatedly tries to hide her Turkishness,[9] she realizes that she cannot escape her foreignness. She feels close to other minorities and social "outcasts," people who are not able, willing, or allowed to feel at home in Germany:

> Somehow we all seemed to belong together. We were a minority and strangers. Squatters, Turks, women...women without family, without the many veils of convention and conformity, women who broke out of the comfortable and cruel securities of the past (20–21).

This description seems to conform to Massey's call for a reconceptualization of home not as a unique geographical place, but rather in relational terms as the place(s) we inhabit with others in the shifting geography of social relations. It is, of course, interesting to note who is included and who is excluded in Özakin's chosen family. While she feels close to other women who fight tradition, she clearly distances herself from women, especially Turkish women, with family.

Despite the fact that she is so proud of her independence, the protagonist misses the security of a stable home. In a conversation with her friend Johannes, who is thinking of leaving Germany and living somewhere else, she remarks sadly, "But, unlike you, I don't have a home that I could long for" (92). This statement is reminiscent of June Jordan's famous quip: "Everybody needs a home, so at least you can have some place to leave, which is where most folks will say you must be coming from" (123). Clearly at this point in her life Özakin's protagonist, and probably the author as well, regards neither Turkey nor Germany as her home. For her as an exile, it is not possible to go somewhere else and then return home, a situation that leads her to ponder the question whether her rebellion was worth the consequences: "Will my rebellion, which I paid for with a loss of home and future, make sense?" (107). It is interesting to note that in this context *Heimat* takes on a temporal aspect in addition to the geographical one discussed earlier. Loss of home is perhaps not equated with but nonetheless closely related to loss of future.

The protagonist's search for a home in leftist and feminist circles is clearly based upon the author's own experiences. In a German newspaper article, rather stereotypically entitled "Eine Türkin ohne Kopftuch" (A Turkish Woman Without a Headscarf),[10] Özakin describes her sense of feeling at home with women. Rather naively, she assumes that women share similar experiences and closeness, a similar love, and a similar hate, all of which lead to a common fight against patriarchy, based on a similar corporeality. Reminiscent of Virginia Woolf's famous declaration against fascism and nationalism, "as a woman, I have no country. As a woman I want no country. As a woman my country is the whole world" (109), Özakin states:

> Now, together with the women...I feel at home. I tell myself that we women don't need any nationality, we are no strangers to each other, we have similar bodies, similar love, similar hate; we all stand against the power of patriarchy and against all domination. Our mental, physiological, and ideological commonalities are greater than the differences in our socialization (9).

While it is easy to decry the naiveté implicit in this statement, it reflects the fact that in 1982 many women believed in sameness and solidarity among women, based solely on gender. Only later in the decade and thanks to the ground-breaking work of mainly American women of color was this assumption of the European and American (white) women's movement thoroughly revised.

The gendered aspects of belonging take center place in Özakin's beautiful poem *Zart erhob sie sich, bis sie flog* (Gently She Lifted Herself Up until She Flew). In this poem, which unlike her prose narratives was written in German, Özakin describes the process by which she became a stranger in her own homeland:

> Als ich mich weigerte
> Eine Decke zu häkeln
> Bin ich fremd geworden.
> Als ich auf das Licht
> Der Straße

Neugierig war
Und mich die Frage
"Wann heiratest du?" ärgerte
Bin ich fremd geworden (52).[11]

It is obvious that already long before she moved away from Turkey she was a stranger in her own culture because of her unwillingness to submit to traditional notions of womanhood in Turkey. Her feelings of estrangement are based not so much on a different cultural background as on the denial of self-determination that she experiences as a woman.

In keeping with Özakin's redefinition of belonging and estrangement, it is ultimately not a place but the memory of her grandmother that becomes the home the narrator needs to survive in the *Fremde*. Her concept of home is no longer purely geographic, or tied to identification with the coinhabitants of the places she regards as home, but tied to memory, to people from her past. The poem ends with her affirmation that she is not a European or non-European, but an inhabitant of the earth (57). Aspiring to belong to a circle of transnational intellectuals and artists, she tries to break down differentiations between Europeans and others. This insistence on cosmopolitanism, which coincides with her desire to find a home in literature, strikes me as overly idealistic in its disregard of existing differences. Her self-definition as a writer, while naive and reductionist on some levels, does, however, open up new possibilities of belonging, of finding a *Heimat* that is not based on and limited by national or geographical borders.

Another Turkish-German woman writer, for whom finding a home in literature has been very important, is Alev Tekinay. Unlike Özakin, however, whose search for a home is mainly limited to her own writing, Tekinay's quest includes the study and teaching of literature. Having graduated from the German school in Istanbul before emigrating to Germany and obtaining her doctorate in *Germanistik* at the University of Munich, Tekinay is well-versed in German and Turkish literature and culture. As she outlined in her acceptance speech for the Adelbert-von Chamisso-Förderpreis, *Heimat* is an important topic for her. After the painful experience of being nowhere at home that she experienced at the beginning of her (albeit voluntary) migration, she now claims two homes, two countries, and two languages as her own. She describes her personal situation as follows:

> I have two home countries and two mother tongues. With two feet I stand in two cultures and two languages, in two countries that have melted into one inseparable unity, one new home.

Similar to many second-generation migrants, she now experiences *Heimat* as comprised of both Turkish and German elements, neither one nor the other, but something new. In her children's book *Das Rosenmädchen und die Schildkröte* (The Rose Girl and the Turtle) she creates an even more poetic image of this same feeling, describing *Heimat* in terms of a turtle that builds a house out of both cultures (49). This concept of a transportable, individual home allows her to hold on to positive elements of both cultures, and thus to create a *Heimat* that is tailored to her own needs and desires.

Not surprisingly, this personal development is reflected in Tekinay's literary texts. *Heimat* figures especially prominently in her earlier work, which consists mainly of short stories. In "Langer Urlaub" (Long Vacation), one of the stories in *Die Deutschprüfung* (The German Exam), the Turkish protagonist, who now lives in Germany, returns to her hometown for a six-week vacation and finds herself feeling and being treated like a stranger. She sees everything with the eyes of a tourist, and even the language, her mother tongue, sounds strange to her. The protagonist tries hard not to attract attention, to readapt to Turkish patterns of behavior and speech. Nevertheless she catches herself translating German proverbs into Turkish, and she also has problems with Turkish phraseology and neologisms. Most people assume that she is German and praise her "almost accentless" Turkish. Upon hearing this she remarks: "Here and there, almost accentless. Only almost, never totally. And here and there I attract attention" (133).

As in many other stories by Tekinay, language plays an important role in "Langer Urlaub." On the one hand, language causes others to see the protagonist as a foreigner. On the other hand, she expresses a strong feeling of being at home in language, in both languages: "I only know that I live in two languages, and for me language is an inhabited and inhabitable realm" (141).[12] Immediately following this claim of living in both languages, however, Tekinay's protagonist points out that living in a language does not automatically mean that one acquires a *Heimat*. She expresses the contradictory feeling of not being at home in either country or, for that matter, either language, of living in-between, traveling 2000 kilometers every day on an imaginary train (141). Despite the fact that at the end of her vacation the protagonist begins to feel "at home" again in Turkey, the reactions of others constantly remind her of the fact that successfully finding a *Heimat*, whether in Germany or Turkey, is not only determined by one's own acts and feelings, but also by the locals' willingness or unwillingness to accept "the Other." Therefore it is not surprising that this story ends with a rather laconic diary entry: "That's the way it is. Here I am 'the one from Germany,' whereas for my neighbors and colleagues in Munich I am 'the one from Turkey'" (143).

Another interesting story that plays with the vagueness and relativity of the term *Zuhause* (at home) is "Die Heimkehr oder Tante Helga und Onkel Hans" (The Homecoming or Aunt Helga and Uncle Hans), published in the same volume of short stories. This time the protagonists are an academic couple who, after their studies in Germany, return to Turkey to assume lectureships at a Turkish university. Despite their efforts to reintegrate themselves into society, they realize that they are considered exotic foreigners in both countries. They have difficulties in adapting and suffer from homesickness, cherishing everything that reminds them of their old home in Germany—for example, their German coffee maker, which they almost never used while they were in Germany, because there they used to drink Turkish coffee. Finally they question their decision to "go home" to Turkey, and decide to "go home" again—this time to Germany.

At the beginning of the story, the title "Die Heimkehr" seems to refer to the couple's move to Turkey, their original home. This perception is then undermined by the story's development. While the move back to Germany can be seen as a second homecoming, it ultimately shows the vagueness of the term and concept *Heimat*, its inability to describe appropriately a person's sense of belonging or non-belonging. It turns out that in some respect *Heimat* is always fiction, in a story as well as in real life. In the same way that Salman Rushdie talks about creating "Indias of the mind" (10), Tekinay shows through her narrator how she creates Turkeys and Germanies of the mind.[13]

While the narrator clearly expresses some sense of belonging in both countries, it is probably more interesting to ask about the circumstances that make it impossible or at least difficult for her to experience either country as *Heimat*. In Turkey she criticizes mainly the lack of privacy that prevents her from living her life as she chooses. Relatives and neighbors expect her to conform to a very limited range of acceptable behavior for a woman. She is expected to be stylish and silent, therefore her relatives take her to the hairdresser and the shoe store, where she is outfitted with a pair of high heels.[14] Despite her efforts to fit in, she has trouble dealing with the constant control and criticism that she experiences. Compared to this scrutiny, the indifference and coldness of Germans, which she criticized before, seems desirable. Nevertheless it is difficult for her to perceive Germany as her *Heimat*. This is mainly due to legal and social constraints. While her friends accept her as an equal partner and fellow citizen, German bureaucracy does not. Specifically she criticizes the border controls that make her feel like a criminal and the condescending behavior she encounters at the *Ausländeramt* ("office for foreigners' affairs"), where periodically she has to apply for an extension of her residence permit.[15]

Saliha Scheinhardt, who was born in 1951 in Konya, a city known as a conservative religious stronghold, is the most prolific of these Turkish women writers under consideration. She graphically describes the situation of oppressed groups, usually minority women, and their search for a home.[16] More than any of the other writers, she elaborates on the different meanings of home, and on the political and private conditions that make finding a home (im)possible. Her protagonists struggle to find a home in the country in which they live, and women especially also struggle to feel at home in their own families.

In her fictional documentaries, which are based on actual case studies and lay claim to cultural authenticity, Scheinhardt presents a vivid portrait of repressive family structures. Her early narratives *Frauen, die sterben, ohne daß sie gelebt hätten* (Women Who Die Without Having Lived) and *Drei Zypressen* (Three Cypresses) focus on the plight of Turkish women caught between patriarchal Islamic family structures and an unwelcoming foreign environment in Germany. While these texts have been criticized for reinscribing and perpetuating stereotypes about oppressive Turkish men and victimized Turkish women, stereotypes that already abound in the West, I think that her literature nonetheless fulfills an important function. Scheinhardt has the courage to speak out against the abusive behavior toward women that occurs within the confines of a supposedly protecting family. In doing so, she subverts the myth of the Turkish family as protection against a cold German society. While acknowledging the desire for a home with protected boundaries, a desire shared by all of her protagonists, she also recognizes the restrictions upon the realization of such a home.

Scheinhardt's recent variation on the theme of migration and family life is the story of a Kurdish family who, in emigrating to Germany, seeks to escape from war, violence, and destruction. *Sie zerrissen die Nacht* (They Demolished the Night) depicts the family's unsuccessful search for a home, first in Turkey and then in Germany. For political reasons, they are unwelcome in both countries; in Turkey they are persecuted because they are Kurds, in Germany they are afraid of right-wing nationalism and hate crimes against minorities. In describing the situation of Kurds in Turkey, Scheinhardt deals with a highly explosive political problem. While condemning violence from both sides, her sympathies are clearly with the oppressed minority. In shocking detail she depicts the persecution, arrests, and interrogations to which Kurds are subjected. After living in constant fear of killings and arson attacks in Turkey, they discover in the wake of Rostock, Mölln, and Solingen that this fear continues to dominate their lives, even in Germany.

This novel exemplifies how *Heimat* serves not only as the object of desire, but also as a justification for violence. In enforcing the "official" *Heimat* Turkey, the Turkish state denies the *Heimat* Kurdistan that most Kurds desire. In hopes of achieving this *Heimat*, a small but not insignificant number of Kurds are willing to commit violence themselves. Similarly, the violence this family encounters in Germany is committed in the name of *Heimat*—this time a *Heimat* that is supposedly reserved for ethnic Germans only. Whether it be in the name of an inclusive Turkish, separate Kurdish, or exclusive German *Heimat*, the effects for this family as well as for countless others are the same. It is not only politics, however, that makes the women's search for a home difficult. Over the outrage and protest of the protagonist Helin and her mother Beriwan, Helin's father Kerim takes a second wife. While continuing to provide for Beriwan financially, from this moment on her husband effectively lives with his new wife. Society's demand that Beriwan stay "at home" clashes with the fact that there is no longer a home in which Beriwan belongs. This is one of the reasons why Scheinhardt so strongly advocates education, especially for women: it gives them independence from husbands and family.

Scheinhardt is very outspoken in deploring the situation of minorities in Turkey and Germany. Especially in this narrative, she gives a thorough overview of the political causes of discrimination and persecution, as well as of their effects on members of this particular family and their acquaintances. In both Turkey and Germany the violence they encounter leads to constant fear and sickness, inscribing itself indelibly on the body. Faced with rejection and discrimination, many immigrants suffer from depression and homesickness—which is made even worse by the knowledge that the home they left no longer exists. One of the many problems they must confront in Turkey is the refusal of many doctors and nurses to treat Kurds who are injured in fights or attacks. In Germany they are told of psychosomatic illnesses.

In this novel as well as in some of her political essays, Scheinhardt also comments directly on the effects of German unification on Germany's minority populations. A good example is a letter from a relative who has already been living in Germany for some time. In this letter, he describes how life has changed since German unification: "For God's sake, Kerim, give it careful thought...life here is pure misery for us, another kind of misery than the one we know.... Since the Germans have been one again, we have been persecuted here as well" (*Sie zerissen die Nacht* 93). This assessment of the effects of German unification corresponds to Saliha Scheinhardt's personal reaction. In an interview with Richard Laufner, Scheinhardt reveals that she locked herself in her room on the evening of German unification. At a conference in 1992, she talks about the fear of losing her German *Heimat*:

> The fear of losing my German home, my intellectual and political home, whose democratic system I have treasured for so long, the foreign homeland that for such a long time has not been foreign to me, the home in which I became an adult and a mother—my son was a soldier in the German army. Now this home abandons me, it slowly becomes foreign to me ("Türkinnen in Deutschland" 69).

Despite perceiving Germany as her intellectual and political home, she is afraid for her life and well-being. Unfortunately, these fears are justified; besides the shocking arson attacks that received broad media coverage, Scheinhardt herself experienced a tear gas attack during one of her readings ("Türkinnen in Deutschland" 69).

In addressing the difficult topic of *Heimat,* Zehra Çirak, the youngest of the Turkish-German women writers under consideration, uses a more playful approach. Born in 1961 in Istanbul, she came to Germany in 1963 and since 1982 has been living in Berlin. The search for a home between two cultures also informs her writing, but her repertoire is more varied and incorporates many different topics, some specific to the lives of minorities, some of general interest. Since Çirak came to Germany when she was only two years old, her situation is quite different from that of the other Turkish women writers I have discussed. Çirak writes from the perspective of a second-generation Turkish woman who grew up in Germany, and she skillfully expresses feelings and thoughts shared by many young people. Her outlook on life is less bitter than that of Scheinhardt. Instead of accusations and dramatic case studies, she reverts to irony and playfulness. Nevertheless she is fully aware of the political situation, of regulations that deny her the right to feel at home in Germany, despite having lived there almost all her life. An excellent case in point is her poem "tatsächlich" (really), in which she contemplates whether Turks, Germans, or all those who live in Germany are her fellow citizens. She comes to the conclusion that it does not matter what she thinks because it is, after all, politics that decides whether or not she is allowed to remain with the people whom she considers fellow citizens. The last lines of the poem read:

> als wir in berlin landeten
> befand ich mich unter vielen landsleuten
> ich frage mich immer wieder
> ob nicht alle in diesem land
> meine landsleute sind
> aber wenn wir heiraten
> ist die gefahr geringer
> aus dem land meiner landsleute ausgewiesen zu werden (88).[17]

Çirak's criticism, however, is directed not only towards German politics. Like Scheinhardt, she also criticizes the situation Turkish women encounter in their families, but because of the different medium she chooses, and probably also because of different personal experiences, her criticism appears less heavy-handed, lighter in tone. She does not engage in finger-pointing, and there is no pathos in her texts. Instead of being overtly didactic and moralistic, as most of Scheinhardt's texts are, Çirak's poems are subtly enlightening—although not without political overtones.[18]

In her poem "nicken mit dem kopf heißt nein" (nodding with the head means no) she specifically accuses Turkish families of condemning their female members to speechlessness, thus curtailing their self-expression and sentencing them to a life of lies. She eloquently expresses the anguish and rage hidden behind the facades of an overly protective home:

> zuhause wird nicht geweint
> da schreien stumme zungen
> augen blitzen ping pong spiele
> allgemeine schweigepflicht
> nicken mit dem kopf heißt nein (49).[19]

Other poems are directed more towards Germans, whose idiosyncrasies she scrutinizes and criticizes just as vehemently. In her subtly satirical poem "Eigentum" (Possessions) she denounces the possessiveness many people feel in regard not only to their house and other material goods, but also to their country, language, history, and family. She plays with familiar words and phrases, and ultimately also with readers' expectations, so that these words and phrases appear in a surprisingly new light:

> Meine Heimat mein Land
> meine Landsleute meine Sprache
> meine Geschichte mein Krieg mein Sieg
> meine Sehnsucht mein(e) Frau (Mann) mein Kind
> mein Haus mein Hab und Gut meine Zukunft
> meine Meinung mein Recht meine Person
> mein Nachbar mein Feind in meiner Zeit
> mein Gott steh mir bei daß mir alles bleibt
> da kommt einfach ein anderer mit seinem mein
> und nichts bleibt mir mehr
> nichts von mir—ach du meine Güte (*Vogel* 86).[20]

The humor inherent in this poem is quintessential Çirak, and it sets her apart from all the other Turkish-German women writers discussed here. Another difference is the level of political involvement, which Çirak shares with Scheinhardt. While Özakin's texts document her ultimate retreat into a more unpolitical intellectualism, for authors like Scheinhardt and Çirak, who are more committed to political change, the matter is more complex.[21] Their politics of home, that is, the manner in which they address the socio-political issues of racism and nationalism as well as the gendered issues of family politics, also place them in the role of spokespersons. Especially after the racially motivated fire bombings of Mölln and Solingen, both Çirak and Scheinhardt emphatically condemned the violence and underlined their right to be in Germany. This outspokenness sometimes put them in a difficult position by exposing them and their families to danger. Examples are the earlier mentioned tear gas attack during one of Scheinhardt's readings as well as the following statement by Çirak:

> My father is worried because I'm giving interviews and making public statements about what happened in Solingen. He's afraid something might happen to me, and he would like me to stay quiet. But my generation feels that we have a right to participate in every aspect of German life. We aren't as timid as our parents (qtd. in Veteto-Conrad, "Zehra Çirak" 350).

Despite the many differences between these Turkish-German writers, there is one underlying similarity: all of them claim Germany as their home. Some, like Çirak whose knowledge of her original homeland was restricted to holiday visits and the stories her parents told, claim it as their only home; others like Tekinay, who only came to Germany after she graduated from high school in Turkey, describe themselves as having two homelands. All of them point out how both Turkey and Germany as nations use concepts of home as a justification for violence and exclusion. Especially Scheinhardt's texts, but in a less outspoken manner also those by the other writers, exemplify how nations enforce their version of *Heimat* through violence and oppression. They draw similarities to abuse committed within the confines of a supposedly protective family, thus pointing to the gendered nature of *Heimat*. By describing how even within the family, the primary home, they are not at home, they point to the tension between the traditional demand that women are supposed to focus on the home as a source of happiness and the fact that they are oppressed at home. This is one reason why *Heimat* is so problematic for these women, and why it is at the same time of such crucial importance.

Besides claiming Germany as their home, all of these writers redefine home in some way or another. They offer a concept of *Heimat* that allows for cultural differences and provides a chance to feel at home in a world of transnationalism and multiculturalism, thus challenging the racist concepts of exclusion or forced assimilation. Because of the racist and sexist nature of most traditional concepts, they deconstruct old notions of home and invest in non-geographical forms of home that range from identification with leftists and feminists, to attachment to people in the past, to feeling at home in language and literature, to creating a *Heimat* based on many cultures, to seeing home as changeable and relational. Altogether, they open up new possibilities of belonging.

Notes

All translations are my own.

[1] Asked about my home / I answer: / My grandmother (Aysel Özakin, Gently She Lifted Herself Up until She Flew).

[2] Turks were also the victims of the fire bombings in Mölln (23 November 1992) and Solingen (29 May 1993), incidents that received wide news coverage because they resulted in the deaths of eight women and children.

[3] There are two other Turkish women writers in Germany: Emine Sevgi Özdamar and Renan Demirkan. Due to the spatial limits of this article, however, I cannot discuss their equally interesting work.

[4] Between 1947 and 1960, twenty percent of all films made in the Federal Republic of Germany were *Heimatfilme*—this amounts to a total of 300 films (Höfig 167).

[5] No fewer than 25 million television viewers saw at least one of the episodes, and the film generated more public debate than any other recent film, with the exception of the American TV series *Holocaust* in 1979.

[6] For a further discussion of these phenomena, see Howard (49–70). Based on the observation that East and West German identities are becoming increasingly polarized, Howard suggests that East Germans can be characterized as an ethnic group within unified Germany. This conceptualization, according to Howard, helps to dispel the myth of a biologically defined German nation.

[7] Özakin started publishing short stories in 1973 and won two literary prizes in Turkey. *Die Preisvergabe* (The Prizegiving) was one of the first Turkish novels to question the institution of marriage. In telling the story of a young woman writer, this novel at the same time portrays modern-day Turkish society, divided between traditional and pro-Western forces and also between city and province.

[8] While Turkish has many words that correspond to the German notion of *Fremde*, there is no equivalent English translation. It implies far more than a foreign place, since it can also refer to isolation and alienation.

[9] She describes how she gets nervous thinking about being unmasked as a Turkish woman: "Hier ist es der Gedanke daran, ich könnte als türkische Frau entlarvt werden" (38).

[10] For an in-depth analysis of the many debates raised by and surrounding the headscarf, see Mandel (27–46).

[11] When I refused / to crochet a blanket / I became a stranger. / When I was curious / about the light in the street / and annoyed by the question / "When will you get married?" / I became a stranger.

[12] This view is supported by Franco Biondi, who makes the connection between linguistic expression and identity: "die Sprache ist der persönliche, individuelle Wohnort jedes Menschen" (language is the personal, individual abode of every human being) (28).

[13] The second part of the title is interesting as well. Apparently it was the son of the protagonist's sister-in-law who first gave the stereotypically German names "Onkel Hans" and "Tante Helga" to the Turkish couple, but these names were then appropriated by the narrator to describe herself and her husband. While the narrator gives quite a few examples of how she and her husband become "Germanized," that is, turned into Germans through the perception of others, it is not totally clear if this self-naming indicates that they perceive themselves as Germans as well or if she uses the names ironically.

[14] In this respect Tekinay's description of Turkish femininity subverts at least part of the German perception of Turkish women. While most Germans also perceive the (stereotypical) Turkish woman as silenced, they generally would not use "stylish" to describe her. This stems in the main from class factors; most Germans' contact with Turkish women is limited to members of the working class. One of the many merits of authors like Tekinay and Özakin is that they introduce the general German audience to a wider variety of Turkish women's lives.

[15] In a personal interview, Alev Tekinay told me that it was mainly this difficulty in traveling that convinced her to apply for German citizenship.

[16] Coming from an oppressive family background herself, Scheinhardt is very sympathetic to the difficult situation of women caught between patriarchy and racism. Ironically, Scheinhardt was the first "foreign" writer in Germany to be officially recognized as a "local" writer: In 1985 she won the Literary Prize of the city of Offenbach and was appointed as city writer (*Stadtschreiberin*) of Offenbach, where she still lives and writes.

[17] when we landed in berlin / i was among many compatriots / i constantly ask myself / if not all people in this country / are my compatriots / but when we get married / there is less danger / of being expelled from the country of my compatriots.

[18] For a more detailed comparison of the works of Saliha Scheinhardt and Zehra Çirak see Veteto-Conrad ("Doppelte Nationalitätsmoral").

[19] one does not cry at home / silent tongues scream / eyes flash ping pong games / universal silence as an obligation / nodding with the head means no.

[20] My homeland my country / my compatriots my language / my history my war my victory / my longing my wife (husband) my child / my house my property my future / my opinion my right my person / my neighbor my enemy in my time / my God help me that everything remains mine / somebody else just comes with his my / and nothing remains mine / nothing of mine—oh my dear.

[21] To a certain extent this is true for Alev Tekinay as well, although I think that her idea of a world without borders, which provides a home for everybody, while well intended, is rather naive.

Works Cited

Applegate, Celia. *A Nation of Provincials: The German Idea of Heimat.* Berkeley: U of California P, 1990.

Bammer, Angelika. "Editorial." *New Formations* 17 (Summer 1992): vii–xi.

Biondi, Franco. "Die Fremde wohnt in der Sprache." *Eine nicht nur deutsche Literatur: Zur Standortbestimmung der Ausländerliteratur.* Ed. Irmgard Ackermann and Harald Weinrich. München: Piper, 1986.

Broder, Henryk M. "Wir lieben die Heimat." *Der Spiegel* 27 (1995): 54–64.

Çirak, Zehra. "tatsächlich" and "nicken mit dem kopf heißt nein." *Freihändig auf dem Tandem: Dreißig Frauen aus elf Ländern.* Ed. Luisa Costa Hölzl and Eleni Torossi. Kiel: Neuer Malik, 1985. 88, 49.

———. *Vogel auf dem Rücken eines Elefanten.* Köln: Kiepenheuer & Witsch, 1991.

Geisler, Michael. "'Heimat' and the German Left: The Anamnesis of a Trauma." *New German Critique* 36 (Fall 1985): 25–66.

Höfig, Willi. *Der deutsche Heimatfilm 1947–1960.* Stuttgart: Enke, 1973.

Howard, Marc. "An East German Ethnicity? Understanding the New Division of Unified Germany." *German Politics and Society* 37 (Winter 1995): 49–70.

Jordan, June. "Notes towards Home." *Living Room.* New York: Thunder's Mouth, 1985.

Kaes, Anton. *From Hitler to Heimat: The Return of History as Film.* Cambridge, MA: Harvard UP, 1989.

Laufner, Richard. "Türkisch war nur Pausensprache: Gespräch mit der Schriftstellerin Saliha Scheinhardt." *Freitag* 15 (5 Apr. 1991): 20.

Mandel, Ruth. "Turkish Headscarves and the 'Foreigner Problem': Constructing Difference through Emblems of Identity." *New German Critique* 46 (Winter 1989): 27–46.

Martin, Biddy, and Chandra Talpade Mohanty. "Feminist Politics: What's Home Got to Do with It?" *Feminist Studies / Critical Studies.* Ed. Teresa de Lauretis. Bloomington: Indiana UP, 1986. 191–212.

Massey, Doreen. "A Global Sense of Place." *Marxism Today* (June 1991): 24–29.

Morley, David, and Kevin Robins. "No Place like *Heimat*: Images of Home(land) in European Culture." *New Formations* 12 (Winter 1990): 1–23.

Özakin, Aysel. *Die Leidenschaft der Anderen.* 1983. Trans. Hanne Egghardt. Hamburg: Luchterhand, 1992.

———. *Die Preisvergabe.* 1979. Trans. Heike Offen. Hamburg: Buntbuch-Verlag, 1982.

———. *Soll ich hier alt werden?* Trans. H.A. Schmiede. Hamburg: Buntbuch-Verlag, 1982.

———. "Eine Türkin ohne Kopftuch." *Die Tageszeitung* 14. Dec. 1982.

———. *Zart erhob sie sich, bis sie flog: Ein Poem.* Hamburg: Verlag am Galgenberg, 1986.
Peck, Jeffrey. "Rac(e)ing the Nation: Is there a German 'Home'?" *New Formations* 17 (Summer 1992): 75–84.
Rushdie, Salman. "Imaginary Homelands." *Imaginary Homelands: Essays and Criticism 1981–1991.* London: Granta Books, 1991.
Scheinhardt, Saliha. *Drei Zypressen.* Berlin: Express, 1984.
———. *Frauen, die sterben, ohne daß sie gelebt hätten.* 1983. Freiburg: Herder, 1993.
———. *Sie zerrissen die Nacht.* Freiburg: Herder, 1993.
———. "Türkinnen in Deutschland: Eine Innenperspektive." *Schwierige Fremdheit: Über Integration und Ausgrenzung in Einwanderungsländern.* Ed. Friedrich Balke et al. Frankfurt a.M.: Fischer, 1993. 68–77.
"Sehnsucht nach F6 und Rotkäppchen-Sekt: Die Rückkehr der Ostprodukte in die Warenregale der neuen Bundesländer." *Frankfurter Allgemeine Zeitung* 14 Aug. 1995.
"Stolz aufs eigene Leben." *Der Spiegel* 27 (1995): 40–52.
Tekinay, Alev. "Dankesrede zum Erhalt des Adalbert-von-Chamisso-Förderpreises 1990." *dergi* (Apr./May 1990).
———. *Die Deutschprüfung.* Frankfurt a.M.: Brandes & Apsel, 1989.
———. Interview with Heike Henderson. 24 July 1994.
———. *Das Rosenmädchen und die Schildkröte.* Frankfurt a.M.: Brandes & Apsel, 1991.
Veteto-Conrad, Marilya. "*Doppelte Nationalitätsmoral*: Social and Self-Perceptions and Authorial Intent of Two German-Language Turkish Women Writers." *Occasional Papers in German Studies* 9 (Aug. 1996): 1–28.
———. "Zehra Çirak: Foreign Wings on Familiar Shoulders." *Homemaking: Women Writers and the Politics and Poetics of Home.* Ed. Catherine Wiley and Fiona R. Barnes. New York: Garland, 1996. 335–60.
Woolf, Virginia. *Three Guineas.* London: Harcourt Brace Jovanovich, 1938.

ABOUT THE AUTHORS

David A. Brenner is Assistant Professor of Germanic and Slavic Languages and Literatures at the University of Colorado at Boulder. His publications include *Marketing Identities: The Invention of Jewish Ethnicity* (forthcoming, 1998) and a number of articles that cross traditional disciplinary lines, combining cultural, film, and media studies with German, Jewish, and gender history. His latest project is a book about the reception of *Schindler's List* throughout the world.

Birgit Dahlke is currently participating in a research project on GDR literary history at the Humboldt University in Berlin, sponsored by the German Research Council. Her research interests encompass twentieth-century literature, particularly the most recent contemporary literary and feminist criticism. She is presently working on a study of how rape is dealt with in literature from the GDR. This article and the interview with Elke Erb are drawn from her 1994 dissertation on women authors in the GDR to be published by Königshausen & Neumann. She has published articles about the inofficial literary scene and about the young generation of GDR women writers, as well as reviews of very recent German literature.

Sara Friedrichsmeyer is Professor of German and Head of the Department of Germanic Languages and Literatures at the University of Cincinnati. Her publications include *The Androgyne in Early German Romanticism* (1983) and the co-edited volume *The Enlightenment and Its Legacy* (1991). She has published articles on German Romanticism, feminist theory, and various nineteenth- and twentieth-century German writers, among them Caroline Schlegel-Schelling, Annette von Droste-Hülshoff, Paula Modersohn-Becker, Käthe Kollwitz, and Christa Wolf. She is working on the representation of "Gypsies" in German literature and co-editing a volume titled *The Imperialist Imagination*. She has been co-editor of the *Women in German Yearbook* since 1990.

Katharina Gerstenberger is Assistant Professor of German and a member of the Women's Studies Program at the University of Cincinnati, where she also serves as book review editor of the *Lessing Yearbook*. She received her PhD from Cornell University. She is the recipient of a

1996–97 Research Associateship at Five College Women's Studies Research Center at Mount Holyoke College in Massachusetts. Gerstenberger has published articles in the fields of autobiography studies and Jewish studies; she is currently working on a book entitled *Truth to Tell: Women's Autobiographies from the Turn of the Century.*

Heike Henderson, Assistant Professor of German at Boise State University, received her PhD in German Literature with a Designated Emphasis in Feminist Theory and Research from the University of California at Davis. This article is part of an ongoing investigation of the politics of multiculturalism and its representations and contestations in literature. Her research and teaching interests include twentieth-century literature, feminist criticism, ethnic studies, and interdisciplinary cultural studies.

Patricia Herminghouse is Karl F. and Bertha A. Fuchs Professor Emerita of German Studies at the University of Rochester. Her research has focused on nineteenth- and twentieth-century literature, particularly on the literature of the GDR and the social contexts of women's writing. Editor of the textbook anthology, *Frauen im Mittelpunkt* (1987), she was also co-editor of *Literatur und Literaturtheorie in der DDR* (1976) and *DDR-Literatur der 70er Jahre* (1983). In addition to on-going work on a book with the tentative title *History, Literature and the Political Agenda in the GDR,* she is currently finishing a volume of short prose works by Ingeborg Bachmann and Christa Wolf for the German Library series and a co-edited volume, *Gender and Germanness: Cultural Productions of Nation.*

Barbara Hyams is a research associate at the Tauber Institute for the Study of European Jewry (Brandeis University). She has taught German Studies at M.I.T., Brandeis, Boston University, and the University of Tulsa. In 1991–92 she directed a study abroad program at Humboldt University, Berlin. She is a contributing co-editor of *Jews and Gender: Responses to Otto Weininger* (1995), and is currently writing a book called *The Art and Science of Suffering: Sacher-Masoch, the Jewish Question, and the Woman Question, 1856–1941.* Her research on Sacher-Masoch was partially funded by an NEH/DAAD Summer Seminar (1995) at Cornell University.

Jutta Ittner teaches German language and literature at Case Western Reserve University. She received her PhD from the University of Hamburg and has given papers on Brigitte Kronauer and published articles on exile literature and language. Her book *Augenzeuge im Dienst der Wahrheit: Leben und literarisches Werk Martin Gumperts (1897–1955)* is forthcoming from Aisthesis, Bielefeld. Her article on Kronauer "My Self, My Body, My World" is included in *Home-making: Women Writers and the*

Politics and Poetics of Home (Garland, 1996). She is currently working on a volume of translations of Kronauer's early stories.

Beth Linklater is a lecturer in German at Oxford Brookes University in England. She wrote her PhD dissertation on constructions of sexuality in GDR literature, a study that concentrates primarily upon the authors Irmtraud Morgner and Gabriele Stötzer-Kachold. She is interested in women's writing, the GDR, and theories of sexuality. She is currently working on humor in German women's writing of the 1980s and 1990s.

Annette Meusinger (PhD) has published articles on GDR women writers (Christa Wolf, Sarah Kirsch, Gabriele Kachold), on Ingeborg Bachmann, and Nawal El Saadawi, as well as on feminist theories. In 1988-90, she taught at Cairo University. She received a DAAD grant in 1992 and a DFG research grant in 1994-96. She is currently unemployed and working on a book-length comparative study of the concepts of identity and body in both feminist theories and in modern women's literature in Germany and the USA.

Daniel Purdy was born in Berlin and raised in New York City. He received his PhD from Cornell University (1992) and is currently an assistant professor in the Department of Germanic Languages at Columbia University. His study of German fashion culture is forthcoming: *The Tyranny of Fashion—The Discipline of Elegance: Consumer Cosmopolitanism in Eighteenth-Century Germany* (Johns Hopkins, 1998). His anthology on *Fashion and Modernity* will appear with the University of California Press in 1998.

Monika Shafi is Professor of German in the Department of Foreign Languages and Literatures at the University of Delware. She is the author of *Utopische Entwürfe in der Literatur von Frauen* (1989) and of *Gertrud Kolmar: Eine Einführung in das Werk* (1995). She has published articles on various nineteenth- and twentieth-century German authors, among them Annette von Droste-Hülshoff, Theodor Fontane, Irmgard Keun, Christa Wolf, Ingeborg Drewitz, and Günter Grass. She is currently working on a book manuscript entitled *Germans as Foreigners, Foreigners as Germans*.

Lynne Tatlock, Professor of German at Washington University (St. Louis), has published a book and articles on Willibald Alexis and articles on an array of seventeenth- and nineteenth-century writers of prose, on representations of war, gendered conceptions of obstetrics and gynecology, male subjectivity, realism and historiography, and popular representations of Turks in seventeenth-century Hamburg. Her edited anthologies include *The Graph of Sex and the German Text* (coedited 1994), *Seventeenth Century German Prose* (1993), *Writing on the Line: Transgression in Early Modern German Literature* (1991), and *Konstruktion: Untersuchungen zum Roman der Frühen Neuzeit* (1990). She recently translated Marie von Ebner-Eschenbach's *Das Gemeindekind* as *Their Pavel* (1996).

Karin A. Wurst, Associate Professor of German at Michigan State University, is the author of *"Familiale Liebe ist die wahre Gewalt": Zur Repräsentation der Familie in Lessings dramatischem Werk.* She has edited and introduced *Frau und Drama im achtzehnten Jahrhundert* (1991), *J.M.R. Lenz als Alternative? Positionsanalysen zum 200. Todestag* (1992), and *Eleonore Thon's Adelheit von Rastenberg* (1996). She has published articles on various aspects of the works of Lessing, Lenz, and Harsdörffer, and on the eighteenth-century women writers Elise Bürger and Elisa von der Recke.

ABOUT THE TRANSLATORS

Karein Goertz, Lecturer in German at the University of Texas at Austin and Adjunct Assistant Professor of English and German at Huston-Tillotson College in Austin, recently completed her PhD in Comparative Literature at the University of Texas at Austin. Her dissertation, "Generational Representations of the Holocaust: Trauma, Memory, and the Imagination," explores issues of narrative truth in Holocaust autobiographies and novels. Her publications include articles on May Ayim, Zehra Çirak, Charlotte Delbo, and Ruth Klüger, as well as translations of German poetry and literary essays.

Sieglinde Lug is Director of Women's Studies and Associate Professor of German and Comparative Literature at the University of Denver. Her publications include a book about an eleventh-century Andalusian Arabic poet, a translation of Brigitte Schwaiger's *Wie kommt das Salz ins Meer*, and articles on both Arabic and German literature. She just finished the translation of Herta Müller's *Niederungen* for the University of Nebraska Press and is now returning to her study of literary responses to Chernobyl and a collection of her mother's postwar stories.

Lynn E. Ries received her PhD from the University of Oregon. She teaches at Chemeketa Community College, Salem, Oregon. She has translated short stories by Barbara Frischmuth for a volume being edited by Karen Achberger and Martha Wallach.

Sabine Schmidt is an instructor of German at Rhodes College in Memphis and a translator and journalist. She received her MFA in Literary Translation from the University of Arkansas in Fayetteville. Her translations include fiction by Milena Moser, Rose Ausländer, Günter Herburger, Saki, Henry Rollins, Paul S. Beatty, and Iceberg Slim. She has published articles on popular music, film, and twentieth-century literature and is co-editor of the German feminist zine "planet pussy." Her research interests include MigrantInnenliteratur, translation theory and the role of the translator, post-Wende film, and feminist approaches to rock and country music.

NOTICE TO CONTRIBUTORS

The *Women in German Yearbook* is a refereed journal. Its publication is supported by the Coalition of Women in German.

Contributions to the *Women in German Yearbook* are welcome at any time. The editors are interested in feminist approaches to all aspects of German literary, cultural, and language studies, including pedagogy.

Prepare manuscripts for anonymous review. The editors prefer that manuscripts not exceed 25 pages (typed, double-spaced), including notes. Follow the fourth edition (1995) of the *MLA Handbook* (separate notes from works cited). Send one copy of the manuscript to each coeditor:

Sara Friedrichsmeyer *and* Patricia Herminghouse
Department of Germanic   Department of Modern
   Languages and Literatures   Languages and Cultures
University of Cincinnati   University of Rochester
Cincinnati, OH 45221   Rochester, NY 14627
Phone: 513-556-2751   Phone: 716-621-1607
Fax: 513-556-1991   Fax: 716-865-5336
E-mail: sara.friedrichsmeyer@uc.edu   E-mail: pahe@troi.cc.rochester.edu

For membership/subscription information, contact Jeanette Clausen (Department of Modern Foreign Languages, Indiana University–Purdue University, Fort Wayne, IN 46805).

CONTENTS OF PREVIOUS VOLUMES

Volume 12

Sara Lennox, Feminist German Studies across the Disciplines: Introduction to Grossmann, Ferree, and Cocks; **Atina Grossmann,** Remarks on Current Trends and Directions in German Women's History; **Myra Marx Ferree,** Sociological Perspectives on Gender in Germany; **Joan Cocks,** On Commonality, Nationalism, and Violence: Hannah Arendt, Rosa Luxemburg, and Frantz Fanon; **Todd Kontje,** Gender-Bending in the Biedermeier; **Irmela Marei Krüger-Fürhoff,** Epistemological Asymmetries and Erotic Stagings: Father-Daughter Incest in Heinrich von Kleist's *The Marquise of O...*; **Helen G. Morris-Keitel,** Not "until Earth Is Paradise": Louise Otto's Refracted Feminine Ideal; **Barbara Hales,** Woman as Sexual Criminal: Weimar Constructions of the Criminal *Femme Fatale*; **Kathrin Bower,** Searching for the (M)Other: The Rhetoric of Longing in Post-Holocaust Poems by Nelly Sachs and Rose Ausländer; **Charlotte Melin,** Renderings of *Alice in Wonderland* in Postwar German Literature; **Helgard Mahrdt,** "Society Is the Biggest Murder Scene of All": On the Private and Public Spheres in Ingeborg Bachmann's Prose; **Frederick A. Lubich,** Interview with Elisabeth Alexander: The Mother Courage of German Postwar Literature; **Karen Hermine Jankowsky,** Remembering Eastern Europe: Libuše Moníková; **Leslie A. Adelson,** Now You See It, Now You Don't: Afro-German Particulars and the Making of a Nation in Eva Demski's *Afra: Roman in fünf Bildern*; **Sara Friedrichsmeyer and Patricia Herminghouse,** Towards an "American Germanics"?: Editorial Postscript

Volume 11

Jutta Brückner, On Autobiographical Filmmaking; **Margaret McCarthy,** Consolidating, Consuming, and Annulling Identity in Jutta Brückner's *Hungerjahre*; **Janice Mouton,** Margarethe von Trotta's Sisters: "Brides Under a Different Law"; **Jenifer K. Ward,** Enacting the Different Voice: *Christa Klages* and Feminist History; **Renate Möhrmann,** "Germany, Pale Mother": On the Mother Figures in New German Women's Film; **Barbara Becker-Cantarino,** "Gender Censorship": On Literary Production in German Romanticism; **Dagmar von Hoff,** Aspects of Censorship in the Work of Karoline von Günderrode; **Lewis Call,** Woman as Will and Representation: Nietzsche's Contribution to Postmodern Feminism; **Alyth F. Grant,** From "Halbtier" to "Übermensch": Helene Böhlau's Iconoclastic Reversal of Cultural Images; **Lynda J. King,** Vicki Baum and the "Making" of Popular Success: "Mass" Culture or "Popular" Culture?; **Katharina von Ankum,** Motherhood and the "New Woman":

Vicki Baum's *stud. chem. Helene Willfüer* and Irmgard Keun's *Gilgi—eine von uns*; **Friederike Eigler,** Feminist Criticism and Bakhtin's Dialogic Principle: Making the Transition from Theory to Textual Analysis; **Imke Lode,** The Body in the Discourses of Colonial Savage and European Woman during the Enlightenment; **Sara Friedrichsmeyer and Patricia Herminghouse,** The Generational Compact: Graduate Students and Germanics.

Volume 10

Richard W. McCormick, Private Anxieties/Public Projections: "New Objectivity," Male Subjectivity, and Weimar Cinema; **Elizabeth Mittman,** Locating a Public Sphere: Some Reflections on Writers and *Öffentlichkeit* in the GDR; **Ruth-Ellen B. Joeres,** "We are adjacent to human society": German Women Writers, the Homosocial Experience, and a Challenge to the Public/Domestic Dichotomy; **Marjorie Gelus,** Patriarchy's Fragile Boundaries under Siege: Three Stories of Heinrich von Kleist; **Gail K. Hart,** *Anmut*'s Gender: The "Marionettentheater" and Kleist's Revision of "Anmut und Würde"; **Brigid Haines,** Masochism and Femininity in Lou Andreas-Salomé's *Eine Ausschweifung*; **Silke von der Emde,** Irmtraud Morgner's Postmodern Feminism: A Question of Politics; **Susan C. Anderson,** Creativity and Nonconformity in Monika Maron's *Die Überläuferin*; **Ruth Klüger,** Dankrede zum Grimmelshausen-Preis; **Karen Remmler,** Gender Identities and the Remembrance of the Holocaust; **Suzanne Shipley,** From the Prater to Central Park: Finding a Self in Exile; **Sigrid Lange,** Dokument und Fiktion: Marie-Thérèse Kerschbaumers *Der weibliche Name des Widerstands*; **Miriam Frank,** Lesbian Life and Literature: A Survey of Recent German-Language Publications; **Luise F. Pusch,** Ein Streit um Worte? Eine Lesbe macht Skandal im Deutschen Bundestag; **Jeanette Clausen and Sara Friedrichsmeyer,** WIG 2000: Feminism and the Future of *Germanistik*.

Volume 9

Ann Taylor Allen, Women's Studies as Cultural Movement and Academic Discipline in the United States and West Germany: The Early Phase, 1966–1982; **Susan Signe Morrison,** Women Writers and Women Rulers: Rhetorical and Political Empowerment in the Fifteenth Century; **Christl Griesshaber-Weninger,** Harsdörffers *Frauenzimmer Gesprächspiele* als geschlechtsspecifische Verhaltensfibel: Ein Vergleich mit heutigen Kommunikationsstrukturen; **Gertrud Bauer Pickar,** The Battering and Meta-Battering of Droste's Margreth: Covert Misogyny in *Die Judenbuche*'s Critical Reception; **Kirsten Belgum,** Domesticating the Reader: Women and *Die Gartenlaube*; **Katrin Sieg,** Equality Decreed: Dramatizing Gender in East Germany; **Katharina von Ankum,** Political Bodies: Women and Re/Production in the GDR; **Friederike Eigler,** At the Margins of East Berlin's "Counter-Culture": Elke Erb's *Winkelzüge* and Gabriele Kachold's *zügel los*; **Karin Eysel**; Christa Wolf's *Kassandra*: Refashioning National Imagination Beyond the Nation; **Petra Waschescio,** Auseinandersetzung mit dem Abendlanddenken: Gisela von

Wysockis *Abendlandleben*; **Dagmar C.G. Lorenz,** Memory and Criticism: Ruth Klüger's *weiter leben*; **Sara Lennox,** Antiracist Feminism in Germany: Introduction to Dagmar Schultz and Ika Hügel; **Ika Hügel,** Wir kämpfen seit es uns gibt; **Dagmar Schultz,** Racism in the New Germany and the Reaction of White Women; **Sara Friedrichsmeyer and Jeanette Clausen,** What's Missing in New Historicism or the "Poetics" of Feminist Literary Criticism.

Volume 8

Marjorie Gelus, Birth as Metaphor in Kleist's *Das Erdbeben in Chili*: A Comparison of Critical Methodologies; **Vanessa Van Ornam,** No Time for Mothers: Courasche's Infertility as Grimmelshausen's Criticism of War; **M.R. Sperberg-McQueen,** Whose Body Is It? Chaste Strategies and the Reinforcement of Patriarchy in Three Plays by Hrotswitha von Gandersheim; **Sara Lennox,** The Feminist Reception of Ingeborg Bachmann; **Maria-Regina Kecht,** Auflehnung gegen die Ordnung von Sprache und Vernunft: Die weibliche Wirklichkeitsgestaltung bei Waltraud Anna Mitgutsch; **Maria-Regina Kecht,** Gespräch mit Waltraud Anna Mitgutsch; **Susanne Kord,** "Und drinnen waltet die züchtige Hausfrau"? Carolina Pichler's Fictional Auto/Biographies; **Susan L. Cocalis,** "Around 1800": Reassessing the Role of German Women Writers in Literary Production of the Late Eighteenth and Early Nineteenth Centuries (Review Essay); **Konstanze Streese und Kerry Shea,** Who's Looking? Who's Laughing? Of Multicultural Mothers and Men in Percy Adlon's *Bagdad Cafe*; **Deborah Lefkowitz,** Editing from Life; **Walfriede Schmitt,** Mund-Artiges... (Gedicht); **Barbara Becker-Cantarino,** Feministische Germanistik in Deutschland: Rückblick und sechs Thesen; **Gisela Brinker-Gabler,** Alterity—Marginality—Difference: On Inventing Places for Women; **Ruth-Ellen B. Joeres,** "Language is Also a Place of Struggle": The Language of Feminism and the Language of American *Germanistik*.

Volume 7

Myra Love, "A Little Susceptible to the Supernatural?": On Christa Wolf; **Monika Shafi,** Die überforderte Generation: Mutterfiguren in Romanen von Ingeborg Drewitz; **Ute Brandes,** Baroque Women Writers and the Public Sphere; **Katherine R. Goodman,** "The Butterfly and the Kiss": A Letter from Bettina von Arnim; **Ricarda Schmidt,** Theoretische Orientierungen in feministischer Literaturwissenschaft und Sozialphilosophie (Review Essay); **Sara Lennox,** Some Proposals for Feminist Literary Criticism; **Helga Königsdorf,** Ein Pferd ohne Beine (Essay); **Angela Krauß,** Wieder in Leipzig (Erzählung); **Waldtraut Lewin,** Lange Fluchten (Erzählung); **Eva Kaufmann,** DDR-Schriftstellerinnen, die Widersprüche und die Utopie; **Irene Dölling,** Alte und neue Dilemmata: Frauen in der ehemaligen DDR; **Dinah Dodds,** "Die Mauer stand bei mir im Garten": Interview mit Helga Schütz; **Gisela E. Bahr,** Dabeigewesen: Tagebuchnotizen vom Winter 1989/90; **Dorothy J. Rosenberg,** Learning to Say "I" instead of "We": Recent Works on Women in the Former

GDR (Review Essay); **Sara Friedrichsmeyer and Jeanette Clausen,** What's Feminism Got to Do with It? A Postscript from the Editors.

Volume 6

Dagmar C.G. Lorenz, "Hoffentlich werde ich taugen." Zu Situation und Kontext von Brigitte Schwaiger/Eva Deutsch *Die Galizianerin*; **Sabine Wilke,** "Rückhaltlose Subjektivität." Subjektwerdung, Gesellschafts- und Geschlechtsbewußtsein bei Christa Wolf; **Elaine Martin,** Patriarchy, Memory, and the Third Reich in the Autobiographical Novels of Eva Zeller; **Tineke Ritmeester,** Heterosexism, Misogyny, and Mother-Hatred in Rilke Scholarship: The Case of Sophie Rilke-Entz (1851–1931); **Richard W. McCormick,** Productive Tensions: Teaching Films by German Women and Feminist Film Theory; **Hildegard M. Nickel,** Women in the GDR: Will Renewal Pass Them By?; **Helen Cafferty and Jeanette Clausen,** Feministik *Germanistik* after Unification: A Postscript from the Editors.

Volume 5

Angelika Bammer, Nackte Kaiser und bärtige Frauen: Überlegungen zu Macht, Autorität, und akademischem Diskurs; **Sabine Hake,** Focusing the Gaze: The Critical Project of *Frauen und Film*; **Dorothy Rosenberg,** Rethinking Progress: Women Writers and the Environmental Dialogue in the GDR; **Susanne Kord,** Fading Out: Invisible Women in Marieluise Fleißer's Early Dramas; **Lorely French,** "Meine beiden Ichs": Confrontations with Language and Self in Letters by Early Nineteenth-Century Women; **Sarah Westphal-Wihl,** Pronoun Semantics and the Representation of Power in the Middle High German *Märe* "Die halbe Decke"; **Susanne Zantop and Jeannine Blackwell,** Select Bibliography on German Social History and Women Writers; **Helen Cafferty and Jeanette Clausen,** Who's Afraid of Feminist Theory? A Postscript from the Editors.

Volume 4

Luise F. Pusch, Totale Feminisierung: Überlegungen zum unfassenden Femininum; **Luise F. Pusch,** Die Kätzin, die Rättin, und die Feminismaus; **Luise F. Pusch,** Carl Maria, die Männe; **Luise F. Pusch,** Sind Herren herrlich und Damen dämlich?; **Ricarda Schmidt,** E.T.A. Hoffman's "Der Sandmann": An Early Example of *Écriture Féminine*? A Critique of Trends in Feminist Literary Criticism; **Renate Fischetti,** *Écriture Féminine* in the New German Cinema: Ulrike Ottinger's *Portrait of a Woman Drinker*; **Jan Mouton,** The Absent Mother Makes an Appearance in the Films of West German Women Directors; **Charlotte Armster,** Katharina Blum: Violence and the Exploitation of Sexuality; **Renny Harrigan,** Novellistic Representation of *die Berufstätige* during the Weimar Republic; **Lynda J. King,** From the Crown to the Hammer and Sickle: The Life and Works of Austrian Interwar Writer Hermynia zur Mühlen; **Linda Kraus Worley,** The "Odd" Woman as Heroine in the Fiction of Louise von François; **Helga Madland,** Three Late Eighteenth-Century Women's Journals:

Their Role in Shaping Women's Lives; **Sigrid Brauner,** Hexenjagd in Gelehrtenköpfen; **Susan Wendt-Hildebrandt,** Gespräch mit Herrad Schenk; **Dorothy Rosenberg,** GDR Women Writers: The Post-War Generation. An Updated Bibliography of Narrative Prose, June 1987.

Volume 3

Ritta Jo Horsley and Richard A. Horsley, On the Trail of the "Witches": Wise Women, Midwives and the European Witch Hunts; **Barbara Mabee,** Die Kindesmörderin in den Fesseln der bürgerlichen Moral: Wagners Evchen und Goethes Gretchen; **Judith P. Aikin,** Who Learns a Lesson? The Function of Sex Role Reversal in Lessing's *Minna von Barnhelm*; **Sara Friedrichsmeyer,** The Subversive Androgyne; **Shawn C. Jarvis,** Spare the Rod and Spoil the Child? Bettine's *Das Leben der Hochgräfin Gritta von Rattenzuhausbeiuns*; **Edith Waldstein,** Romantic Revolution and Female Collectivity: Bettine and Gisela von Arnim's *Gritta*; **Ruth-Ellen Boetcher Joeres,** "Ein Nebel schließt uns ein." Social Comment in the Novels of German Women Writers, 1850–1870; **Thomas C. Fox,** Louise von François: A Feminist Reintroduction; **Gesine Worm,** Das erste Jahr: Women in German im Goethe Haus New York.

Volume 2

Barbara Frischmuth, Am hellen Tag: Erzählung; **Barbara Frischmuth,** Eine Souveräne Posaune Gottes: Gedanken zu Hildegard von Bingen und ihrem Werk; **Dagmar C.G. Lorenz,** Ein Interview: Barbara Frischmuth; **Dagmar C.G. Lorenz,** Creativity and Imagination in the Work of Barbara Frischmuth; **Margaret E. Ward,** *Ehe* and *Entsagung*: Fanny Lewald's Early Novels and Goethe's Literary Paternity; **Regula Venske,** "Männlich im Sinne des Butt" or "Am Ende angekommen?": Images of Men in Contemporary German-Language Literature by Women; **Angelika Bammer,** Testing the Limits: Christa Reinig's Radical Vision; **H-B. Moeller,** The Films of Margarethe von Trotta: Domination, Violence, Solidarity, and Social Criticism.

Volume 1

Jeanette Clausen, The Coalition of Women in German: An Interpretive History and Celebration; **Sigrid Weigel,** Das Schreiben des Mangels als Produktion von Utopie; **Jeannine Blackwell,** Anonym, verschollen, trivial: Methodological Hindrances in Researching German Women's Literature; **Martha Wallach,** Ideal and Idealized Victims: The Lost Honor of the Marquise von O., Effi Briest and Katharina Blum in Prose and Film; **Anna Kuhn,** Margarethe von Trotta's *Sisters*: Interiority or Engagement?; **Barbara D. Wright,** The Feminist Transformation of Foreign Language Teaching; **Jeanette Clausen,** Broken but not Silent: Language as Experience in Vera Kamenko's *Unter uns war Krieg*; **Richard L. Johnson,** The New West German Peace Movement: Male Dominance or Feminist Nonviolence.